THIS IS MY BELOVED

JEWISH CHRISTIAN LADY EVANGELIST. Combinations of these words can cause a fuss. A little over a century ago, even more so. Back then, crowds of thousands of women and men, of all classes, in cities, towns and villages across Australia, New Zealand, North America and Britain, flocked to hear Emilia Baeyertz tell her story and exhort them to follow Jesus the Messiah.

For decades, a ticket to hear Mrs Baeyertz was one of the hottest going. Yet, Emilia has been largely forgotten, even among those many whose spiritual ancestors found new lives through her message.

We have no sound recording yet we do have her voice. She published her own lectures and biography. Everywhere she spoke, the newspapers recorded what she had to say and how her audiences responded. Drawing from some of those records, and from what we have had to imagine, we present for you Emilia's remarkable true story of romance, tragedy and hope as an historical novel.

THIS IS MY BELOVED

THE STORY OF
EMILIA BAEYERTZ
JEWISH CHRISTIAN
LADY EVANGELIST

Betty Baruch and Amanda Coverdale

Emilia Baeyertz Society
Melbourne

Published by Emilia Baeyertz Society Inc.
5 Laughlin Avenue, Nunawading Victoria 3131, Australia
© 2017 Emilia Baeyertz Society Inc.

Authors: Betty Baruch and Amanda Coverdale
Editor: Garth Coverdale
Producer: CATTAC PRESS
Printer and distributor: Ingram

The image of Emilia on the cover is from the September 1886 edition of
The Pioneer published in Launceston, Tasmania.

For acknowledgements, please refer to Authors' Notes and The Story
Behind The Story at the end of this novel. For notes, a chronology, a
character list, a collection of extracts and attribution of sources and quotes,
please refer to *This Is My Beloved Companion* edited by Garth Coverdale
and published by Emilia Baeyertz Society Inc.

All Bible quotes are from the King James Version.
Words in italics are described in a Glossary by Merle Roseman.
Typeset in Garamond Premier Pro.

National Library of Australia Cataloguing-in-Publication entry
Creator: Baruch, Betty, author.
Title: This is my beloved : the story of Emilia Baeyertz, Jewish Christian
    lady evangelist / Betty Baruch & Amanda Coverdale.
ISBN: 9780994572400 (paperback)
Subjects: Baeyertz, Emilia, 1842–1926–Fiction.
    Women evangelists–Australia–Fiction.
    Evangelists–Australia–Fiction.
    Biographical fiction.
Other Creators/Contributors: Coverdale, Amanda, author.
Dewey Number: A823.4

This is my beloved and this is my friend,
O daughters of Jerusalem.
SONG OF SOLOMON

To David Perry
with thanks.

Contents

Cast of Characters

Emilia Aronson, our subject
George Aronson, Emilia's brother
John Aronson, Emilia's father
Maria Aronson, Emilia's mother
Charles Nalder Baeyertz, Charlie's son
Charlie Baeyertz, a bank manager
Charles Baeyertz, Charlie's father
Marion Baeyertz, Charlie's daughter
Mary Anne Baeyertz, Charlie's mother
Abraham Berens, Eliza's husband
Eliza Berens, Emilia's sister
Christopher Bunning, a pastor
Martin Langmore, a doctor
Emily Macartney, a vicar's wife
Hussey Macartney, a vicar
Robert Newfield, a suitable young man
Sarah Perrin, an evangelist
Thomas Rae, a doctor
Henry Reed, an evangelist
Boswell Reid, a surgeon
David Rosenthal, a jeweller
Mary Thomson, an evangelist
Henry Varley, an evangelist
Nancy Wait, a teacher
William Wood, a vicar

All but two of these characters are historical. For the complete list, please refer to *This Is My Beloved Companion*.

PART ONE

At Home in Bangor

1855 to 1864

CHAPTER 1

Bangor, Wales
Thursday 29 March 1855

MARIA ARONSON SANK INTO HER CHAIR, RESTED HER FEET ON HER footstool and gazed across the table at the ruins of her daughter's lavish lunch. 'Have you enjoyed your party, Emilia?'

'Oh yes, Mama, thank you. Everyone came home to celebrate my birthday. Cook made my favourite food. It's been lovely; just look at all the presents!'

'Why not open them now?'

Without wasting another moment, Emilia turned to the small table that was covered with parcels of every description, picked up the topmost one, tore at the string and asked, 'Let me see if my family or friends are mind-readers.'

Her mother laughed. 'There has been no need in this house for anyone to have to read your mind. All that is required is sharp ears. I never knew such a girl for dropping hints, subtle and otherwise.'

Emilia scarcely heard. She was fully occupied by unwrapping gifts and keeping up a flow of comment as each was revealed. 'Not gloves again! Why does Aunt Rachel always buy me gloves for my birthday?'

'Most probably because you lose your gloves from one year to the next', murmured her mother.

'And Aunt Dora never fails to present me with flowered handkerchiefs.'

This time her mother spoke in a voice that demanded to be heard. 'They are beautiful handkerchiefs, Emilia. Very like those I saw you admiring when we were out together last week.'

Her daughter swung round to face her and spoke as to a child, 'No, Mama, those were lilac. These are blue.'

And Maria, feeling guilty, regretted that she had not returned to the shop quickly enough to secure the ones that Emilia had so admired, for her sister-in-law had asked her to buy handkerchiefs that her daughter would like. Suddenly Maria found herself enveloped in a grateful hug while Emilia flourished a copy of *Lamb's Tales from Shakespeare*.

'Mama, you are a darling to give me what I most wanted! How did you guess?'

Maria patted her hair back into place and gave her daughter a long look. 'Put it down to second sight, Emilia, or more correctly second hearing, although I swear it was more like five times that the title of that book found its way into our conversation in recent days.'

Emilia stepped back from her mother's chair and with her head to one side asked, 'Can you guess why I especially wanted *Lamb's Tales*, Mama?'

Her mother pretended to think. 'Mmm, let me see now. Could it have anything to do with the fact that your father and I took your brothers and sisters to a matinee performance of *Romeo and Juliet*? 'Twas such a pity you were not well enough to accompany us that day.'

Emilia's face fell at the memory so Maria asked, 'Have you seen your father's present yet?'

'Yes. He gave me a paperknife.' She went quickly to the table again, found what she was looking for and brought it to show her mother. Emilia had given her father's gift the barest glance when she had unwrapped it, but now she saw the lustre and the attractive design. 'Is it silver, do you think, Mama?'

'It certainly is silver, Emilia, and will need polishing every few weeks. You will have to do that you know. I cannot have you handing it over to the servants to look after for you.'

'Did you go with Papa when he bought the paperknife, Mama?'

'No, a jeweller has his own sources. As soon as he brought it home he showed it to me. He is tired of you borrowing his whenever pages need cutting.'

'Well, I cannot be blamed for that. So many of the books in Papa's library have uncut pages still. Now I have my own paperknife I will not have to ask.'

She threw her knife into the air and caught it, chanting, 'My own paperknife, my very own paperknife, my very own paperknife.'

Her mother leant back in her chair and watched. It was good to see Emilia active, happy and in relatively good health. There had been times … but Maria would not allow her thoughts to dwell on the many occasions on which she and John had almost despaired of seeing their third daughter grow into girlhood and beyond. Yet God had been good, and she was still with them, each year becoming stronger and more like the other children who were at school. 'Do you realise, Emilia, if I had been told that morning thirteen years ago that my baby was a boy, you would now be celebrating your *bar mitzvah*?'

The knife clattered to the floor. 'Oh Mama, how thankful I am the baby was a girl. Just think, I would have to read the portion for the day in the Synagogue. I would probably swoon away and give everyone a fright!' Her brothers each in their turn would learn Hebrew for months on end for the occasion.

'I do agree with you, Emilia, it is fortunate the occasion will not arise. You have had quite as many frights as we could possibly stand—more than your share, in fact. And now that I think of it, you really should be taking a rest on your bed until dinner time. You know that tonight Aunt Rachel has been invited to dinner.'

As she took a deep breath to protest loudly, which she always did at the first mention of a rest in her room, Emilia was interrupted by the announce-ment of a late visitor.

The footman stood at the drawing room door and stated, 'Dr Isaacs, Ma'am.'

Maurice Isaacs soon found his favourite chair. Despite his comfort, he gave, as doctors so often do, the appearance of readiness to leave at any moment.

'It is good of you to find the time to come at all, Maurice', said Maria. 'Emilia, I am sure, appreciates it very much.' She offered him a selection from the leftovers on the tea table, but he shook his head saying he would trouble her for no more than a cup of her excellent tea.

After several thoughtful sips, he rose to bring a low stool to the side of his easy chair and invited Emilia to take her place by him. As she settled herself, Emilia was disconcerted to find his searching gaze fixed on her. 'So you are thirteen years old today, Emilia Louise Aronson?' His tone held a kind of wonderment. 'When my mind goes back to the day I placed you, a tiny newborn in your mother's arms, and I look upon you now on the threshold of womanhood, I am at a loss for words.'

'You hardly expected the little one to see thirteen summers.'

'Why Maria, I would swear I never put such a thought into words.'

'You did not need to. I myself was often aware that my dear child's life was hanging by a thread.' Maria went on softly, 'John and I can never thank you enough, Maurice, for your unstinting care of Emilia through the years. When I consider the countless occasions we have had to call you out, regardless of the time of day or night!' She shook her head slowly. 'Where Emilia was concerned, you never spared yourself.'

Dr Isaacs waved his hand. 'Let us not speak of those times now, Maria. From the day I first started out as a family physician I have accepted the conditions under which I work. Think how glad I would be if all my patients responded to my ministrations as Emilia has done.' A smile that had been playing around Emilia's mouth was swiftly replaced by a scowl. 'I am aware that our last winter has been a taxing one for Emilia, and it is my considered opinion that her headaches and other symptoms have been aggravated by her exposure to all weathers while attending school.'

At this point Emilia burst out, 'But I was always kept home when the weather was really bad!' She looked to her mother for confirmation.

'That was according to my instructions, Emilia.' The next moment he slapped his knees and rose briskly to his feet. While smiling into his patient's troubled face, he gave her a quick pat on the shoulder. 'You are old enough now, Emilia, to be done with school. Once you are at home and spending your days with your mother, I expect to see a distinct improvement in your overall health. When the schools close for the summer, that will be the ideal time for your school days to draw to a close.'

He slipped a forefinger into his waistcoat pocket, withdrew his gold hunter, snapped it open and glanced at the time. 'Hmm! Later than I thought.' Feeling about in his various pockets he eventually produced a small parcel which he held out to Emilia saying, 'A very happy thirteenth birthday, my dear, and may there be many more.'

Emilia had seen parcels as small as that before. It could only have come from a jeweller. Her smile grew wide in anticipation as she turned it over to look for the knot in the string.

Dr Isaacs leant forward and planted a fatherly kiss on her forehead. 'Now had you been a boy', he told her, tweaking one of her curls, 'I should have had to go to a great deal more expense for your *bar mitzvah*'.

By this time Emilia had succeeded in unwrapping a jeweller's box and was further engrossed in opening the minute clasp. Suddenly, it yielded to her plucking fingers and, as the contents were revealed, she gasped with delight.

'Oh, Dr Isaacs, thank you! What a heavenly brooch!'

Standing at her shoulder to get a view of the dainty filigree oval, Maria exclaimed, 'No, Maurice, you should not give her anything so expensive. It is far too good for a girl her age. She is only a child after all!'

The tone of her voice revealed that the brooch pleased her as much as it did her daughter. He did not answer her directly, saying only to Emilia, 'Wear it in good health my dear and, whenever you pin it on, spare a thought for your old doctor'.

As her mother ushered him out of the room, Emilia took her newest acquisition to the window. She was intrigued to discover that what she had taken for a random design was in fact her own entwined initials, ELA.

The delightful brooch did not prevent Emilia from feeling cheated. She would not complete as many years of schooling as her brothers and sisters. Perhaps with some strong words on her part she could persuade her father to take up the cudgels on her behalf. She would appeal to his sense of justice, for each of her brothers and sisters would receive a Continental education. How unfair then, that she should be deprived of the last few years of her education! If not her father, then George would stand with her. She could count on George. Though younger by five years, her favourite brother had been her greatest ally.

Conscious of a pricking under her eyelids, Emilia reminded herself that while she was often teased by her family for acting younger than her years, her brothers and sisters had not been able to call her a cry-baby, for she had always been able to summon anger to overcome tearful self-pity.

Now, hearing the footsteps of her mother returning, Emilia faced the doorway ready to do battle. She was exhilarated by the knowledge that her temper was rising. As the door opened, she flung words about her—heedless words, useful only in that they fanned the flames of her anger. 'So it is all decided, Mama. I am to leave school at thirteen. No-one bothered to ask what I think about my education being abandoned in this way, nor does anyone care! You have just made up your mind that I am to stay at home with you, to be trained as another servant in a house already full of servants.'

Her mother, who over the years had gained painful experience in handling these eruptions, took the time to settle herself upon the sofa. Only then did she pat the seat beside her. 'Come, sit by me. It is time we discussed this matter.'

'Oh yes, there can be any amount of discussing, but I know that in the end it will come out exactly as you have planned it!'

'Emilia, come!' Waiting until her daughter had deliberately dawdled her way to her side, Maria drew a long breath and began. 'There is no reason in the world, Emilia, for you to look upon the wise counsel of your doctor as a sentence of servitude. It may seem unlikely, but the day might well come when you enjoy the time we spend at home together.'

Maria's oblique glance met a sceptical look. Undeterred, she continued in the same quiet way. 'Do you remember the woman who visited us when you were ten years old?'

'Why do you change the subject? We were talking about school.'

'I still am. That incident has some bearing on the matter.'

'No, I don't remember.'

'We have not talked about her visit much, but whenever you are sick I wonder what she meant.'

'Oh yes, now I remember. A woman we'd never met before came. Eliza sent me into this room alone.'

'Yes, you did come in with a fearful expression. It took me some time to assure you.'

'She ruined a perfectly good day. That woman happened to visit us when we were all at home. The boys were all here because none of their sports were playing. Julia, Eliza and I had no piano lessons. We were having a lovely time being pirates and the Royal Navy.'

'The woman said she had a special message about one of my children so she asked to see you all. I was puzzled, especially since she was a stranger, but she did come with a good reference.'

'Nurse despaired over the creases in our clothes but all she could do was brush our hair and tell us to be on our best behaviour.'

'After you'd stood in line, the visitor indicated that she wanted to talk to me alone. That's why I sent you all back to the nursery. Then she described one of my daughters, so I sent for Eliza.'

'Eliza wasn't away for long. When she came back, she was bewildered and told me that they didn't want her, but they wanted me. I was very afraid.'

'It turned out the woman had forgotten your names and she'd wanted to talk to you from the beginning. Eliza is two years older and her name also begins with an "E". When you were sitting in this room with us, the woman said, "This one will be the best and cleverest of them all, when she grows up, of that I feel sure".

'When I ran back and told the others, they teased me and said the woman must have been joking. I got angry. I'd repeated her words exactly.'

'I'm not surprised, Emilia. No one likes to hear their younger sister boasting that she will be the best of them all. Besides you were sick so often. You've missed so many days of school.'

'Why have you reminded me about that dreadful day?'

'If that woman is right and you are to become the best and cleverest, you must continue your education, at home with me. Tell me what you think of this list of what we might do in the days that lie ahead. Of course, our mornings will be taken up with household matters, for between us we must ensure that the house runs smoothly and, believe me Emilia, there is more to that than meets the casual eye. It will be useful experience against the day that you have a house of your own.'

Sensing that her daughter was about to burst forth with some ill-considered remark, Maria hurried on. 'Each day, after luncheon, we shall both be the better for a short rest, after which we can choose from a variety of pastimes. There will be calls to pay on some afternoons ... '

Here she was interrupted as she fully expected to be, by Emilia's scornful voice at her side. 'Mama, you know how I detest visiting!'

Her mother looked at her calmly. 'I hope our calls help overcome your timidity. Not that we shall be making calls every day, for that would defeat the purpose of your staying in with me to benefit your health. I am referring to occasional visits to our friends, or to the park or the beach, when the weather is at its mildest. There will be "At Home" days and I do admit to requiring your help to entertain. If you would care to, we can spend part of each day with a good book. Your father and I have built up an excellent library and since I enjoy reading aloud as well as being read to, we shall be able to delve into as much of the classical literature as we choose. In that way we shall continue and extend your education as well.'

Another brief glance assured Maria that her words were having at least some beneficial effect on her daughter, for the pout was not quite so much in evidence. Could there be the beginnings of a small reluctant smile?

'After *Lamb's Tales*, you will want to read *Romeo and Juliet* as Shakespeare wrote it. I love Shakespeare, and Macaulay, because they are written in the purest English.'

This time, when Maria stopped to draw breath, there was no immediate outpouring of objection. 'We could also attend concerts and lectures presented by scholars when they visit Wales. Now I think of it, the warmer weather is upon us. There is really no reason why we cannot ask Mrs Melrose to pack us a picnic hamper whenever we want to drive along the coast or go into the mountains or cross the Menai Strait. Nurse and the little ones who've not yet begun school can join us. Why should only visitors benefit from our magnificent scenery?'

This last suggestion brought a meditative look to Emilia's face. Perhaps she was, after all, coming to accept the necessity of remaining at home with her mother. Maria had never been so sanguine as to believe that her daughter would actually welcome the months which lay ahead, but if she could settle down with some degree of contentment, they would all be more than satisfied.

As for Emilia, she had entirely forgotten that it had been her intention to enlist her father and George on her side in the battle. Somehow the situation had resolved itself acceptably, and she now felt quite at ease about her future. All anger had left her and, when her mother began to stack the plates onto the tea tray, Emilia, without being prompted, worked alongside her. Maria acknowledged, as she seldom allowed herself to do, that this daughter, despite her difficult nature, held an especially warm place in her heart.

CHAPTER 2

Bangor

1855 to 1863

AFTER THE FIRST SIX MONTHS OF STAYING AT HOME, EMILIA HAD TO admit to herself that, though she was missing the competitive spirit of her school days when she had always to prove she was at least equal to her class, she had not become as melancholic as she feared she might. On the whole she was enjoying her life away from school, and it was only partly due to the improvement in her health. There was now scarcely a picnic spot nearby that she had not visited with her mother, nurse, sister Emily and younger brothers during the summer months. They also explored several mountain glades, and even two of the heights.

Emilia also found herself adjusting to the constant round of daily household tasks. Although the At Home afternoons were her least-favoured times of the week, Emilia gradually developed skills in conversation and being the hostess. Emilia also became more willing to accompany her mother on visits to other homes because she understood the social requirements. When she attended concerts and lectures given by famous musicians and intellectuals, Emilia discovered that the audience included many of the people she had met elsewhere.

Even though she gained much entertainment through the social scene, Emilia really only came to life when she and her mother settled down comfortably in their library.

She had always loved this room, especially in winter when the flames from the fireplace reflected in the lozenges of glass that protected the books. On the shelves were leather-bound sets of Dickens, Scott, Thackeray, Trollope and the Brontë sisters. There were Jane Austen's novels, old and valuable editions of Shakespeare's plays and works in German, French, Yiddish, Russian and other languages. She spent many happy afternoons with sea charts and art folios that she discovered in the drawers of a cabinet.

Mother and daughter sometimes read quietly and at other times read poems and speeches aloud to each other. Although the pronunciation of certain words took some practice, the printed text was easier to understand when spoken aloud. When they took up a play they divided the roles and also read aloud. Maria was blessed with a beautiful speaking voice and when she was portraying a character, Emilia could see the person clearly in her mind's eye. Her own turn to read aloud brought forth complimentary remarks from her mother that fell agreeably on her ears. Emilia would, in time, become grateful for these hours spent reading for an audience of one.

The years, as they sped, brought little of apparent importance. In a country town, to a girl in her teens, life is apt to appear monotonous. Yet, as her health steadily improved, one great event loomed like a glittering star.

CHAPTER 3

Bangor
March 1863

AFTER TWELVE MONTHS OF PREPARATION, THE DÉBUTANTE BALL WAS only three weeks away. Anticipation filled Emilia with excitement and, on occasions, panic. She had to remind herself she had been praised by her dance and etiquette teachers for mastering the skills required of débutantes. She had also made new friends amongst the other young ladies.

It had been soon after her twentieth birthday when her mother had said she was ready for the next Social Season in Bangor. Emilia protested that she could not curtsey for the Mayor.

'Of course, you don't know how to curtsey; you haven't been to the classes! However, you are healthy enough and you've had enough practice meeting people in many situations. You'll be able to manage a ball.

'I'll submit applications for you, and three of your brothers, to attend the same ball. The boys should experience at least one even though your father has other plans for them. I expect Saul, Charles and George, at eighteen, seventeen and sixteen, are already interested in certain young ladies, but they've not yet mentioned any names to me. They do know that John and I must promote them in society and find them suitable wives.'

Emilia assented and so went away to mull over what she remembered of the experiences of Julia, Eliza and Lewis at balls.

Maria Aronson had all the qualifications required for her children to participate. She had debuted to the society of her day and since then she had remained in the right social circles to ensure that her own children would debut.

As everyone expected, Maria's applications were accepted. The Aronson house was filled with joy and Emilia and her brothers were promptly sent to their classes. The boys were instructed in protocol and dance and Emilia in deportment, dance and conversation. Emilia returned home from these sessions wondering how she would ever understand the nuances in the behaviour of young men and their parents. Fortunately, dancing did not present the same difficulties. Emilia was usually one of the first to pick up the steps: her body, arms and feet seemed to know instinctively what movements were expected of them.

She found she had no time for leisurely afternoons in the library; instead there were visits to warehouses, linen drapers, shoemakers and markets. Their dressmaker became a daily visitor. Emilia was excused from household duties in the face of these more important considerations. She was allowed to rise later and even, at times, had breakfast brought to her bedside. Emilia's daylight hours passed in a daze of excited activities.

During the day of the ball, six Aronsons prepared for the evening. A maid helped Emilia into a gown of purest white, with a skirt held at the fashionable oval shape by a crinoline. The high neckline was softened and set off by swans-down. Then Emilia sat down at the mirror to allow the maid to prepare her dark brown wavy hair for an evening of dancing. She looked at herself carefully. No longer was she the adolescent who learned how to manage a family home and retreated into the world of books. Now that she was nearly twenty-one, she could see the size and shape of an adult.

Her brown eyes stared out of a face which had a neat chin and pale skin. The absence of tan was evidence of her care to protect her face from the direct rays of the sun.

Her father had hired a magnificent landau to transport them all. As the horses moved off, Emilia felt her breathing quicken. Hoping to stave off the panic that threatened to overwhelm her, she resorted to an old trick to take her mind away from the ordeal. She began to count things she could see as they drove along High Street.

The mild evening had allowed her mother to remove her shawl so Emilia was able to count the seed pearls embroidered into the neckline of her gown. Those pearls, and matching pearls at her throat and ears, caught the glow from the gas lamps they passed in the street. Emilia counted the dark buttons on the evening suits of her father and brothers. She counted the rosebuds in her own bouquet, and then she counted their leaves. When she could find nothing further to count, she turned her gaze again to her mother.

Maria Aronson had excellent taste when it came to clothes and this night, in Emilia's eyes, she had surpassed herself. Maria's gown of royal blue silk with its wide oval crinoline skirt was a masterpiece of the dressmaker's art. Her habitual air of distinction set off the gown to perfection.

Emilia had often lamented that she had not inherited poise and refinement from her mother's side of the family. Never had she felt the lack of it as keenly as she did that night. She knew her appearance could not be faulted. Then why, she asked herself, did she feel inadequate to meet the demands of the evening ahead? Any lack lay with her. Of that she had no doubt, for she had never been able to measure up to her own expectations.

She should have had the sense to insist on coming to the ball as a guest only. Whatever had possessed her to agree to be presented to society? She knew well the answer. She had done it to please her mother, and it was far too late to withdraw. She fiddled with the ribbon of her bouquet. In a few more minutes they would arrive at the Hall.

Emilia could never have guessed it, but her father had been averse to attending the evening's entertainment altogether. He too was lending his presence to please Maria. He had said to her weeks before, 'You go to the ball, my dear. I have been to balls more times than enough, though I know you always enjoy them. After the first dance or two, Emilia will be carried off by the various young men she knows, leaving Saul free to stand in for me and so provide you with a partner. Really my dear, I do think that would serve quite well.'

But Maria had insisted. 'We cannot do without you, John', she had said. 'Who will hire a carriage and act as chaperone to Emilia? A man is needed for this role.'

'My dear Maria, is not our Saul a man?'

'Indeed he is, but he cannot act as Emilia's father. Any young man at the ball interested in Emilia will be looking for an introduction to her father before writing to him. I must say, John, your distinguished air can only enhance our daughter's prospects.'

As usual, John had conceded. He had now to put as a good face on the whole thing as he could and support Emilia.

Covertly, he watched his daughter closely enough to see that she was a bundle of nerves. Surely it would have been kinder never to have started this business. No, Maria had stoutly maintained that the ball was the only way to launch a young woman into the Season, as such an occasion showed her to best advantage. While he agreed, John kept a tender spot in his heart for this delicate child of theirs and fervently hoped that the evening would not prove too much.

Emilia caught her father's smile and was warmed by his nod of encouragement. She returned the smile but could not think of what to say.

Her father winked at her to try to raise her spirits then said, 'You look beautiful tonight. Your dress reveals you to be the elegant young lady you have become. I'm sure all those dancing and deportment classes will come to your aid.'

Maria glanced at Emilia and decided that this was the time she'd been waiting for. 'I've been meaning to tell you what your Aunt Dora said. As you left your last deportment lesson, she remarked that she is sure of success in your dances and curtseys. We agreed that you have matured into a capable and confident young woman. I'm pleased you are here. I've often seen you feel anxious before an event but after you arrive you fit in easily. I'm sure you will do that tonight too.'

George had turned to look at Emilia too. When she looked at him, he gave her his saucy wink. It was all right for him, Emilia thought crossly, to feel so carefree. What was to her an ordeal was to him in the nature of a lark. Her brothers would not be the focus of all eyes as she and the other young ladies would be, when they entered the Hall.

George was in fact planning to make the most of his night out. Once his duties to his sister and mother were discharged, he would be free to mingle with the other guests, choose his own dance partners and chat with his male friends. He was also looking forward to the supper which, if he had been correctly advised, would of itself make the evening worthwhile.

Emilia relaxed back into the cushions of the carriage and released her tense arms and hands. She no longer grasped her bouquet but let it lie in her lap. Her mother's hand rose to comfort Emilia with a pat, but it was arrested in its movement, for Maria's attention was caught by something said by her husband.

He and George were talking business, of course, and Saul and Charles were intent on listening. Maria's hand came to rest on Emilia's wrist while her eyes rose to heaven as she asked herself if her menfolk ever talked of anything else. She herself followed the fortunes of their business, but there were better times and places. Since their voices were lowered, she listened carefully so as to miss none of it.

Her husband was saying, 'Even Donahue at the bank has been heard to say that this is the ideal time to be expanding into the Australian colonies. Gold and wool are available in such quantities. He said there is more money in Melbourne than there are goods for the people to buy. So what do you say George? Would you be prepared to go to assess the possibilities? If everything we hear should be true, and the openings for trading in jewellery and wool are all we could hope for, it may be just a question of time before a branch of J. Aronson & Sons has its opening in the colony of Victoria.'

Before either George or Maria could comment, Saul burst forth, 'Why are you talking to George about this? He has just come back from school. I'm sure either Charles or I could be your representative in the colonies.'

'There is no need to be jealous boys; I have been considering your futures too. We shall discuss the matter soon but not tonight.'

Before George could say a word, his mother broke in. 'My goodness me, you do seem in a hurry to send our son to the very end of the earth! He is only sixteen and has just returned from the Continent. He is too young to establish a business alone even though he seems wiser than his years. Give him a little more time to settle in here and look around. When he has found himself a wife there will be time enough to think of sending him half-way round the world, for then they can provide each other company on the long sea voyage out there. What sort of a life would he have, all alone in a strange country?'

John assumed an aggrieved expression. 'You cannot have forgotten that Eliza and Abraham also live in the antipodes, in the very same town. I seem to remember that you objected when Abraham first wrote to me from Melbourne with his hope of marrying Eliza, yet now her letters are full of news regarding the host of friends and associates they have in the Jewish community there. You cannot imagine that George will be starved for companionship? Why, it might be there that he finds a young Jewish lady to his liking.'

'It is the long sea voyage that concerns me most. If only there was a companion for him during those months at sea. Eliza and Abraham at least had each other.'

George realised that while these words were directed at his father, they were also meant for him, and judged now was the time for delaying tactics. 'Papa,' he said, 'I am flattered to think that you consider me qualified to be sent to the Australian colonies. I trust that means you are satisfied with the reports from Vienna?'

His father nodded gravely. 'Yes, my boy, I am entirely satisfied. You were quick to go beyond the rudiments of their languages that your mother had taught you and wasted no time in getting down to study. In Melbourne, needless to say, you will not have to master their language.'

'I am glad to have met with your approval, Papa. I would not want you to think I found school easy. They went out of their way to share their knowledge and show kindness.'

His father gazed at his son contently. 'Great kindness awaits you in Melbourne, of that I have no doubt.'

'Nor have I any doubt about that Papa. My doubt is in myself. I cannot feel the same confidence you do and prefer to have experience working here. I have not spent enough time in our shop. If you have no objection, I would like to learn the jewellery and cloth trades first. As well as that, I need to better understand the market in Australia.'

After consideration, his father nodded his agreement. 'Very well, George, I will give you more hours around the shop and copies of reports from our suppliers. The newspapers indicate that great numbers of wool bales are exported from Port Phillip. Also, our jewellery skills could be applied to some of the gold found in the Australian colonies. I will write to Abraham to ask what he can tell us. Certainly, he has a better vantage point in Melbourne. There will be plenty for us to do here until then—that includes all three of you, boys.'

John Aronson settled back in his seat with an air of accomplishment and again became aware of his daughter's strained expression. He put himself out to jolly her along. 'I must say, Emilia, it's not as bad as you may think. You will be just one of many young women to curtsey before the Mayor and Mayoress of Bangor tonight. My role in the ceremony is to support you and be proud to be the father of such a vision of loveliness!'

Her mother was not slow to add her encouragement. 'Your father is right, Emilia. You are looking exceptionally well, if a trifle pale. Try slapping your cheeks and biting your lips to bring up the colour.'

If Emilia had been pale before she began listening to the men's conversation, she had grown paler still. Before long George would be lost to her. Of all her brothers, she was closest to George and depended on him for support when the others teased her about her health. During the time he had been in Vienna, she had missed him more than her parents realised. The thought of him leaving for an even longer period appalled her. How she was to face such a prospect, she did not know.

Fortunately, she had no time to brood on the matter. A loud clatter of hoofs on cobble-stones gave notice of their arrival. The carriage swayed between the stone gate-posts that guarded the entrance to the forecourt of the City Hall. When they came to a halt, George, who had the best view, gave his opinion that they would have a fair wait as there were a good number of vehicles ahead of them.

'Anyone we know?', asked his mother.

'I thought I saw Mr and Mrs Morris pass through the entrance door, Mama.'

'It could not have been them, m'boy,' said his father. 'Jacob Morris has taken his wife and the girls on a tour of the Continent.'

Maria gave her husband an impatient look. 'They have been home these two weeks past. I did tell you. Due to his mother's illness, they have been obliged to return early. You seem to have forgotten.'

'Well', said Mr Aronson mildly, 'Since George saw them going into the ballroom, you must be right as usual.'

Saul, Charles and George discussed the Morris girls until their landau could draw up into the oblong of light thrown from the open doors of the Hall. There they helped their mother down, then Emilia. Together, they all climbed the shallow steps into the brightly lit interior and the base of the magnificent staircase.

CHAPTER 4

Bangor
March 1863

GEORGE TOOK POSSESSION OF EMILIA'S CLOAK. HER HANDS NOW WERE free to gather up the folds of her very full skirt and hold her bouquet during the ascent.

Once inside the ballroom, Emilia drifted over to the bevy of young ladies which opened to include her. Now George had returned from the cloakroom, Emilia became more at ease with her surroundings. Her fixed smile relaxed into her natural one. She soon lost sight of her parents and brothers yet felt quite secure hidden among her friends. She joined in the complimentary remarks passing between the débutantes, for there was not one who was not looking her best. Some, dressed with exquisite taste, drew gasps of admiration.

Emilia rose onto the tips of her toes to peer into the farthest corners of the ballroom. She craned her neck in every direction, glad her mother was not near enough to rebuke her for this unladylike manoeuvre. It was not for just anyone that she was demeaning herself in this way; it was simply that she knew of the possibility of a certain young man attending the ball.

She had met him at her aunt's garden party last autumn and had enjoyed his company. There had been such a crush at the Lazarus house that day. Mr Newfield had been briefly introduced to Emilia. She had later learnt from a friend that his first name was Robert. As she searched for some sign amidst the great throng in the ballroom, Emilia repeated his name softly to herself; the mere sound of it gave her assurance. If he should be in the ballroom, he would come to her; of that she was convinced.

It was her father who came to claim her for the first dance. The next few dances were with young men who were relations of her friends. Later in the evening, when she had resorted to looking for one of her brothers to dance with, she felt her wrist firmly clasped.

'Miss Aronson, please wait!'

Emilia turned in surprise to find Robert Newfield at her side.

He seemed very unsure of himself, and asked doubtfully, 'You do remember me I hope, Miss Aronson?'

She gave him her broadest smile. 'Yes, of course, I remember you. We met last year.'

He was visibly relieved, and took heart at the sight of her welcoming smile. 'Then may I have the next dance with you, Miss Aronson? Please!'

Emilia looked around to see the friends with whom she had been chatting disappear through a door with a 'see you later'.

The musicians were warming up for a waltz, so it seemed the most natural thing in the world for Robert to take her hand, place his other gloved palm at her waist and lead her into the orbiting movements.

Emilia realised at once that she was in the hands of an accomplished dancer. As their steps synchronised, she felt the glorious sound of the piano and strings take hold of her in a way she had never experienced before. She was now completely relaxed and borne along by music which spoke to her of the joyous anticipation of young love. Yes, she had to admit that for the first time in her life she was stirred by love, and it was love for that very man whose arms now led her around the floor. Why this should be so she had no idea. He was handsome enough. He was of slight build, but then so was she. Her indifferent health had left its mark. She never could gain weight no matter how hard she tried.

Happily drifting in a universe that contained only Robert and herself, she longed for the dance and the music to go on forever. After a long time the musicians slowed and brought that music to an end. Much against her will, they returned to this world and came to a reluctant stop. After a second dance, Emilia was surprised when he stood his ground and suggested a third.

'Sorry, Mr Newfield. I am sure my mother would frown upon my having the same partner for more than two dances. Unless, of course, there is some kind of understanding between us.'

Fearful that Robert would be dismayed by her rebuke, Emilia caught what appeared to be a pleased smile on his face, and was amazed when he said quite eagerly, 'I take it then, that your mother is here this evening'.

'Yes, Mr Newfield, and so is my father.' Her heart lifted as she listened to his next words.

'I should very much like to meet your parents, Miss Aronson. Do you think an introduction to your father would be acceptable?'

Emilia, who had been gazing at the floor and holding her breath as he spoke, now looked up at him, her eyes sparkling. 'My father,' she said demurely, 'is at present standing at the edge of the dance floor to your right'.

Robert swung around immediately and saw that there were indeed several men to his right. They had formed a tight knot that would, in his opinion, be hard to approach. With a slight lift of his shoulders, he turned to Emilia for help, and she too realised they faced a difficulty. John Aronson was in the midst of the group of men, and his head was down as he listened to a gentleman of a stature smaller than his own. In such circumstances, how was she to attract his attention?

After spending a fruitless few moments waving her hand at him, Emilia moved to a position behind him and stretched her arm in his direction as far as it would go. Her fingers caught hold of his sleeve and tugged it firmly.

John swung round, saw her and said impatiently, 'Emilia, can you not see I am engaged with Mr Morris? We do not wish to be interrupted.'

'This is more important, John.' said Jacob. 'I am happy to be interrupted when your daughter wants to introduce her dance partner.'

At this, her father excused himself from his immediate company and stepped back beside Emilia. Throughout the introduction his eyes were on Robert with a piercing intensity.

'Newfield did you say? How do you do, Mr Newfield. I believe I may be acquainted with your father.'

'Yes, Mr Aronson, I think you and my father have met at times in the way of business.'

'Are you Daniel Newfield's eldest son?'

'His second son, Mr Aronson.'

'If I am not mistaken, both your father and your uncle are in tea.'

'That is so, Mr Aronson, and you are in jewellery and wool.'

Emilia heard Robert release his breath in a sigh as a smile expanded her father's face. Robert's family had been approved, and that had taken them over the first hurdle.

In the action of turning to join his friends Mr Aronson said dismissively, 'I am happy to have made your acquaintance, Mr Newfield.'

Robert, having progressed so far, was not willing that a further opportunity be denied him.

'May I have a word with you in private, Mr Aronson?'

John Aronson swung back to face Robert again, ready now to give him his undivided attention.

'In that case,' he said, 'we shall have to seek quieter surroundings. Come with me.'

Emilia, realising she had been entirely forgotten, stood a moment irresolute, watching the two men walk away. Before she could decide what to do next, she heard the announcement requesting the evening's special guests to line up for the presentation. Suddenly all her former terrors returned to plague her and so she hurried to seek courage with the other ladies who were gathering, as nervous as she, in the centre of the ballroom.

It was not the first time that John Aronson had attended such occasions, and he knew that the place most likely to provide the privacy they needed was the supper room. The main doors would not yet be open, but he knew of a small swinging side door ... ah yes, there it was. He threw his weight against it and passed through with Robert close behind him.

The tables with their heavy white cloths were already laden. There were platters of fish, baked, steamed, and fried, as well as a superb salmon in aspic. There were roast fowls and pheasants, sliced tongues, large bowls of various salads, dishes of fruit preserves and, occupying the whole of a small table, a score of pitchers of fruit punch.

This sparkling array was barely noticed by the two men, who wasted no time finding a corner out of the way of hurrying waiters. They stood facing each other, neither at first able to find words with which to break the silence.

Now that he was alone with Robert, John Aronson shed his customary air of dignity, and in doing so was making it clear that whatever was to pass between them from that moment forward, would be on the basis of man to man.

CHAPTER 5

Bangor

1863

'WELL, MR NEWFIELD, YOU ASKED IF YOU MIGHT HAVE A WORD. DOES this word have anything to do with my Emilia?'

Robert, not normally at a loss for words, on this occasion was momentarily speechless. He cleared his throat several times before he was able to say, 'Er, yes, Mr Aronson, it does. I would be glad of your permission to call at your house to see her.'

Now that the words had actually been said, John was happy to assume his most genial air. 'Well now, Mr Newfield, I see no difficulty about that.' He paused to think. 'We shall be celebrating Passover quite soon. It would be best if you would come to us for *Second Seder*, if your family has no objection. In that way we can all get to know you. I trust that will suit?'

Robert, who had suffered agonies while waiting for his answer, was quick to agree. He had hoped he might be invited to come visiting that very week, but as he was obliged to wait, then he would do so as patiently as he could. 'I'm sure that my brother could undertake my *Second Seder* duties.'

Having done his duty rather neatly, John set off to resume business with his companions. He led the way back through the side door into the ballroom where he was surprised to find the ceremony under way.

Each young woman was announced in turn. After a short walk to the dais, she was presented to the Mayor and Mayoress, and then, prompted by a soft chord on the piano, sank into her curtsy. Polite encouraging applause greeted each effort. When Emilia's turn came, both Robert and her father noted with undisguised pleasure that her sense of balance was superb, and heedless of disapproving stares directed their way, they applauded vigorously and at length.

His face shining with pride, John led his daughter onto the floor for the dance that followed, though he willingly stood aside for Robert when the dance immediately after it was announced as the supper dance. He watched the two young people join the crowd streaming in the direction of the supper room, then turned away to begin his search for Maria. He found her sitting on a sofa resting her feet and would have been glad to join her but she jumped up as he arrived.

'I believe the suppers here improve with each year that passes. Let us sample this year's effort, while you tell me about that young man. I confess to being quite ready for whatever is available to eat.' Her husband offered her his arm and they joined the press.

Once inside the supper room they were fortunate to find two empty chairs side by side, and with small sighs of relief took possession of them. No sooner were they seated than Saul, Charles and George appeared. The boys divided between them the tasks of collecting food and drink for their parents, and successfully delivered laden plates and full cups without spilling any of them, despite the crowd. The boys then left to satisfy their own appetites.

John did not wait until their plates were empty before he began to tell his wife of Mr Newfield.

'Newfield?' she asked him. 'Son of Lily Newfield?'

'He is Daniel and Lily's second son, Robert. He asked my permission to call at the house to visit Emilia.'

Maria continued to gaze at him with a questioning eye. 'What did you have to say about that?'

'What do you think I said? I certainly let it be understood that we would have no objection to his calling at the house, but at the same time I did not want to give the impression that we were in any hurry to hand our daughter over to just any young man. I suggested that, to begin with, he should come to us for *Second Seder*. That seems the best way to start things off. At least I think so, and I hope you agree.'

'Perhaps it is. Our family will be out in force that night. He will certainly have his courage tested.'

'That is the most acceptable way to bring two young people together for the first time—in the bosom of the family.'

His wife pursed her lips and said nothing further. Her doubts, though unspoken, centred on the person of her husband's elder sister, Rachel. Any young man would be sufficiently unnerved on his first visit to a strange family without having to meet the gimlet eye of Aunt Rachel. But she did agree with her husband; there was no need whatsoever to hasten the friendship between this Robert Newfield and their daughter, though she could not deny that it was only a question of time before she would have to steel herself to face the loss not only of Emilia, but of George as well.

She dreaded the thought. Should Emilia marry Robert, she too would leave the Aronson home. She hoped that few of her many children would be as eager to venture so far from home as Eliza had.

Maria tried buoying up her spirits with the thought that, should Emilia become engaged in the not-too-distant future, George's departure would certainly be delayed, but this ploy was only marginally successful. 'John, should Robert Newfield in time write to you, and should you reply with a suggested dowry, remember to insist that he insure his life.'

'Of course. Before Eliza was married I saw evidence of a life insurance policy from Abraham. When the occasion arises with any of our other girls, you may be sure I shall do the same.'

Maria shrugged. 'In any case it is early days to be thinking of such things. At present the two barely know one another.'

But John was no longer listening. He was busy listing in his mind the enquiries he would have to set in motion the following day. It was his responsibility after all, to go carefully into the matter of Robert Newfield's character and prospects.

CHAPTER 6

Bangor
16 Nisan 5623

EMILIA SLIPPED INTO THE DINING ROOM TO CHECK THAT ALL WAS ready for *Second Seder*. Her parents, brothers and sisters were still in the drawing room. With them were a few relatives, who were usually not invited until the second night of the Passover. This year there was also Robert Newfield. It brought a warm glow to her heart to hope that this personable young man would be calling regularly at the house to see her. Since the night of the ball she had indulged in many agreeable daydreams, all of them anticipating their engagement and the joy of preparing for their wedding.

Tempted again to drift into flights of fancy, Emilia took herself firmly in hand. Her mother had left the finer details of the Passover meal in her charge so her thoughts were centred on her duties. She began checking off on her fingers ... the candles, the *matzot*, the horseradish, the *charoseth*, the roasted egg, the parsley, the salt water, and the lamb's shank bone. And yes, there was the napkin with the three *matzot* folded within it. The cutlery gleamed, the wineglasses sparkled and the table napkins were in place, neatly folded. There was the place for Elijah the prophet with his special wineglass to mark it; everything was ready.

After a quick visit to the kitchen to thank Cook and the maids who had taken such pains again to maintain her mother's exacting standards, Emilia knew there was no further excuse for delay. As she came back down the passage, though her heart leapt at each thought of Robert, this was the time, not to run, but to be restrained, sedate and composed.

Her mother lit the candles and recited the *ma'ariv prayer*. Her father, seated at the head of the table, raised the first cup of Passover wine and intoned, 'Blessed art Thou O Lord our God, King of Creation and of the fruit of the vine. Blessed art Thou, for we are chosen from among many nations and people, we are sanctified by Thy holy commandments, and to this very day we have been spared to celebrate the Feast of Unleavened Bread, the memorial of our freedom from slavery.'

John raised his wineglass again and this time drank from it, and everyone else at the table copied his actions. As she replaced her wineglass, Emilia stole a peep at Robert seated opposite her, and at that moment he glanced up and returned her smile. How handsome he was, she thought, with his *yarmulke* flat on his dark hair and his brown eyes glowing. The fact that this was his first appearance in the midst of her family seemed to worry him very little. The service continued, and Emilia made a determined effort to concentrate. Her father washed his hands in the small basin placed at his side and dried them on the hand towel alongside it. He then continued to read aloud from his *Haggadah*. 'Blessed art Thou, O Lord our God, King of Creation, and of the fruit of the earth.'

Taking a head of parsley, John dipped it into the dish of salt water and, breaking pieces from it, passed these down the table on both sides for everyone to eat. Emilia could not remember when she had first been told that salt water represented the bitter tears shed by their ancestors during the time that they were slaves in Egypt. Knowing well what would follow, Emilia watched her father closely.

John Aronson raised high the cloth which had first been folded into four to form three pockets, in each of which there was a cake of *matzo*. With every eye fastened on him, John by-passed the first cake, did not so much as uncover the third one, but removed the second cake of unleavened bread and held it in both his hands. A hush descended as John broke the cake in half. Reserving one section, the *afikoman*, until the meal was over, he repeated the blessing upon the other half which was then broken into morsels and distributed to all present.

'Eat of the bread of bondage which our ancestors ate in Egypt, and come celebrate the Passover. This year we celebrate it here in Wales, but next year in God's goodness, in our own land, in Jerusalem!'

Through moisture-laden eyes, Emilia looked about her and saw that others at the table were equally moved as they raised their wineglasses and echoed, 'Next year in Jerusalem!'

The bitter herbs, in the form of horseradish, were eaten next. Her father placed a little grated horseradish paste onto pieces of unleavened bread and distributed them around the table. Emilia reminded herself that this was a representation of the bitter bondage suffered by her ancestors in the days of the Pharaohs. Never had the Passover been more meaningful for her. She wondered if Robert's presence was the reason for this. Could it be that her growing love for him was awakening all her emotions?

At every place at the table a second cup of wine was being filled, and Emilia knew that now would come the four questions. Nuriel was too young and Fred had asked last year so she heard her brother Arthur ask, 'Why is this night different from other nights? On other nights we eat either leavened or unleavened bread, but tonight only unleavened.'

Down the table from Emilia, Emily was reading from her *Haggadah*. So familiar were the words that Emilia momentarily lost interest. Of their own volition, it seemed, her eyes sought out Robert's, which were following her sister's finger along the page. This made it possible for her to observe him undetected.

What was there about Robert, she asked herself, that she found him so attractive? Was it his fine-drawn features, or could it be the way his hair with slight waves framed them? His face, like his body, followed closely the outlines of his bones. And to think, she told herself, she was often advised that she needed filling out!

At that particular moment Robert leant back in his chair and, as if he could feel her gaze upon him, looked up. Caught unawares, Emilia blushed and lowered her eyes. To cover her confusion she raised her *Haggadah* and switched her attention back to the service just as the second question was being read.

'On every other night we eat any kind of herbs, but tonight only bitter herbs. Why is this?'

It was no use, she just could not pay attention to the reading. Her thoughts possessed a life of their own now, and they would keep returning to the young man whom she had come to regard as her young man.

Aunt Rachel was seated next to Robert, and for some time she had been watching Emilia with a speculative gleam in her eye. Emilia was blissfully unaware of her aunt's gaze because she had deliberately avoided looking at her.

Her father was reading again, in answer to the questions that had been asked. 'Because when we were slaves in the land of Egypt, the Lord our God brought us out with a powerful hand and a mighty arm. Therefore it is necessary that we repeatedly tell of the departure from Pharaoh's kingdom, year by year, and those who do so are to be commended.'

The wonderful meal of soup, fish, stuffed goose and compôte of fruit with macaroons was finally over, and John brought the Passover service to a close. His eyes on the *Haggadah* text, he read aloud, 'This remembrance Passover meal, in all its customary observances, has now come to an end. Grant us, O Eternal Who Dwelleth Above, that we may be soon found in Zion, our Homeland, rejoicing.'

Emilia rose from her place and asked to be excused. Only the Passover songs remained to be sung and the lemon tea, which was to round off the meal, was her responsibility. In spite of Aunt Rachel's gaze that she suspected was still fixed on her, she took the risk of throwing Robert a brief smile as she left the room.

The grandfather clock in the hall was chiming midnight as the guests, well rugged-up against the cold, moved towards the front door. Having caught a sign from Robert, Emilia had waited behind in the dining room and was deep in a discussion with him regarding a proposed visit to his grandmother.

In the hall, Aunt Rachel was being enveloped in her cloak. As Maria helped her with its folds, Rachel asked, 'Is that young man one of Daniel Newfield's boys?'

'Yes, Rachel; he is their second son, Robert, as I may have said when I introduced him to you.'

'And is he paying court to Emilia?'

'One could hardly say that, Rachel. This is his first visit to the house.'

'Hmm! So painfully thin! In my opinion he needs fattening up. Looks as if a puff of wind would blow him away.'

Maria, by a masterly effort, managed to keep resentment out of her voice. 'You have said the same thing about Emilia on more than one occasion.'

'Well, Maria, it can be said of Emilia with equal truth. But then your daughter has been an ailing child her life long. Is this Robert also a martyr to poor health?'

Maria had to remind herself that her husband's sister was widely known for her plain speaking, never considering the feelings of others. With more than usual thankfulness she handed Rachel over to her brother. John could accompany Rachel to her carriage while Maria saw to their other guests. Maria had had enough of Rachel!

In the dining room, Emilia and Robert were making plans for a day in the country. 'My grandmother lives at Highcliffs. Have you been there before, Emilia?'

'Is that the place about five miles from here?'

'Yes, thereabouts. I told grandmother that I had met a special young lady at a garden party, and she said at once that I must bring you to visit her. Do say that I may take you? I have no doubt you will like my grandmother, for everybody does.'

Emilia needed no persuading. She was happy to fall in with any plan that Robert might make. His very presence filled her with the confidence to face society.

So it was decided. On the first mild day that would suit Robert's grandmother and Emilia's mother, the visit would be made.

CHAPTER 7

North Wales

1863

ONE COOL FINE DAY, EMILIA, ROBERT, HER MOTHER AND THEIR DRIVER set out in a hired coach to fulfil their luncheon engagement at the home of Mrs Susannah Moss. Each time the sun appeared, it soon slipped back behind clouds as if to prepare for its next appearance.

Emilia was blissfully happy. She filled her lungs with fresh air and told herself there was nothing she liked better than being courted. This new status that came with having her name linked with that of a male companion was really most agreeable. Her former routine existence had given way to one full of excitement and novelty, something quite outside her experience. By far the best part of it all was the companion in her life, Robert Newfield!

Seated beside Robert, Emilia spent some time viewing the unfamiliar parts of High Street. She then allowed her hand to drift along the leather of the seat towards Robert, and her heart leapt as his hand, in search of hers, came to rest upon it.

As the cobbled thoroughfare gave way to a country road, she realised that this was the way to Cardiff, which she had travelled before.

Soon they reached the hamlet where Robert directed the driver to his grandmother's house. Mrs Moss was at the door to greet them and lead them into the hall where they divested themselves of their coats and scarves. Once in the drawing room, their hostess saw to it that they were all comfortably seated around the hearth of a fire that glowed brightly.

Had it not been for her head of silvery hair, Robert's grandmother might well have been taken for a much younger woman. Her movements were as quick as many a younger person's and her energy was radiant. As she leapt to her feet to attend to some imagined lack in Maria's comfort, something quite small was dislodged from the occasional table by her chair. Robert bent to retrieve it. Once his grandmother was re-seated, he gave it to her.

'Oh thank you, Robert! It is my precious miniature of dear Mary Anne Disraeli.' She turned the face of it towards her guests and asked them, 'Do you not think it a good likeness?'

Maria's eyes met her daughter's, and she answered for them both. 'We have not had the pleasure of meeting Mrs Disraeli. Is she a friend of yours, Mrs Moss?'

'Yes, she is a dear friend indeed. This small portrait was her gift to me last year. She and her husband are such fine people. What a pity you do not know them.'

Emilia asked if she might hold the tiny painting, and when it was in her hand, she looked with pleasure into a dainty face framed in dark side curls. With mock severity she said, 'Robert, you never so much as mentioned that your family has such famous friends. You must be more secretive than I could ever have guessed.'

Robert held up his hands in protest. 'They are not my friends, Emilia, though I must confess to having met them here once.'

When the miniature had been returned to its place on the small table, Susannah looked at it for a moment with her head to one side as if contemplating its perfections.

She then said quietly, 'My husband and I came to know the Disraelis, oh, it must be twenty years ago now, in Brighton. They were then staying at the same hotel we had been going to for many years. It is strange, is it not, how one can take to previously unknown people? That is what happened to the Disraelis and ourselves; we took to one another on sight. Mary Anne's bright chatter and Dizzy's clever remarks combined to make our first meeting a most memorable one. My husband and I had never been much interested in politics, but after that we both have followed his parliamentary progress with interest.'

'It is only too clear,' put in Robert, 'that the papers rarely have anything good to say about Mr Disraeli. It seems that they save their comments until such time as they are able to quote some speaker from the opposition who has made reference to him in derogatory terms. Then they appear to take delight in reporting every wounding syllable.'

At that moment, luncheon was announced so they followed their hostess into the dining room. Here also, a fire was blazing. As they took their seats, Susannah determined to change the topic of conversation, for she did not want to bore her guests by speaking again of people not known to them.

But in this case she found that the Aronsons were charmed by the name Disraeli, and were eager to hear anything she could tell them about both Benjamin and his wife. In answer to a question put to her by Emilia, Susannah told them, 'Yes, Mary Anne does call her husband "Dizzy", even when there are others in the room. He seems to like it.'

The soup had been brought in, and Maria, enjoying each spicy mouthful, determined to ask her hostess for the recipe. She knew that some cooks did not reveal their culinary secrets, but perhaps the one in this house would be more obliging. Now Susannah was speaking again, and Maria set aside her thoughts to listen.

'Many of our friends ask me, "Why, when he was born of a Jewish mother, does Mr Disraeli lay claim to be Christian?" I am rather tired of answering.'

Robert, who had come to the end of his first course said, 'You cannot stop there.'

His grandmother smiled at him, then turned the same smile upon Maria and her daughter. 'It is a matter that causes great perplexity I know, particularly among our own people. It was Mr Isaac D'Israeli, Dizzy's father, who arranged for all four of his children to be baptised into the Church of England. Dizzy was then about twelve years old, and so had not celebrated his *bar mitzvah*.'

Maria murmured that yes, they had heard something of the sort, before adding, 'But why, when his father had departed this life, did Mr Disraeli not choose to return to the Synagogue?'

The second course, a delicious fish stew, was now brought in and conversation languished until everyone had been served.

Mrs Moss took up her fish knife and fork, glanced down the table to assure herself that her guests had everything they might require, and only then did she address the question, with a small sigh. 'When I tell them what Dizzy told me, they are often anything but pleased.'

She placed a little of the fish on her fork. 'The reason he has not returned to the Synagogue is that his allegiance is now to the Jesus of the Other Testament.'

The silence following these words could almost be felt. Susannah was left to continue the story. 'I heard Dizzy say that he was convinced that Jesus came to complete all that had been spoken of by our prophets, and to fulfil in every regard the law given us by Moses. He asked, "Who can deny that Jesus is the incarnate Son of God?" I was not the only Jewish person there that day, but I heard no voice raised against him.'

Robert was incensed. 'You cannot mean to tell us that every Jewish person there agreed with him?'

'Not at all, Robert. I meant only that we were impressed by the conviction with which he spoke. No-one could bring himself to enter into controversy against the outstanding man of our age.'

Mrs Moss then made another determined effort to change the topic of conversation from the one she had initiated. She paid particular attention to Emilia, drawing her out to tell of her interests, her likes and dislikes, and her hopes for the future. As she firmly reminded herself, getting to know this friend of Robert's had, after all, been the main purpose of the visit.

The afternoon passed swiftly, and dusk was near when Maria rose to leave. Delighted with the recipes she had been given, she bid adieu and was followed into the hall by Emilia and Robert. Their horse had already been fed, watered, harnessed and put to the coach so they could be off. Maria was anxious to be home before darkness set in.

As long as their hostess could be seen, Emilia continued waving her handkerchief. Not till then did she lean back and say happily to no-one in particular that she had enjoyed the afternoon immensely.

'I do not doubt it,' responded her mother dryly, 'since the subject of conversation was your favourite one'.

'Whatever can you mean, Mama?'

'It seems to me, Emilia, that we spoke of little other than yourself.'

This made her daughter pause.

Maria continued. 'However, we did speak of other things and, I must say, a little of what I heard was most disturbing. Mrs Moss said that Mr Disraeli, whom we all look up to, chooses the Christian's understanding of God rather than our own. This is very distressing. Has he altogether rejected his own heritage, Robert? Does he then deny the truth of the Scriptures?'

Robert's concern equalled hers. 'No, Mrs Aronson, I cannot believe that he has turned his back on his heritage, for on that occasion when I talked to him, he actually said, "Mark my words young man. The time will come when vast communities in America will still find music in the songs of Zion and seek solace in the parables of Galilee." Does that sound like a man who has forsaken his Jewish roots?'

Maria, only vaguely comforted, had heard enough about the Disraelis. She began to speak of other things. When they reached the street in which the Newfields lived, the horse slowed to a halt.

As they opened the coach door, a blast of cold air rushed in upon them. Robert was farewelled hastily amidst final good wishes to his family so the door could be closed against the unwelcome evening air.

Following the short ride to their own house, Emilia and her mother warmed themselves before their drawing room fire. After some thought, Maria said, 'That would have been a strange conversation that Robert had with Mr Disraeli on the one occasion they met. He mentioned "the parables of Galilee", did he not?'

'Yes, Mama. I have only once had a Christian's Bible in my hand. A girl at school showed me hers. Our Scriptures take up almost the whole of their Bible. Their Other Testament is tacked onto the end. The parables of Galilee must be in there.'

'Well, of course, I have always known that they rely a great deal on the teachings of Moses and the prophets, which has always seemed to me rather odd. But then they add to our Bible and make Jesus out to be the Anointed One, the Messiah, or as they say, the Christ, when we all know he was like all other Jewish men, no better and no worse. It worries me that Robert's grandmother is so tolerant of Mr Disraeli's Christian leanings. Should Robert ever speak to you of such things again, Emilia, I want you to let him understand that you are not interested.'

Emilia was about to ask why when her mother spoke again.

'It might be best if your father did not know anything about our conversations on this trip. I imagine he would be far from pleased. We will say nothing to him or indeed to anyone, and we will try to forget it ourselves.'

Relieved of her pent-up feelings, Maria left the fireside to make her way upstairs, and Emilia followed her, chewing her knuckle in uncertainty. That she was not to broach the topic with her father she could well understand. It was really no-one else's business, but she could not take seriously her mother's prohibition on her talking it over with Robert. He was the very person who could help her see the matter clearly. When the opportunity presented itself, this was what she would do.

CHAPTER 8

Bangor

1863

ROBERT NOW CALLED AT THE HOUSE EVERY SPARE MOMENT HE HAD. Whenever he could beg time away from his work, he was there to take tea with Emilia and her mother, to escort them to galleries and museums and even, on occasion, to accompany them on their picnics. Robert also accompanied Emilia to the important events of the Season. Her friends called her a social butterfly and pointed out that they'd have never expected to use that name about her.

When Emilia, in bubbling high spirits, would tell her father of their latest outing, John Aronson would grumble that Daniel Newfield was more lenient with his sons than he had been with his.

'The trade in tea must be flourishing. It might be worth my while investing a little in some of their shares.'

But nothing could dampen Emilia's bliss throughout this time. She would have been happy to let it go on indefinitely, but Robert was insistent that the time had come to seek positive approval from her father so that they might be engaged and could then begin planning their wedding.

After exhaustive enquiries regarding Robert's standing in the business and Jewish communities, John Aronson was satisfied that there could be no valid objections to a union between him and his third daughter. But there was still one question that required an answer.

After dinner one evening, when the remains of the meal had been cleared away and Maria and the children had left their places to go to the drawing room, John detained Emilia. He suggested that she sit beside him in her mother's place. Knowing what was to come, she ran forward eagerly.

'Now, about that young man of yours. He has written to say that he will not be satisfied until he has my approval for an engagement. Before I can give that, there is something I must hear from your own lips. How do you feel about it all? Is Robert Newfield the man you choose to marry?'

A most searching gaze accompanied the last question, for John Aronson knew his daughter well enough to be confident that should she have even the slightest doubt, it could not be hidden from him. But it appeared his fears were groundless, for her response came freely.

'Yes, Papa, Robert is the man for me, and I want to be married to him, more than anything in the world.'

John was conscious of the solemnity of the moment, but was far from convinced that Emilia was. He lowered his voice so that she had to pay strict attention to what he was saying. 'It is necessary for a young woman in your situation to face reality, Emilia. An engagement is not just an excuse for a round of parties designed to make you the envy of your friends. It is not an arrangement to provide you with a pile of gifts with which you scarcely know what to do. Where our people are concerned, an engagement is a very serious matter indeed. It is a betrothal that leads on to the *chuppa* as surely as night follows day. Afterwards come family responsibilities, and they are what I am not sure about. Are you ready for those, Emilia?'

'Oh, I am, Papa. Of course, I am!'

John gave this daughter of his a long considering look. He was remembering her history of poor health, her long drawn-out battles to be placed on an equal footing with others her age. Dare he allow her to take this decisive step from which there could be no withdrawal? Did not wisdom decree rather that she be made to wait a few more years? With due care to avoid antagonising her, John tried to put these thoughts into words. It was as if he had touched a sensitive nerve.

'Oh no, Papa! Please do not ask us to wait any longer! Robert wants the wedding to take place as soon as it can be arranged, and that is my wish too. Will you not allow us to be engaged this very week? Please give us your consent tonight, please Papa!'

Her father lowered his head in thought. He asked himself whether he and Maria had been better prepared for the responsibilities of life at the time of their engagement, and came to the reluctant conclusion that they had not. Like every couple they knew, they had of necessity to learn as they went along. Emilia and Robert would just have to do the same. He sighed, rose from his chair, leant forward and planted a kiss on his daughter's forehead. 'Very well, my dear. When Robert comes for his answer, I will tell him that he has my approval, and the engagement may be announced as soon as the dowry is settled.'

Emilia, her face alight with joy, caught his hand and kissed it. Then she rose to her full height and hugged him tightly. 'Thank you, Papa! Thank you, thank you!' She then leapt for the door and, as her father followed more slowly, she sped towards the drawing room to break the good news to her mother and siblings.

Soon after Maria's brother, Alexander Lazarus, and his wife Dora, arrived at the house where Emilia and Robert were to celebrate their engagement, Emilia found herself enveloped in a great kissing hug. 'To think that you two first met in our garden!', exclaimed Dora.

Alexander assured Robert, in the best tradition, that he had shown excellent taste in choosing such a special young lady.

Soon the engaged couple began the ceremony of Sitting for Joy, meeting a steady stream of family and friends coming to offer their felicitations and to add to the ever growing layers of gifts.

Early in the afternoon, Emilia's smile had been wide and welcoming but, as time progressed, the muscles of her face began to ache intolerably. Her smile lost its spontaneity. She turned slightly in her seat to see how Robert was faring. Were his neck and shoulders feeling the strain too? While engagement had much to commend it, she was forced to the sad conclusion that the same could not be said for Sitting for Joy, which to her mind could be described in no other way than as a test of endurance.

For Emilia, the months leading up to the wedding passed in a kind of dream—an exciting dream of a future with her own house and servants. Her mother took her to London to purchase her trousseau. Her father booked the carriages. The invitations went out. The dress was delivered. She lived through each day as though the bustling activity, into which the household was thrown, had nothing whatever to do with her—despite being consulted on all kinds of matters as if her word were law.

In vain was Maria's constant effort to bring her daughter down to earth. Finally, as the wedding date drew inexorably closer, she set aside a time to discuss the really important practical issues. 'Meet me this afternoon in the library, Emilia. I simply must talk to you. There is not only the wedding itself, you must prepare for all the years ahead as Robert's wife. Do you have any idea what that will entail? I will see you at two o'clock. Please be on time.'

Even after being taken severely to task, Emilia found meeting her mother's expectations more and more difficult. How could she put her mind to mundane matters, when this rosy world of joyful anticipation enfolded her?

One mundane matter to which she did attend was to remind Robert to arrange his life insurance.

CHAPTER 9

London, England
1863

THE NEXT DAY, ROBERT SET OFF FOR LONDON WHERE HE FOUND A room near Euston Station.

The following morning, after the short cab ride to Harley Street, he had no difficulty finding the recommended insurance office. With the cheque for the first premium safe in his coat pocket, he climbed the stone steps to the entrance and went in. After a few preliminary questions at the desk, he was ushered into the consulting room of the company's doctor where he was politely requested to remove his coat, waistcoat and shirt. He was then subjected to the most thorough examination he had yet undergone. He was aware that he was in the hands of a most conscientious medical practitioner. Not once, but several times, the doctor repeated the sounding of his lungs and heart and recorded his findings with meticulous care. He then indicated that Robert might dress, after which he invited him to take a chair at the side of his desk.

Robert sat watching the doctor pinch his upper lip between his thumb and forefinger. Surely he had only to say, 'I find you in excellent health, Mr Newfield. Please take this report to one of our insurance agents in the next room.' What was wrong with the man? Why was it so difficult?

Finally the doctor spoke. 'I regret to have to tell you, Mr Newfield, that my tests prove that you are not a fit person for life insurance. I am afraid I cannot pass you.'

Robert gazed across the neatly arranged desk and wondered if he had heard right. 'Not pass me as fit? I should like to know why not!'

The answer could not have been more clearly put. 'Mr Newfield, you are suffering from tuberculosis in an advanced form. Its more common name is "consumption". Your life expectancy at present is a few months at best, and then only if you move to a warmer climate immediately.'

Robert sprang to his feet. 'I do not accept your findings, nor do I believe what you are telling me. There are other insurers in London. I shall avail myself of their services without delay!'

Still muttering to himself about that fool who dares to practise as a doctor, Robert hurried down the steps to the street and looked about him. He saw a likely sign in a window further down, strode in its direction and there presented himself once more to an insurance society's physician. In a short while, he was back on the street seeking yet another insurer, then another. By the time his watch showed a quarter to five, he had visited six insurance companies and been turned away from them all.

Several of the doctors had spent a fair amount of time with him while others were at once satisfied that they were dealing with the victim of a fatal malady. Tuberculosis! Consumption! The words were repeated like a death knell in consulting room after consulting room where sombre faces refused to be moved from their findings by his scathing denials. The final doctor, who was older and more understanding than the rest, had shaken his head at him sorrowfully. 'Would that I could agree with you, Mr Newfield. If only it were true. It is not my task to support you in your unfounded hopes; I must present the facts to you as they are.'

It was then that Robert, for the first time, bowed his head in defeat. Something within him withered and every fond hope died. He thanked his examiner for his patience and returned to his hotel.

On the train journey home, Robert searched his mind desperately for the words with which he might acquaint Emilia of the perilous state of his health, and finally realised that there was just no way to soften the blow. Robert had to steel himself for the task that lay ahead. After pacing the Bangor station platform for what seemed a long time, but was actually only two minutes, he squared his shoulders, pushed open the door and entered the railway tea room.

Emilia and her mother were seated at a table in an alcove, the teapot and cups before them, awaiting his arrival.

His first action was to apologise for keeping them from their tea.

They both smiled at him. 'Nonsense, Robert!' Maria waved him to the place beside her daughter. 'The pot has been brought just this minute. We ordered it when your train came in.'

As he drew his chair up to the table, Emilia caught a glimpse of something in his face that warned her all was not well. Her mother, across the table, also found her eyes drawn to his face, and both she and Emilia, disturbed without understanding why, put their anxiety into words at the same time.

'Has something happened, Robert?'

'Robert, you are so very pale.'

He did not answer them at once and Emilia, who was still looking at him fixedly, wondered why. He gazed instead across the room, though what had caught his interest there other than empty tables and bare walls, she could not see.

Leaning closer to him, she whispered, 'Robert, is there something wrong? If there is, you know you can tell us.'

Ever the practical one, Maria poured tea for them all, and Emilia placed Robert's cup where he could not fail to see it. This thoughtful act broke into his reverie, and he turned again to face them.

'Mrs Aronson, Emilia, yes, there is something I must tell you, though how I am to find the words ... '

They heard his deeply indrawn breath and waited. Pity stirred in them both.

'I am afraid it has not been possible for me to insure my life.'

Their relief was so great it had to express itself in words. 'If that is all that is worrying you ... ,' began Maria.

Her daughter chimed in, 'There's bound to be a suitable agency in Liverpool.'

One look at Robert's face made it clear to them that they had somehow failed to lay hold of the heart of the problem.

'Please allow me to explain. It will not be possible for me to insure my life anywhere, ever. I have been told that I have almost no life left to insure. Every doctor who has seen me, and I have been examined by many, has said that I am a consumptive in the final stages. I might live another few months if I sail for the south of France this week. So you see, Emilia, we cannot continue to plan our future together. I have no future.'

The shock was so severe that neither Emilia nor her mother could speak. There was therefore no protest at first when Robert rose to his feet. 'I must ask you to excuse me now. I have to let my own family know. Goodbye, darling Emilia! Goodbye, Mrs Aronson!'

'Robert!' The cry was torn from Emilia's throat, but he only turned back for a moment.

'It is best that I go now, Emilia. God bless you my dear, dear girl.'

Maria put out her hand to take her daughter's. 'Let him go, my child. Robert belongs to his family now.'

Stunned and appalled beyond measure, Emilia slumped back in her chair. Her heart was fluttering as though desperate to escape from a body that had in a matter of minutes turned to ice. Her breathing became ragged, and she began to experience again the terror she had known so frequently in childhood. But, before she could be overwhelmed, she heard the sound that had always spelt security: the scraping of her mother's chair on a polished floor. At once, Emilia cast herself into her mother's arms. There she shuddered uncontrollably while the tears that might have eased the pain, however slightly, refused to come.

CHAPTER 10

Bangor

1863

MARIA CAME OUT OF HER DAUGHTER'S BED ROOM AND SOFTLY CLOSED the door. She smothered the sigh that had risen within her, for she had done too much sighing of late. Since the day that Robert returned from London to break the shocking news, gloom had descended on two households—not only gloom, but sharp anxiety. Emilia's health had broken down completely and she now kept to her room, eating almost nothing and speaking scarcely at all.

There had been a letter from Robert. He had written that his arrival in Paris had taken place without incident, and he would soon be on his way to the villa that his father was renting for him on the Riviera. He begged Emilia not to grieve for him, but to take care of herself and to adapt to a contented life without him. He sent her his fondest love and asked to be remembered to her family.

Maria had kept this letter for some days, waiting for the right moment to show it to Emilia. If only she could be certain that seeing Robert's handwriting would not waken afresh her daughter's sense of desolation and her inconsolable despair. Emilia's mind had become so overwrought with grief that her mother hesitated to place upon it even the lightest burden.

She paced up and down the landing outside Emilia's bed room weighing the benefits against the possible harm, and decided finally to judge from her response whether to take the matter further. She entered the darkened room again and leant over Emilia's listless form. 'My darling, a letter has come.' As this was greeted with nothing but silence, Maria continued, speaking very softly, 'It has a French postmark, Emilia, and Robert's handwriting. Would you like me to read it for you?'

This time a gentle sigh escaped the blanched lips of the young woman on the bed, and taking this as a sign that some interest had been aroused, Maria unfolded the letter and began to read. But before the first sentence had come to an end her daughter's head rolled back and forth on the pillow and tears welled up between the half-closed lids.

'Very well, Emilia', her mother said hurriedly, 'if it upsets you so much I will read no more. But Robert has not forgotten you, and cares for you still. I shall leave the letter here by your bed so that when you feel ready you may read it yourself.' Kissing her daughter tenderly, Maria murmured, 'Poor darling dear', and tip-toed from the room.

That evening Maria sought out her husband. 'It is time we did something more for Emilia than just watch her suffer! It is beyond our power to do anything for poor Robert, but that is not the case with our daughter. We must get Maurice here for a consultation.'

Her husband looked up from his newspaper in surprise. 'Dr Isaacs, unless I am completely mistaken, is in this house every week or so.'

'Oh yes, he is his usual attentive self where Emilia is concerned, and has succeeded in bringing about some slight improvement in her state of health. But I am speaking of something quite different now. She is behaving like the young girl she was rather than the woman she has become. We need his advice to help her to face the future and to take up the threads of her life. After all, at twenty-one years of age she has still a great deal of living ahead of her.'

On the first evening that Maurice Isaacs was free, he accepted Maria's invitation to dinner. As soon as the coffee had been brought into the drawing room, she wasted no time in asking for his advice.

Pursing his lips, as was his habit when giving a matter his deepest consideration, Maurice gave it as his opinion that the weight of medical evidence regarding the restorative value of sea voyages could not be ignored. 'For Emilia, a long voyage will have the added benefit of removing her from all places that are associated in her mind with Robert Newfield and the tragedy that has befallen him.'

Little could have been more unpleasant for Maria to hear, but she did not interrupt.

'Everything about this house, this town, these hills, is a reminder to Emilia of all that might have been. I am hopeful that the proven double remedy of sea air and sunshine, will take her out of herself as nothing else could do.

My advice, since you have asked for it, is that you send Emilia away by sailing ship, as soon as possible.'

Now Maria could no longer restrain herself. 'But Maurice, she cannot be sent away in the state she is in at present! You have seen her, thinner than she has ever been, for she eats little. It is beyond reason to expect her, in such a run-down condition, to stand up to the rigours of a sea voyage.'

Maurice Isaacs looked across at her with compassion. 'It has been my experience,' he said gently, 'that patients in a decline such as Emilia's often recover once their interest in life around them is reawakened. This does frequently happen at sea. I strongly recommend that you begin making enquiries.'

But Maria, who was not yet ready to give up the fight, had found another objection. 'There is the matter of a chaperone, Maurice. A young inexperienced woman of Emilia's age cannot travel great distances by sea unaccompanied. It is unthinkable!'

'Not as unthinkable as you might suppose, Maria. In these days of mass emigration, many young women sail long distances by themselves.'

John Aronson had been a silent listener to the exchange between his wife and Maurice Isaacs without feeling any need to contribute to the conversation. At this point, he rose from his seat and went to stand with his back to the fire. He cleared his throat several times as though to give notice that he was about to speak, but still took another moment to set his thoughts in order. 'Maria, I am entirely in agreement with you that it would not be seemly to send our daughter on a sea voyage of any length without providing someone to accompany her. But can you not see that there is someone to go with her? George is ready now to represent our firm in the antipodes and it is high time he was given his chance.'

Maria glanced up sharply at her husband. He had not a devious bone in his body. She would have to come to terms once again with the fact that the great oceans of the world would come between her and her beloved children.

'You will remember, Maria,' John was saying, and she made a visible effort to concentrate on his words, 'that over recent weeks we have been discussing sending George to Melbourne. Now, with Emilia requiring a long sea voyage for her health, we have an answer to the question of a travelling companion for him, as well as one for her. It seems to me a neat solution for them both.'

Maria, her expression stony, said through stiff lips, 'When I receive news of the safe arrival of both my children and learn that Emilia has been restored to full health, then and only then, will I concede that what you consider a neat solution has in truth been best for all concerned.'

John Aronson took it upon himself to obtain two first-class tickets on *Empire of Peace*, a White Star Line clipper sailing from Liverpool to Melbourne on 8th February 1864. Now Maria and George had to break the news to Emilia.

Maria was at her most encouraging when she entered her daughter's bed room with George. 'Here is George come to see you, darling. You cannot imagine what it is he has to say to you. Something you could never guess!'

She then stole quietly from the room, but not before she heard a small voice ask, 'What is it?'

Leaning forward as though sharing a secret with his sister, George said in a low voice, 'It has been decided at last, Emilia, I am to go to Melbourne for Papa. It's time I went to investigate the jewellery and wool trades in the colonies.'

Was he mistaken, or had a moan arisen from among the bedclothes? A moment later his sister raised her head from the pillow and turned on him a pair of woebegone eyes in which there trembled two large tears.

'I hope those tears mean that you will miss me, Emilia?' He could not mistake the two very firm nods that came in answer to this question. 'Then come with me! It is a fearfully long journey to make alone. It would be altogether different if you were there as well. Do say you will come!'

For a brief moment, Emilia's eyes lit up. A nod of affirmation followed. And another.

'Good girl, I knew you would not let me down.' George judged from her eager nod that his sister was as ready as he to be on her way. After they had informed their mother, they began to plan to their heart's content all that needed to be done.

PART TWO

Bon Voyage

February to June 1864

CHAPTER II

At sea

February 1864

SHE DREAMED OF ROBERT OFTEN, WITH AN INTENSITY THAT MADE the dreams more real to her than the life to which she later awakened. That night's dream was no exception. As she again drew near to the gate leading into the garden, the air was filled with the perfume of spring flowers. The gentle hum of bumblebees was like the purring of a well-contented kitten.

Robert was waiting for her in his usual place in the shade of a spreading oak. As she hurried towards him, she could hear the river at the bottom of the garden chuckling over its stones and pebbles. The last time she had been here she had wondered if there might be a punt that could take them out onto the water but she had forgotten to ask.

He had heard the click of the gate and had raised his head from the book he was reading to call to her. 'Emilia, my darling. You are here at last! I have been waiting for you to come.'

He rose to his feet, stretched his arms wide and, as she ran into them, gathered her to him. She laid her cheek against his and blissfully closed her eyes, waiting for his welcoming kiss. But Robert eased her down onto the seat beside him, and then reluctantly drew away from her. 'We cannot be too careful Emilia, for your sake.' He took both her hands in his. 'How very delighted I am that you could come. I would not have believed it possible to miss anyone as much as I have missed you.'

Through tears, Emilia said softly, 'As I miss you, Robert. Each time I come I look for some improvement so in time we can again be together.'

Robert shook his head sadly. 'No my dearest one, there can be no improvement, only decline. The disease is following its usual course, and much as I would like to surprise you with news of a miraculous cure, I have long since given up the expectation of any such thing.'

This grim fact was discussed each time they met, and now, to counter the gloom that followed close upon it, Emilia happily remembered the punt.

'Would it be possible for us to go out on the river? Have you seen a punt that we might use?'

'There is one, though I have not seen it. The day will come for me to take the punt out onto the river, but that day is not yet.'

It distressed Emilia to see that far from lightening the atmosphere, her query about the punt had plunged Robert into an even deeper melancholy. Fearful of causing him further anguish she remained silent, her hands growing cold in his. And so they sat for what seemed to her a very long time, until Robert released her and reached for the book he had put aside at her approach.

'Emilia,' he said hesitantly, 'there is something here we ought both to look at. Read this to me, and tell me what you think.' He found the page he wanted, and with his finger marking the line, placed a Bible in Emilia's lap.

She knew this passage. It was from the Prophet Isaiah. She began to read aloud.

> Behold, the Lord's hand is not shortened that it cannot save;
> neither his ear heavy, that it cannot hear: But your iniquities
> have separated between you and your God, and your sins have
> hid his face from you, that he will not hear. For your hands
> are defiled with blood, and your fingers with iniquity; your
> lips have spoken lies, your tongue hath muttered perverseness.

Looking into Robert's face, Emilia could not contain her indignation. 'Who is being spoken of here, Robert? It cannot be you! Your tongue does not speak lies or mutter perverseness.'

'I am not blameless, Emilia, and I do not know of anyone who is, do you? I have not lived for twenty-five years without telling a lie, and if perverseness means wilful wrong-doing, then I am guilty of that too.'

Provoked beyond reason, Emilia demanded hotly, 'But that can be said of every person who has ever lived, Robert!'

He sighed softly, 'Emilia, how can I use the sins of others to excuse my own? We both know well, my darling, that my life is drawing to its end. At some time in the not-too-distant future I will be required to give an account to the Most High God of the years that have been allowed me on earth. What have I ever done that I might be deemed worthy to stand in His presence? I look back over my life and see nothing that I have done, or said, or even thought that was not motivated by selfishness. Can you wonder then that I stand condemned by the words you have read, knowing that what is written applies to me? I am separated from God!'

Emilia was filled with dismay to see that a mist of tears covered Robert's eyes, and she searched her mind for another, a lighter topic of conversation, so that they might still enjoy this time of being together.

But Robert was already speaking again, his voice very low, 'I have never admitted to anyone, not even to myself, how long I have been resisting the Lord God, refusing to let Him into any part of my life. And now that I need Him so desperately, I do not know how I might find Him.'

He lifted his head to face her and his next words came as a cry from the depths of his being. 'I am on the very edge of eternity, Emilia, and I am not ready!'

Her heart swelling with an aching pity, Emilia offered what comfort she could. 'Robert, do any of us give thought to the life after death unless circumstances compel us? My darling, in your situation we would all be just as you are.'

She drew him to her and as his arms went about her she could feel the shuddering of his sobs. And it was then that she experienced a division of herself. She was at the same time an onlooker, fearing the scene would fade and leave her to lament. She knew then that it was another dream onto which she could not hold. She became aware of her tear-dampened pillow and a grey porthole through which the morning light was streaming.

She turned her pillow to its cooler side and for some time tried to recapture her dream, but could not. She realised again that she and Robert were parted for all time, and that every hour was taking her further and further from him. A familiar head-pain now threatened to overwhelm her. With a determined effort, she sat up and swung her feet to the bare boards.

She padded her way to the writing desk in the corner of the cabin and sat there wondering if she would ever become accustomed to the wearying sound of wood under stress, and the creaking and groaning of every piece of bolted-down furniture around her. All in all, she considered she had done well to adjust so quickly to shipboard life, though the constant scurry and bustle of men out on the decks was far removed from her normally placid life at home. She reached across for a sheet of foolscap, chose a sharpened pencil from a box, and began to write.

My dearest Mama,

It is some days now since George and I said goodbye to
you all at Liverpool and set sail on 8th February. How often
I think of you all with the tenderest feelings imaginable.
Tell Papa that we are so thankful for his prayer that gave
us up to the God of Abraham, Isaac and Jacob and asked
for the blessing of the angel that redeemed us from all evil.
I shall never forget the faces of our brothers and sisters
gathered to farewell us. Emily cried. It was heart-wrenching
to hug my nephews and nieces, not knowing how much
they will have grown by the time I return to Bangor.

My tears were stilled when Papa took George and me aside
and gently laid his hands on our heads and began to recite
that beautiful Aaronic Blessing.

'The Lord bless thee and keep thee. The Lord make his face to
shine upon thee, and be gracious unto thee. The Lord lift up
his countenance upon thee, and give thee peace.'

Never have I seen my father so moved as when he drew
us, first one and then the other close to his heart. I was
overwhelmed with love for him then, and know I will love
him always. You too, Mama, I miss you both so much!
How I wish I could have you here with me, at least for a little
while, but alas, every hour is driving me farther away from you
until such time as I return Home, whenever that might be.

I miss you dreadfully, Mama, especially so this morning after
dreaming of Robert again last night and waking to another
day without him.

Here she paused, aware that should she continue in this vein, her mother
would worry. She must avoid that at all costs. Resolving to introduce a
brighter note, she continued,

Thank you Mama, for the paper, postage stamps and pencils
which I found packed in my cabin trunk. Who but my
darling mother would be so thoughtful as to include these?

Now there is no excuse for my not writing home, but there was little danger of that ever happening as I want to tell you about all the excitements that have taken place on board since we set sail.

The first and most amazing thing is that George and I have found we are not subject to seasickness! Do you remember when Eliza and Abraham were on their way to Australia? How they suffered that first week at sea? George and I fully expected that we too would endure the same fate, but it seems we are blessed with strong stomachs, inherited no doubt from Grandfather. You once told us he was the only member of his large family who did not suffer from mal de mer. You may imagine what a happy circumstance it is for me, Mama, to be one of the healthy few on board when hundreds are confined to their beds!

Since we left England, only three first-class passengers have attended all meals, Miss Nancy Wait, George and me. As a consequence we have been able to enjoy a good deal of Miss Wait's company.

George has observed that there is a resemblance between us. We both have dark wavy hair with some curls, brown eyes and neat chins. Her complexion is more brilliant than mine. Unlike me, she has a light dusting of freckles across her nose. She is perhaps a year or so older than me, and a little taller.

We share many interests in common. She was a music teacher at Thornvalley Hall. Miss Wait is travelling to the colony of Victoria to take up a position as a governess and music teacher in the Western District.

A glance at the porthole was enough to show Emilia that the morning was now well advanced. Forsaking her desk, she hastened to prepare herself for breakfast. A knock at the door revealed a girl, a mere child, with a ewer of hot water for her wash.

As Emilia placed the last pin in her hair, George appeared to escort her for a stroll on deck until the gong should sound for the first meal of the day.

In the early days, Emilia's innate reticence made meal times awkward. When seated at the Master's table, and thus obliged to respond to the gambits of Captain Clark, she could scarcely concentrate on her food for nervousness. Those officers seated at the same table, were mostly young men who reminded Emilia of her brothers at social events in Bangor. Gradually, she became comfortable with the company of staff and passengers in the dining saloon and on deck.

Indeed, there were times when Emilia surprised herself by engaging one or two of the officers in a few words of light chatter whenever their paths crossed. The ship's doctor, though a little older, was also pleasant to talk to. Later, when she wrote of him to her mother, Emilia said she could not understand how he was able to care for the dozens of seasick passengers, both above decks and below, as conscientiously as he did.

Not only Emilia's shyness, but her general health as well, was deriving benefit from life on board ship. The sea air, the frequent sunshine, the good food and no doubt the days of leisure in an unfamiliar setting, were proving as effective as any tonic that might have been prescribed for her. In one of her letters, she remembered to thank her mother for her forethought in ordering clothes that were a little larger in size. It was only a question of time, she wrote, before she would need to wear them.

CHAPTER 12

At sea

February 1864

OUT ON THE DECK EARLY ONE MORNING, EMILIA BREATHED HER FILL of the crisp air and gazed at the heaving ocean with serene contentment. It was much better here than in her confined cabin. Leaning on the ship's rail, listening to the thrumming of the wind in the canvas above her and the rushing of the water against the bow, she would have been happy to stay in the same spot hour after hour. The movement of the deck beneath her feet, the massive rolling and regular pitching exhilarated her, and though she would have not objected to remaining there alone, she looked up gladly when a shadow fell along the deck at her side.

'Good morning, Miss Aronson. You are out early, I see.'

She saw that it was the ship's doctor approaching the rail, his face raised blissfully to the sunlight. It was an arresting face. Apart from its obvious intelligence, there was a variety of colour to catch the eye, for combined with his grey-green eyes and warm brown hair, he wore a neatly trimmed beard the exact shade of ripened wheat.

'Good morning, Dr Langmore.' Aware that she had been staring, Emilia blushed beneath his smiling gaze and shyly turned her head away.

'Miss Aronson, I am delighted to find you out taking the air. If all my patients were to adapt to life on board a sailing vessel as quickly as you have done, there would be little for a ship's surgeon to do, and I could well find myself without a situation.'

Emilia was about to respond to this when they were interrupted by a sudden loud cry coming from the direction of a life-boat further down the deck. It was followed by the sound of an indignant voice raised in protest.

'Let me go, you beast!'

But it appeared that the beast had a very secure grip and, in spite of a volley of impolite comments, was sufficiently in command to haul into their view a scrawny ill-clothed youth. 'A stowaway, sir! Hiding in that there lifeboat.'

The youngster appeared to be no more than fourteen years old and Emilia could not help but be curious as to what would befall the boy.

'Take him to the captain, Wilks. He always prefers to deal with stowaways himself.'

'Aye aye, Sir!' And to the stowaway, 'Quick march, me lad!'

As they watched the two climbing a companionway which would lead them to the bridge, Emilia could contain herself no longer. 'What will become of him, Dr Langmore?'

Martin Langmore smiled at her reassuringly. 'Oh, he'll be all right. The captain will put the fear of death into him so that he will wish he had never been born, and after that will place him in the care of one of the older seamen who will see to it that he works out his passage. No stowaway is treated harshly on this ship.'

With relief showing on her face, Emilia said, 'I am so glad to hear you say that.' There was a moment's pause, and Emilia looked up into his face enquiringly, for it was evident to her that he had something on his mind to say.

He met her gaze ruefully. 'Miss Aronson, I have been hoping for some days to find you and your brother together so that I might speak to you both. But as it has not happened that way, may I ask you to tell him what I will now make known to you?'

'Yes, of course, Dr Langmore.'

'Miss Aronson, it is usual for the ship's surgeon to take his turn conducting Divine Service when there is no clergyman on board to do so. It may be helpful for you and your brother to know in advance the hour and place of meeting. It will be my pleasure to make sure that you are always notified in good time.'

Emilia's eyes left his face and focused on a line of waves out to sea. 'Thank you, Dr Langmore. That is a very kind thought, but neither my brother nor I will be attending church services. Our family is of the Jewish faith, and has been so for countless generations.' It had not been her intention to startle him, but she could see that she had done so.

He was instantly contrite. 'My dear Miss Aronson, forgive me! Of course, the name Aronson should have alerted me, but it is no use being wise after one has had to be told. I confess that my only thought till now has been that it is a handsome name for an equally handsome young lady. But please allow me to say how delighted I am that we have two of the Lord's own people "according to the flesh" in our midst.'

'Are my brother and I the only Jewish people on board the ship, Dr Langmore?'

'Now that I think about it, Miss Aronson, I do believe there is a Jewish couple, newly married as I understand it, among the eleven first-class passengers. They are Mr and Mrs Louis Monash. You have not made their acquaintance as yet?'

'Not yet, Dr Langmore, but you may be sure we will look out for them and make ourselves known.'

'Mrs Monash, I regret to say, is at present indisposed with seasickness. She is not familiar with the English language, but whenever I attend her, Mr Monash is kind enough to interpret for me.'

He smiled upon Emilia in the warmest manner possible. 'I must try to express to you my special interest in the Jewish people, Miss Aronson. I have long entertained an abiding respect and, more than that, a love for your people.'

Emilia was intrigued. 'May I ask why?'

'It surprises me that you should ask, for there are to me obvious reasons. Perhaps the first one I should mention is your gift to us of the Holy Scriptures. You cannot be unaware that by far the greater portion of the Christians' Bible consists of Jewish Holy Writ?'

Again fixing her gaze on some point beyond him, Emilia nerved herself to say, 'It grieves me to have to remind you, Dr Langmore, that Christians have added to our Tanakh that which is not lawful for us to believe.'

'You are no doubt referring to the later writings.'

'Yes, I mean the Other Testament. It is not for us, Dr Langmore!'

He moved slightly until he was standing squarely before her. 'The New Covenant was foretold by your own Prophet Jeremiah who declared, "Behold, the days come, saith the Lord, that I will make a new covenant with the house of Israel, and with the house of Judah." There is more, though at present I cannot recall it. Look in your Scriptures, Miss Aronson.'

Emilia, who had never heard of such a verse, determined to ask George about it at the first opportunity. Just then she heard his voice.

'Emilia!'

Startled, both she and Dr Langmore swung round. George was striding towards them, slightly out of breath.

'Good morning, Dr Langmore. I see you have found my sister. In spite of looking everywhere for her I have not been as fortunate as you till this minute. Where have you been, Emilia?'

Emilia had drawn a deep breath, and seeing that she was preparing to speak her mind to her brother, Dr Langmore broke in with a firm voice.

'May I ask you both if you would care to accompany me in a stroll along the deck until we hear the gong for breakfast? I would like your opinion about something that has been on my mind of late.'

Murmuring their willingness to be of help if they could, brother and sister fell into step at either side of the doctor as he began.

'Most of my patients are at present suffering from seasickness, not at all unusual during the first days of any sea voyage, and I had fallen into the habit of thinking that it must always be so. Until this voyage, when I have been asking myself whether the number of days that passengers remain prostrate could be shortened if an incentive were given them to rise from their beds sooner. I would like to test this theory by organising some activity that will appeal to almost everyone on board, and this is where I would value your advice. Whatever we arrange cannot be of too strenuous a nature and ought to take place while the weather is still mild. What form do you think this activity should take?'

Glancing at George, Emilia saw that his brow was knit in thought, but when she raised her eyes at him questioningly, he only shook his head. In the meantime an idea, vague at first, was gradually being revealed to her.

Before she could put words to it the breakfast gong sounded and all three quickened their steps. On the way to the dining saloon, Martin Langmore suggested that the Aronsons meet him at his surgery after the meal to discuss the matter further. They also agreed to his suggestion that it was time they began to use their first names.

Martin, Emilia and George arrived at Nancy's table. George chose to sit beside her. His sister took the chair that he had drawn out for her on his left. Only after she was seated did Emilia realise that Martin was at her other side.

Hesitantly at first, but then, as the meal progressed and she sensed his deepening interest, she shared her idea. 'Originally, what I had in mind was a costume ball but, since so many will have recently risen from sick-beds, perhaps it might be simpler to have a costume party during the afternoon. Do you not think so, Martin?'

'Yes, I do!'

Encouraged, Emilia expanded her idea. 'There must be limitations placed on lavishness of dress, permitting only things normally found on board ship and among passengers' own luggage. No-one need feel disadvantaged.'

Dr Langmore, who had been listening intently asked, 'Should we also restrict the costumes to those of living people?'

But there Emilia had to differ. 'Speaking for myself, I will be hard pressed enough without having that as an added difficulty.'

He nodded. 'Very well, I will let it be known that characters from any period of history will be acceptable. Do you think we should also allow figures from literature?'

'Oh yes, and nursery rhyme characters too. My guess is that these will be the most popular of all. When do you suggest?'

'Today, while the weather is mild and the winds are abating. I will consult Captain Clark now and then inform my patients on my rounds. That may inspire some of them to get out of bed. Please excuse me.'

Emilia turned to George and Nancy to ask their opinion. George readily concurred. 'Now we have the vexing question of the characters we are to assume. Do either of you have good ideas? My mind is a blank.'

Nancy's teacup hovered above its saucer while she gave this question her earnest consideration. 'Well,' she said at last, 'you and Emilia could dress as the Dish who ran away with the Spoon, in which case I must insist that Emilia appears as the Spoon. Or you two may have a preference for representing Dick Whittington, in which case ... '

George raised his hand imperiously, 'You may count on me as a gentleman to stand aside in Emilia's favour ... and allow her to be the cat'.

Nancy, who had been quietly enjoying the picture her mind had conjured up of George in whiskers and a furry tail, was piqued. But she chose to swallow her disappointment along with her tea, and to put her mind to other possibilities, with the result that barely half a minute later she was exclaiming, 'Of course, what could be better! You and Emilia can be the King and Queen of Hearts!'

'Indeed! I must say I like the thought of being announced as the King of Hearts better than that of the Dish that ran away with the Spoon. Really, now that I think of it, I am looking forward to that moment and the matter of finding appropriate costumes fades into insignificance. We will find something suitable with which to clothe ourselves, never fear.'

Emilia interrupted their conversation to suggest Florence Nightingale. 'Since George wants to be the King of Hearts, I suggest that Nancy be the nurse.'

'Why, that is a delightful idea. How clever you are. Since I don't have to spend long preparing my costume, I'll help you both make your crowns and see if I can acquire jam tarts from the galley.'

CHAPTER 13

At sea

February 1864

My dearest Mama,

We have been most fortunate till now in encountering the mildest weather imaginable, and are reminded by various officers that there will be foul weather waiting for us before we reach the Cape.

Last night I again dreamed that I was in the garden where Robert sits under the oak tree reading his Bible. He showed me that verse from the Psalms which tells of the goel who forgives all our iniquities and who redeems our lives from destruction. But wherever there is a redeemer, he must pay the price for our redemption, as with the *Pidyon haBen* when the first-born son is redeemed. Money has actually to change hands. So who, Robert asked me, has paid the price for those of us whose lives are redeemed from destruction? Of course, Mama, I do not know. The only acknowledged redeemer, the *goel*, must be a kinsman. So my dream was over-shadowed by this perplexity. I imagine Robert is failing in health wherever he is.

Now I must tell you Mama, of the Costume Party that took place yesterday afternoon. I am sure that had you been with me you would have taken as much pleasure in it as I did. In addition to the lavish tea provided, the costumes on parade were a treat not to be missed. Almost everyone on board was there, most having not long before risen from sick beds, and there were very many in fancy dress with historical, biblical and literary figures well represented. As you would expect there were also nursery rhyme characters such as Bo-Peep and Miss Muffet.

A father and son from intermediate-class came as William Tell. It appears that the father and Miss Wait are related and neither knew the other was on board until they met at the party. She speaks of him as 'Cousin Will', and the boy she calls 'Tommy'. I have now learned that their surname is Blackland.

To my mind Mama, the most spectacular of the costumes were worn by two sisters, seamstresses, who were dressed as The Queen of Sheba: Before and After meeting King Solomon. The Before sister was only moderately splendid, if that is not a contradiction in terms, and the After sister was clothed in what appeared at first glance to be cloth of gold but must have been a clever copy. She was weighed down with ropes of pearls and golden chains and armlets—also copies I am sure—but the result was well worth seeing!

While I was thinking about a character whose costume would be easiest to create with our limited luggage, George and Miss Wait decided upon the King and Queen of Hearts for us both. The idea of Florence Nightingale finally came to my mind. Miss Wait took my idea to be Florence and then she helped me to find a dress suitable for the Queen of Hearts and to prepare the jam tarts I had to take to the party.

Passengers are continuing now to recover from their seasickness, and George and I are meeting more of them on our promenades on deck, and at the meal table. We have made the acquaintance of Mr and Mrs Louis Monash. Mr Monash has already established himself as a merchant in Melbourne. George hopes to learn something from them.

Here Emilia paused, having heard noises from the deck. Listening intently, she was able to distinguish the sound of raised voices. Something out of the ordinary was taking place, and she was in no frame of mind to be left in ignorance of what it might be. She laid down her pencil, checked her appearance in the glass and hurried out on deck. She could see a crowd gathering and quickly joined it, for at its centre was a ship's officer with a telescope to his eye. Gazing out to sea in the same direction, Emilia saw, half-way to the horizon, the sails of another ship. So that was the reason for all the excitement! Before she could add her questions to those of the other passengers, the officer began to speak.

'She is the *Lady Leonore* on her way to London from Bombay. She has seen us now and is changing course so we can exchange mail.'

He lowered the instrument to urge those who had letters they were writing, to finish them in good time for the mailbag call.

Back at her desk, Emilia picked up her pencil again to write.

> Mama, a homeward bound sailing ship has been sighted!
> I will end my letter now in the hope of catching the mailbag.
>
> My fondest love to Papa and all at home, and the biggest and best of hugs and kisses to you, my darling Mama.
>
> From your ever-loving daughter,
>
> Emilia

With the letter to her mother clasped tightly in her hand, Emilia hurried back on deck. The rails were now almost fully lined with passengers, and spying an unexpected opening ahead of her, Emilia swiftly stepped into it. The next moment she was joined by George, also with an envelope in one hand. In the other he was clasping a small telescope which, after Emilia had relieved him of his letter, he wasted no time in raising to his eye.

The other ship was now fast approaching them and, after what she considered quite long enough for her brother to be taking pleasure in its wide sweep preparatory to coming alongside, Emilia plucked his sleeve.

'Let me see, George!'

Reluctantly, he passed the telescope to her and she gave him the letters so she could grasp the telescope securely. Emilia raised it expectantly and with the barest of turns she had it correctly focused and was amazed at the clarity of the scene that met her eye. Of the men and women crowding the ship's decks, many were in Indian dress. The colourful saris of the women captured her attention immediately, and for a time she had eyes for little else.

Emilia asked George to estimate the number of passengers.

'Well, the *Empire* has about 270; perhaps 150?'

The two ships were soon within hailing distance. Speaking trumpets enabled the captains to exchange news and weather and to arrange the exchange of mail. Excited chatter followed on both ships.

George told Emilia, 'There will be no difficulty lowering a boat today. The sea is as calm as I have seen it since we left England. I will see if I can find the sailor with the mailbags.'

Eventually, all the letters and packets were collected in canvas bags, securely tied together then lowered on a rope to seamen waiting in the ship's boat which had been lowered in readiness. Soon outgoing mail was drawn up onto the deck of the *Lady Leonore* to resounding cheers from both ships. Only once the boat had returned and the mailbags for Melbourne were taken on board did the passengers lose interest. By the time the two ships drew apart to resume their original courses, no more than a handful of passengers remained to wave their farewells.

Later that day, Emilia came across Nancy who was out on deck to blow the cobwebs away. As they fell into step, Nancy asked, 'Did you know that there is a school for passengers' children held every morning on the lower deck?'

'No, that I did not know. Who is the teacher responsible?'

'There are three, the Misses Gantry, all experienced in the handling of children. My cousin Will has been to see how the school is progressing, and he told me that for all their training the Gantry sisters are not finding it easy to manage the great numbers who come to them for tuition. Will tells me that many children and parents attend who have never learnt their letters. The Gantry sisters are almost at their wits end.'

Emilia's eyes narrowed as she looked searchingly at her friend. 'I can see that it is just a question of time before you offer to help them. They, of course, will be very pleased to have you. All your experience at Thornvalley should prove invaluable.'

Nancy did not answer at once. Her thoughts had flown to the years she had spent in Thornvalley, such happy years, and she only came down to earth when she heard Emilia ask, 'I am not mistaken, am I? You will be offering your help, Nancy?'

'Yes', she said at last. 'I did think I might talk to the Misses Gantry and see what I can do to help them.' Then she turned to Emilia with a question of her own. 'But what about you? From all I hear, two helpers would not be too many. I am sure there would be smiles all round if you were to come with me.'

Emilia at once became flustered. 'But I have no experience whatever! I would have to be shown what to do which would waste someone's time.'

'You could begin with the very youngest children. No-one has to take you through the alphabet, surely!'

For a full minute, Emilia turned over in her mind the possibility of helping in the school. Inexperienced as she was, the need was so great that something would have to be done. Finally she looked at her friend and said ruefully, 'You have persuaded me Nancy, rather against my will, I must confess. But I may be able to deal sufficiently with the little ones. At least I will try. Would you like me to go with you now to see the Misses Gantry?'

'Not immediately. We have scarcely been out on deck long enough to enjoy this refreshing breeze that has sprung up.'

Quite late in the day, the two young women went down between decks to offer to help teach in the school.

CHAPTER 14

At sea

March 1864

My dearest Mama,

A few days ago, Nancy and I enjoyed a pleasant stroll along
the deck as she told me much of her story. She had taught
in the school at Thornvalley and was pleased that she could
earn sufficient to keep her widowed mother in a fair degree
of comfort, for when her father had been alive, they had lived
very comfortably indeed.

Because she had always loved music, she had received
instruction in the pianoforte and, a little later, in singing as
well. A day came when she was delighted to receive a request
to provide the children at Thornvalley Hall with musical
instruction twice a week. There she composed a children's
march and some other piano pieces. Nancy was also a private
tutor for the children of several families in the district.

Sometime after her mother passed away, the children no
longer required tuition. Many had achieved the musical
skills they sought. Other students had grown older and were
sent to boarding schools. Even though some families still
engaged her as a music teacher, Nancy could not gain enough
income. She began to seek positions in neighbouring counties.
Then she found newspaper advertisements from the colony of
Victoria. Nancy has secured a position with the Williamsons,
a wealthy family in the Western District. She is to be
governess to the children and music tutor at a nearby school.

When she received confirmation from Mr Williamson, Nancy
happily made herself ready for the journey and came aboard
where we did, at Liverpool. It is such a story of a young

woman's courage that my eyes misted. As I began to tell her all that had befallen me, you may imagine how our tears flowed.

The weather has changed, and for the worse. After all the pleasant days we have experienced, we have now run into a series of storms. Annoying for us in first class, it must be especially unpleasant for the passengers in steerage. Nancy and I have been down there. Whenever there is heavy rain, or if the seas sweep over the decks, the hatches must be battened down to stop the between-decks accommodation being flooded. This means that steerage passengers are without fresh air and daylight for hours and even days at a time.

This inclement weather has closed down our school, Mama, which was being held out on deck each morning. There have been so many pupils, both children and their parents, that Nancy and I volunteered to help with the teaching. I asked for, and was given the youngest children, expecting these to be the easiest to manage. I soon learned my mistake! Most had not yet been taught to pay attention or to listen. As soon as our first morning's work was done, Nancy and I descended on George in his cabin and would not release him until he gave his promise to help on the following day.

But our victory was short lived, for the very next day the wind was so boisterous that I could not make myself heard, and school was dismissed. Since then strong winds and high seas have continued, and we all have no choice but to keep to our cabins, where there is so little to do apart from resting on the bunks and reading. Without our books George and I would be cast into utter boredom, and even so we have not escaped the numbing lethargy that results from the constant buffeting of winds and waves. Dr Langmore says this is common.

He tells us that he is planning something to revive everyone's spirits, but so far no-one has discovered what.

My very loving greetings to all the family, and my special love to you dear Mama and to Papa as well.

Your fond daughter,

Emilia

On a day when the wind had dropped sufficiently, George and Emilia promenaded the deck with Nancy between them. They saw crew carrying planks on their shoulders to an open space on the foredeck. Enjoying, as people do, the spectacle of others at work, they asked one another what the purpose of it all could be.

Not until they saw benches being brought up and placed in a wide semi-circle, did George exclaim, 'This has to be in preparation for whatever Martin is planning in the hope of raising the passengers' morale.'

Nancy, who was on the point of agreeing said instead, 'And here he is, coming to see how it is all progressing.'

It was indeed Dr Langmore who, seeing them, raised his hat politely. 'I am delighted to find you all here together. There is so little time, for this spell of fine weather cannot last beyond forty-eight hours, after which we will again no doubt be battered by storms. I wonder if you would help me make it widely known that we are to have a soirée at eight?'

George nodded. 'Yes, when I asked the captain about the weather he said the same thing. So we must make the best use we can of today's calm. Just what do you have in mind for the soirée, Martin?'

'I had hoped originally to arrange an evening of passenger participation for tomorrow night, but dare not take a chance on the weather. It will mean a great rush for everyone but it does cut short agonies before performance.' He glanced at his pocket watch. 'Please forgive my haste. I see all is going well here. You will favour us with a song this evening, Nancy? And you, George, no doubt have a recitation for us? And may I count on you, Emilia?'

George took it upon himself to answer for them all. 'We will not let you down.'

With a brief wave of his hand in parting, Dr Langmore strode off to employ his time involving as many passengers as he could in the coming entertainment.

My dearest Mama,

Last evening an entertainment was arranged for the ship's passengers by Dr Langmore. It was a right royal affair, made especially enjoyable for two members of the Aronson family and their friend Nancy Wait. The weather could not have been more suitable for an evening out on deck, as the full moon had risen by the time we were to start so there was no need of lanterns, and there was only the slightest breath of wind.

Nancy and I were both listed early on the programme so had but a short wait for our names to be called. Afterwards we were at liberty to enjoy ourselves watching and listening to the other performers. There were musical instruments played, a flute, a concertina and a violin, all undertaken by little more than beginners who received great ovations led, of course, by their own kith and kin.

The readings and recitations were more to my liking, especially the ballads, one of which was presented by George, but I must say that I did enjoy a violin duet played by Will and Tommy Blackland. Tommy's violin was smaller than his father's but it produced a very sweet tone, and he played it exceptionally well for an eight-year-old. The evening concluded with a one-act-play, an Irish Comedy, with three men and a woman from the Emerald Isle making up the cast. It ended with their singing of an old Irish folk-song, a lover's lament that was so haunting it brought out many a handkerchief, both of the male and female kind. It was as well that encores were kept to a minimum, for the entertainment, as so often happens, ran on far longer than had been expected.

Next morning the predicted storms had not yet arrived, and Nancy and I were able to take our usual stroll on deck.

We were stopped countless times to receive congratulations on our efforts of the night before, she on her beautifully expressive solo, and I on my dancing. One of the lady passengers impressed on Nancy that her rendering of *Home Sweet Home* had brought tears to the eyes of her husband who, when it came to matters of sentiment, was usually the most hardened of men.

Your loving daughter,

Emilia

The following evening the wind again rose as had been expected, heralding the onset of more stormy weather. But in spite of it Emilia slept soundly, and again dreamed of the garden where Robert awaited her. She felt the sun upon her, hotter than on her previous visits, and the fragrance coming to her on the faintest of breezes was that of summer roses. She could see Robert in his usual place beneath the oak with his coat beside him on the bench and his shirt-sleeves rolled up to the elbows. How gaunt he was becoming, and how pale. He rose to meet her, but the effort set him coughing, so she ran to gently ease him back. Seated beside him, Emilia chatted about anything that came to her mind, filling in the moments until he was ready.

Robert took her hand in his and said softly, 'I cannot tell you how glad I am that you have come today, Emilia, for it is to be a special day for me, and I so wanted you here. In a little while we will go together to look for the punt that is somewhere by the river's edge, but first there is something I particularly want you to know.'

Robert paused. 'When you were here last, I talked of our kinsman-redeemer. I can now tell you that I have found our *goel* at last, or should I say rather, that he has found me? Can you imagine the joy that I now have, my darling?'

Not only his eyes but his whole face was filled with a joyous light.

'I have accepted for myself the price he has paid for me, Emilia. I am not my own, I have been bought with a price, and that I am now washed, I am sanctified and I am justified!

Emilia could answer him nothing for she did not understand. Above all else, she was happy that he was happy.

Emilia lifted his hand, entwined firmly in hers, and lightly pressed her lips to it. If she was expecting to capture his attention, she failed, for Robert's mind was obviously elsewhere. 'Let us go down to the river now. It is time for our farewells. Come, my darling. Come with me.'

Hand in hand still, they followed the path to the shallows and almost at once found the punt half-hidden by reeds. Stretching down, Robert drew the punt to him and stepped into it. He bent for the pole, grasped resolutely and, even as Emilia extended her hand for him to help her in, pushed out away from the riverbank and into the current. As the boat picked up speed, he called out. 'Goodbye, my dearest! Do not be sad for me. I am going home to my redeemer-lord. Seek for him as I did, my darling, and let him guide you.'

As the last of his words floated across the water, Emilia saw Robert look up as though he were listening to a voice from above him. The pole that had been propelling him fell from his hands and his knees buckled. Just before a bend in the river hid him from view, she saw his hands go to his mouth and bright red blood well up between his fingers to stain his wrists and drip slowly into the boat.

Shaken by great wracking sobs, Emilia slowly became aware of a sodden pillow and desolation so deep that she scarcely took note of the shrieking of the wind in the rigging and the thundering of hail on the deck. Not till many dark hours had passed did she turn her pillow and make an effort to settle herself to sleep again. Even then memories of Robert would not leave her, and when at last her porthole began to let in a poor imitation of daylight, she rose from her bunk to seek what solace she could in a letter to her mother.

> My dearest Mama,
>
> Another dream tore at my heart last night. I dreamt that
> Robert is dead and I wept as I have never wept before.
> All round me nature is grieving with me, the very sky in
> tears as if to show its sympathy. During the night there was

a great storm, and we have been told we may expect many
more, so that it could be a long time before we see the sun
again. But what does that matter to one who has had every
likelihood of sunlight taken from her? I have heard people
say repeatedly that I am young with my whole life ahead of
me, but Mama, where am I to find another Robert? I look
into the future with no hope of finding the kind of happiness
I knew with him, and I am convinced that whatever the years
may bring it can only be second best.

Emilia

On a sunny morning of a cool Sunday in June, the *Empire of Peace* sailed
through the heads of Port Phillip Bay, waited several hours in mid-channel,
then slipped into her berth at Station Pier, Sandridge. Her long journey from
Liverpool was finally over.

PART THREE

Love's Arena
June 1864 to October 1865

CHAPTER 15

Sandridge, Victoria
5 June 1864

'STAND STILL EMILIA, AND LET ME GET A GOOD LOOK AT YOU!'

There had been hugs and kisses enough to satisfy even the two sisters and George, feeling he had fulfilled his duty, followed his brother-in-law back to the ship to see to their trunks.

In the face of her sister's close scrutiny, Emilia's mouth quirked into a mischievous smile. 'Well Eliza,' she asked, 'does what you see please you?' Emilia twirled about to reveal every possible view of herself to her sister's gaze.

Eliza's eyes grew round with amazement. 'My dear girl, I am finding it hard to believe what I see; and I don't mean your dress! When I call to mind the thin, pale, undersized scrap of humanity I left behind in Wales, I wonder if you can be the same person.'

Emilia laughed delightedly. 'It may not be easy for you to believe, Eliza, but I have George to vouch for me.'

'I cannot complain of your appearance Emilia, for in that direction there is a distinct change for the better, but what of that temper of yours?'

Emilia's eyebrows came down and her mouth formed itself into what her family had always called her puffy pout. Why were older sisters like this? They never failed to remind you of what you had been like as a child. She was relieved when Eliza changed the subject, for what could she have done other than to protest that she had long since grown out of childhood?

Instead, Eliza declared, 'I've been looking forward to wearing the dresses Mama sent for me. We are never sure of London fashion. But your clothes are coming apart at the stitching! What a good thing I have a dressmaker who can work wonders, though there may not be sufficient cloth there to let out the seams further.'

Before Emilia could declare that the matter of her clothes could wait, Eliza continued. 'I would not have you think that I am complaining, my dear.

It is a joy to see this happy outcome of your long sea voyage, and I know Mama will be delighted when I write to tell her.'

'Mama will be sure to let Dr Isaacs know and, if he were not such a gentleman, he would say, "I told you so!"'

Eliza drew Emilia's arm through hers. 'We must find somewhere to sit out of this crowded wharf and squally weather. We were driven here by Dinsley's. Abraham's business is one of his best customers.'

They soon found a covered street-waggonette with DINSLEY LIVERY STABLES neatly painted at the back and sides. As Emilia followed Eliza up the steps, the driver came to ask if they wished to be taken anywhere. Leaving Eliza to explain that they would be resting until such time as they were joined by the men, Emilia leant back on the padded seat and closed her eyes to shut out the swaying movement that affected everything within sight.

'Eliza', she asked plaintively, 'how long must I wait to get back my land legs? I feel as though I am still at sea.'

Her sister smiled sympathetically as she sat opposite. 'I have not forgotten how I felt when I arrived. My greatest fear was that I might again become seasick, which, of course, did not happen. Mal de mer passes after a few hours. Be patient.'

Knowing that patience was not easy to put into practice, Emilia was grateful when Eliza's next words gave her something else to think about.

'I must tell you our news. We have moved into our new house. But, before we tell you about that, you must let me have all the news from Home, Emilia. It seems an age since Abraham and I heard anything worthwhile. His family are poor letter-writers, always claiming they have too much going on to bother, and Mama, whom we rely on for most of our news, gave us little else but details of your departure and likely arrival, with next to nothing about the rest of the family.'

By 'Home', Eliza meant Bangor, or Wales, or sometimes even Britain or Europe. Her own house in St Kilda was home, but not Home.

'How were Mama and Papa when last you saw them?'

'Just as well as can be, Eliza. If I should tell you that Papa keeps as busy as he always did, and that Mama has few spare moments in her day, you would be sure to say to me, "Then nothing has changed since I was Home". Indeed, everything is as it was. Yet I do have more news which I will impart later. You won't be surprised to learn that Mama was reluctant to allow three children to be so far away from Home at once. She misses you greatly and delights in receiving your letters.'

Eliza gave a sigh of satisfaction. 'Then there is nothing to be anxious about on their account. When I write to tell them of your safe arrival, I will be able to say that here too, all is as well as can be. It cannot be long now before Abraham is made a partner at Cremayne Brothers. It has already been talked about, and may take place as early as next year.'

'Oh Eliza, I am pleased! Now tell me about your new house. You wrote to us some time ago saying that building had begun. Is it finished yet?'

Eliza's sigh, this time, was one of exasperation.

'How long everything takes in this country! As far as the outer stonework is concerned, yes, that has been completed for some time, and the scaffolding has been removed at last. The roof is finished and so are the inside walls. But though the glazier has been to do his work, there is no sign of the painter for the doors and window frames, and so much other work remains to be done that I wonder sometimes if we shall ever be in a position to receive guests.

'Beatrice, our maid, is busy all day dusting and sweeping to keep the house clean. Cook presents delicious meals even without all the implements we had in Bangor. There will be extra work now that you have joined us so our neighbour's second maid will help Beatrice on some days. Today, Beatrice has been next door to help them prepare a little party for you and George. Some of our friends are looking forward to meeting you both this evening and hearing the latest news from Home.

'You will be pleased to know that we do have beds in each of the bed rooms, so you and George will at least have somewhere to sleep, but there is still a difficulty about your clothes. Will you be greatly inconvenienced by having to keep everything in your trunks until the wardrobes are delivered?'

Emilia's eyes twinkled. 'After our four months at sea, Eliza, do you really have to ask? George and I are by now thoroughly trained in such matters and shall be able to manage very well indeed.'

'That does relieve my mind. Abraham and I have been living in our new house less than two weeks, and the difference from our previous home must be hard for someone like you to imagine. Our tiny slab cottage had an earth floor and calico walls and ceilings. That was difficult with our baby. Whenever it rained there was mud everywhere, and it was worse after a storm, for then we paddled about in several inches of water. You might think it was better in the summer, but the dry weather was equally as bad, for the hot north wind blew in clouds of dust which settled on everything and warned of the danger of bush-fire.

Fortunately, Cremayne Brothers were pleased with Abraham's work so promoted him to Manager. He could then apply for a loan to buy our land in St Kilda near the railway station and the beach. So now we have grounds in which to grow vegetables and a yard for hens, turkeys, ducks and a pond. Since we first came to the colony the prices of all kinds of food have fluctuated wildly, so it is only sensible to provide ourselves with as much as we can.

'The neighbours have said that when we organise the cages and purchase the livestock, their groundsman will help us establish our vegetable garden. They are so generous to us. They came from Poland and share our faith. They were wealthy enough to build a large house as soon as they arrived in the colony.'

Emilia had listened carefully. It was important to learn all she could of this new country where life was so different from the one she had left behind. 'I can imagine that your new house will have a host of advantages for my niece. Speaking of whom, when do I get to hold her?'

'Soon enough. She is in the care of Nurse today. Remember, that every new advantage we have, must be weighed against our greatest disadvantage, the debt we have incurred, which is always worrisome. And,' Eliza continued, 'in case you are labouring under the illusion that we are building ourselves a grand mansion, I must tell you that you are bound to be disappointed, particularly at this early stage when we still lack many pieces of necessary furniture and curtains. You will see that there is not one foot of fencing on the place, nor any garden walls, and as for flower-beds, there is, so far, only a sandy waste with tussocks of wild grass, clumps of tea tree and patches of saltbush. There is no gravel sweep up to the door, nor will there be one, as we have built the house quite close to the street in keeping with our neighbours.'

'But Eliza, now you have George here, the garden around the house will surely take on an improved appearance. In a matter of weeks, I would dare to say, he and Abraham's contractors will have begun to tame the landscape to the likeness of an English park.'

Emilia could not be sure, but she fancied that, as Eliza bent her head to look at the watch suspended on a fine chain around her neck, she heard her mutter, 'I shall believe that when I see it.'

What she said aloud was, 'The men have been gone a long time. It is just possible that Abraham is waiting for the appearance of the carrier he has engaged for the luggage, but where in the world can George be?'

As if on cue, George's head appeared to stand beside their open vehicle. 'There you both are! Abraham told me to look for a Dinsley waggonette, but I did not ask where it was likely to be.' He gazed doubtfully at Eliza before saying, 'I hope you will excuse Emilia, but something unexpected has happened and her help is needed.'

George addressed Emilia as he opened the small door at the back. 'I have just come upon Nancy in a distressed state of mind. She has been given some painful news, and I cannot think of anyone she would rather see just now than yourself.'

CHAPTER 16

Sandridge

5 June 1864

WITHOUT A MOMENT'S HESITATION, EMILIA TOOK THE SUPPORT OF George's hand and stepped down to the ground.

'What has happened? Where did you find her, George? Point her out to me if you can.'

Taking her a little to one side, George indicated the direction in which she should look and, as soon as Emilia caught a glimpse of her friend, she set off towards her. George remained behind to explain to Eliza who Nancy was, and how greatly both he and Emilia had come to appreciate her friendship on their voyage.

Lifting her skirts, Emilia edged past several groups of her fellow passengers whose numbers had swollen by the arrival of their family members and friends. Wild with excitement, children of all ages ran in every direction, dodging loaded pony-carts, dog-carts, hand-carts and wheel barrows.

As a space opened briefly in front of her, Emilia dived through, and then she could see Nancy plainly, sitting on a cabin trunk. No use calling, for any sound she made would only be swallowed up in the general hubbub. Not until she was almost upon her did Nancy see and hear Emilia.

When Emilia appeared, Nancy dabbed her red eyes and white face with her damp handkerchief. No belated attempts to remove the symptoms could hide their tale—she had been crying without restraint, having believed she was among strangers.

Emilia stooped down, flung her arms about Nancy's shoulders and hugged tightly.

'What is it Nancy? What happened?'

At first Nancy could not answer for lack of breath, but then she was able to gasp, 'I have just been given the most dreadful news, Emilia! It's about the Williamson family. Their solicitor, Mr Colman, met me here and explained that Mr Williamson has been severely injured in a farming accident. He has had to employ a manager to run his farm and to move his whole family into town. He can no longer afford to employ me. Their local school is unable to offer me any more teaching hours either.'

Emilia stood up to consider this news, staying close enough to embrace Nancy's shoulders. 'But surely the Williamson family has an obligation to find a position for you since you have travelled from Home to work for them?'

'Mr Colman said that he has been looking, on behalf of Mr Williamson, for a position that is suitable for me. The only one he has found is as a music teacher in a private school for boys in the colony of New South Wales.'

'Has he made a commitment on your behalf that you will take up that position?'

'The solicitor said that he has sent a letter to them but has not received their reply so there is no role for me yet.'

'I think it would be unfair of him to assume that you will now go off to New South Wales when you have been expecting to stay in Victoria.' Emilia drew her brows together in thought. 'Tell me, is Mr Colman still here?'

'Yes, he has gone to collect my other trunk, and is really being as helpful as he can be.'

'Well, that is all to the good, I must say!'

'He told me that he is doing everything he can to find a suitable solution. He has engaged a room for me at a hotel in the city where I can stay until he finds a position.'

'And who,' said Emilia judicially, 'would be in a better position than he? I think you should leave it all in his hands. Try not to worry too much.'

But Nancy had embraced Emilia's waist and buried her face in the folds of the dress—her words could no longer be heard.

Gently Emilia smoothed back the dark curls clustering at Nancy's forehead. She was about to say something else comforting when, at that moment, she felt a hand on her arm and looked up to see George. Emilia could not hide her relief. Behind him was their sister, so they both stood aside to allow Eliza to speak to Nancy.

Eliza approached Nancy with her warmest smile. 'We have not been introduced but let us not stand on ceremony. I am Eliza, Mrs Abraham Berens, Emilia's sister. You are, I take it, Miss Wait? George has explained that among your present difficulties is the fact that you have a room in a hotel but you don't want to stay by yourself. I hope I can help you with this matter.' She nodded at Nancy encouragingly.

'I speak for my husband as well, Miss Wait, when I say that you would make us very happy if you should come to be our guest for as long as it may be convenient. We will have no trouble in fitting another bed into the room we have allocated to Emilia.' Eliza extended her hand and, after only a brief hesitation, Nancy stood and accepted her warm grasp.

'Now we have to find Abraham and Finny.' Eliza gazed purposefully about the crowd and then continued, 'Finny is Dinsley's carrier. We three ladies and our handbags will go first on their waggonette. Finny will take George and Abraham home with the cabin trunks and the rest of the luggage.'

Suddenly, she pointed and then began to wave. 'Oh, look George. There's Abraham; he's standing on top of Finney's cart and waving at me now.'

George could now lift Nancy's cabin trunk onto his shoulder and set off.

Eliza's eyes lingered long enough to be sure that her brother was moving in the right direction. Then she said, 'Let us go back to the waggonette now.'

Nancy followed her friends until she stopped and gasped, 'Oh Emilia! I had completely forgotten about Mr Colman.'

Nancy turned a stricken face to Emilia, then realised that to Eliza the name meant nothing. The words tumbled from her as she tried to explain. 'Mrs Berens, happy as it makes me to accept your invitation, I cannot leave here without letting Mr Colman know where to send on my big trunk and any news he may obtain concerning a vacant position. I am sorry to cause this delay, but I cannot see how it may be avoided.'

So they waited where they were—Nancy pink with embarrassment and Eliza thinking about her poor feet and wondering how much longer it would be before she could put them up.

At last, a finely dressed figure broke through the crowd, pushing towards them a trolley bearing a heavy trunk. He did not lessen his pace until he was face to face with Nancy, though his quick glance had also taken in her two companions. 'Are these friends of yours, Miss Wait?'

'Yes, Mr Colman. Mrs Berens, Miss Aronson, may I present Mr Colman? Mr Ernest Colman is acting on behalf of Mr Williamson. Miss Emilia Aronson is my friend; her sister, Mrs Abraham Berens, has been kind enough to invite me to stay with them for a little time.'

After resting his trolley and doffing his hat, Mr Colman shook each hand in turn. When the introductions were over, Eliza led the way to the waggonette.

Mr Colman addressed himself to Miss Wait as he pushed the trolley. 'As

I explained, Mr Williamson is willing to pay for your accommodation in Melbourne. I selected a hotel near my office so I can visit you quickly whenever I have news. I am willing to take responsibility for you, on behalf of Mr Williamson, until such time as we find a suitable position for you. Are you prepared to ignore Mr Williamson's generous arrangements and go off with these people, Miss Wait?'

As Eliza watched them approach from her seat, she could discern the tenor, if not the actual words, of their speech. When they arrived, she declared, 'Mr Colman, Miss Wait ought not to be kept standing. Since you were the bearer of the news that has caused her distress, I anticipate that you wish to have her comfortably seated. Please be so kind as to allow her to join me; then you will be free to discuss whatever you please.'

Emilia helped Nancy climb up the steps at the back, then followed and sat beside her.

This gave Mr Colman time to think. He turned to Eliza and said, 'Very well, Mrs Berens, may I have your address so I can visit Miss Wait when I have any news?'

Nancy was relieved to hear his question. 'Thank you, Mr Colman, for understanding that I would rather stay with friends than be alone in a hotel. No doubt you chose a suitable hotel, but I have just endured a long sea voyage only to discover that my trip was unnecessary. My friends will provide the company I need to recover from my surprise and disappointment.'

Eliza withdrew her calling card from her purse. 'Mr Colman, I am pleased that you have accepted our arrangements for Miss Wait. Here is my card. You are at liberty to visit her at our home in St Kilda.'

By now George had returned to the women, so he was introduced to the solicitor. 'Thank you, Mr Colman, for finding her other trunk. It must have been difficult amongst all the baggage unloaded from the hold. Please follow me to the cart.'

The driver of their waggonette was now free to close the door, mount his seat at the front, take the reins and ease his horses out into the traffic on the pier.

Emilia placed her arm about her friend's waist and said, 'You must stay with us until you have fully recovered from this terrible shock.'

Eliza, who had been thoughtfully smoothing the fingers of her tight-fitting gloves, broke in to say, 'If Miss Wait would be so kind as to give my husband all the particulars about the position she would like to obtain, he and George can begin making enquiries.'

'Thank you, Mrs Berens. How kind of you to offer assistance.'

Back at the cart, Finny and George loaded Nancy's larger trunk. Mr Colman waved as the four-wheeled sprung cart took Finny, George and Abraham away. He then set off to return the trolley.

George said to his brother-in-law, 'Poor chap. He still looks confused. I guess very little has gone according to his plans today.'

Abraham replied, 'I'm puzzled too; we appear to be taking more luggage and people home than I'd expected. I'm sure Eliza will explain it all later. Meanwhile, look around as we travel; our house is only three miles along the coast at St Kilda.'

They left Sandridge behind as the sun set. Seated beside her friend and opposite her sister, Emilia was able to assess the changes that time had worked upon Eliza's face and figure.

Emilia had always accepted that Eliza was the beauty of the family. As far back as Emilia could remember, admirers had flocked to their parents' house, each one, it seemed to her youthful mind, more handsome and eligible than the last. Some had been spoken of as possessing exceptional prospects; others as belonging to old and highly respected families. Still others had been widely acknowledged as brilliant and marked out to go far. Yet her sister, in spite of family promptings, had not responded to the most highly regarded of her many beaux, nor had she succumbed to the charms of the most handsome. Eliza had settled her affection on Abraham Berens, the one furthest away from Bangor.

Abraham was six years older than Eliza, from Posen in Poland, and was the first person the Aronsons knew who had gone out to Melbourne. There he had found work as an importer and wholesale jeweller until, five years before, he had returned to Bangor to marry Eliza.

Emilia told herself that Eliza had, after all, been proved wise in her choice of a husband. When it came to working with figures or anything of a financial nature, Abraham could not be bested, being able to work out in his head in seconds, what others, even with pen and paper, struggled long minutes to achieve. It was this ability, coupled no doubt with his cheerful good nature, which had raised him to the position he now held with Cremayne Brothers, and which would soon gain for him a partnership.

Curls still complimented Eliza's girlish air and at first glance her beauty was undiminished. Further scrutiny revealed that her former pale complexion had not altogether escaped the consequences of the Australian sun. There were now fine lines radiating from the corners of her eyes and those curls were now worn in a more mature style. Her appearance reminded Emilia that her sister was two years older and that during those two years she had borne Amy.

On entering the Berens's house, Emilia and Nancy were welcomed by Beatrice and shown to their bed room. Beatrice then left to find a bed for Nancy. When the cart arrived, George and Abraham brought inside the three cabin trunks and the extra trunks that had remained in storage throughout the voyage. They then set up the bed that Beatrice had found and left her to make it up. Eliza informed Cook about the additional guest who would be joining them for a week or two.

On seeing her guests settled, Eliza said, 'As I mentioned on the way, our neighbours have invited some of our friends here in St Kilda to a party to honour George and Emilia.'

Nancy asked to be excused. 'I'm sorry. I'm not ready to attend a party. I am still shocked so would provide little entertainment tonight. No-one is expecting me so no-one will notice my absence.'

Eliza replied, 'We fully understand. Perhaps you could help Emilia select a suitable dress from her luggage?'

CHAPTER 17

St Kilda and Melbourne, Victoria 6 June 1864

IN THE MORNING, ELIZA AND ABRAHAM TOOK THEIR GUESTS ON A guided tour of their new home.

Emilia exclaimed, 'You have a perfectly delightful house, Eliza. I don't know why you insisted that it was humble when I can see the builders have made every provision for extensions when the need arises and your budget allows. Furthermore, I would be disappointed to come to the other side of the world and find a replica Welsh village here. You need to build houses that suit the climate and the location.'

Before she opened the door to the Nursery, Eliza said, 'Amy doesn't stay asleep once the birds start their morning chorus. I expect Nurse has given her breakfast by now.'

The three visitors followed Eliza into the room. Emilia had to restrain herself from rushing to embrace her niece until Nurse had been introduced to George, Nancy and herself.

Once she was invited to, this stranger with the warm smile lifted the little girl out of her cot to give her a cuddle. 'I'm so pleased to see you. Your Mama has filled letters to your Grandmama with stories about you.'

'Amy is nineteen months old now.'

'I'm going to enjoy being here if I get to see Amy most days.'

As the party of five were sharing breakfast around the table, Eliza said, 'Now that you have been shown where everything is to be found in the house, please consider it your home. You are no longer guests, but family, even you, Nancy. You have met Nurse and Beatrice. You will meet Cook shortly. We are most fortunate to be able to employ these women because good and trustworthy servants are rare in the colonies.'

*

'Here we are, Emilia. This is Bourke Street.' They had walked up the hill from the Melbourne Terminus next to the Fish Market on Flinders Street.

'What wide streets, Eliza! So different from the High Street in Bangor.'

'Yes, it was one of the first things we noticed on our arrival. There can be no doubt this city was planned with an eye to the future. Do you not agree, Nancy?'

'Yes, indeed', said Nancy as she watched two young women holding up their skirts to avoid a puddle.

Eliza took the opportunity to introduce her favourite topics for visitors. 'You will soon discover that between the wide streets there are lanes conveniently interspersed for the use of trades-people and their carts. Victoria, unlike some of the other colonies, was not a convict settlement, though since the finding of gold here in such vast quantities, we have been hosts to ticket-of-leave men and great numbers of people from around the world. Gold, of course, has been the making of Melbourne. These large buildings you can see have gone up all over since gold started arriving from the diggings. In only thirty years, it has become the city you see around you.'

'Eliza,' Emilia interrupted, 'at Home we were told in all seriousness that the gold here was just lying about waiting to be picked up. That cannot be true, can it?'

'Well, Emilia, strange as it may seem to you, there were nuggets of gold taken up from the surface of the ground when the gold rush began in 1851. But now all the places where gold was found in this way have been worked over, as have the river beds, so that today most gold has to be obtained the hard way, by mining. This has given rise to the many mining companies in the colony, as well as trading houses that supply their provisions. As you may imagine, they do a roaring trade. Certainly Cremayne Brothers, which is one of them, is a thriving concern.'

They were now in the very heart of the city. Traffic moved in every direction, and the resulting chaos made it difficult for Emilia to see through the shop windows much more than tantalising glimpses of goods of impressive quality. To amuse herself, Emilia read aloud the signs high above the windows—'BUCKLEY & NUNN, THE COLONIAL GOLD & JEWELLERY COMPANY, HENRY FRANCIS CHEMIST & DRUGGIST, COBB & CO. COACH OFFICE, ALBION HOTEL.'

This visitor experienced a thrill of joy. Here she was, Miss Emilia Louise Aronson, and nobody in particular at the age of twenty-two, yet privileged to see with her own eyes a street in a new land, a land which she suspected would tax her to her limits. She was ready to meet every challenge that could come her way. Not since the days of Robert's courtship had she felt so sure of herself. She knew now that, while still treasuring memories, she was happy and willing to open her heart once more.

CHAPTER 18

Melbourne
Late July 1864

'ARE YOU SURE, NANCY, THAT YOU WILL NOT CHANGE YOUR MIND AND come with us tonight?'

'Do forgive me Emilia, but I do not have the capacity to attend as many dinners, operas, balls and card parties as you do. I realise I might learn of a family who wants to employ a governess or a music teacher at these events, but I went out with you last night and I would appreciate staying home tonight.'

'What a selfish creature I am to keep asking you! But I must fly. Now where did I put my shawl?'

The shawl, made from the same bolt of emerald-sprigged muslin as her dinner gown, was found after a brief search and placed around her shoulders. With a parting wave to Nancy, Emilia hurried down the hall to where Eliza, Abraham and George were awaiting her.

'How lovely she looks,' Eliza commented to Abraham. 'That brilliant green suits her to perfection!'

Abraham replied, 'Your family's "ugly duckling" has become a beautiful swan. I remember her as timid and fragile; she has become a radiant young woman.'

George commented, 'When we are out and about, I am asked whether my sister is spoken for. I am not surprised. I shrug my shoulders and say, "Not that I know of" because she is just as friendly with that fellow as she is with every other one she meets.'

✳

The highly polished silver sparkled on the smooth white cloth with its crisply ironed table napkins. Everything in the Vogel dining room was of the finest quality, and the fire had been lit early and then allowed to die down so that the room was pleasantly warm.

It had not taken Emilia long to notice that, apart from the Vogel's eldest daughter who could not have been more than sixteen years old, she and George were by far the youngest among the guests. Not until later did another gentleman come, offering apologies to his hostess. This latecomer was about her own age, Emilia judged, and when introductions had been completed and everyone took a place at the table, it was he whom she found seated on her left.

The food that evening was excellent. The elderly gentleman on Emilia's other side certainly thought so for, as course followed course, he did not so much as raise his eyes from his plate, showing a marked lack of interest in anything other than the food set before him. Across the table from her were George and the daughter of the house, who appeared to be getting on so famously that it was no time at all before George had reduced her to help-less giggles. Watching them with envy, Emilia was wishing that she had been seated in their company when she heard herself addressed by the young man on her left.

'Miss Aronson, do I understand correctly that you and your brother have only recently arrived in the colony?'

On turning to face the speaker, Emilia came within the compass of his engaging smile, which so unnerved her that his name was driven from her mind and a crimson tide of embarrassment swept up her neck to flood her face.

Not put out in the least, the young man took upon himself the task of carrying the conversation. He told her of his family's arrival in the colony when he had been just a boy, and amused her by his descriptions of the various adjustments they all had to make to fit into colonial life. He paused to give her the opportunity to begin relating some of her own experiences, but when he saw that she had not yet regained her composure, he told her instead the story of his horse's lameness, which had caused the delay in his arrival at the Vogel's dinner party.

'My father warned me, Miss Aronson, that all was not well with my riding horse. He suggested I walk him up and down to test his leg, and I did this and could find nothing wrong. But there must have been a stone there which gradually worked its way deeper under his shoe, for I had not been long on my way here before he stopped, refusing to go any further. I carry a small pebble knife with me, of course, but I had quite a struggle to free the stone, and it was this that made me late.'

Emilia smiled at him shyly. 'We were late arriving too, and it was my fault.' The conversation was not difficult; if only she could remember his name she would not appear to be so lacking in manners.

The young man beside her had not noticed. His thoughts were not disapproving. He was, in fact, congratulating himself on being seated next to the most charming young lady at the table, and he wondered whether she had yet reached her twentieth birthday.

In the brief silence that now descended, Emilia could hear snatches of the conversation around her. One of the men was pouring scorn on someone in Parliament whose name appeared to be McCulloch, and another name, that of Higinbotham, was being mentioned here and there. The words 'asinine', 'lunatic', and 'criminal' were being applied rather liberally, while fears generally were being expressed that negligence on the part of Victorian politicians could yet bring an end to the current prosperity of the colony. The ladies, meanwhile, had not yet exhausted the topic of lavender being among the colours to be worn in the coming season.

When an argument among the men appeared to be getting out of hand, their host appealed to the young man seated at Emilia's side, and it was then, on hearing him addressed as Charles, that her memory sprang to her aid. Yes, she remembered now; he had been introduced to her as Mr Baeyertz. Being at last in possession of his name, Emilia relaxed and took upon herself a greater share of the conversation.

By the time they had finished eating dessert they were on friendly terms and Mr Baeyertz hoped to continue talking with her. However, as custom dictated, the dinner guests were separated for some time. The women followed their hostess into the drawing room while the men remained in the dining room. When the men finally joined the women, both Charles and Emilia were claimed by others wanting to talk to them, and so they drifted from one group of guests to another. From time to time Emilia would glance up to see if Charles was still in the drawing room and, on the odd occasion she caught his eye, there passed a rueful smile between them. Eventually, to her relief, she found Eliza beside her, murmuring that they were about to make their farewells.

CHAPTER 19

St Kilda

August 1864

'HOW ARE YOU FEELING, ELIZA? ABRAHAM TOLD ME THAT YOU ARE not at all yourself this Sabbath morning.'

'Emilia! I thought you would have left with the men.'

'I offered to stay home with you today and I knew Abraham would be pleased.'

Eliza sighed. 'That is most thoughtful of you, Emilia, but not, I think, really necessary. I was not able to eat any breakfast, and I know that worried him, but it is, after all, only a headache. If I were to be rid of that I know I would feel better. It could be the late nights and the rich food we have been having all this week that are responsible. I'm sure a day in bed is all that is needed to set me right.'

'Is there anything I can get you for your headache?'

'There should be some of that mixture that Dr Ledler makes up for me. Please look in the hall cupboard, Emilia.'

Emilia returned to the bed room bringing a bottle with her. 'Is this what you meant, Eliza?'

'Oh, you have found it. Good! I am to take a teaspoon only when I really need to. Make sure you shake it well.'

'Eliza, there are just a few drops left. Have you another bottle anywhere?'

'If there is not one in the hall cupboard, that is all there is.'

'Then we will have to go into the city to get you some more.'

'On the Sabbath, Emilia? I shall just have to do without.'

Emilia recognised the moment had come for some very plain speaking. 'When I discovered how little was left in the bottle, Eliza, I went at once to talk to Nancy. Please do not make difficulties when I tell you that she has offered to go to Dr Ledler's and get a fresh supply of your mixture.'

Eliza lay back on her pillows as though the conversation were just too much for her. 'But Dr Ledler's shop is in the city, and I have no idea how often the trains run on Saturdays.'

'No need to distress yourself, Eliza. Nancy can get a seat on a Dinsley's waggonette.'

Eliza acknowledged the sense in Emilia's suggestion. 'Very well,' she murmured. 'Please tell Nancy that I am most grateful. Dr Ledler's shop is in Swanston Street and we are account-customers. I have always found Mr Dinsley very obliging.'

Emilia crossed to the window to adjust the blind to shut out as much light as possible. She tiptoed to the door and, with a last quick look around to see that her sister wanted for nothing, went out, closing the door softly behind her. When she had first been made aware of Eliza's illness, she had marvelled that it should be someone other than herself who was laid aside by sickness. Always, throughout her life, it had been she who was the frail one needing constant attendance, so that now it was a rare pleasure for her to take on the care of her sister.

Six days had passed since the night of the Vogel family dinner party, and Emilia had not heard from Mr Baeyertz. Nor had their paths crossed during the social round of evenings spent in the homes of Eliza's friends. Was he known only to the Vogel family? Could this mean that he was not Jewish, as the Vogels were not? As she had explained to Nancy, if that were so, there was no certainty that they would meet again, which to her mind was a pity. She had been looking forward to their becoming friends. But perhaps it was not to be, she sighed inwardly, and told herself she should try to forget that she had ever met him.

Emilia returned to the door of the library where she had left Nancy. Her friend was still there, engrossed in writing. Nancy paused and raised her head to listen as Emilia explained, 'Eliza is most grateful that you have agreed to go to the pharmacist on her behalf. Give me a few minutes. I will write the notes to Mr Dinsley and Dr Ledler and then you can be on your way. How is your letter progressing?'

While Nancy replied, Emilia gathered together pen and paper and sat where they could share the inkwell.

'By the time you have written yours, Emilia, I should be ready to seal mine so that I can take them both into town. I have been writing to my cousin, Will Blackland.'

Emilia was puzzled. 'I thought he and Tommy were in Melbourne.'

'They left a few days after we landed. They went by steamer to Portland, then took a coach to Tarryever.'

'Tarryever? Is that the name of the town?'

'No, it is a sheep station. Cousin Will is the new manager. He was engaged by a company in England.'

Emilia had bent her head to begin her own letter, but suddenly looked up again. 'If you have a little space still, please remember me to them both.'

Nancy nodded her head in reply, and soon the silence was unbroken except for the scratching of pens.

Will Blackland was aware of the circumstances surrounding Nancy's employment situation and she had hoped that by now she would have more cheering news to give him. Mr Colman was still searching for a position for Nancy. Abraham and Eliza, though as willing as ever, were at a loss to know what to try next. While Nancy was grateful for their unstinting hospitality, she had already made up her mind that she must soon advertise herself as a music teacher in the Melbourne papers and begin to earn her own money. She had included a hint of this in her letter. The two young women soon finished writing and addressed their envelopes.

The short walk to the livery stables did not take Nancy long. There, on the presentation of Emilia's note, she was told that if she cared to climb aboard the waggonette that was even then on the point of leaving, she could be taken into Melbourne without delay. Nancy enjoyed the three-mile journey in the sunshine. Soon they had crossed the Yarra River. When the driver stopped and began to assist his passengers to alight, Nancy gathered her skirts in one hand.

At the shop bearing the gilded sign, DR D. LEDLER, PHYSICIAN & DISPENSING CHEMIST, she pushed open the heavy door and went inside.

Having come from the brightness of the street, she could see little in the dimness. At first, she thought herself alone until a figure emerged from the shadows to enquire whether there was any way in which he might assist her. As her eyes adjusted, Nancy made out a black coat and above it an elderly face half-hidden by a full grey beard.

She responded, 'May I speak to Dr Ledler, please?'

'I am Dr Ledler, may I be of help to you?'

Nancy proffered Emilia's second note and an empty bottle.

'I have come on behalf of Mrs Abraham Berens of St Kilda. She has a dreadful headache but her bottle of headache mixture is empty. She is at present in urgent need of it. May I please wait and take the bottle back to her?'

'Ah yes, I am aware of Mrs Berens's severe headaches. It is most unfortunate that she suffers from such a debilitating condition. Please excuse me.' The elderly man disappeared through a door, returning very shortly with a large storage bottle which he was shaking vigorously. 'Ah, Miss … ?' His eyebrows rose questioningly.

'Miss Wait.'

He nodded acknowledgement. 'I am glad that this contains enough laudanum to fill her eight-ounce bottle. Since my shop assistant left his job here last week I have not had enough time to make up more. If you would care to be seated, Miss Wait, I shall not keep you long.'

Nancy sat in the chair he had indicated, and allowed the silence to wrap itself around her. No sound could penetrate the thick glass of the street window, and the door was inclined in such a way that it closed itself firmly.

Into the silence there now came the clink of glass on glass and a subdued gurgling of pouring liquid.

When Dr Ledler pulled out brown paper and scissors, Nancy rose to her feet to stand by the counter. She asked, 'What sort of person do you require to fill the role of shop assistant in your dispensary?'

Dr Ledler replied, 'I shall finish this task before I answer your question. I need to be sure I have secured the medicine correctly.'

Nancy watched his fingers as Dr Ledler formed a parcel with the brown paper. He creased flat the folds and secured the ends with softened sealing wax. Then, from a roll under the counter he snapped off a length of string and deftly twisted it lengthwise and again across the width of the parcel before finishing off with a loop for the customer's finger. As the note instructed, he recorded the transaction on Mrs Berens's account. Finally, he offered the package to Nancy who accepted it and leant against the counter while the doctor considered his answer.

Dr Ledler said, 'Since my previous assistant left I have not had time to find someone suitable. I look for someone who is industrious, is willing to learn how to handle the medications and has experience in serving customers because I am not always here. It is more important to find a person of suitable temperament with whom I can work than someone who's had experience working with a chemist. I can teach the person all they need to know.'

Nancy explained that she knew of someone who might be suitable. Thanking him for the information, Nancy suddenly became aware of the passage of time. They would be waiting for her back at the house, and by now Eliza would be desperate for relief. 'I must take this to Mrs Berens now.'

'Certainly. Please remind her to take only one teaspoon at a time.'

Nancy pulled open the heavy door, stepped out into the street, set off for the nearest pillar box, posted her letter and then looked for a Dinsley stop.

'I might have found a job for George, Emilia! I think he would enjoy working with Dr Ledler in his dispensary.'

Nancy had run from the Dinsley depot to blurt out her news. Emilia, startled at the unexpectedness of it all had pleaded, 'Give me a little while to pour out this mixture for Eliza. I will hurry back as soon as I can.'

In her sister's bed room, she measured out the required dose and watched Eliza gulp it down. Emilia then tucked in the blankets and quietly left the darkened room. She sought Nancy in the garden. Abraham and George had placed a wooden seat in a shady corner and it was there that Emilia found her. 'Now, what do you mean about a suitable job?'

Nancy explained about the vacant position at Dr Ledler's practice. 'I thought the job might suit George better than me. He's worked in a shop. Besides, I've been thinking of advertising for piano students.'

Emilia agreed. 'It may be of interest to George. We must tell him when the opportunity arises and find out how to put your advertisements in *The Argus*.'

CHAPTER 20

St Kilda
August 1864

SUNDAY DINNER WAS NEARLY AT AN END. NANCY AND EMILIA HAD helped Beatrice with serving the meal. Eliza had insisted that she was fully recovered from the previous day's illness. The women withdrew with a tea tray to the sitting room, where Emilia and Nancy each took up their needlework. Neither hinted that they were itching to talk to George.

The men joined them and sat in comfortable chairs. Abraham asked George. 'So what was David Rosenthal's word last week regarding a possible partnership in his jewellery business?'

George replied, 'He said, and I can only agree, that at present his warehouse cannot support two partners. Should Papa increase his regular trade with him, he could then move the business to Bourke Street and that might be the right time to take me as his partner.'

With a look of enquiry, Abraham asked, 'Will you recommend this proposal to your father?'

'What do you think? Should I support Mr Rosenthal in this?'

Abraham, who on his first visit to Melbourne had worked closely with David Rosenthal, replied, 'There should be profit enough for two eventually.'

Plainly the idea of waiting did not satisfy George. 'I would prefer to be employed at once. I don't want to be dependent on Papa any longer.'

Nancy immediately took the opportunity to speak. 'George, when I went to Dr Ledler's chemist yesterday, I discovered that he is in need of a shop assistant. I thought you may be interested so I asked what sort of person he wished to employ.'

'That was very enterprising of you but, while I have worked in my father's shop, I don't have any experience of pharmacy.'

'Dr Ledler is willing to teach his assistant all he or she needs to know about dispensing the medication and the needs of his patients. He said he puts more value in a shop assistant he can work with than expertise in medication.'

'It is rather difficult to apply for a position when I don't know what sort of person the employer wants or how much he is paying.'

'I can see that. Dr Ledler said he wants an industrious person with experience working with customers. I have not served in a shop. My skills are teaching and music.'

Before he could say anything disparaging, Eliza commented, 'George, you have the very qualities Dr Ledler is seeking. He is my dispensing chemist and highly regarded by my friends. You are already experienced in selling, and you want to earn a wage. I do hope it all works out well for you.'

Abraham added, 'You would do well to be associated with Dr Ledler. You would learn a new line of products. You would also meet many people who could be of great benefit when you run your own business here.'

'I can see you are all determined that I investigate this job.'

Eliza offered Abraham another cup of tea. 'No, thank you my dear. George has been foolish enough to tell me that he would rather work, and as there is still a great deal to do outside, I am happy to oblige him. Come on, George, we can discuss that position while we work in the garden. Please excuse us, ladies.'

George did not hesitate to follow, leaving the ladies surprised at their hasty exit.

Nancy said, 'Eliza, there is something I want to talk to you about. I would be glad of your advice.'

After offering more tea and noting the shaking of heads, Eliza prepared to listen.

'Mr Colman has been sending notes informing me of his progress. No opportunities ever come of them. I have decided I must advertise my services in newspapers as a music teacher because I don't want to keep presuming on your generosity. Besides I would like to earn income to purchase some things for myself.'

'You must not worry about staying here. We were pleased to provide a home when you were so new to the colony and had found that your expectations had not been met. Your fine piano playing in the evenings has been most enjoyable and our favourite tune has become the children's march you composed at the school. We'd be happy to recommend you to our friends. Just the other day one of my friends said she was looking for a piano teacher for her daughters.'

Emilia had been thinking. 'I can see the wisdom in your decision, Nancy. By taking students here people will discover that you are a competent teacher and they will happily recommend you to others. That may lead to a permanent job in the city or elsewhere in the colony.'

Eliza said, 'You are most welcome to use the piano to conduct lessons in the drawing room. We can investigate opportunities for teaching in a public building when the number of your students increases. I wonder if the town hall rents a room for music lessons? We'll have to ask Abraham to place advertisements in the papers for you while he is in the city.'

On the following morning, George rose carefully from his bed and, after dressing, adopted an unusual posture with which to walk into the dining room.

Eliza, Nancy and Emilia looked up from their breakfast bowls to watch him find a comfortable position on his dining chair.

'I'm not surprised to see you in so much pain this morning, brother dear. You moved more rocks and soil yesterday than you have in recent weeks. I wondered if you would have a painful back today.'

Abraham, who had arrived while Emilia was speaking, commented, 'You did say you wanted to do some work and I appreciated your help with the garden. We have made enormous progress.'

Eliza added, 'What George needs is some of Dr Ledler's embrocation to rub into the sore muscles.'

'I have not forgotten what Nancy told me yesterday. I'll go this morning to obtain some and enquire about the position.'

CHAPTER 21

St Kilda

August 1864

THE FOLLOWING AFTERNOON, NANCY WAS IN THE LIBRARY WRITING A newspaper advertisement promoting pianoforte tuition, when she was interrupted by Emilia with the mail delivery.

One letter was from Mr Colman. In it, he explained to Nancy that he had news from Mr Williamson and asked where they could meet to discuss the matter of her employment.

Eliza entered the room just as Nancy finished reading. Emilia looked up from her needlework when Nancy said, 'I'm glad you are both here. Please look at this and recommend a suitable location.'

On reading it, Eliza said, 'I do not expect to entertain other visitors this week. You can invite him to afternoon tea on Wednesday. If you write a reply now, he can receive it tomorrow morning and reply with the afternoon mail.'

Several times on Wednesday afternoon, Nancy glanced at the clock on the chimneypiece. How slowly the hands were moving, it must surely be running down! But when she asked Eliza to check the time with the watch on the chain around her neck, the mantel clock was found to be actually two minutes fast. It was not until the hands finally pointed to six minutes past three o'clock that there came a knocking at the front door.

The three ladies had been waiting in the drawing room, although Eliza had tried to insist that Emilia need only to be present with Nancy. 'It is a private matter,' she had said, 'and Emilia knows you better than I do.'

But Nancy had pleaded, 'I want both of you to stay with me. Emilia may have known me longest but you, Eliza, have had more experience with the way business is done in this colony than either of us.'

After Beatrice had shown Mr Colman into the drawing room, she went to collect the tea tray.

Eliza politely asked Mr Colman to sit down while indicating empty chairs with a sweep of her hand. Mr Colman gladly complied after placing a portfolio on the table between them. The four exchanged greetings and spoke of their meeting at Sandridge.

Beatrice interrupted the discussion when she brought in a loaded tea tray and left it for Eliza to serve her guest. After pouring and handing around three cups, Eliza began. 'Mr Colman, I fully understand that you may not have expected to find yourself speaking to three women this afternoon, but Miss Wait asked us to join her. She is unfamiliar with the business world and so asked for our assistance. We will be most discrete.'

'Thank you for your explanation, Mrs Berens. I do understand that Miss Wait would like the support of her friends. I will get out the papers that Mr Williamson has asked me to deliver.'

The women sipped at their teacups while they watched him select some envelopes from his case.

'Miss Wait, I am pleased I could speak to you this week. Mr Williamson again apologises to you for the unforeseen change to your positions as governess to his family and teacher at the school. We have been searching for suitable employment for several months. Nothing has become available even though we expected that we would have found a position for you by now. He is aware that you were depending on him for an income and he also expects you have grown weary waiting for a position. Furthermore, Mrs Williamson has been aware of your situation and has been pestering her husband to resolve your difficulty.

'Mr Williamson has decided to write you a cheque for the salary you would have earned as a governess in their home from the time you arrived in Victoria to this week.' Mr Colman held up an envelope addressed to Nancy.

'Mr Williamson has also written a letter explaining the circumstances in which you came to the colony and assuring future employers that you made the voyage on the understanding that you had obtained a position with a reputable family.' Mr Colman held up a second envelope addressed to Miss Wait.

'Mr Williamson feels that he has fulfilled the spirit of his arrangement with you. He wishes you great success in gaining employment and in finding a home for yourself in the colony. Mrs Williamson regrets that she was unable to make use of your assistance and trusts that her husband's new arrangements will suit you.'

After he had finished speaking, Nancy sat still for a while. She had heard what Mr Colman had said and also what he had not. Mr Williamson was concluding his association with her and so she had to seek work by herself.

The clock ticked loudly in the hush that had fallen upon the room. Eventually, Eliza felt that something should be said. 'Mr Colman, I think Miss Wait is surprised to learn that Mr Williamson will no longer seek work on her behalf, through your careful administrations, and that she is to be cast out alone into this colony.'

'I appreciate your concern, Mrs Berens, but she will not be without assistance because Mr Williamson has provided a substantial cheque. The money will allow her to take her time to find a position before she has to depend upon her own efforts.'

Nancy was still immobile in her shock, so Emilia rose from her chair, accepted the two envelopes from Mr Colman, took three steps and handed them to Nancy.

Nancy snapped out of her trance to grasp them and pass them on to Eliza. 'I do thank you for bringing me the news. Mrs Berens is right; I am shocked. I had every hope that you would deliver an offer of a job today. The cheque and the reference will be most helpful to prove that I came to the colony for virtuous reasons. I will write to thank Mr Williamson when I have recovered my composure. I regret that I have not met Mr and Mrs Williamson since my arrival.

'I wish to thank you too, Mr Colman, for the things you have done on my behalf and for conveying news from Mr Williamson. It has comforted me to know that someone was seeking a position that would suit my skills.' Nancy did not know what else to say so she smiled shyly and reached for her teacup.

Once Eliza had inspected the contents of the envelopes and placed them back on the table, she filled the breach by thanking Mr Colman for conveying them and continued with some small talk until neither she nor Mr Colman could think of anything else to say. She saw him to the door and farewelled him.

When Eliza returned to the drawing room, she found Emilia embracing Nancy, while tears slipped down the latter's cheeks. Eliza poured another cup of tea for each of them and was pleased to see that Nancy readily accepted hers.

Nancy wiped her face and said, 'Thank you so much for your help. You have both given me support at the times when it is sorely needed. I could not wish for better friends. I do know that I am not alone in this world but I have been shocked by this news. Now I need to decide what to include in my advertisements.'

Eliza said, 'Why don't you take a nap now? We will talk to Abraham and George about the changes in your arrangements when they come in for dinner. I'm sure they'll give some helpful suggestions.'

After they had been dining for a while, Abraham said, 'Nancy, it is most unlike you to play with your food. What has happened?'

George responded, 'I gathered from Eliza that something occurred here this afternoon.'

Eliza looked at Nancy and waited for her nod. 'Mr Colman came to tea this afternoon to talk to Nancy about her employment prospects.'

George remembered meeting Mr Colman on the dock. 'He appeared to be a reliable chap.'

Eliza, interrupted occasionally by Emilia reminding her of omitted details, told them everything that had taken place while Mr Colman was there.

George asked, 'Do you think that Mr Colman's explanation is the only reason why Mr Williamson wrote the cheque and reference letter?'

Eliza shook her head in perplexity. Emilia, beginning hesitantly, said 'I do think there is another reason. I expect that he has felt the weight of responsibility for Nancy's welfare. However, her needs have prevented him from pursuing anything new for his own family and business prospects. He has been unable to move away from Melbourne until the matter was settled. By this excuse, he is no longer bound by his obligations to her. Mr Williamson probably instructed Mr Colman to explain his actions as if his only thought was for the good of Nancy so as to conceal his desire to be rid of her claims on him.'

Eliza gazed at her younger sister in admiration. How clever of Emilia to see it all so clearly.

Nancy gasped and reached for her handkerchief as tears ran down her cheeks again.

Emilia hugged her and said, 'Perhaps you could look upon it as a release from your obligations to the Williamson family too. You are no longer obliged to take any position they may have found for you. Instead, you can please yourself as to what you do. Indeed, you can start teaching piano right where you live.'

Abraham said, 'You now have a large sum of money in your name. You can provide for yourself while word gets around that you now offer piano lessons.'

Eliza added, 'Neither will you have to feel that you are relying on our generosity either. You should be eager to get that cheque deposited into an account in your name. If you are well enough tomorrow, I will go into town with you to the National Bank of Australasia.'

Abraham interrupted, 'I will write a recommendation to the bank for you to take to Mr Larcham. I am sure he will be most helpful, Nancy. I have always found him reliable.'

'Thank you', said Eliza. 'I had thought of Mr Larcham because you've spoken so highly of him in the past. Come with us Emilia; you can get what you need from town.'

'I've promised myself a morning of catching up on my mending. I've put it off so often that I really must attend to it now.'

Eliza looked at George and asked, 'You must have visited Dr Ledler by now. Your posture is much improved from what we saw on Monday. Have you made any arrangements with him?'

'Yes, I start working with him next week. We will have a trial period. He can test my aptitude and I can test my ability to learn. I do hope, though, that I will soon be channelling my energies into selling articles commonly found in chemist shops.'

CHAPTER 22

Melbourne

August 1864

'HERE WE ARE, NANCY, THE NATIONAL BANK IS THE ONE WE WANT.'
Eliza led Nancy up the steps, through the heavy doors and across to a window
marked ENQUIRIES. Nancy saw the bank official on duty there regretfully
shake his head. Mr Larcham had been transferred to a country branch just
the week before.

Eliza was clearly put out. 'My husband especially recommended Mr
Larcham to us, for it is he who has had the charge of Cremayne Brothers
accounts for the past several years.'

'May I know your husband's name, Madam?'

'Mr Abraham Berens.'

'Of course, Mrs Berens. We know your husband well. He has been one of
Mr Larcham's special clients. We now have a new Manager in his place. I will
at once enquire whether he is free to see you.'

They had not long been seated in the chairs provided before a young man
came to take them to Mr Baeyertz, who would be pleased to attend to them
immediately. As they followed down a narrow corridor, Eliza asked herself
where she could have previously heard the name 'Baeyertz'. Try as she might,
the memory eluded her. Nancy, on the other hand, recalled only too well.
Their separate speculations were interrupted by their guide who stopped at
a door and ushered them into an office with a large desk. The young man
behind it rose to his feet.

After the introductions, Eliza gave the reason for their visit and Nancy
was able to take note of the manager with the same name as the young man
of whom Emilia had spoken. If this was indeed he, then Nancy could well
understand why Emilia's description had included a delightful smile and a
marked charm of manner. Nancy spent the next few moments checking off
in her mind other virtues which stood above average.

She felt a gentle nudge from Eliza, and heard her murmur in her ear.
Nancy quickly pushed the envelope she had been holding across the desk.

Eliza gave an indulgent little laugh and then explained, 'You will have to be patient with Miss Wait, Mr Baeyertz. This is her first experience in dealing with financial matters in Melbourne.'

Nancy smiled at him shyly. 'That is quite true, Mr Baeyertz. I am not in the habit of handling cheques.'

He nodded understandingly. 'You may rest assured, that almost any young lady would be obliged to say the same.'

Mr Baeyertz read the cheque and Abraham's letter with care. 'Mr Berens writes that you are not yet married. Is that correct? Very good. Given his recommendation, we will be pleased to open an account in your name. If you would be so kind, please let me have a few particulars about yourself.'

He withdrew from his desk a form on which he wrote the answers to his questions.

Although she had not expected to be, Eliza was most favourably impressed by this new young manager, and thoughts of Mr Larcham faded from her mind. It was during this time that she was visited by what she later described to her husband as a flash of insight. Here in this very room was the most personable young man Nancy could ever hope to meet. Surely, with the right kind of encouragement on her part, and with Abraham's help, something lasting might come of it. With the perfect timing of the introduction of Mr Baeyertz to Nancy, the void that had been opened up in her life by Mr Williamson could be nicely filled.

For some weeks, Eliza had been planning to hold a soirée, and she now determined that when the time came, she would send an invitation to this young man. A soirée would be ideal for the purpose she had in mind. Nancy and the piano could occupy centre-stage for a good part of the evening. After that, events could be left to shape themselves.

Eliza stood at the door leading to the dining room where everything was laid out ready for supper. Coming from the drawing room that had been transformed into a music room, she checked that there were sufficient chairs for everyone. She caught her husband's eye and accepted as no more than her due, his nod and smile of approval. There could be no doubt that the evening had proved to be a resounding success, for she had chosen her guests carefully. Eliza had been fortunate to be able to include a violinist of some renown in the colony. Added to this were a husband and wife, whom she would have invited in any case, who sang duets in voices that blended most pleasingly.

Eliza was especially gratified to note that everyone's favourite that night was Nancy who, as was hoped, earned several recommendations to friends with daughters ready to learn piano. First, she accompanied herself with a sensitive rendering of a medley of Scottish airs and laments. For her conclusion, she chose the children's march that she had composed. Among those who had contributed to the singing and applause was, Eliza was delighted to see, the young man to whom she had sent a special invitation, Mr Baeyertz. What Mrs Berens failed to see was the attention that Mr Baeyertz and Miss Aronson paid to each other.

CHAPTER 23

St Kilda

January 1865

IN THE WEEKS THAT FOLLOWED THE CONCERT, AS ELIZA HAD CONFI-dently expected, events did begin to shape themselves without the need for her presence in her drawing room on Sunday afternoons. After all, what need was there for a further chaperone when Emilia was always present at such times?

George had worked for Dr Ledler long enough to know that jewellery, not pharmacy, would be his career; his Sunday afternoons were filled with the preparation for his return to Bangor.

At first Charles had come to visit only when invited to do so. Then, as the hot weather advanced, he became a frequent visitor and better known as Charlie. So it was that only Emilia and Charlie were present to hear Nancy read aloud a letter from Tarryever.

> My dear Nancy,
>
> How very pleased Tommy and I were to receive your recent letter! We were glad to hear that you have work even though Mr and Mrs Williamson weren't able to find you a job.
> You must be quite busy now that you have several girls and young women coming for lessons on the piano. It sounds as though the Berens's have worked hard to promote your skills because your letter said your students are mostly people from the Jewish community there.
>
> We have both settled in well here, though one can still see on every hand the neglect that has been such a cause of concern to the Company. The work still needing to be done will keep us busy for many a long day. This does not worry Tommy in the least, as he is quite happy to be spending his days working with the men. But I am deeply troubled that there is no

school for him to attend, the closest one being more than fifty miles away.

On a visit to neighbouring properties, I found a Committee being formed to look into the possibility of opening a school ourselves this year. I could not help but be interested, and when my neighbours saw this, they invited me onto the Committee without more ado. Since then I have received written permission from the Company representative in Melbourne to offer a disused shearing shed for the school house. It will need extensive repairs and, as well as that, additional rooms will have to be built for a teacher's dwelling. It is centrally situated in the district, and conveniently close to the main farm buildings where there is a general store.

On behalf of the School Committee, I have been given the task of asking you to consider taking on the post of School-Mistress here. The Committee was pleased when I put forward your name. They said they have every confidence in my recommendation of you, and I know I do not need to add how very delighted Tommy and I would be to have you here with us. But we do not want that to influence you. Come only if you are sure the post is right for you.

It will be several months before the building work is done, and details have by no means been finalised, but the matter of remuneration has already been discussed and I do not believe you will have cause for disappointment in that regard. At this stage we expect to be opening the school with nineteen children, and this number will, of course, be increased as younger brothers and sisters reach school age. After seeing you put your undoubted skills to good effect on board *Empire of Peace*, I do not believe there is anyone better suited to fill the post we are offering.

I have not forgotten, Nancy, that you travelled half-way around the world for a governess position with the Williamsons, but it may well be, dear cousin, that for a season

here in this far-flung corner of the colony you will find
freedom and independence that you will learn to value, rather
than the support of someone else's family.

As soon as I have word that you mean to accept our offer,
I will inform the Committee, and when all is in readiness
I shall come to Melbourne to collect you. Whatever your
decision may be, Tommy and I want you to know that we
wish you well now and always.

I remain

Your affectionate cousin,

Will Blackland

Nancy folded the letter back into its creases with a thoughtful frown.

'What do you think, Nancy? Will you accept?'

Although her manner had not betrayed it, Emilia was disturbed by the contents of the letter, and was most anxious to learn her friend's likely response to it. Should the School Committee's offer be accepted, Emilia knew she would be losing not one friend, but two. She and Nancy had not been slow to discover that it was not for Emilia's benefit that Eliza constantly urged Charlie to come to the house, and it had been the cause of a great deal of hilarity between them when they were alone together. In the event of Nancy's leaving for Tarryever, Charlie's visits to the house would come to an end.

Nancy was nibbling a knuckle in indecision. 'It all needs a great deal of thought, Emilia. There are several good reasons for my going, among them the fact that I have trespassed on your sister's generous hospitality long enough. I must not dismiss this offer without careful thought.'

Emilia let out a sigh of relief. 'If you still consider you are misusing Abraham and Eliza's hospitality, it will not do! We all enjoy having you with us. Just think how I will miss you if you should go.'

Nancy turned to Charlie, seeking his opinion of the post that had been offered her. But he was no help. 'My dear Miss Wait, I hardly know how I should advise you. From the letter, there is an undoubted need for a teacher at Tarryever. Whether you should fill that post is not for me to say.'

Nancy had bowed her head, and now spoke very softly. 'If my father was still alive and here with me, he would say that this is a matter that needs prayer. And then he would pray with absolute confidence that God would provide him with the answer. Every morning it was his habit to start the day with the Bible and prayer. How I would like a faith such as his. The truth is that I begin my day rushing to attend to things left from the day before.'

'But you do pray before going to sleep Nancy. I know you do!'

'Not every night, and even then it is a hurried affair at best.'

Silence followed Nancy's words, but before it could continue too long, Charlie said apologetically, 'I must confess that my unfailing habit each morning, especially in the summer, is to pray as I walk along the St Kilda beach.'

Emilia was at once interested. 'Do you find many people about so early in the day?'

'I think it would surprise you, Miss Aronson, to see just how many people are at the beach at an early hour. Ever since the St Kilda Sea Baths opened five years ago, they have been very popular.'

Emilia and Nancy looked at one another and laughed. 'We have been talking for some time of going to the Baths for a dip in the early mornings', said Emilia.

Nancy chimed in, 'And we had made up our minds to start this week, Emilia; let us make tomorrow our first day!'

'In that case,' said Charlie with a twinkle, 'I will meet you at the Sea Baths to see whether you keep your resolution.' He glanced at the clock on the chimneypiece and said, 'Regrettably, it is time now for me to go. How glad I am that I do not have to wait a whole week to see you again, and need only say, "Until tomorrow!"'

When the door had closed upon him, Nancy drew her friend down upon the sofa with her and said, 'Emilia, that young man's fondness for you is growing with each week that passes. It can only be a question of time before you receive a declaration from him.'

Emilia gasped with astonishment. 'You cannot mean it! A declaration from Charlie? No, that is the last thing I would expect to hear!'

'It is the custom, my dear, for hopeful young men to try to discover if their affection for the young lady of their choice is returned.'

Emilia said crossly, 'I know very well what the custom is, Nancy. What I do not accept is that Charlie would be so lacking in common sense as to make a declaration to me! If Eliza had the least idea that something of that nature were in his mind, he would never cross this threshold again. No such alliance is possible between us, for I am Jewish and Charlie is not. It is as simple as that.'

CHAPTER 24

St Kilda
January 1865

'ARE THESE SEAGULLS THE SAME AS THE ONES WE HAVE AT HOME? LOOK, Emilia, they have red eyes, red beaks and red legs and their upper wings are a soft powder grey. In England, we saw bigger gulls with the same coloured feathers but their bills were yellow and their legs were pink.'

The two young women were being escorted back to their house after their early morning swim. Charlie was carrying the basket filled with damp bathing costumes and towels, and was cheerfully confessing that they had astonished him. In spite of their stated intention, he had not expected them to keep their early morning appointment. He offered, by way of recompense, to share with them what little knowledge he had of Australian birds. 'These are silver gulls and I think you are talking about the herring gulls that are found in the northern hemisphere.'

Emilia, recalling her childhood in Wales, said dreamily, 'I have such happy memories of the herring gulls back Home. When we threw them crumbs, how they swooped on each piece, squabbling and fighting over it! Are these gulls as greedy as that, I wonder? Nancy, we must remember to bring stale crusts for them tomorrow.'

'Oh!' Charlie had an air of surprise. 'You will be coming to the beach again tomorrow? I thought that having once proved yourselves willing and able, you would not consider it necessary to repeat this morning's remark-able feat.'

At this, the young ladies turned on him and let him know in no uncertain terms that they resented this low opinion of themselves, for they intended to visit the Sea Baths every morning throughout the summer, whether he took his early morning walks or not.

*

As well as his weekly visits at the Berens's house, Charlie was now meeting Emilia most mornings on the sands of St Kilda Beach. Nancy was their constant companion and, as day succeeded day, her interest in the silver gulls increased. Although she still went into the water with Emilia, she was never sorry to return to the soft fine sand where she could watch the birds alighting, lifting their smooth wings in flight and arching their proud necks at the close approach of any of their own kind. When bread was thrown to them they proved themselves no different from their northern cousins, having the same bullying tactics towards one another and the same greed for food.

After that first morning, Nancy brought with her the sketching book that she had long neglected, hoping to commit to paper the graceful movements of these handsome sea birds. As the days grew increasingly warm, more and more people came out in the early morning to take advantage of the sea air. Soon there were not only the birds for Nancy to sketch, but small children and, sometimes, their pets as well.

Sometimes Charlie came to stand beside Emilia as she watched Nancy at work, shaking his head in wonder, impressed by her artistic ability. Then, as likely as not, he would suggest to Emilia that she join him in a stroll along the water's edge where the sand was firmest. There they shared the sounds of the breaking of waves and the crying of the gulls and, from time to time, their own speech or song. For both, the tranquillity was a welcome contrast to the remainder of their busy days. When they did converse, they found many interests in common. Emilia had to admit to herself that even with Robert this had not always been so. She had to make a distinct effort not to compare her present companion with her former one. She chastised herself when she slowly came to understand that she had been more in love with the idea of running her own household, than with Robert himself.

One day, she could never really understand why, Emilia told Charlie about Robert. She had not dreamed of him since her mother wrote with confirmation of his death. She began well—until she came to relate the turmoil that overtook their household when the wedding was cancelled. Then, her throat tightened and she was unable to go on. In spite of herself, her eyes filled with tears and the sobs that she was unable to hold back shook her unmercifully. She could never explain how she came to be wetting Charlie's coat lapels with her tears, but afterwards she had a faint recollection of a gentle hand drawing her to him, and of two strong arms holding her comfortingly. Even though her weeping intensified, it could not shut out the sound of his tender words.

'To think that all these weeks I had not an inkling of the sorrows you have had to bear. My poor, poor dear! If only I might be able to make up for your sufferings in some way.'

Did she imagine it, or did his arms really tighten about her? For what seemed a time without end they stood together with waves lapping at their feet. Then as her sobbing eased and she began to stir in his arms, he reluctantly released her.

After a hasty but unsuccessful search for her handkerchief, she was saved from the unladylike embarrassment of wiping her face upon her sleeve by Charlie thrusting his own folded handkerchief into her hands.

Peeping past its folds, Emilia was glad to see that the only person on the beach at that moment was Nancy, sitting hunched over her sketching book with her back to them. After several more deep breaths, Emilia was ready to resume their walk along the damp sand when the sun suddenly broke through a cloud. Emilia raised her hand against its glare and was glad of the resulting shadow on her face for Charlie's next words caused her eyes to fill again.

'I must confess to envying Robert this one thing Emilia, that you held him in such high regard that you agreed to marry him.'

Emilia turned away from Charlie to gaze out to sea.

Refusing to be discouraged, he continued, 'Perhaps it is too soon to speak of such things with you Emilia, but should you ever feel the same towards me, you would make me the happiest man in God's creation'.

Emilia was startled. Her hand slid from his arm and her heart sank like lead. 'Charlie.' Her throat caught on the name and she had to begin again. 'Charlie, it cannot be right for you to speak of such things. There can be no future of that kind for us, not ever! It is impossible for me to consider anyone not of the Jewish faith in that light.'

The smile which had lit his face faded as his eyes rested upon her. 'Very well,' he said at last, 'I understand. I have a similar problem. We will not speak of such serious matters. If we must, we shall confine ourselves to friendship.' He took her hand and would not allow her to reclaim it until they reached the place where Nancy was waiting for them.

CHAPTER 25

St Kilda
February 1865

CHARLIE CAME IN TO BREAKFAST TO FIND HIS FATHER THERE BEFORE him.

Charles Baeyertz, sen., had grown up in his sister's home in England, working as a law clerk for his brother-in-law. When he could, he joined the Royal Navy. After serving as Private Secretary to a Governor in the West Indies, he had migrated to Melbourne in 1852 with his wife, Mary Anne, and two children, Suzette and Charlie. Their third child, John, was born three years later.

Trustworthy and competent, Mr Baeyertz was suited to his role as Warehouse Keeper of Trades and Customs. In a port where the love of gold afflicted weaker men, he was worth every penny of his annual salary of £700.

'Ah, Charlie! I am glad there are just the two of us here. There is something I particularly wish to discuss with you.' He watched while his son flicked open his table napkin and then glanced up at him enquiringly.

'Yes, Father?'

'It has come to my ears that you are being seen in the company of young ladies not known to your mother or me.'

The tone of his father's voice was pleasant enough, and while he was often funny and generous, this time his son wondered whether the pleasantness would be sustained.

His father thrust his face across the table and asked, 'May we be privileged to know the names of these no-doubt-charming lasses?'

'Certainly, Father. Their names are Miss Emilia Aronson and Miss Nancy Wait. While it is true that they are unknown to you, we can easily remedy that.'

'"Aronson"? Did you say "Aronson"? What sort of a name is Aronson?'

'You must bear in mind that whatever kind of name Aronson may be, she will change it when she marries.'

His father chose to return to what he considered the main issue. 'I dare say, you would agree with me that Aronson is not what one would regard as a good English name?'

Charlie responded mildly. 'It is about as near to a good English name as Baeyertz is.'

The older man's back stiffened. 'I do not need to tell you, that our family name has been English for generations and has always been well regarded ... I could even say with truth, highly respected. Your sister made a respectable match with Richard Gibbs.'

Charlie nodded across the table at his father and said with a smile, 'In that case, you will be pleased to know that the Aronsons are also highly regarded in Wales, and though not Welsh, the name originates from a most respectable source—the Bible.'

His father, about to lift a spoonful of porridge to his lips, paused with his hand in mid-air. 'A Jewess, is she?'

'As you say, Father, a Jewess. One whose family connections go back much further than ours.'

Anger flared in his father's eyes. 'I can do without any cleverness from you, my lad. An assistant bank manager in the city you may be, but as long as you continue living under my roof, you are still my son and subject to my wishes. Let me therefore tell you that if any woman can be said to be unwelcome in this house, it is a Jewess. You will stop seeing her. That is my final word!'

As he once more dipped his spoon into his porridge, Charles Baeyertz, sen., was struck by an unpleasant thought. 'You have not been so great a fool as to make her any promises, I trust, nor given her cause to make a court case of it?'

His hopes of a peaceful exchange between them fading fast, Charlie met his father's gaze squarely. 'You need have no fears on that score for similar reasons. Miss Aronson is not at all anxious to link her future with mine. Quite the reverse! So there can be no question of promises having passed between us.'

His voice full of satisfaction, his father exclaimed, 'Good! Very good. I am greatly relieved to hear it, and have no doubt that she will take the break with you philosophically enough, seeing she has no choice in the matter. Give the Hebrew his due, he is quick to accept hard facts when he has to.'

By the time his father had come to the end of these remarks, what had started as mere satisfaction had lapsed into the worst kind of smugness. But then as he looked upon his son with genuine affection, his tone changed again. 'You are young yet, Charlie. There will be someone for you in time, a young lady we can all be proud of, who will fit comfortably into our family and feel at home with us.'

But Charlie had risen to his feet. 'Perhaps I have not made myself plain. I want to marry Emilia, if I should be so fortunate as to persuade her to change her mind. I hope that she will have me, and I can spend the rest of my life with her by my side.'

His father's attitude hardened. 'I am warning you, Charlie. If you persist in your plans to bring that woman into our family, I will not have you in the house!'

Once his father's strident tones had faded, Charlie replied in as calm a voice as he could manage. 'Very well, Father. I shall take a room on The Esplanade. I'll go and pack now. Tonight I shall return to take leave of everyone, and then you can count on my having departed for good.'

And though he had eaten nothing, Charlie left the breakfast table to begin the task of removing from his room every trace that he had ever been its occupant.

His father was sure that his son would soon see that his choices were faulty. After all, he had faced many difficult decisions in his own life.

CHAPTER 26

St Kilda
February 1865

ELIZA, BUSY WITH THE BED LINEN, WAS NOT WITH HER SISTER WHEN Nancy came into the sitting room holding an opened letter from Will Blackland.

'It appears,' she told Emilia, 'that the Committee is prepared to be extremely generous in their terms of employment. As well as my accommodation, they have offered to supply me regularly with all kinds of provisions. They mention meat, vegetables, milk, butter, cheese, flour, tea and sugar.' She referred to the written page to be sure she had left nothing out. 'Oh, and wood too, of course, for fires in the house as well as the school room. If I do decide to go to Tarryever, the villagers have arranged for my cousin Will to escort me on the voyage.' She seated herself at the work table opposite her friend and raised her shoulders as though to say, 'Who could ask for more?' She then put it into words. 'It all sounds so tempting that I do not see how I can refuse.'

Emilia's response was accompanied by a glance that was more than a little sceptical. 'Well, of course, their whole aim is to tempt you. The parents who make up that School Committee are naturally anxious to secure the very best teacher they can get.'

Nancy said dubiously, 'I cannot help wondering whether Cousin Will has made claims regarding my teaching abilities that will be hard for me to prove valid. I would never describe myself as anything other than a teacher of average capabilities.'

'How can you say that? As well as the usual qualifications, you teach pianoforte, singing, drawing and French. Where else are the Tarryever families likely to find a teacher with your gifts?'

Nancy laid aside the letter and took up her piece of embroidery. 'I must confess, Emilia, that the conditions of this post do appeal to me, and the remuneration offered, which I haven't yet told you about, is considerably above what I was expecting.'

Emilia paused in the act of threading her needle to ask wistfully, 'Does this mean you will soon be writing to accept? I am selfish enough to wish you would stay. I shall miss you most dreadfully.'

'I have not finally made up my mind, but rest assured that you will be the first to know my decision, well before I write to my cousin about it.'

After this, there seemed nothing more to say. The two young women sat plying their needles, each lost in their own thoughts. Emilia's were all of Charlie, and her very real fear that once Nancy was gone she would lose any opportunity to see him. Nancy's were centred on the position at Tarryever. Once there, she would be able to forget about the way her plans had not worked out and could start out on a new life.

Thirty minutes later, Nancy put down her embroidery and said, 'I have decided to accept. I remember that Will's January letter said that the shearing shed will need extensive work to convert it into a school house and add accommodation for a school teacher. The sooner I reply, the sooner the builders can begin. I will write a letter to Will now.'

On the following Sunday afternoon, the pleasant weather led Charlie to suggest that, rather than stay in the drawing room, the three of them should take a walk along the beach. Nancy ran to get her sketching book and pencils while Emilia collected their hats. After they had found a suitable spot on the beach for Nancy to sit, her eyes were attracted to a handful of interesting shells. She hardly noticed when Charlie drew Emilia away to pace with him the narrow sweep of damp sand.

'By the end of the year, I will be a lonely bachelor living in sparsely furnished quarters above the National Bank in Bridge Road, Richmond. I am, of course, proud to be offered management of a brand new bank building, but it has been designed for a whole family to live upstairs rather than just me. My only company at night will be my library and ledgers from the rack downstairs.'

Charlie had chosen his words carefully. But he had not succeeded in hiding the truth. She had suspected that she was the cause of his leaving his father's house and now she was certain.

Her heart warmed to him as she saw the measure of his willingness to sacrifice for her, not only his family's good opinion, but all the comforts of home. In return, she felt that there was nothing she would not do for him. In a rush of tenderness she put out her hand to him and he, taking it, tucked it beneath his arm, so that their footsteps were drawn closer together at the edge of the flowing tide.

'Tell me ...' Charlie drew her arm even closer. 'Does Nancy know when she will be travelling to Tarryever?'

'No, Charlie. She only sent her letter last Monday. They won't have it yet. The men at Tarryever have a substantial task to prepare the shed for habitation, which will take many months. I'm hoping that wet weather and lack of timber will delay the work, so that she's here for a long time. I will miss her dreadfully.'

'You do realise that when she leaves to go there, it will no longer be seemly for us to meet at your sister's house on Sunday afternoons.' Waiting only for her nod, he went on, 'In ordinary circumstances, I would write to your father to ask if he has any objection to me courting you in the usual way.'

Emilia was horror struck! 'On no account, Charlie. You must do nothing of the kind!'

Charlie had stopped and swung round to face her, saying, 'I am fully aware that these are not ordinary circumstances and that in our case it would be far from a sensible thing to do.'

'How right you are, Charlie! He would refuse and write to Eliza who would then bundle me on a ship for Home. You do see why? She would be free of all responsibility for me, and no blame could then be laid at her door. If I were to marry you, Eliza and Abraham would have the worst kind of shameful sorrow. I dearly love them. I don't want them to be shunned by their Jewish friends.'

Charlie could only stare at her.

She continued, 'Why should you think that strange, Charlie? Was the reaction of your own family very different? When they discovered that your young lady was Jewish, did they not pack you off like a naughty schoolboy?'

He sent her an anguished look, for he had hoped to spare her the knowledge.

'You did not have to tell me,' she murmured, 'I knew it must have been so. It often happens where our people are concerned.' She shrugged lightly and then said, 'As for women like me, it is laid down that we should only consider men who are Jewish. I must confess: in general, that meets with my full approval.'

But now Charlie had regained his voice. 'Emilia, I want you to know that in spite of the likely objections of our family and friends, I intend to go on seeing as much of you as I possibly can. My dear, since my intentions are of the most honourable kind, it is only fair to warn you that from this moment on, I consider us to be courting.'

In the coming weeks, Emilia tentatively and privately discussed the implications with a few friends she could trust. All, except Nancy, counselled against such a marriage.

CHAPTER 27

St Kilda

March 1865

'I CANNOT UNDERSTAND IT, ABRAHAM! THAT YOUNG CHARLIE BAEY-ertz has been coming to the house all this time and still he has not declared himself. I do hope he is not just toying with Nancy's affections.' It was quite late, the others having gone to their beds, when Eliza stood up from the table to collect together her letter writing instruments and paper.

'Now Eliza, remember that all the circumstances are not known to us. It may be that he has put out feelers, so to speak, and has not been encouraged by the response.'

'Well, if Nancy has not considered that marriage would solve her problem of an income, I feel sorry for her. Here she has a good-looking, intelligent young man with excellent prospects visiting her, and if she is not careful she may find she has missed her opportunity. It cannot be long now before she leaves us for Tarryever.'

Abraham raised surprised eyebrows. 'Nancy is to leave us? You have mentioned nothing of this to me.'

His wife said defensively, 'I have only known it but a day or two. She has been in correspondence with that cousin of hers, and he has been able to secure for her a most suitable teaching post in the west of the colony. Still, I shall be sorry to see her go.'

'Do you suppose Charlie knows about this?'

'If he does not, it may be just the spur he needs. Now, if you were to speak to him ... '

'Me? What on earth do you expect that to achieve? At his age, and I believe he is twenty-two, one would presume that he knows what he is about.'

'Yes, yes, it would seem so in the normal course of events, but in this case it would be a great pity if something were not done to hasten things along. It is fortunate that there are still some months before Nancy leaves us. Time, I am optimistic enough to think, for almost anything to happen.'

CHAPTER 28

St Kilda

September 1865

'WHEN IS THE *JINDIMINE* DUE TO ARRIVE IN MELBOURNE, EMILIA?'

'The date that was given in Will Blackland's last letter is a little over a month away.'

'Now that I am lodging in Hawthorn to be near the building site, I make do with walks along Bridge Road.'

Their eyes met. Emilia waited for Charlie to put into words the thought that was uppermost in her mind as well as his.

'And with Nancy gone, I will have no possible excuse to call at the house on Sunday afternoons, as I have today.'

Emilia's voice was low with misery as she answered, 'There is nothing at all that we can do, Charlie—at least, I know of nothing.'

He did not respond at once. Eventually he said, 'There is one thing, if only you will be agreeable to it, my dear. The day Nancy's ship sails for Portland, we must be married. I will not need an excuse to visit the Berens's home after that day because you'll be in mine. Does that meet with the prospective bride's approval?'

'Oh, Charlie, if only we could!' Why her eyes should fill with tears at the thought Emilia could never have explained, but the happy result was that once again she found herself within the circle of his arms.

CHAPTER 29

St Kilda

November 1865

CHARLIE BOUNDED UP THE PATH LEADING TO THE FRONT DOOR OF HIS old home, knocked impatiently, then had to wait some minutes to be admitted.

When the door opened it revealed his mother, who gasped, 'Come in, Charlie, come in.'

'Good evening, Mother!'

He followed Mary Anne Baeyertz into the entrance hall where he gave her a brief hug. She took his hand to lead him into the sitting room but he hung back saying, 'No, I must not stay long, lest Father come home and find me here.'

His mother stepped back into the hall. 'Oh, Charlie, how I have missed you! But tell me about this young lady of yours. Will she make you happy?'

'Mother, you cannot imagine the joy she brings me. I can see nothing but happiness ahead for us both.'

'Then that is all that matters to me. Bless you, my darling boy. My blessings on you both!'

'We are to be married on Thursday week, on the morning of November 16th. You will come, Mother? The wedding is to be at Christ Church in Hawthorn.'

Tears gathered in her eyes. 'If only I could, Charlie. But you know how your father feels about it, and if my being there ever came to his ears ... '

Her son took her hand in his and squeezed it gently. 'Yes, I know. He would see it as the worst kind of treachery, and never allow you to forget it.'

'But I will be thinking and praying for you both throughout the whole of that day,' she murmured through her tears, 'and I have a wedding gift for you. Have you bought the ring yet, Charlie?'

'Not yet. We will visit a jeweller one day this week.'

'Then wait just a moment. I have something for you.'

Expecting that at any moment he would hear his father's footsteps approaching the gate, Charlie waited by the open door.

When his mother returned, breathless, he chided her, 'You should not have hurried so, Mother.'

In no condition to waste her breath in argument, Mrs Baeyertz gasped, 'Here you are, my son. This belonged to my mother, and I want you to have it for your bride.' As she spoke, she opened her fingers to reveal in her palm a gold wedding band. Rolling it into a ball in her handkerchief, she pressed it into his hand. 'Now go quickly, before your father gets home. Goodbye, dear Charlie. God bless you always!'

Fearful that she may have detained him too long, she gave Charlie a slight push as he stepped onto the verandah. Then, through her tears, she watched him stride down the path, out of the gate and towards the St Kilda railway station.

CHAPTER 30

St Kilda

16 November 1865

THAT THURSDAY, EMILIA LEFT THE HOUSE AT THE SAME TIME AND ON the same path that she used each morning. Under the towel and costume in Emilia's basket that day were several items that were none of Eliza's business.

While she strode, she remembered the first day the three friends had met on the beach. They had been excited about the adventure and the hot January weather had made the cool seawater deliciously refreshing. During winter, brisk walks in the cool air of early mornings blew away sleepiness from their eyes and their thoughts. They'd only stayed indoors when too much rain or wind would have counteracted the benefits.

As she approached the St Kilda pier, in fear of Eliza glancing out of the window and in anticipation of what was to come, Emilia increased her pace a little.

Charlie was not waiting for her.

'What if something has happened to him and he does not come?' A strange sense of desolation assailed her. She was cutting herself off from her family. Should she turn and walk to the sea baths while she had the chance?

No. Memories of Charlie had crowded into Emilia's thoughts. She wanted to jump with joy. Jumping would attract unwanted attention. She paced instead until, while facing the way she had come, Emilia heard footsteps behind her. Might they belong to Charlie? They did! She ran eagerly into his arms. In the hansom cab he had hired, she held his hand tightly throughout the trip to the church.

Discrete enquiries had revealed to Charlie that most clergy and rabbis would rather not be asked to perform such a ceremony. To his relief, the Reverend William Wood was not only willing and able but felt obliged as the vicar of the Church of England parish where Charlie then resided. Only much later would Mr Wood know the significance of his work that spring morning.

There was no great feast, nor fancy dress, nor choir at Christ Church, Hawthorn. Neither family nor friends attended for neither had been invited. Their only guests and witnesses were the vicar's maid and the church's gardener. Had the bride and groom not been convinced that their union was ordained in heaven, this would have greatly grieved them both.

Nancy had, of course, been told of their plans and had kept them to herself until she sailed west with Will that very morning.

When Eliza heard the news that afternoon, she was furious. If she had known what was working, she would have put Emilia on a homeward bound vessel and never left her till she was safely outside Port Phillip Heads.

Nurse was as surprised as Eliza but Cook and Beatrice had been happy romantic conspirators, considering it a runaway match, not fully understanding the shame Eliza would endure.

Eliza dismissed them both for not warning her. Before they could pack their own rooms, they had one last task from Eliza—the collection from the public rooms of all the objects that belonged to Emilia. Eliza did the same in Emilia's room. They found items scattered all over the house and packed them. After Beatrice and Cook accepted their outstanding wages and most satisfactory references, they walked together around to Dinsley's depot. There, Eliza arranged both for a waggonette to transport the two women and their belongings to The Esplanade so they could find a room, and for a carrier to call in the morning for a delivery to Richmond.

When Emilia received the boxes and saw there was no note from Eliza, she realised afresh the consequences of her actions. She had cut herself off from her family and from her Jewish friends and neighbours. She cried for a long time as her sorrow battled with her joy of knowing that Charlie Baeyertz was her husband.

As soon as they heard the news from Cook and Beatrice, Charlie arranged for them to be employed by his bank. He could use a maid and a cook at the Richmond branch. They were grateful and so accepted his offer, after a little hesitation, for Emilia could be touchy.

CHAPTER 31

Richmond, Victoria
November 1865

A WEEK AFTER THEIR WEDDING, EMILIA SAT DOWN IN HER NEW HOME to write a letter. She looked down at the blank paper before her and sighed.

She had postponed this task because, every time she thought of it, grief and delight rose together to swamp her thoughts. Her news would be painful, but she must honour her parents and so tell them of her decision. She must impress upon them that Eliza was not at fault.

My dearest Mama and Papa,

I am writing to bring you the most wonderful news imaginable! My name is now no longer Miss Aronson, but Mrs Charles Baeyertz, and you will need to write to me care of National Bank of Australasia, 231 Bridge Road, Richmond, Victoria where Charlie is the new branch manager.
The building was completed a few weeks ago so we could both move into the empty flat above on the very afternoon of our wedding.

Charlie is just five months younger than I am. His family are English immigrants. No, the Baeyertz family are not Jewish. Charlie and I were married not in a Synagogue, but in a Church.

We have agreed to respect each other's religion and not try to convert one another.

If only you knew my dear husband as I do, you would understand how it is that we have chosen one another as marriage partners for life. I am, of course, sorry, if it is possible to be both sorry and deliriously happy at the same time, that my marrying out of the faith cannot help but bring sorrow and shame upon our family.

To tell the truth, it is not a matter of regret that I have taken this step but far otherwise, and I trust that you and all the family will, in spite of everything, be happy for me.

You must not blame Eliza because she did not know anything. She behaved as an older sister and hostess should at all times.

If you can, please be happy for us. Do not sit shiva for me and do not allow anyone in the family to do so. I regret for all our sakes that my new husband is not of our people; rest assured that nowhere could there be a better son-in-law to bring into our midst. Charlie joins me in sending love and trusts that it will not be too long before he is able to meet all of you in person, when I am sure he will set at rest any fears you may be harbouring on my account.

Give my love to all my brothers and sisters and most of all to you my dear, dear Mama and Papa,

From your ever-loving daughter,

Emilia

CHAPTER 32

Bangor
February 1866

NOW THAT JOHN HAD STEPPED DOWN FROM THE DAILY MANAGEMENT of the business, he could retreat to the library for an hour or two before joining Lewis in the shop. As always, Maria Aronson remained at the breakfast table to sort through their mail. This morning, she caught a glimpse of familiar handwriting. With gladness in her heart and Emilia's silver paper knife in her hand, she pounced on the envelope, unfolded the pages and began to read.

As she laid down the letter, Maria stared unseeingly before her. Then speaking softly to herself, she said, 'It is too late now for anything to be done. It is not as if she were under age.' But then a thought came to her. Of course there was something still to be done! Maria lifted up her heart in prayer. 'O Holy One of Israel, watch over my child. May the foundation of this marriage be solid, and free from further sin, and in the years ahead may her joys far outweigh the sorrows. Let me bring my husband before Thee as well, O Lord. Guard his heart from the shock that must come with the reading of this letter, and comfort him. May he see that only time can prove whether this step that she has taken will be the ruin of her life as we fear it may be. Help John to forgive what will appear to him her desertion of the faith of our fathers and the turning of her back on our godly heritage. And may it be that Thou, the God of our Fathers, wilt be pleased to forgive her as well. Amen.'

Giving no thought to the rest of her husband's mail, Maria poured him a fresh cup of tea, placed it together with their daughter's letter on a small tray, and carried it to the library. Without waiting to make her presence known, she went straight in and placed the tray on the desk in front of him. John looked up sharply at the interruption, but the sight of the letter from Emilia drove all other thoughts from his mind.

'A word from Emilia at last! What has the little minx been so busy about that she could not write to us before this?' Humming quietly under his breath, John reached for the closely written pages with keen anticipation.

Maria withdrew quietly into the hall where she stood by the slightly open door and waited. At first she heard nothing but the humming, until there came a muffled exclamation followed by the slamming of a hand on the desk. A chair scraped, causing her to wonder if her husband had risen to his feet. But there was no sound of footsteps to break the silence. Just as she came to the conclusion that her husband would be ready to talk the whole matter over, she heard the heart-wrenching sound of a grown man crying.

New Beginnings

1867 to 1877

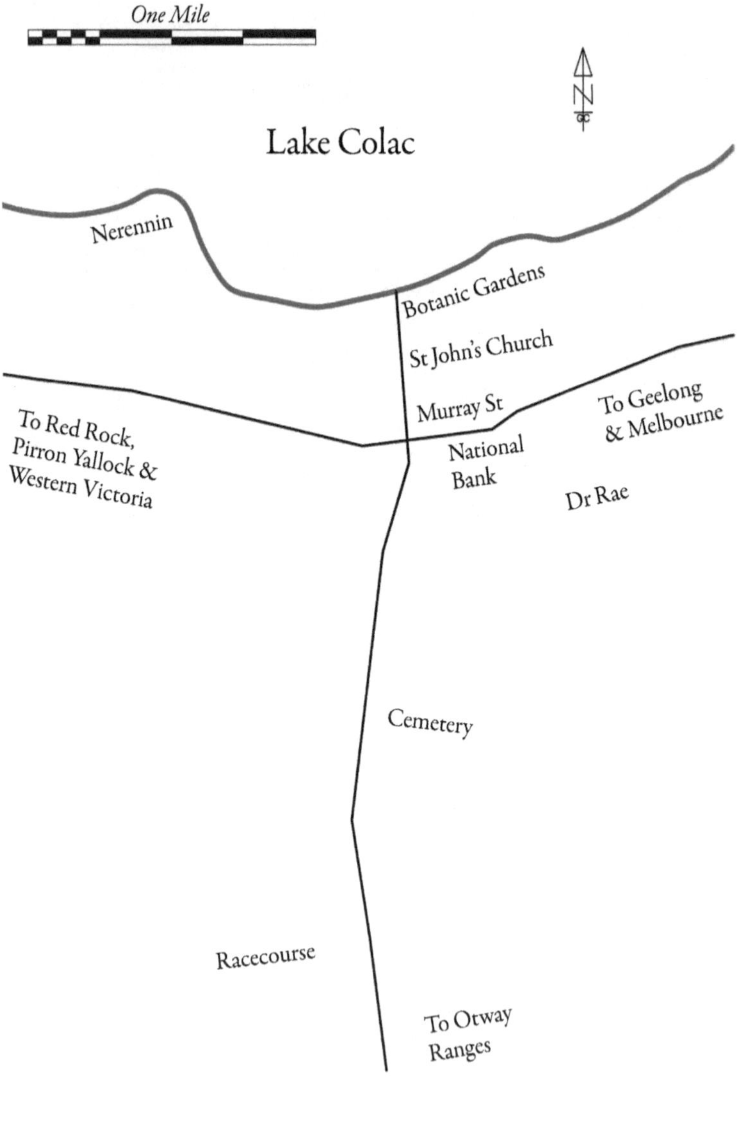

One Mile
Lake Colac
Nerennin
Botanic Gardens
St John's Church
Murray St
To Geelong
& Melbourne
To Red Rock,
Pirron Yallock &
Western Victoria
National
Bank
Dr Rae
Cemetery
Racecourse
To Otway
Ranges
N

CHAPTER 33

Colac, Victoria
1867

WHEN NEWCOMERS TO THE WESTERN DISTRICT OF VICTORIA CLIMB
Red Rock, they discover a vista of extinct volcanos with scoria cones, ancient
lava flows and crater lakes. On looking southwest, they see a huge body of salt
water called Lake Corangamite. To the southeast, their view is of the smaller
freshwater Lake Colac that has a surface area of seven square miles.

In 1837, pastoralists began to establish large properties to run sheep and
cattle here on the fertile undulating plains. Several hamlets slowly grew up
around the Lake. The largest, on the southern shore, became the township
of Colac.

By the time the Baeyertz family arrived in 1867, Colac had a population
of 1500. There was no synagogue but churches, schools, hotels, stores, trades,
professions, a post and telegraph office, a newspaper, a Shire Hall and a
bank had all been established. The family soon eagerly contributed to Colac
society.

Mr Charles Baeyertz, jun., was the new Manager of the National Bank.
Colac suited Charlie, for outdoor pursuits, of which he was passionately
fond, were plentiful.

Emilia wasn't so keen on horses; they made her nervous. Yet, the country
life was her idea; she had suggested the transfer. Here, they could escape
the worldly life of the big city. They could enjoy picnics beside the cool lake.
Charlie could build his own boat to row and sail upon the tranquil waters.
He could show off his rifle shooting and join hunting parties with his well-
trained bird dogs.

They brought with them their son, Charles Nalder Baeyertz, who had
been born in December the previous year while they lived above the bank in
Richmond. Cook and Beatrice accompanied them, taking the change as an
opportunity to see the country.

The Baeyertz family of three lived at number 26, on the south side of Murray Street. Here, as in Richmond, their brick building housed both their accommodation and the bank.

The stuccoed stone façade gave the impression of a solid and dependable institution in a dusty street where there were few others. Any bushranger would have trouble breaking in. A finely carved stone cornice ran the length of the building above the doors and windows of the ground floor. The roof above the first floor was out of sight behind a carved parapet that stood atop the front wall.

No verandah yet shaded the six windows that gathered light and warmth from the sun for the six rooms. On the ground floor, the big room on the left with the wide window was the banking chamber.

The room on the right, with its own door to the street, was their parlour. George's wedding gift, a beautiful white marble clock, sat on a shelf. A sash window gave Emilia a view of Murray Street. A window through the back wall allowed her to see the yard behind. A back door allowed her to enter the yard from the parlour and then mount the timber steps that led to a gallery beside the four bed rooms on the upper floor. Emilia was grateful that they were not living in a bark hut.

Their main bed room was directly above the banking chamber; each could be warmed by a hearth and share the chimney. No one would break into the bank from the ceiling as long as the manager occupied that room.

A second bed room was allocated to Beatrice, a third to a nursery for baby Charles, and a fourth to a new nurse. Marion Cecilia Baeyertz was born above the bank, in March 1869. Marion was her aunt Eliza's middle name.

In the back yard, we can imagine a scene typical of the colony at this time. Three structures stood in line along the western fence. The closest was the kitchen and the cook's bed room. Beyond was the bath room and washhouse. The third was the outhouse. Emilia could observe Beatrice and Cook moving around the outbuildings while attending to their tasks.

Emilia took great delight in the flower garden beside the vegetable garden. A good deal of thought had been put into the location of the gardens to make the most of the sunlight. Chickens enjoyed roaming in the back yard during daylight, unless the dogs were out. The fowls were always carefully returned to their coop at dusk as the red foxes, so recently acclimatized to the colony, had already arrived in Colac.

Billy, their groundsman, was often to be found at the stables and kennels at the southern end of their property which abutted Bromfield Street. He was a Colac man who had his own holdings nearby.

CHAPTER 34

Colac

1869

IT WAS HERE, AMID THE PURE JOYS OF A HAPPY HOME AND IN CONSTANT company of her devoted husband that Emilia began to realise that true religion was something more than a tradition or a creed.

One evening, when they had retired to their bed room, Emilia commented that it was time to arrange a christening service for Marion. She then surprised Charlie when she said that she wanted to be christened too! He'd been careful not to speak about his faith, according to their agreement.

They were, however, not prevented from praying for one another and Charlie devoted time at the end of each day to prayer. After he had knelt for a long time in silence, with his eyes closed and hands clasped, Emilia often asked, 'Why do you pray so long? And for what do you pray?'

'I pray for you,' Charlie would reply. 'I must not talk with you of Christ, but I can speak to Him of you, and beseech Him to show you Himself and in some way to reach you.'

When Emilia spoke of being christened, she explained to Charlie that every day she saw that he possessed some wonderful inner power which was the spring of his life and action. She did not realise that she could see the character of Jesus revealed in Charlie because she did not know that the Holy Spirit lived within him.

Instead, Emilia hoped that she would gain the fullness of life she saw in Charlie if she undertook the church's sacraments of christening and confirmation. These rituals would also help her to raise young Charles and Marion with the right knowledge.

During one discussion, Charlie said, 'Since you appear to be willing to talk about the Christian faith I want to tell you about an amazing thing that has overtaken me.'

'What amazing thing might that be?'

'Well, I scarcely know how to describe it to you. It happened first in the moment when the midwife allowed me to see our newborn son.'

'I remember that day so clearly.'

'Yes, I was surprised when regular customers to the bank cheered at the news. Do you remember that some wives of the men who worked with me gave us gifts of newly made baby's clothes? I digress. When I saw our son, I became convinced that I was looking upon a gift that had come from the Father Himself, and at the same time felt that I was in His very presence.'

The expression on Emilia's face was a mixture of doubt and perplexity. 'I would never have known, Charlie. You said not a word of this to me.'

Charlie, who had closed his eyes as on an inner vision, now opened them to say apologetically, 'No, my darling. I am sorry. Several times I did try to tell you, but the words just would not come. Then too, we had made a pact and I could not in all conscience speak of my God, the triune God, as I would have had to do. That might have offended you.'

Emilia nodded but did not interrupt him.

'In the normal course of events I have allowed the memory of that experience to fade in the adjustment of our daily lives to include our precious boy.'

'And then I gave birth to Marion here.'

He drew a deep breath to say softly, 'Yes, then Marion joined us, the most perfectly adorable tiny being imaginable. When she came into our lives she was clearly another gift from a loving God. I was completely overwhelmed that He should consider me deserving of such a child. I, who had allowed God into my life at my confirmation but still knew myself to be unworthy, could only offer Him my poor efforts at thanksgiving.

'Emilia, to say that I was caught up in the consciousness of God's love does not begin to describe how I felt at that time. The tears just streamed down my face. I could not stop them. It came to me then that He wanted a deeper relationship with me so I would have to give God all of my life. In my day-by-day life with you and the children, I have been more than happy but, since Marion's birth, I've been spending more time reading the Bible and I've been seeking the presence of Almighty God.'

'Aha, that's the reason why you've been reading the Bible more often.'

Some days later, after Charlie had finished his prayers and climbed into bed beside Emilia, she said, 'I've spoken to our vicar. He wants us both to attend a class to explain why the Church of England christens children and adults.'

Charlie said, 'I'm happy to go with you to hear what our vicar has to say. I don't know what the vicar told my parents when they had me christened, but I remember what I learnt during the lessons for my confirmation. It was during those sessions that I became a more diligent seeker after the truth, and the One Whose Name is Truth led me to the reading of His Holy Word. While I read those pages I met Him face to face. I saw clearly what Jesus had done for me in His life and death. What could I do Emilia, but bow in humble adoration?'

Charlie blinked back tears. 'And that is how I submitted myself to Him. I acknowledged that as a sinner I stood in urgent need of a Saviour, and there could be no doubt that He was the One Sent From God. I learnt that His name "Jesus" means "Saviour". Another name is "Emmanuel", which means "God with us." I also learnt that Jesus had come from His home in Heaven for the very purpose of taking upon Himself our sins. Because He died, redeemed sinners live and, by the mercy of a loving God, I am one of the redeemed. So you see, my dear, I welcomed Jesus into my life at my confirmation. I pray that you will know Jesus as your Saviour and receive His strength to live each day as His disciple.'

CHAPTER 35

Colac

1869

AFTER THEIR CHRISTENING SERVICE, EMILIA WAS DISAPPOINTED TO discover that she found no rest in her spirit from her compliance with this ritual. However, she did not stop attending church. Indeed, none of the church members would have guessed that she was Jewish. They saw her play the piano as rostered and competently read from the prayer book. Furthermore, Emilia was an eager participant in many aspects of the work in the region. During those years, the good people of the church presented her with a handsome silver tea and coffee service on which was inscribed, 'In grateful acknowledgement of Mrs Baeyertz's invaluable services in connection with St John's Church, Colac.'

One day, Beatrice interrupted the cup of tea Emilia was having with a friend to give Mrs Baeyertz a letter. Emilia opened the envelope to find papers from the vicar, the Reverend Mr Thomas Sabine, in response to her request for confirmation. She tossed the papers over to her guest saying, 'You know more about this sort of thing than I do; please answer those questions for me.'

Some weeks after she had been confirmed, Emilia joined in at the communion service, thinking that this would be the crowning deed of the religious course she had set herself. During the service the congregation turned to the Creed. Emilia recited, 'I believe in God, the Father Almighty, Maker of heaven and earth and in Jesus Christ, God's only Son, our Lord ... '

Emilia could not finish. She was overwhelmed by a sense of being farther from God than ever. Her conscience thundered, 'How can you? How dare you say the creed when you don't believe that Jesus Christ is God's Son, our Lord? You really believe that He was a mere man and, therefore, an imposter.' She had noticed this fundamental problem the first time she visited a church and heard the creed. It had not gone away.

She dared not speak the words nor go to the Lord's Table. At home each day, Emilia kneeled with Charlie, held his hand while he prayed and wished that she had been born without a soul. That would have spared her all the anxiety and confusion of considering her fate. She could not reconcile the faith she was born into with the faith she had chosen, so she hid her confusion from everyone, throwing herself into the delights of living in Colac, the tasks of daily life and the formation and training of the church choir.

CHAPTER 36

Colac

25 February 1871

THAT SATURDAY, EMILIA WALKED THE THREE BLOCKS TO THE CHURCH of St John the Evangelist and opened the doors to allow the refreshing breeze to flow through. The building had been opened the year before on the corner of Hesse and Pollark Streets with an effective and pleasing choir. Now the Blundens were in charge of the choir and organ, she was content to accompany the soloist from time to time.

As she practised some pieces for the following day, she heard familiar footsteps approach so looked and smiled. It was indeed her Charlie. They exchanged a fond greeting.

'I love hearing you play the hymns; once is not enough.'

Emilia turned to the music for the solo. She was not surprised to hear Charlie's rich voice rise as she played the first notes of one of his favourite hymns.

> O Paradise! O Paradise!
> Who doth not crave for a rest?
> Who would not seek the happy land
> Where they that loved are blest?
> Where loyal hearts and true
> Stand ever in the light,
> All rapture through and through,
> In God's most holy sight.

Her eyes were moist with checked tears, but her fingers still mechanically pressed the keys as her loved one sang on, of 'the world growing old' and the longing to be 'at rest and free'. Emilia's heart yearned with an unutterable longing for the rest of which he sang. She still struggled to understand because she did not possess the assurance of eternity in heaven.

Once her fingers had found the last notes, Charlie explained that he would leave her now to lock the church and go home while he arranged a treat. She would be driven one and half miles from the bank to Nerennin where they would meet for dinner with his parents. Now he needed to organise their transport home later that evening.

Emilia kissed her children good night and left them in the care of Nurse, with instructions that the staff were not to wait up and to leave her bed room unlocked. In the buggy, she chatted with Billy and enjoyed listening to the regular beat of the horse's hooves against the road.

The homestead at Nerennin had a beautiful vista of the lake. Charles and Mary Anne had retired here with a generous pension to live near their grandchildren, son and daughter-in-law.

The attitude of Charlie's father had changed. He had slowly warmed to his daughter-in-law as he watched her take good care of his son and grandchildren. In his company, Emilia chose her words carefully and often spoke of her father-in-law's interests instead of her own.

After the delightful summer evening and sunset at the farmstead, at nine o'clock it was time for Emilia's treat. The four adults walked together down the slope from the house to the side of the lake. The senior Mrs Baeyertz draped a cloak against the cool night air around the shoulders of her daughter-in-law. Charlie graciously, tenderly, settled his wife into his boat. He pushed off, got in and then gently pulled away as she waved their farewells.

What a perfect night it was! Emilia trailed her fingers in the silvery waters while Charlie slowly stroked for the shore below the Botanic Gardens under the waxing crescent moon and myriad stars. The dipping oars, creaking rowlocks, murmuring wavelets and their own hushed tones were the only sounds to break the wonderful silence and beauty of that night of sacred purity. Emilia breathed in the tranquil air, laden with the scents of the Australian bush, and wondered that anyone could be so happy.

Charlie's care for his wife was shown in his thoughtful scattering of rugs and cushions about the boat to reduce the hardness of the bench seat and beautify their transport. His thoughtfulness reminded her of the comments of Colac residents about his approach to his role as bank manager. How many times had she been stopped in the street by women of the town who told her that, young as he was, Charlie Baeyertz held a position of high regard in the business circles of the district? She had smiled her thanks and gone her way hugging to herself the supreme satisfaction of knowing that this man of integrity was the husband she loved. He was only twenty-eight but he had become her whole world.

As she gazed on him fondly their eyes met, but his dreamy expression scarcely changed. Emilia knew what it meant to have one's cup running over. After letting the boat drift for some time, he asked her, 'Is this evening special for you too? Do you feel as I do, at one with God's wonderful creation? I do not want this idyll to end.'

Emilia was not as ready as he to shatter the atmosphere that held her spellbound. She volunteered only a very soft, 'Hmm' and even then was not sure just what she meant by it.

When the time came to look for the jetty, Charlie saw that he did not have to row very far. He tied up the vessel securely and assisted Emilia to step out onto the planking which led to the shore. After he tucked the cushions and mats into a large sugar bag to be collected the next day, Charlie followed Emilia to solid ground. Emilia put on her cape and together they walked slowly up the hill outside the fence that protected the young plants in the Botanic Gardens.

Beyond the top, the streets had been set out north to south and east to west on level ground. While they ambled through the moonlight along Queen Street, Emilia linked her arm with Charlie's.

As Emilia compared the gardens of the houses they passed, she became aware that her husband wanted to talk. Mindful of the late hour, he spoke in a whisper as he prepared to ask Emilia something. He looked down at her and, in a changed voice, asked, 'My very dear wife, I would be glad to hear from your own lips how high a value you place on the last five years of your life, the years in which we have been man and wife'.

Emilia frowned at him. 'Do I detect an unworthy motive in that question? It occurs to me, sir, that someone is hopeful of hearing words that abound to his credit.'

'My dear Mrs B! Surely you do not harbour such thoughts about your poor spouse. Is it not a fact that his fondness for his wife passes the bounds of reason?'

'And my dear Mr B., is not your unfortunate wife an even worse case? How can anyone doubt that from the day on which she became your blushing bride, she has been in a very heaven of delight? I cannot understand how such a question came to arise.'

By this time their giggles were becoming difficult to suppress, yet something in Charlie was not yet satisfied. 'Am I to be blamed, my darling, for uprooting you from the midst of a loving family in a bustling city to be brought to a country town where every day is nothing more than a repetition of the day before?'

'You are no doubt waiting for me to complain that you brought me here and then left me to my own devices. Well, it seems I need to remind you that not only did you bring me here on my suggestion but you brought our son as well and since then Marion has joined our little family. Where do you think I would want to be, if not here with you and the children? As for each day being the same, let me tell you that since we arrived I've found much to do at church and the women of Colac have warmly invited me to join all their associations. What's more, a duke visited.'

'Mmm, yes! I do seem to remember,' her husband murmured, 'that His Royal Highness Prince Alfred was presented to a certain young lady.'

She raised her finger to him, 'And your dogs were selected for use by the royal hunting party.'

Her husband's lips twitched, 'I do not recollect, my love, any voice of complaint.'

'Of course I voiced no complaint. I was in a state close to perfect bliss, as you very well know, and I strongly suspect that was your condition!'

They broke off their conversation to take care as they crossed Murray Street. Bright as the moonlight was, it might not prevent them from being run down by a Cobb & Co coach.

They did not go in through the parlour. Instead, Charlie swung wide the gate beside the bank.

Charlie stepped back and, as Emilia passed by him into the yard, remarked casually, 'Then I need not fear that my wife is among those in the town who spend their idle hours in dreaming of what might have been, if only?'

Emilia stopped and turned to stand before him wearing a look that could not be mistaken for anything else but exasperation. Charlie cast glances up and down the moonlit street, took her in his arms and soundly kissed her. Then, grasping her firmly by the hand, he led her along the path to the wooden stairs, where they crept up in their socks, slipped through their door, bolted it quietly behind them and then tiptoed to their bed.

CHAPTER 37

Colac

4 March 1871

A WEEK LATER, CHARLIE ENTERED THE PARLOUR AND SAT DOWN AT the dining table after the usual half day of work on the Saturday.

'I'm famished because I had no time for morning tea. There were so many customers!'

Emilia said, 'The noise of the crowd in Murray Street waiting for the doors to open this morning was louder than usual. It attracted Beatrice and me to the parlour window. We saw certain respectable people in the crowd but we didn't like the look of some of the others. When we first arrived here both Beatrice and I felt concerned that we were living so close to the bank. I made it clear to her that each of us ought to take notice of what was going on, to be aware of discontented customers and untoward activity.'

'Naturally you are concerned, my dear, but I saw a policeman today keeping an eye on the crowd. Policemen often come past the bank when we are open and I haven't heard of bushrangers in this area for a while now. Sometimes the price of goods in Melbourne makes people mutter and rumours travel with Cobb & Co. By the way, Harry came to tell me that quail are breaking cover whenever the horses gallop. Their numbers have increased since I looked last month at the racecourse.'

'It's fortunate Cook knows what to do with quail. They are such small birds that they can't be left in the oven too long. When are you thinking of going?'

'This afternoon. The weather is ideal.'

'I'd hoped we'd practise the new hymn for tomorrow's service. I told Godfrey that we would.'

'I'll ride up the hill on Nimrod and come home directly after sunset in the moonlight. I'll be back in plenty of time for dinner and a music practice at the church this evening.'

'I was afraid you'd forgotten. While you are away this afternoon, I'll visit a friend who has invited me.'

'You'll arrive in time for High Tea.'

'We can both be productive this afternoon and this evening. Please remember not to get carried away with the dogs and birds, as you often do. Stop shooting well before sunset, please.'

When they finished their lunch, Charlie put on his hat and said, 'I'll go to find Billy so he can help me to prepare Nimrod and the dogs to go out.'

Since Nurse and the children were having their afternoon naps and Cook was tidying up after lunch, Emilia could attend to her mother's news from Home that had come in the post.

One of Maria Aronson's earlier letters had explained that she had forgiven her daughter, although Maria hoped Emilia would not regret her choice of husband. Her father had crossed Emilia's name out of the family record in the great Bible, but he could not utter any curse against her because she was still his treasured daughter. Since then, Emilia and Maria had enjoyed exchanging letters and would do so for the remainder of Maria's life.

Having read the letter through, with the smile still lingering on her face, Emilia let her thoughts wander. She was soon thinking about the way their families had changed their attitudes towards her and Charlie. His young brother John, his sister Suzette and her husband Richard had enjoyed their company on a recent visit to Nerennin from Ballarat.

Last month, Emilia had taken the children to see their grandparents for an afternoon. When she'd returned, Emilia had explained to her husband the funny song that Mr Baeyertz had sung for her and his grandchildren. The children had also happily played with their grandmother who loved them dearly. Emilia had realised that the friendship she shared with her mother-in-law was growing stronger every month. Emilia could forget her difficult courting days now they were both at peace with Charlie's family.

The chime of the marble clock brought Emilia back to the present which was a quarter to four. She could not afford to indulge in reveries if the children were to be ready to see their father off. Upstairs in the nursery, she met Nurse helping the children from their cots. Dividing the tasks between them, the women dressed the young ones, brushed their hair, put their shoes on and took them out onto the gallery where they all looked through the rails down into the back yard.

Nimrod was tied to a post by the vegetable garden. Charlie waved, indicating that Emilia should join him. When she reached the yard, she was quickly surrounded by dogs enjoying freedom from their kennels. Careful not to step on the excited animals, Emilia wove her way between them to stand beside Charlie.

'Is Nimrod fit for a ride?'

'He's ready for a gallop and you can see the dogs are straining to get out of this yard.'

Nimrod's coat shone in the sun. Banjo, Charlie's favourite dog, pranced around Nimrod's stationary feet. Billy held Nimrod while Charlie mounted. Charlie checked that the shotgun Billy handed him was unloaded and strapped it into its leather scabbard.

Charlie and his children waved to each other. As always, he had a bright beautiful smile and a tender word of good-bye.

He then turned to thoughts of the hunt. He called the dogs and urged Nimrod to start the journey to the racecourse paddock through the south gate.

Emilia turned back to the house and, with her heart full of joy, sang as she went tripping up the stairs to her bed room.

There she removed her housedress, cleaned her hands and face at the basin on the corner washstand and then, with a towel thrown about her shoulders, attended to her hair. Emilia then put on her second-best visiting gown, her bonnet and her shawl, went to down into the yard where her children were now playing with Nurse and Billy, bid adieu and set off.

CHAPTER 38

Colac

4 March 1871

THE AFTERNOON'S VISITING PASSED PLEASANTLY AND EMILIA WAS home again in good time. Once she had changed for dinner, she was free to take her place in the parlour by the open window with the view of Murray Street, along which her husband would return.

Emilia had asked Nurse to bring Marion and Charles downstairs once they were dressed ready for bed. While Emilia held her daughter, her son stood upon a chair and prattled away in his sweet childish fashion as they watched the traffic in the road.

After an hour or so, an uneasiness Emilia could not dispel came to possess her mind. Telling herself that a watched pot never boils, she looked away sometimes to play with the children. By and by, through the window, she made out the figure of a neighbour passing with the keys to the church in his hand. She called to him, 'Come in please, or send up the keys, as we want to practise tonight.'

His clouded expression was replaced with relief and he said, 'Oh, then I'm thankful that Mr Baeyertz's accident was not as bad as I heard it was.'

'Accident! What do you mean?'

He stared at her in dismay. It had not occurred to him that she should still be ignorant of all that had taken place. 'Mrs Baeyertz,' he stammered, 'I felt sure that you would already know, but I see that you do not. I regret to have to tell you, your husband has had a shooting accident.'

Emilia made out men's voices further down the road and hoped they had better news.

Beatrice and Billy had by this time arrived to warn Mrs Baeyertz. They found Emilia already in flight. She asked Billy to wait for her. Emilia raced upstairs to don her bonnet and cloak. Nurse hurried downstairs behind Emilia to help Beatrice with the children.

Emilia and Billy rushed out into Murray Street. They first met Banjo. Halting in front of Emilia, he looked up at her. Something was amiss because he was not his usual boisterous self. She bent to hug him and murmured, 'What's happened to your master?'

As the voices approached, Emilia could see in the twilight a farm wagon with a draft horse put to its shafts, accompanied by four or five of Charlie's friends. Emilia went to the wagon, climbed up and found her husband lying flat out upon a mattress. She sat down and rested his head on her knee. One of the men said that another had ridden Nimrod to Dr Rae's house to report the accident. Someone else explained that Charlie's other gun dogs were being looked after.

The procession stopped at their residence. Emilia climbed down while Billy opened the gate and cleared the men's path.

One of the men gave a word of command which set them all to lift up Charlie on the mattress. Billy collected the saddle and gun from the cart and, with Banjo, led the men into the yard and to the foot of the stairs. Charlie was then carefully carried to his own bed. Heedless of the men crowded into the room, Emilia leant over and cradled his head in her arms.

'Charlie! My poor, poor darling, what has happened to you?'

His eyes opened and he made a valiant attempt at a smile. 'My fault, my dear ... an accident. My gun discharged itself, and there was I in the line of fire. Give it a few days ... I will then be myself again and this will all be behind us.'

Emilia gazed into the pale, drawn face and was overcome with dread. Yet her voice gave no sign of this as she said very gently, 'What you need is a long, long rest, and I will see to it that you are given every opportunity to recover fully. Trust me, my darling.'

Becoming aware of the other men in the room, Emilia spoke to them from a full heart. 'Your kindness to my husband is very much appreciated. I cannot thank you enough. But now you will be wanting to get to your own homes where there will be a meal awaiting you. I will not keep you.' Smiling her gratitude, Emilia asked Beatrice to see them all out so she could be alone with her Charlie.

She was sitting on the bed beside Charlie when she heard banging on the front door downstairs. She arrived at the head of the steps to find Beatrice directing the doctor up the stairs.

When he saw Emilia, Dr Rae asked, 'How are you my dear? I have a good idea of what I will see in my patient because one of his friends has explained what happened. Please take me to him.'

'Thank you for coming so quickly, Dr Rae. Please follow me.' Emilia turned and led the way.

After Dr Rae had inspected Charlie for a short time, Emilia was surprised to hear that he was going to leave them.

He explained, 'I must send a telegram to the hospital in Geelong. Dr Reid is the closest surgeon and he is over forty miles away. I'll need his help. May I ask you to sit with Charlie while I'm at the telegraph office? Have you eaten dinner yet? You were waiting for Charlie to return home, I suppose? When I return, I'll sit with Charlie while you have your meal.'

When Dr Rae returned, he found Emilia answering his knock on the front door.

When she saw the question on his face, Emilia said, 'I've just finished eating dinner. Cook was worried that the food would spoil. Besides, she and Beatrice insisted that I eat the meal that had been prepared because they think I'll be awake for much of the night. Beatrice has been sitting with Charlie while I was dining and so I am about to relieve her.'

'They are right you know. I should have thought of that. You've been blessed with good staff. I've sent the telegram. Let's go up to see Charlie again.'

As they turned to leave the parlour, an urgent rapping was heard on the front door. When Emilia opened it, her father-in-law rushed into the room.

'Where is he? What's happening now? Ahh, Doctor, it's good to see you here. We came as soon as we heard the dreadful news. Billy is seeing to the horse and buggy while we're inside because we can't stay the night. There is no more room in this house.'

'Mr and Mrs Baeyertz. We were just going up to see Charlie. Why don't you join us?'

As the men reached the gallery, Mary Anne remained at the head of the stairs to link her arm with Emilia's. 'How are you, my dear?'

'I'm bearing up. Charlie said he'd recover from his wound in a few days. It can't be that simple if Dr Rae wants the help of a surgeon.' She could say no more because tears had begun running down her face. Mary Anne released her hold so Emilia could find her handkerchief in a pocket.

Dr Rae held the door open so his companions could enter the bed room. Beatrice stood up and Emilia said, 'Thank you so much, Beatrice, for allowing me to eat dinner. I feel much refreshed. I don't think we'll need you for a while now so I'll leave you to help Cook clean up the kitchen. I'm sure you would both like to finish your work for the day and rest.'

CHAPTER 39

Colac

5 to 9 March 1871

AT ABOUT THREE O'CLOCK ON THAT SUNDAY MORNING, EMILIA WAS woken from dozing in her chair at Charlie's side by the clattering of a four-in-hand, the voice of Billy and knocking. Emilia was coming down the stairs as Dr Rae opened the front door.

Dr Reid was waiting. 'Thanks for coming so promptly, Boswell. Mrs Baeyertz, this is Dr Boswell Reid.'

'I came as fast as we could. I even changed horses at Winchelsea. There are lights shining in almost every house in the town. How is your patient, Thomas?'

Clearly word had got around about their bank manager. Emilia let the doctors examine the patient on their own upstairs while she hung the kettle to boil the water then stirred the fire beneath it. After Emilia had made the pot of tea and was setting out the teacups, both doctors returned.

As soon as they entered the room, Dr Rae said, 'We've examined Mr Baeyertz again in the lamplight and we don't think that it will be necessary to amputate his arm. In any case, it would be best to wait until daylight before we make a final decision. Charlie is dozing at the moment. You might want to go upstairs to resume your vigil, Mrs Baeyertz, until the sun shines into the room.'

Dr Rae and Dr Reid were so tired that they easily fell asleep in the comfortable chairs in the parlour. They awoke when Beatrice entered the room to stoke the fire. The doctors accepted the offer of a cooked breakfast and then, while Beatrice returned to the kitchen, the men went upstairs to assess their patient.

Emilia opened the curtains to let daylight flood into the bed room so the doctors could carefully examine Charlie. She heard comments that did not sound at all hopeful. Later, at the breakfast table, Dr Rae explained, 'The daylight has revealed that the charge entered between the left shoulder and breast and passed out at the top of the shoulder. It is clear that amputation at the socket is compulsory if we are to save Mr Baeyertz. His prospects are good because he is strong and healthy. I recently performed a similar operation and that patient has survived.'

Chloroform was administered at Emilia's request. The difficult operation was over before Charlie woke. When the doctors were happy that the wound would not bleed much, Dr Rae summoned Emilia. 'Your husband is bearing up with great fortitude. Now you have no cause for fear about his recovery. Dr Reid can return to Geelong.' Emilia was mightily relieved.

Time seemed to move through treacle during Sunday and Monday. Dr Rae and Emilia left the sick room as little as possible and nursed Charlie. Over the days, the doctor recognised the signs of deterioration in his patient, while Emilia saw small improvements as proof that he would recover.

Friends of the children took little Charles and Marion out to play. Mr and Mrs Baeyertz visited the patient each day. Cook and Beatrice not only made bigger meals but kept up a steady production of food to serve with cups of tea offered to the visitors.

Evidence of the popularity of the bank manager was seen in the number of people who called at the house offering support. Dr Rae soon had to arrange for a public notice requesting that townsfolk refrain from visiting.

On Monday evening, Dr Rae came downstairs to find Emilia, Mary Anne and Charles, sen., in the parlour. They had just finished dinner and were discussing their plans for nursing Charlie that night.

The father asked the doctor, 'Am I right to think that my son's health is not as good as you'd hoped after the operation?'

Dr Rae held up his hands. 'It's time I spoke to you all frankly. At first I thought that our amputation of his arm would allow Charles to recover from the shooting. Today I investigated his wound again and saw that our amputation did not remove all the damaged and dead flesh. When the charge entered the shoulder, it struck the bone which shattered within Charlie's chest. We removed the bone fragments but we hoped that his body would deal with his damaged flesh through the normal inflammation process. It appears that the damaged flesh lost its blood supply and died. It has now become toxic and that is what is keeping him ill. Emilia, your husband is dozing for longer periods and I think that sometime tonight he will die.'

Emilia cried out, 'No, that can't be true. He is my very life.'

The doctor continued, 'While Charlie is awake now and able to speak, you should all go to see him.'

Little Charles was staying with some friends that night and there was no time to get him back. He had already been into the sick room that day so knew his Daddy was unwell.

After Charlie's parents' had spent some time with their son, Emilia, with tears slipping down her cheeks, went upstairs to take Marion in to join them. The sick man was hardly recognisable as her lively loving Papa, so Marion was relieved to be taken back to the nursery by her grandparents.

Alone at Charlie's bedside once again, Emilia was overjoyed to see his eyes open, seeking her out. 'My darling,' she asked, adjusting his pillow, 'are you comfortable? How are you feeling?'

His voice, though weak, was quite steady as he said, 'The doctor has sent you because he can see I am getting worse.'

She swept back his hair from his brow as she said tenderly, 'He told me you are still unwell so he advised I stay with you.'

'You've seen me getting worse tonight. There is no doctor who can be of use to me, my love. I am sorry to have to say it, but it will not be long before I must leave you.'

'No, no, Charlie, do not even think of such a thing! You can't leave me after the life we've made together. You are all I have.' She had become greatly distressed even as she spoke, and now the tears filled her eyes so that she could scarcely make out her husband's face. But she could hear him, and his words came as a knife to her heart.

'Dearest Emilia, do not be distressed when I say that I know I cannot remain long with you. Be happy for me instead, for I am going to Heaven to be with Jesus. I have settled my account with God and am at peace.'

Kneeling by her husband's side, Emilia saw that his eyes were now focused beyond the confines of the bed room, fixed upon a scene that did not include her.

'Charlie,' she whispered, 'I am here beside you, my darling.'

But it was clear that he could not hear her. If the expression on his face was anything to judge by, he seemed to Emilia already part of another world, listening to voices other than hers. A moment later, a wonderful change came over Charlie. Even as she watched her husband's face, she saw a light.

Not a light that shone upon it, but a light that radiated from it, and she heard Charlie's well-loved voice. 'He has come for me. My Lord Jesus has come to take me home! I will be in His presence for all eternity. Praise His blessed name!'

Soon after his joyful declaration, Charlie lost consciousness. He died two hours later, at 11.00 p. m. on Monday 6th March 1871.

Dr Rae felt for some thread of heartbeat that would provide at least a little hope for the distraught wife who was loudly crying beside the bed. But his fingers could detect nothing, and a glass held to the mouth showed not a sign of the breath of life.

Emilia was unaware of Dr Rae and her parents-in-law, who also sat by the bed, because her storm of weeping blocked out all other things. As the tears ran down her cheeks, Emilia promised herself that she would not rest until she was certain that she would join Charlie in eternity, where even now he was rejoicing.

After verifying the death of Mr Baeyertz, Dr Rae turned to Emilia. It became clear to him that while her husband was quite beyond medical aid, she was not. He drew her to a chair and eased her into it, assuring her that she would be more comfortable sitting down. He urged her parents-in-law to comfort Emilia while he opened his doctor's bag.

Emilia cried out, 'Charlie has gone, and I do not know how I am to bear it!'

Dr Rae poured from a small bottle a spoonful of brown mixture which he urged her to swallow at once.

Only then did he feel free to return to the bed and to lower the eyelids of the once-vital man, and to pull the sheet as far as it would stretch to completely cover the body. With that gesture, it was borne in on him that he had done all that he could do now. It would be up to Emilia's family, her church and her town to provide for her.

On the Tuesday morning, Dr Rae instructed several men to visit the residents of Colac to inform them of the death of their much-loved bank manager. The distribution of the news could be tracked by the position of the blinds or shutters at each residence. Homes that had received the melancholic tidings had pulled down their awnings and soon a gloom settled over the whole community.

That afternoon, the Magistrate heard from the witnesses and found that the death was accidental. The whole story made that evening's *Colac Herald* and Friday's *Colac Observer*.

On Thursday, the Shire Hall and most businesses adjourned after lunch so all could attend the funeral of Mr Charles Baeyertz. Hundreds followed the cortege of thirty carriages and many horsemen to the cemetery where his son sprinkled a basket of flowers onto the grave. Later, a tall and dignified tombstone surmounted by a veiled urn was, as the marble fixed to the base declares to this day, 'Erected by many friends to mark their esteem for his memory'.

Immediately after the funeral, the Presbyterian minister's wife took Emilia and the children to the manse for a few days so they were not left at home alone in despair.

Once Emilia felt able, they returned to their home above the bank. When people came to try to comfort and condole with her, she would look at them and say 'You have not lost your husband. Your heart is not broken. I wish you would leave me alone.' At last she said to Beatrice, 'You must not send anyone else up to see me. I believe I shall go out of my mind if these people come and talk to me.'

However, one lady declared that, despite entreaties from Beatrice, nothing would keep her away. She went up and sat beside the grieving widow. She did not talk like the others—she too had lost the husband of her youth. Instead she took Emilia's hand and sat beside her. Emilia felt a hot tear fall right down on the back of her hand. Those tears, from her friend's heart, comforted, helped and soothed her more than all the words the people had spoken.

CHAPTER 40

Colac

Autumn 1871

EMILIA SOON ACCEPTED THE INVITATION FROM MR AND MRS BAEY-ertz to stay at Nerennin with the children and Nurse. Little Charles and Marion were thrilled. They had always enjoyed visiting the farm animals and now their own horses and dogs were also there.

Whenever Emilia could slip away from the house, she would lie on the newest grave in the cemetery to be with Charlie. There, while shedding many bitter tears, she would list her complaints before God. Why had He felt it necessary to keep her among the living when the light of her life had been taken from her? Could He not have arranged things so that her life too was brought to an end? How was it that a God whose mercy was a byword throughout the earth, dealt so unfeelingly with her?

She reminded Him that she had given up all that was dear to her when she married Charlie. She had lost her family, her inheritance and her Jewish community. Her father could not reinstate her. Her brothers and sisters might not want anything to do with her. She was alone to look after the children. To them, everything seemed to go on just the same without their father. Sometimes she longed for death.

Hour after weary hour she put her case, reminding the Almighty that she was only twenty-nine years of age with her life still ahead of her. Could the Almighty really mean her to travel that long road without the one who meant everything to her? Was God's heart so stony that He would not spare her the endlessly barren and dreary future that lay ahead?

One damp misty evening, as she returned from the grave, Banjo met her in the lane to Nerennin.

'Dear faithful old dog; you don't forget me.' She knelt down and put her arms around his neck and cried. Then she walked home with him and a lighter heart.

*

On the Saturday night, four weeks after her husband's death, Emilia felt so utterly desolate that the four walls of the house seemed like an awful prison. She yearned for the open face of Nature. No desert or forest depth was near, but there was the lake shore, with its cool murmuring water and so she took her weary heart yonder.

'If there could be healing in any place for me, if any balm could drop upon my heart,' she told herself, 'surely it would be by Charlie's Lake!'

There she remembered many happy incidents she and the children had shared with Charlie. The murmurs in the evergreen trees standing beside the lake reminded her of the way Charlie would say kind things to them. The waves formed by the breeze were reminders of him teaching her to row. The children had been afraid of getting into the boat until Charlie had carefully shown them how to be safe.

His boat lay upon the beach, just where he had hauled it. His hands were the last to have rested upon the gunwale. Every timber and rivet of the dear inanimate thing spoke of him. He had handled every plank, every nail and every rivet; for he had built her with his own hands from his memory of the example shown by his father. He had talked to Emilia while he worked and she sat nearby watching the children play. The characteristic light-hearted tone of Charlie's voice echoed in her thoughts. He'd remained excited throughout this long project to float what was, as far as he knew, the first boat on the lake.

When he'd last hauled it ashore, Charlie could not have foreseen that he would never return to his little boat. He would never again row his family out into the middle of the lake and teach them songs from his childhood while they sat rocking on the waves.

Tears ran down her cheeks, unchecked. Emilia crept into the boat where she lay and pulled the cape around her shoulders. 'Oh Charlie, my own darling, I cannot, cannot, live without you. I have no God! No Christ to comfort me!' The gentle noises of the wind in the trees and the waves on the lake subsided into the background as sobs enveloped her.

Sometime later, she could hear footsteps on the shore. The evening walker was making slow progress but the feet were definitely coming towards her. Emilia wondered if she should flee from the stranger, but she was too exhausted to get out of the boat. Besides, what did it matter if she was attacked? Nothing could be worse than losing Charlie.

The footsteps paused close by the boat. Emilia kept her head bowed in the hope that the visitor would not recognise the shape in the boat was a person. A gentle hand was laid upon her head and she heard a sweet voice broken with anguish say, 'We must bear it, dear.'

Emilia looked up to see her mother-in-law crying too, with the starry heavens in the background. Mary Anne had seen her from Nerennin, on the hill above the beach, and knew that her daughter-in-law needed comforting.

After she helped Emilia to climb out of the boat, they embraced. Their arms may not have been those of Charlie, but they shared a grief and the hug gave comfort to each woman. A bond of love was formed that night between them which deepened and gave solace to each one as the years went past.

A few days later, the children were having their afternoon nap and Nurse was enjoying some time to herself. Emilia joined her parents-in-law in the drawing room. This room was her favourite as they could enjoy the excellent views of Lake Colac framed by the windows.

While she watched Mary Anne pour out tea into cups, Emilia said, 'I have received a letter from the National Bank informing me that they will appoint a new manager soon and so require me to move out of the dwelling. They are happy for Beatrice and Cook to stay. There are so many things to do that I feel overwhelmed. I don't even want to get out of bed most days.'

After accepting a full teacup, Mr Baeyertz announced, 'We'll help you find a cottage to rent in Colac.'

His wife continued, 'You are not alone Emilia. We moved to Colac so we could be near you and Charlie. We're eager to help you make decisions. Our lads will move your furniture to your new place. Send a message or come here whenever you need help.'

'Thank you very much for your willingness. I'm comforted to realise that I'm not really alone in the world. I don't know where to start though.'

Mary Anne handed Emilia her cup of tea. 'When you move, keep Nurse with you until you can manage the housework and two children by yourself. I am happy to look after Charles and Marion from time to time. You will enjoy living on a quieter street. We can start looking for a cottage tomorrow'. She then took up her own cup and relaxed into her seat.

CHAPTER 41

Colac

May 1871

THE STILLNESS OF THE AFTERNOON WAS DISTURBED BY A KNOCKING at the front door of her cottage. Emilia rose at once and hurried down the hall. By the time she had succeeded in releasing the heavy door knob, her visitor was already raising a hand to knock again.

For a long drawn-out moment, the younger woman inside and the older one with the suitcase outside on the porch stared at one another, and then began to speak at the same time.

'Eliza! What a lovely surprise!'

'My darling girl, how are you?'

In each other's arms, hugging as if they never intended to do anything else, each sister was eventually forced to free one hand to dab at streaming eyes.

Emilia then took charge of Eliza's outdoor things, draped them upon hooks and led the way into the parlour.

'I'm impressed by this delightful cottage. It's in a charming little spot. And you are keeping it clean.'

'My parents-in-law helped me find this cosy nook to rent. It is just the right size for us. You will have to meet little Charles and Marion for the first time when they wake up and Nurse when she returns. How wonderful it is to see you, Eliza. How kind of you to come all this way to see us.'

'Of course, I had to come. You haven't written to us with your news. You have not replied to my letter. I wrote just as soon as Abraham heard about poor Charlie at the bank. Otherwise, we might still not have known.'

Emilia let her gaze drift out through the window. It seemed hardly the right time to mention the rift that her runaway marriage had caused, especially as her sister now seemed determined to forget it.

As if she had been reading her sister's thoughts, Eliza leant over to pat her hand. 'My dear, a tragedy such as you have suffered pushes all else to one side, and Abraham and I want you to know that whatever may have passed between us before does not alter the fact that you are my very dear sister. As

I wrote, nothing would please us better than to have you and the children come to live with us in St Kilda. We have a minyan now, enough members to start a shule.'

Deeply touched, Emilia had to fight back tears to offer a choked, 'Thank you.'

Eliza spent a moment busily smoothing her gloves. 'I do not want you to think we are prying but Abraham urged me to ask you how you are situated financially.'

Lifting her eyes to her sister's face, Emilia could see that the question was kindly meant.

'We hope,' Eliza added, 'to be of some help to you. Will you have the means to live comfortably on what Charlie has left you?'

It was what Emilia might have expected. Apart from her own husband, she had not known a sweeter-natured man than Abraham. She was glad to be able to say to her sister, 'Oh yes! The life insurance will be more than sufficient. And Charlie made a small investment in land. We have not been left destitute. He was most careful. We shall have enough, thank you.'

Her sister sent her a penetrating look. 'Hmm! If I am any judge of character, and I pride myself that I am, I would incline to the belief that whatever sum Charlie left will be spent on your children. If any scrimping is to be done, it is you who will suffer.'

Overwhelmed by such kindness, and wanting to delay a response, Emilia asked, 'What does George have to say about it?'

'George will support me in this. You need not worry about him. He has done very well for himself. He returned Home for a while but is back in Melbourne working for David Rosenthal, the jeweller. Lewis married Leah and is a leading citizen of Bangor. Saul, Charles and Frederick are all now jewellers and are planning to follow you, George and me here.'

'Is that so? What about you and Abraham? I expect your house is fully built by now but is your garden fully planted out?'

'Yes, the garden looks wonderful due to the expert care of our groundsman.' Eliza tilted her head to one side. 'But I came here to help you. If you have a spare bed, I'd like to stay for a while.'

*

After a few days of Eliza's precious sympathy, Emilia trusted her sister enough to break the news.

'Eliza,' she began hesitantly, 'you and Abraham are the most generous people I know, and the most forgiving too, when one considers all that took place when I was with you last. But there is something that you are not yet in a position to take into account.'

'If you are worried about having to break the lease, I am sure the landlord will understand.'

Emilia replied, 'There is that. And I have only just unpacked our boxes. Besides, I don't want to leave the friends I have made here.'

'You can ask your Colac friends to give you some names and addresses of their friends in Melbourne. Take all the time you need for repacking. Shall we say six to seven weeks from now? I will come down about then to help you with whatever still needs to be done.'

Emilia was beginning to feel like a coach careering downhill. Hoping to bring the runaway to a halt, she said, 'But, if we go away from Colac, I shall no longer be able to take the children to visit their father's grave. They will be most distressed about it, as of course, will I.'

Eliza's gaze held genuine compassion. 'Perhaps that might be for the best. I have spoken to Dr Rae about possible remedies for your listlessness and lack of sleep. Your doctor was most clear; you will break down completely, if you do not leave Colac, meet new people and seek a new vocation. Do not think me hardhearted, but have you considered that you may have grieved long enough?'

Seeing her sister's eyes grow moist, Eliza's voice became even gentler. 'You are still young, Emilia. You have the greater part of your life ahead of you. It is your duty to give thought not only to your children's future, but your own as well. Come home. We will buy you a cottage by the beach.'

Emilia had listened to her sister with her head lowered, but peering through her lashes, she realised that while Eliza spoke of future and duty, behind her generosity she had in mind a second marriage for her, and this time Eliza would see to it that the gentleman concerned was sound, wealthy and Jewish. She straightened her back, lifted her head and explained that she had vowed to herself never to go back to that old life.

Emilia was disconcerted to see that Eliza's face showed not surprise, but instead a complacent smile, which broadened as her sister went on to say,

'Well, of course, we fully expected that it would not be long before Charlie had made a Christian of you. A wife usually tries to please her husband in such matters. When we first heard of your marriage to Charlie, Abraham exclaimed, "It will not be long now before that Jewish girl is lost to the faith", and it seems that time has not proved him wrong.'

Emilia answered her thoughtfully. 'Yet neither is he entirely right. I am not yet a believer. It is not to please Charlie that I am trying to learn how to follow Christ. It is so that I can bring my children up to have what Charlie had. He never discussed with me what he believed, for I had forbidden him to do so. Eliza, when I saw my husband facing eternity, and saw the radiant joy that lit up his face as he entered the presence of the One whom he loved and worshipped, I set out on my own search to be with Charlie again.'

Eliza was now staring at her intently. 'Tell me, Emilia, have you been baptised into the Christian religion?'

Recognizing that this was a most vital question to her people, Emilia replied, 'Yes. I've been christened and confirmed at the church here.'

Eliza replied, 'So you are no longer Jewish'.

'As long as I live, I shall always be Jewish, for that is my birthright. I have not forsaken my heritage in the nation into which I was born.

'Perhaps you and Dr Rae are right. If I have to leave here, I would like to go to Geelong. It is a thriving town with Corio Bay and beaches and sea baths and piers and railways and factories and people from all over the world. I can help others there.'

CHAPTER 42

Colac

June 1871

AFTER ELIZA HAD GONE HOME, EMILIA FACED AN IDEA THAT HAD BEEN creeping around at the edges of her sorrow for days. Not only would she be without Charlie for the remainder of her life, she was no closer to joining him in eternity. It was altogether too much! Her friends at church had told her there was *only one* solution to this problem. But how could she make herself acceptable to the same Lord whom Charlie had come to know so intimately?

Every time she reached this point in her argument, Emilia would conclude that she could only learn about that eternity by studying his Bible. After all, hadn't he told her that he'd learnt more about Jesus by regularly reading this book?

Early one morning, well before the children were awake, Emilia searched out his Bible and opened at the first book of the Other Testament that was forbidden her by the rabbis. There came to her a memory of her father pointing out, when she was quite small, that these teachings were to blame for the terrible persecutions which had followed their people down the centuries.

With his words still echoing in her mind, Emilia hesitated. With an effort, she began to read the Gospel of Matthew. Almost at once, she became engrossed, for at the outset there was a family tree of the son of David, the son of Abraham. This was written for her own people. She read on.

The next morning again found Emilia with the Bible in her hands and she was able to finish Matthew before her daily duties descended upon her. The following day she began to read the next book, Gospel of Mark. It was not until, as day succeeded day, she reached the end of the fourth Gospel and called a halt. She had read that the figure central to the Gospels had been taken from the earth by a cloud. There could be nothing for her in the chapters to follow. It was He who had stirred her interest and won her admiration. She wanted to know more of Him.

Emilia turned back to immerse herself in the four books again.

The days stretched into weeks, and now Emilia grudged every minute that took her away from her Scripture reading, so precious had the Bible become to her. Now she pressed on through The Acts of the Apostles and The Epistles to The Revelation of St John the Divine at the end. Only then did she return to the Tanakh. The Teaching, Prophets and Writings appeared to be all there, but strangely out of order. The gentle Spirit of the Living God opened her eyes to begin to understand anew what was written there. As her perception deepened, she began to see an unbroken harmony between the Scriptures she had known from childhood and the Gospels where she had read of the One who said, ' … had ye believed Moses, ye would have believed me: for he wrote of me'.

In the Scriptures, there was One who was promised to the Jewish people, the Lord's Anointed, the Messiah, who came in the person of Jesus of the New Testament. Was there not a psalm which made mention of sufferings similar to those endured by Jesus? Emilia checked and found Psalm 22. How could King David have described therein a death that would not take place for hundreds of years, if it were not that the Almighty had revealed it to him? Death by crucifixion, described by the words, 'they pierced my hands and my feet', and 'all my bones are out of joint', was wholly unknown to the Hebrews of King David's day.

Slowly she became aware that the Jesus who she was coming to know through the Bible, and who had so wonderfully revealed Himself as the One sent from God to redeem her people, was now waiting expectantly for a response from her.

Her friends, the Calvert family, invited her and her children to stay a little while at their estate at Pirron Yallock to the west of Colac. One day, while everyone else was out tending to the farm, Emilia sat alone in the house. There God's voice thrice sounded in her heart to read more. She picked up Charlie's Bible and, as she read again the account of the crucifixion in the Gospel of John, she was aware of a presence with her which was sweet and beautiful. This presence opened up the Word to her. She saw things as she had never seen them before.

'He suffered all this for me. Christ has died for me!' She went into her bed room and kneeled down and worshipped the Lord Jesus as God. She sobbed aloud not for sorrow, but for joy. From that time, she was sure that Jesus was God: the Christ, the Redeemer; who died on the cross for her sins.

Now when she visited the grave, she remembered Charlie kneeling beside the bed praying for her night after night. God had indeed answered those prayers. He had taken Charlie, for a short time, and given her the rich gift of His Son.

CHAPTER 43

Geelong, Victoria
Spring 1871

My dear Nancy,

In my last letter, I covered quite a few pages in telling you how it was that I came to faith in the Redeemer of my soul, Jesus of Nazareth. As there was not much other news in that letter, I am now writing again as promised, to let you know all that has taken place with us over recent weeks.

The decision to move to Geelong was the beginning of an extremely busy time for me. I had to repack all our worldly goods in preparation. Eliza and Mrs Baeyertz came to help me, and I don't know how I should have got on without them. When I moved from the bank manager's residence, Mr and Mrs Baeyertz handled all that had belonged to Charlie, as I could not bring myself to touch any of his things. This time, when I left the little cottage, there were fewer things to pack. I have grown especially close to Mary Anne since we both mourn the loss of our dear Charlie.

A real estate agent in Geelong, Mr Cutler, was happy to send me descriptions of suitable houses I could rent before we left Colac. I signed the lease for a small house near the town and the beach and returned it to him by post. He waited in the house while the furniture movers unloaded our belongings three days before we arrived in Geelong. The children and I felt like we were in a wonderful dream when we unlocked the door and found our belongings already placed in the rooms, still in boxes, but mostly in the right rooms. The experience was really the culmination of answers to many prayers to our Heavenly Father.

The task of unpacking is proceeding slowly. The children always want my company so we go for walks most days to learn together what is where. When the weather is fine we go to the beach or the sea baths. We always meet someone new. We have been visited by the friends of people we knew in Colac and little Charles and Marion have met children their own age. Everyone has been kind to us. I am beginning to feel as if I will belong.

When I've been lonely I've talked to my neighbours. Many women do their housework during the day, when their husbands are at work, and they are usually happy to receive a visitor and share a cup of tea. I've heard some sad stories and prayed with those women on several occasions.

Since moving here I've found many opportunities to tell people about Jesus. The town is small enough to walk to the beach, churches, shops, factories, infirmary and gaol.

Charles and Marion send oceans of love to Nancy. They hope that very soon they might have the joy of meeting her for the very first time, to give her the hugs and kisses that they have been saving for her. As always, dearest Nancy, with this letter I send my very fondest love.

I remain,

Ever your friend,

Emilia

CHAPTER 44

Geelong
Spring and Summer 1871

EMILIA OFTEN VISITED THEIR NEIGHBOURS. MOTHERS WELCOMED A sociable stranger into their daily routines of housework and caring for children. She presented a novel interruption and many were intrigued by the Jewess who wanted to speak about the Gospel.

After attending her local Church of England for some weeks, Emilia offered to teach a Sunday school class. The vicar asked her to lead a large class of lads aged fifteen to twenty.

Sometime later, Emilia was invited to join church members in visiting patients in the infirmary. She found a neighbour who was willing to care for Charles and Marion and added her own name to the list of visitors.

Emilia was a cautious student as she accompanied her colleagues to the Geelong Infirmary and Benevolent Asylum. She had very little experience of hospitals. When she was a child, hospitals were considered a danger to one's health rather than a place of healing. Her father had arranged for Dr Isaacs to visit the Aronson home whenever they required medical advice.

Her church friends assured Emilia that, since her childhood, advances had been made in the treatment of patients and the cleanliness of the hospital. The Geelong hospital, opened twenty years earlier, treated the poor and distressed. Strict guidelines on who could gain admittance limited the number of patients who had contagious diseases or complicated conditions. Although the rules had been relaxed over the years, the visitors rarely contracted a disease.

The Benevolent Asylum, on the ground floor, provided a home to destitute elderly citizens and the incurable patients. The Infirmary, on the first floor, was established to afford medical and surgical aid to paupers and casualties.

A church member introduced to Mrs Baeyertz the Master and Matron of the Infirmary and some of the male and female nurses who were on duty. The Master supervised the nurses and they cared for the patients. The Matron, on the other hand, was responsible for the housekeeping duties in the Infirmary. While Emilia was being shown how to navigate the Infirmary wards she crossed paths with a doctor.

Her guide said, 'Mrs Baeyertz, may I present our Senior Surgeon, Dr Boswell Reid?' 'Dr Reid, Mrs Baeyertz has agreed to become a visitor to our patients. This is her first day here.'

Emilia shook the proffered hand and said, 'Dr Reid, I should have expected to meet you here. I was most grateful that you came to Colac to help us, despite the inconvenience.'

'It was a dreadful case. I thought the amputation would save Mr Baeyertz. When I received the news that your husband had died, I was very sad for you.'

'I was distraught and I still feel his absence keenly.'

'What are you doing in Geelong?'

Emilia's guide answered his question. 'Mrs Baeyertz and her delightful children moved here some months ago. She seems to have an endless source of goodwill to help people.'

Emilia continued the explanation. 'Everyone at church has been most kind to us since we arrived. After Charlie died I was consumed with grief and spent many hours at his grave. My sister and my parents-in-law were concerned. Dr Rae feared that I would never recover if I remained in the town that was full of memories. He spoke highly of Geelong and suggested that I might find a new vocation here. I would rather be in Colac, near Charlie's grave, so I must keep myself busy.'

'I am pleased to see you are eager to help others. I'm sure that will help you recover from your grief, in time. I will not hold you up any longer. No doubt I will see you again.'

'Thank you, Dr Reid, for your kind words.'

'Not at all. Good day to you both.' With that salutation, Dr Reid departed.

On resuming their tour, Emilia's guide explained the roles of the different staff they'd encountered. She then introduced several of the patients to Emilia, thus thrusting her directly into the work.

✻

'Oh, no! I could not pray in public. It would be utterly impossible.'

Mrs Simpson replied, 'I am surprised you don't believe you can pray in public because you seem most confident to me. You speak well and it's obvious you had a good education as a child. Everyone in our Presbyterian Mothers' Prayer Meeting knows of your visits to women around town.'

'Well, I'm happy to speak to one or two women at a time but speaking to a room full of women seems daunting.'

'You wouldn't really be talking to everyone. You'd be talking to God and we'd be saying "Amen" alongside you. I was fearful of speaking in public the first few times. I'm still embarrassed to ask for directions when I'm lost in Geelong, yet you visit women whom you've never met to tell them about your faith. Someone from my church mentioned last week that they've seen you walking great distances from your home. We're beginning to think you'll have visited more families in Geelong than any of us ever will. What about writing out your prayer before the meeting so you can organise your thoughts? You could even read out your prayer if that will stop you getting confused.'

'What a good idea. I guess I don't have to give a long prayer?'

'No, not at all. Short prayers allow other mothers to have a turn. Why don't you pray about a woman you are visiting in her home or at the Infirmary?'

Emilia sighed. 'All right, I'll write down my prayer so I can pray aloud at the next meeting.'

'I think you'll discover it's not as hard as it looks.'

The day of the next Mothers' Prayer Meeting was hot. Emilia carefully chose a dress and purse that would allow her to carry her handkerchief, fan and note. By the time she arrived at the manse, her anxiety about speaking in public had been eclipsed by her dislike of the hot north wind.

After entering, Emilia waited until her eyes adjusted to the dimmer light inside. In the drawing room, the curtains had been pulled almost shut to reduce the heat seeping into the room. It would soon be stuffy.

Emilia greeted the women who were already seated and chose a chair near the door that might catch a breeze. She put her purse beneath the seat and confirmed the location of her note. She had spent much time writing and rewriting her prayer to say something meaningful in the fewest words.

Once most of the women who usually attended had arrived, the leader began proceedings.

'Ladies, thank you for coming to this prayer meeting, particularly when the hot weather makes it so uncomfortable to walk. You will have read in the papers that there was a drunken brawl at the pub on the weekend and several men are in the Infirmary while others are in gaol. I was afraid for my sons. This morning's theme for our prayers will be God's guidance for our sons and daughters. If you have other concerns for prayer you are welcome to include them too. We start our prayer time with adoration of God and thanksgiving for all He has done before we offer up our supplications.'

Emilia was relieved that the prayer topic was broad because she wanted to pray for some women in the Infirmary. When her turn came, Emilia pulled out her piece of paper and made sure she was holding it the right way up. She did not try to read it closely because she remembered how her prayer had started. After she began speaking, she looked down at her notes and realised she could not see her handwriting. The light was too dim and as she was sitting in a corner it was hard to move elsewhere. What was she to do? She felt dizzy.

She didn't want to disappoint Mrs Simpson, so she shoved her note back into her pocket and looked up to heaven, just like she did at home. She prayed silently for God to help her and soon remembered what she'd written. She spoke to God as a child speaks to a parent whom they trust and love. As she explained her concerns, she lost sight of others in the room. When her prayer came to its natural finish, Emilia opened her eyes and gasped at finding ten women looking at her.

Before she could apologise for speaking so long, the leader spoke first. 'Thank you Emilia for praying aloud in our group. I think that's your first time. We appreciated your contribution. While we prayed with you, we learnt more about the church's ministry in the Infirmary. We'll keep you and the patients in our prayers as we go about our daily tasks.'

On entering the Infirmary one day, Emilia received an unexpected request from the Master. 'I'm aware you only wanted to visit female patients but, now you are familiar with the work, I wondered if you'd be willing to speak to men? The nurses have mentioned some are not in good spirits. Are you willing to speak to two or three of the men today?'

When Emilia agreed to his request, the Master said, 'Let's go to the men's ward now.'

One elderly gentleman was physically weak but he was a lively conversationalist. Emilia asked, 'Do you have many visitors? Does your family live a long way out of town?'

'My wife died some years ago and my sons own the business I began. I'm not worried that they don't visit often because they are making the business successful. Besides, I've enjoyed conversations with my fellow patients.'

Emilia said, 'Have you considered what will happen at the end of our lives?

'I went to Sunday school when I was a bairn, but I decided church wasn't for me. I've done many good deeds and I've been a generous benefactor. I'll be right when I get to heaven. '

'May I tell you what the Bible says?'

'You might as well. I'm not going anywhere.'

Emilia said, 'When you were born into this world you received a nature, a life from your parents, by your birth, and that life is an evil nature. It is a nature that is condemned. It is a nature that can do nothing else but sin. It is a nature that cannot love God. It is impossible for any man or woman to love God or to fulfil the law in any way with that one old evil nature; and God calls men who have only that one nature dead, because although the body is alive, and people can walk about, eat and drink, and enjoy themselves, the soul is dead.' She produced her trusty pocket King James Bible, and read aloud, 'Verily, verily, I say unto thee, except a man be born again, he cannot see the kingdom of God.'

'You can't frighten me about my sins. I'm a good man. I've raised a family and worked hard to make my business successful. I've served the Geelong community and I've given a lot of money to the poor.'

Emilia smiled. 'The Gospel of John also records Jesus saying, "I am the resurrection, and the life: he that believeth in Me, though he were dead, yet shall he live: and whosoever liveth and believeth in Me shall never die." Jesus was saying that it's only your attitude towards Him that will determine how you will spend eternity. Good deeds are commendable but it's only if you accept Jesus' death and resurrection for yourself that you will get into heaven.'

'Don't you talk to me about Jesus or the Bible! You have no right to pass judgement on me. You don't know anything about me other than what I've just told you. If you ask the Mayor what I've done for this town, he'd give you a long list. In fact, I'll tell you myself since I'm here to stay.'

While Emilia listened to his accomplishments, she considered what else to say. When he began boasting loudly she realised that he would not listen to anything else. His voice grew louder and echoed from the high ceiling.

Emilia saw the nurse threading his way through the ward so she interrupted the patient. 'I see the nurse is coming. No doubt I've excited you too much and that is not good for your health. I'll leave now. May I visit you when I make my rounds each week?'

'Yes, you may look in on me but nothing you say will change my mind.'

Several weeks later, Emilia entered the Master's room to enquire after the patients. He informed her that the elderly gentleman had called his lawyer, because his health was failing. He would appreciate a visitor. Could Mrs Baeyertz please avoid distressing him?

When Emilia approached the bed, the patient said, 'Please do not go away. I will be done with my lawyer in a minute'.

Emilia went to see some other patients in the same ward and returned after the lawyer had departed.

The patient seemed to have had a great burden lifted from his shoulders. He beamed with pride. 'I am all right now. I have £300 in the bank—all the money I have in this world. I've instructed my lawyer that I'll leave the money to the hospital; that will be another good work, and I shall be all right. As I've said before, I've been a good man and done the best I could in everything.'

Emilia looked at him and wondered what to say. Nothing she had said in the past weeks had changed his mind. Nothing could enlighten this man or awaken conviction. He would die in his sins—not resting in the finished work of Jesus but in his belief of his own righteousness.

CHAPTER 45

Geelong
Winter 1872

SINCE HER DAYS IN COLAC, WHERE SHE HAD STRUGGLED TO ACCEPT Jesus as the Christ, Emilia had searched the Bible to learn more about the one whom her forefathers had rejected. She was saved, she knew that, yet her character was unchanged. She could allow her impatience and quick temper to dominate.

Some twelve months after Emilia had invited Jesus into her life, she noticed that a number of the vicar's sermons gave advice on how to be holy. He preached on 1 Thessalonians, so Emilia read through the epistle. She was struck by Paul's instruction to believers in chapter 2.

> 'As ye know how we exhorted and comforted and charged
> every one of you, as a father doth his children, that ye would
> walk worthy of God, who hath called you unto his kingdom
> and glory.'

About the same time, the leader of the Mother's Prayer Meeting drew attention to Paul's Epistle to Titus. Chapter 2 instructs older women to be reverent in their behaviour so they can teach younger women how to love their husbands and children and be self-controlled.

As she walked home from the meeting, Emilia wondered at the number of times she'd recently read Bible passages about exercising self-control. Perhaps the Holy Spirit was prompting her to consider her behaviour? She'd been serving her Saviour fervently, but she'd not realised God wanted her to improve her behaviour too. Memories of her responses to the children came to mind. Because small inconveniences bothered her, she'd tried to control the children's behaviour with rules. Perhaps too many?

That night, Emilia read the whole of Titus. She was relieved to find she did not have to make changes to her character by herself. Jesus would help her—Jesus the Christ 'gave himself for us, that he might redeem us from all iniquity, and purify unto himself a peculiar people, zealous of good works.'

Before she got into bed, Emilia committed herself to being more holy in her attitudes and behaviour.

The following afternoon five-year-old Charles sat at the piano to practise scales in preparation for his lesson. His mother sat beside him to help but, once Charles had mastered the task, he said she could go now. When Emilia stood up, she found Marion behind her, seated on the floor, happily playing with a toy.

Observing that the children were occupied, Emilia went into the kitchen to cut the vegetables for a stew. She would buy some meat while Charles was at his lesson. She realised she'd forgotten to collect an onion and some potatoes from the washhouse and called Marion to the kitchen. While giving her daughter instructions about where to find the vegetables, Charles shouted out for more help.

Having demonstrated the next scale on the piano, Emilia began walking towards the kitchen. It was only Marion's warning shout that prevented her from stepping on a doll. Emilia replied, 'Don't shout at your mother. Why are there toys in the middle of the room? You know you should always put your things away when you've finished playing with them.'

When she saw Marion's dismay, Emilia realised she had been unreasonable. 'I'm sorry I snapped. You'd gone to collect the vegetables for me and you haven't finished playing. I was surprised when you called out because I was listening to Charles play. Thank you for getting the vegetables. Here, let me hug you. I know you try very hard to do as I ask. You were clever to stop me standing on your doll, 'specially since we can't afford to buy another like this beautiful one from Uncle George.'

Cutting an onion excused the tears that slipped down Emilia's cheeks. Why was she so quick to snap at her daughter? Marion was only three, after all. Perhaps her own grief made it harder to be self-disciplined. Nevertheless, Emilia told herself she would make greater efforts to control her temper.

Another incident came to mind. She'd been impatient when Mrs Simpson reminded her that the Mother's Prayer Meeting had to gather elsewhere the following week. She'd replied, 'Oh, how annoying! I'd planned to do an errand in the vicinity of the manse. I'll have to find another day. It's most inconvenient when I am doing such a lot for the church.'

Mrs Simpson replied, 'I doubt that your tasks are of greater importance than the work of the minister and his wife. I know you walk great distances in Geelong so I'm sure an extra trip won't damage your health. Here's a note with the date and the address of the next meeting. You'll get over your annoyance soon, I hope.'

Some days after she began to pray about character faults, Emilia knelt at her bed with an urgent need. 'Heavenly Father, I've been trying to be patient with the children and to control my temper, but I can't do it in my own power. The least little thing puts me out. I know this dishonours You and keeps me powerless.'

'I've prayed every morning asking for Your help with my temper but I still struggle to control it. I've heard people at church talk about "the blessing". What is that? You give me blessings every day so I'm puzzled. How can I get more of Your help to overcome my impatience?' While she waited for some guidance, Emilia had a feeling of great rushing and being lifted out of herself, and her rapture was so great that she didn't know if she was in the body or out of it.

Over the following days Emilia's character faults were no longer so troublesome. She didn't have to struggle to be gracious towards others and it was easier to manage her temper. When Charles and Marion were not admonished for forgetting to obey one of their mother's rules, they knew that something wonderful had happened.

Before Emilia accepted the vicar's invitation to join those who ministered at Her Majesty's Prison, she asked for lessons from an experienced visitor. Emilia had never been inside a prison and felt overwhelmed at the thought of entering the gates. Her first visit to the prison introduced her to a new community she'd known nothing of. There were so many new things to learn that her grief receded into the back of her thoughts.

Two months after receiving that blessing, Emilia caught herself being critical of a small thing Charles had done. She saw her son look wary and step away from her. She explained to him why she'd been annoyed and bent down to gather him into her arms. He reluctantly let her hug him and she knew she'd have to plead with God for help again.

When Emilia knelt at her bed that night, she talked to God about her experience. 'As long as the feeling from the rapture lasted I found it easier to live as You want me to. Now my evil temper has gained control over me again. I struggle to be patient with the children and my irritability confuses people who know I follow You. Please help me to be more patient with everyone.' God answered her prayers by sending her a blessing again. The rushing sensation embraced her and she was enraptured for a second time.

CHAPTER 46

Geelong

1873

WHEN EMILIA NOTICED THAT THE FEELINGS FROM HER FOURTH blessing experience were waning, she made time that evening to devote to prayer.

Ever since she'd learned that God wanted her to reflect His nature, she had admonished herself on her every failure. She considered that her quick temper and irritability were her besetting sins and often muttered, 'I'm such a sinner'.

She forgot that Father God could forgive her and that it was the Holy Spirit's role to make her more like Jesus. Emilia could not see that her criticism of others meant she set high standards for herself and those with whom she worked. She approached every task with the intention of doing the best she could rather than only what was necessary. When expounding the character and sacrifice of Jesus to audiences unaware of her turmoil, she presented an engaging message of how His death and resurrection some nineteen hundred years before related to them.

That night, she prayed, 'I cannot live any longer dishonouring You as I am now doing. Lord, tell me the secret. Deliver me from my sin and let it be a permanent thing. I don't expect to raise my hands and be delivered instantly from these faults. I understand there is a work to go on in my soul but I want You to change me forever.'

While she waited for God to answer her prayers, Emilia drove herself to such an extent that she became gravely ill and was threatened with paralysis. A friend took Emilia home to nurse her while another family cared for Charles and Marion.

As she lay in bed, Emilia prayed to the Lord over and over again, 'You can do what you like with me, only save me from sin'. She was not as anxious about her health as she was about deliverance. She gave herself to Him in a whole-hearted consecration. She left herself in His hands, choosing His will and surrendering all liberty of choice.

After the Lord had healed her of the illness, through the prayers and ministrations of her friends, Emilia attended a prayer meeting. She was not looking for manifestations but only delivery from her character faults. She prayed, 'I can no longer lead such a wretched life'. A verse came to her, which was, 'Then I will sprinkle clean water upon you, and you shall be clean'. The Lord helped Emilia to take hold of this promise.

When the prayer time finished, Emilia noticed a lack of strange sensations. She'd said she didn't want any signs. They would have been comforting. She couldn't feel any changes within her either, so she would have to trust God's Word as it had come to her.

That night, Emilia found that verse in the writings of the Prophet Ezekiel:

> Then will I sprinkle clean water upon you, and ye shall be
> clean: from all your filthiness, and from all your idols, will I
> cleanse you. A new heart also will I give you, and a new spirit
> will I put within you: and I will take away the stony heart out
> of your flesh, and I will give you an heart of flesh. And I will
> put my spirit within you, and cause you to walk in my statutes,
> and ye shall keep my judgments, and do them. And ye shall
> dwell in the land that I gave to your fathers; and ye shall be
> my people, and I will be your God.

It was only when she encountered the routines of daily life that Emilia saw what God had done. In circumstances where a few days before her temper would rise, Jesus now put His own gentle power within her. Things that once annoyed her no longer moved her to rebuke.

During the next few weeks, Emilia learnt that when she was tempted to yield to sin, she could look to Jesus. While she trusted in Him, He either fought the tempter in her presence or He took the temptation away. She also learnt to look constantly to the Father for His help, and recognise that His answers to her prayers came through the Holy Spirit. As she explained to others, 'it is not so much a blessing to be got and lost as it is a life to be lived.'

On thinking back to the prayer meeting, Emilia reasoned that if God had given her a special feeling she would have rested on that feeling and not have learned this lesson of believing the promises in the Bible and depending on the Holy Spirit.

One Sunday the vicar preached about believers being effective messengers for God in everything they did. When Emilia and the children left the church to stand in the warm sunshine, she looked for Bob.

She spied her friend and, walking over to him, said 'I'm glad I found you, Bob. I want to talk to you about the sermon this morning.'

'What did the vicar say that made you think of me?'

'He did not speak of you directly, of course, but he spoke about the eternal effectiveness of the ministry of those who visited institutions in town. You know I am doing no end of evangelistic work. I keep teaching Sunday school even though the lads make it difficult most weeks. I've visited many homes in this town and I've been asked to speak to some women next week. I go twice a week to the infirmary and I go to the gaol every fortnight. But all this work is in vain; not one person I've spoken to has been converted.'

Bob replied, 'You're not the only one who has talked of this matter. I've been considering a prayer retreat for those who visit the infirmary and prison. What do you think of gathering for three hours a day for six days to seek the enduement of power for service?'

'What a most excellent suggestion. It would be easier to find women who are willing to mind Marion for three hours rather than for a whole day. Furthermore, I'll be able to return before Charles comes home from school.'

'I expect it will take about three weeks for me to make the arrangements. I will send you a message.'

'Thank you. I look forward to hearing from you.'

One

Just as he'd planned, three weeks later Bob welcomed several men and women from different churches to the prayer retreat. They introduced themselves by stating their names, their church and the ministries in which they were engaged.

Next, Bob taught about prayer and the work of the Holy Spirit. Worship began with liturgy from the *Book of Common Prayer* and two hymns before participants were encouraged to spread out in the church hall to spend time alone conversing with the Lord.

While she knelt in the quiet, Emilia said, 'Loving God, you know that I'm visiting many people where they live. However, none of them have accepted Jesus as their Saviour. I'm following the advice I was given for this work but I haven't seen any conversions. I need Your power so I can represent You.'

Emilia had hoped that she would receive God's power so she could speak with His authority. She wanted her words to carry the weight of God's truth and prompt people to recognise Jesus was the Messiah. She found, instead, that God had a different approach.

Emilia became aware of getting right into His Presence in a way that was new to her. God's Presence surrounded her and she was lost to all but Him. God searched her through and through. With the revelation of God there came such a terrible sight of her own sinfulness that she was overwhelmed.

God also showed her the nature of sin. Sin is ugly because it blocks a person's relationships with Him and with others. Sin oppresses those who are caught in it. Sin is so destructive that God had to provide a way to free people from its grip.

In the awful light of His glorious holiness, Emilia could not move or speak. How long it lasted she did not know, but as God gradually withdrew His Presence, she moaned, 'Stay Thine hand, take Thine awful Presence from me.' She felt that she should have died if it had lasted much longer.

While God hovered over her, Emilia forgot about the others in the room. However, they'd heard her moaning and wondered what had occurred. When she opened her eyes, Emilia saw a woman she'd only met that day named Violet Jackson looking at her with great concern.

Violet moved to sit beside her and hold her hand. 'I heard your mumbled words; what has God done in you?'

'I don't really know. I've never had this experience before. I'd asked God for the power to be able to speak for Him but He showed me the awfulness of my sin instead. He seemed to hover over me and I couldn't move. I could neither lift up a finger nor speak. I just knelt there in fearful terror—it was the most awful experience I've ever had in my life.'

Violet replied, 'I've learnt, over several years, that God knows me very well. If I didn't have a correct understanding of who I am in relation to Him, I would have become proud. God taught me the lesson He's just given you some years ago. It's only because of His blessing on my work that I am able to help the women that I do. It seems God is teaching you a similar thing.'

After they had talked for a while, Emilia said, 'I feel God has broken and emptied me and I don't have anything more to give Him. I don't want to keep praying at this retreat because God might take more from me.'

Violet said, 'I think God has done the most important work in you on the first day. He took you at your word and is preparing you to become more effective in speaking for Him. He did not answer your prayer as you expected, but He does love you and wants the best for you. He will want to build you up again with His love because you can't serve Him well if you remain afraid.'

When she watched Emilia shake her head back and forth, Violet said, 'Come back tomorrow and we'll sit together when we pray.'

On the sixth day, Emilia said to Violet, 'Thank you for your encouragement this week. It was only because of your support that I returned each day.'

Bob gathered the participants together and said, 'We have been asking God to equip us with His power for service. What happened to you this week?' After hearing their stories, he asked each one, 'Are you going to take the power?'

When it was Emilia's turn to answer she said, 'No, I feel no change.'

Others also doubted that God had answered their prayers, so Bob said, 'Every blessing must be received by faith. Please open your Bibles at Mark, chapter 11, verse 24. Emilia, please read the passage aloud for everyone to hear.'

Emilia read, 'Therefore I say unto you, what things soever ye desire, when ye pray, believe that ye receive them, and ye shall have them.'

Bob said, 'Another passage that helps us here is John, chapter 16, verse 24. Violet, can you read that for us, please?'

She found the page and read the passage. 'Hitherto have ye asked nothing in my name: ask, and ye shall receive, that your joy may be full.'

Emilia joined her colleagues in kneeling down and praising God that they, by faith, would receive His power to serve Him better. After she took her seat again, Emilia waited and watched the reaction of others. None of her companions exhibited outward signs of power. No one shouted, sang, clapped or lifted up their hands.

Emilia was disappointed; she did not feel great ecstasy. However, there came into her soul such a hush, such an intense quiet and such a brokenness of spirit that she had never known before. She felt that God was now sending her forth to serve Him. He had chosen to work in her and graciously gave her the ability to serve in His name.

The people she'd met at this prayer retreat also became precious to her. Emilia would often seek advice and prayers from Bob or Violet whenever she was faced with a new aspect of ministry in Geelong.

Emilia's conversations about Jesus changed due to her encounters with God. She placed more emphasis on how sin ruins people's relationships with each other and God. This allowed her to explain why Jesus became the Lamb of God and a sacrifice on behalf of every person who lived.

Her listeners also warmed to Emilia's stories about her recent encounters with God. People could see that Emilia had a vibrant relationship with God and that He really was a loving Heavenly Father. Fellow believers were also comforted to hear that Emilia struggled, like them, to live the life the New Testament authors recommended.

On her routine visits to women in their homes and to the infirmary and prison, Emilia was surprised and then delighted to discover that people began to choose Christ as their Saviour. Emilia also recognised God's hand in many of her other tasks and was comforted to know that He was using her to bless others.

The changes did not pass unnoticed. One day, Chris Bunning, the local Baptist pastor, showed Emilia a leaflet. The Reverend Mr Hussey Macartney, vicar of St Mary's Church of England in Caulfield, a suburb near St Kilda, was to host a conference of 'ministers and laymen of different denominations' at his church the following year.

'Hussey has heard from me of your recent experiences and your public speaking. He has asked me to ask you to present a paper.'

'Surely not. I have never done such a thing.'

'Just write as you would talk to a meeting of ladies'.

'But there would be gentlemen there. I couldn't teach men, especially men who know their Bible better than I.'

'I can check your paper for suitability. Mr Macartney has volunteered to read the paper out himself. That way no-one will know it was yours.'

CHAPTER 47

Geelong

August 1876

AS THEY WERE FINISHING LUNCH ONE SATURDAY, EMILIA SAID, 'Charles and Marion, I want to talk to you both, so don't leave the table after we've eaten our apples. I want to show you what's in that pile of papers.'

After the apples, she sat down with the papers and asked, 'Do you remember when we had our likenesses taken at Turner's Portrait Rooms in Moorabool Street? It was the year after we'd moved to this little house. We had to wear our best clothes. The photographer gave us lots of instructions about standing or sitting still.'

Marion replied, 'Yes, Mama. I remember I had to stay still even though my nose was itchy and I really wanted to scratch it.'

Charles said, 'I wanted to see what the photographer was doing with the camera but he got angry when I asked questions. When I cried you asked me to stop because I had to look happy in the photograph we were going to send Grandmama in Wales.'

Emilia answered, 'The photographer did sound upset and I understood why you began to cry. I think he was just annoyed at you. He had to use a new invention and I think he was worried he'd forget to do something important. Instead, he forgot that he was talking to a five-year-old boy. We got a lovely letter back from Grandmama Aronson saying she was pleased to have received the photographs.'

'Uncle George was happy to see the photographs too, wasn't he?'

'Yes, Charles. He paid for our likenesses to be taken so Grandmama could see my children. I've talked about having our likenesses taken because we found it was a difficult thing to do. However, you obeyed my instructions and we got some pleasant photographs. We had to do a lot of new things together in those days, didn't we?'

'Yes, but we belong in Geelong now. I've made good friends with the boys at school and I like this town', replied Charles.

As she sorted through her papers, Emilia said, 'I've been glad to see you going off to school in a happy mood each day. You'll be celebrating your tenth birthday in December, so I think it's time you went to a better school with music and language classes.'

'To which school do you want me to go?'

'Wesley College. These papers are from that school.'

'Why do I have to go to another school? I like it here with my friends and Marion.'

Marion joined the conversation. 'I like our school some days but, when the other children are nasty to me, I wish I could come home.'

'That's what happened to me too. I enjoyed learning to read and write, but I didn't like the other students teasing me about missing school whenever the weather was really bad. Despite my mother's caution, I seemed to get sick too often.'

Marion asked, 'Were you sick, Mama? You're not sick very often now'.

'It's a surprise to me too, Marion. I sometimes wonder if it's the dry climate here that keeps me well. Your teacher told me she's delighted you're in her class. That's nice to hear isn't it?'

Marion nodded thoughtfully.

'Now, Charles, your teachers say you always do well in your school work and they hope you will develop into a brilliant student. Your Aunt Suzette, Uncle Richard and I think you'll get a better education by going to a good church school. The Gibbs have generously offered to pay your school fees so you can get an excellent education. They believe you are a worthwhile investment.

'Wesley College will give you a good foundation for whatever you do as an adult. You'll gain skills that will help you get a good job and make an important contribution to society. Many of your classmates will become important to the colony.

'We've decided on Wesley because it teaches subjects we think necessary for boys and encourages students to practise their Christian faith. The teachers lead prayers and Bible readings in the assemblies and give a Christian point of view when lessons include matters of faith. The school was opened in the same year you were born and has developed a fine reputation.

'The school is forty-five miles away from here, in St Kilda Road near the City of Melbourne. You could live in their boarding house but Aunt Suzette has found a nicer alternative. She has a friend who lives near the school and takes in boarders. You can live with that family during school terms. On some weekends, Marion and I will come on the train to visit you.'

At this point, Charles objected. 'Why can't I go to Geelong Grammar School? Some of my friends from church will be going there; it's much nearer to home.'

'That's true, but I prefer the Methodist approach to education. This letter from the headmaster invites us to visit Wesley College next week. All three of us will go on the train to Melbourne and then be driven to the school. We will meet the headmaster, some of your teachers and some children in your year. You'll be shown your first classroom.

'At the beginning of term, I will take you back to settle you in the house where you will board. The headmaster assured me that the teachers will help you fit into the classes and show you how things are done. Then, after the Christmas holidays with us here, you will start school next year with all the other pupils.

'While we're in Melbourne we'll stay for a few days with the Berens family. I'm looking forward to seeing Aunt Eliza and Uncle Abraham again and I'm sure you'd like to play with your cousin Amy in her wonderful house. We'll also visit Aunt Suzette's friend so we can meet her family and see your bedroom.

'Your Uncle Saul will come to Aunt Eliza's to have dinner with all of us one evening. We haven't seen him for two years, since he became the manager of David Rosenthal & Co. in the city. Uncle George may also come if he's in town. You will be able to see them more often when you're living in Melbourne.

'Marion will keep going to school here and we'll look after each other. Last week your piano teacher told me she wants to introduce Marion to the next grade.

'Any questions?'

CHAPTER 48

Geelong
January 1877

AS EMILIA WENT OUT TO THE LETTER-BOX, SHE NOTICED THE WARM morning that warned of another tiring, hot summer day. She looked forward to the afternoon breeze from Corio Bay that would cool down the house and give her relief just when the heat would be stifling.

Amongst the pile of mail in the letter box, Emilia recognised an envelope from the Reverend Mr H. B. Macartney, jun., BA. She'd been waiting for this letter and wondered what decision she should make.

Before going inside, Emilia went through the gateway and looked up the street to see that Marion and Charles were playing safely in a neighbour's garden. A woman waved and called out that the children were having fun with her youngsters.

Emilia made herself a pot of tea and placed it on the tray with a teacup and saucer, milk, cake and letters. In the morning room, she poured herself a cup of tea, and reviewed the things she'd learnt from Mr Macartney.

At the end of the previous year, he had sent a letter informing her of his desire to establish a ministry at St Mary's to the many Jewish residents of the Caulfield and St Kilda area. He believed that she could make a valuable contribution to the work. Emilia had replied with interest and questions. She also explained she was responsible for Charles, who was at Wesley, and Marion, who also attended school. She would not neglect their needs.

Emilia took a sip of tea. The water was a little too hot just now. She replaced the teacup and opened the new letter. Mr Macartney was most understanding about Emilia's responsibilities to her children. Many of the other women at St Mary's had the same concerns. He proposed that the men and women visit their neighbour's homes while the children were at school. That would, no doubt, suit everyone concerned.

Emilia began to think aloud. 'Now I have to determine whether it is God's will to work alongside Mr Macartney. I have been praying about it since I sent off my first reply.

'Do I feel that I am capable of taking on a new ministry? Certainly Pastor Chris has been most encouraging. Ever since I learnt that the Holy Spirit helps me to be more like Jesus I have become less concerned about my besetting sins. I've learnt I can call out to Jesus whenever I am intemperate and then He helps me. That discovery freed me from seeking the blessing which would only give me special feelings for a month or two. It is not my own nature that is lived out. I must be controlled by the mighty unseen power of God, who is "able to subdue all things unto Himself".

'Well, have I had enough experience talking to people about Jesus? Yes, I think I'm rather well qualified. During my visiting ministries here, I've met people in a wider variety of circumstances than I'd ever met before. I even made myself sick because of my eagerness to tell as many people as possible about Jesus. My illness taught me that it is not my task to draw people to God, but the work of the Holy Spirit.

'I also learnt valuable lessons in the prayer retreat I attended some years ago. I asked God to give me His power so I could speak for Him more effectively. I wanted to speak with such authority that people would accept Jesus is the Messiah. Instead, God gave me a vision of my sinfulness. I thought that was a poor way to answer my prayer, but I've since seen that when others gain a similar revelation of their sinfulness they can then understand the value of His painful death. Many people have responded by giving their lives to Him. That's why I produced those tracts telling my story.

'Another revelation from the retreat was that if God had given me the power to attract people to Himself in the manner of Jesus, I would have taken it for granted and not spent much time praying. By not giving me that power, He taught me to depend on Him every time I seek to draw people to Jesus. I pray for His guidance about the Bible passages I should talk about and that my message will be relevant to the audience.

'I always pray for His guidance during ministry in the infirmary, the prison and in people's homes. When I accepted the leadership role of the Presbyterian Mother's Prayer Meeting, I noticed that I received His help in every task I undertook.'

After this reflection, Emilia drank quite a lot of the tea in her cup. When she put it down again she said, 'When I think back over all the things I've done for the first time here I'm rather astonished. It seems I've been in school again. Joining this new ministry at St Mary's seems to be an appropriate use of my heritage and of the things I've learnt. It would also allow me to act on my great burden for my people.

'Living in Caulfield would make it far easier to visit Charles and the Berens and Aronson families. There seem to be more advantages in moving to Caulfield than remaining here. We will be sad to leave the many friends we have found here but trains do run between Melbourne and Geelong so we may be able to return occasionally.

'I'll have to resign from committees and finish my visiting ministries here. I'll need to make arrangements to have our belongings and furniture transported to Caulfield. I guess that will take some time to organise. I'll pray for God's guidance while I prepare. The next thing to do is reply to Mr Macartney.'

PART FIVE

A New Vocation

1877 to 1881

CHAPTER 49

Caulfield, Victoria
Late February 1877

'MARION, CAN WE COME INTO YOUR BED ROOM? DR BERNARD AND HIS family go to St Mary's. The vicar asked him to visit us this afternoon.'

'Yes, Mama, you can come in. I've put my nightie on again even though my tummy and back are so itchy.'

Dr Jonathan Bernard sat down on the bed. 'Hello Marion. I have a daughter who is about seven, like you, and she would be complaining too if she was as sick as you are.' He got a tongue depressor out of his medical bag and put the bag under the bed.

Emilia sat down on a chair beside the bed and held Marion's hand.

'When did your red rash start? Let me feel your itchy skin. Now I'll feel the glands in your neck and look into your mouth. When I put this on your tongue say "Ahh". You did that well. Hmm, your tongue isn't the normal colour is it?'

'No, it's bright red,' her mother said. 'Marion began complaining about a sore throat and a headache two days ago. When I realised she had a temperature I put her straight to bed. Every so often she complains about feeling cold and reaches for the blanket. I can't believe she needs it when she's only just complained about being too hot.'

After more examination, Dr Bernard reported his conclusion. 'It's pretty clear, Marion, that you have scarlet fever. I expect you met a child who still had the infection while you were living with the Macartneys this last fortnight. So many visitors go in and out of that vicarage I'm surprised Emily's children don't get sick more often.

'You did the right thing, Mrs Baeyertz, to put Marion to bed. She'll need lots of rest and good food. Do you have calamine lotion? Dab it all over her skin because it will help her to stop scratching. I have some medicine to reduce the pain because scarlet fever is a common illness here.

'You are going to have to keep an eye on Marion. Scarlet fever either clears up after several days or it develops complications. I'll come back every day to see how she is. I'll also ask Mrs Macartney to organise the church ladies to bring soups, jellies and junket for you both.

'Now Marion, Your body needs food to fight the fever. You won't want to eat anything chewy with such a sore throat. Even if you throw up your food, try to have soup or drink water often so that you don't lose too much liquid.

'You'd better put a bucket beside the bed, Mrs Baeyertz. It's just as well that young Charles is still living with his school family because scarlet fever is contagious. You'll have to make sure that your visitors don't spend too long with her while Marion is sick because they can get recurrent bouts of the illness. Perhaps we should move your bed into Marion's room so you can get some sleep.'

Thirty minutes later, the doctor and mother walked down the passage to the front door. Emilia said, 'Thank you for coming so quickly, Dr Bernard. You have been very kind to give us so much help. I've been busy for weeks moving from Geelong and I didn't know what else to do for Marion.'

'I can see you're exhausted, Mrs Baeyertz. Mr Macartney told me you'd only moved into this house yesterday and now you've discovered that Marion is seriously ill. Let's go into your drawing room for a moment to commit Marion to the Lord and pray for strength for you too.'

After seeing out her guest, Emilia locked the front door and returned to the bed room to find Marion dozing under the influence of medicine. Emilia made up her bed on the floor. She and the doctor had removed the mattress and not the bedframe because two furniture removers had complained about the difficulty of reassembly the previous day.

As the sun set, Emilia made herself store away the food after their dinner and wash those implements that needed cleaning, even though she was desperately tired. She had not yet discovered whether there were pests in the house that would welcome a free feed.

The warm February air slowly cooled. Emilia had a sponge bath at the washstand, put on her nightwear, made sure the window was open, carefully examined her daughter, turned out the lamps and then got into her own bed.

As she lay in the long twilight, surrounded by an unfamiliar house and concerned about her daughter, Emilia felt alone. Cheerfulness for Marion's sake was no comfort now. In fact, it seemed as if a plug had been pulled out and all her cheerfulness had drained away.

Accusations came into her thoughts. She realised that Marion might still be well if they had stayed in Geelong. The more she thought about her decision, the more she felt she had not considered all the factors. She hadn't even gone to Caulfield to confirm it was the right place for them to live.

She forgot about the careful and prayerful way in which she'd compared her skills with the needs of her new ministry and so concluded that she'd done the wrong thing. The tears that ran down her cheeks out of self-pity now turned into a desperate flood.

Marion turned over in her sleep and muttered something loudly enough to startle her mother. Emilia sat up in her bed. 'What was that, Marion? What do you want?' When Marion did not reply, Emilia stood up, dried her face with a handkerchief and stepped over to the child's bed. Marion's breath rose and fell in the regular pattern of sleep.

Now that she was standing up, she noticed her Bible. 'That's a very good idea.' She lit the candle on the stand, then picked up the book and sat on Marion's bed. After reading Psalm 23 twice, Emilia asked her Father God for His comfort and strength in this difficult time. She prayed that God would prevent her from succumbing to the devil's suggestions that she should have stayed in Geelong. Remembering Dr Bernard's kind words, she got off Marion's bed, tucked her Bible under the edge of her pillow, blew out the candle, snuggled into the sheets and allowed sleep to embrace her.

CHAPTER 50

Caulfield
6 March 1877

SOME DAYS LATER, DR BERNARD'S EXAMINATION OF MARION MADE HIM frown. He gave the appropriate medicine and made her as comfortable as he could, then indicated to Emilia that they needed to talk outside the bedroom.

After they sat down in the drawing room, Dr Bernard said, 'You remember I said that scarlet fever either clears up quickly or gets worse? Well, this afternoon, I can definitely say that Marion's illness is developing complications and they are serious. I'm afraid that it will be tonight when we find out if she will live through the disease or it will become fatal. I've given her the best treatment I can so now we need to pray. Let me hold your hands.'

Tears were sliding down Emilia's cheeks by the time Dr Bernard said 'Amen'. She dabbed her face with her handkerchief, embarrassed that the doctor saw her in such circumstances.

'There's no need to feel awkward about crying, Mrs Baeyertz. I'm worried about Marion too, but I've done the best I can and we've committed her to God. Shall I ask Emily to visit you later today? I don't want you to be alone for the whole afternoon.'

'Yes, please. If Mrs Macartney could come, I'd be very thankful. I've been unpacking boxes while Marion has been sleeping but I would appreciate some company today.'

An hour later, the cheerful knock on the front door interrupted Emilia from her housework. She was not disappointed when she opened it to find two ladies on the doorstep.

Emily Macartney greeted her and said, 'Let me introduce Mrs Porter to you. She and her children live near you.'

'Pleased to meet you. I'm Alice.'

'Emilia.'

After this exchange, Emily continued, 'We had just been talking about bringing you a stew and soup when Dr Bernard came to tell us of your distress. It's good you live nearby because we had no trouble carrying these dishes and our bags.'

On the way to the kitchen, Emily asked, 'Have you unpacked a vase yet? My neighbour insisted we cut some of her flowers. She enjoyed Marion's help with weeding the garden and hopes that these flowers will remind her of their fun. Now summer's over, they will last longer in water.'

Emily and Alice put down the casseroles, wrapped in towels, onto the kitchen bench. While the other two organised afternoon tea, Mrs Porter withdrew the flowers from one bag and arranged them in the vase taken from another bag. The vase was put into Marion's room when they looked in on her.

After that, the tea tray was taken into the drawing room where the women enjoyed a chat. Half an hour later, Emily asked if Emilia needed any help moving furniture or other belongings. Her offer was quickly accepted because Emilia had been hoping for someone to help her store boxes in high cupboards.

Fifteen minutes later Emily said, 'You've done very well to unpack so many boxes while you've also been nursing Marion. You've turned this house into a lovely home.'

'Thank you for your kind words. I've noticed you looking a few times at the watch on your neck-chain. I expect it's time you went home. There are probably lots of people at the vicarage wondering where you are.'

'We were happy to come. We've both had children with scarlet fever and we know how harrowing the days and nights can be. I feel I must return because our daily maid will have finished her work by now. I'll ask my husband to organise a prayer meeting for tonight and I'll send a message to the Ladies Prayer Group so they can pray for you too.'

After farewelling the vicar's wife, Alice wanted to hear from Emilia why she had moved to Caulfield, so they refilled the teapot and returned to the drawing room.

Some hours after her new friend had left for home, Emilia stored away the left-over soup and the remains of Emily's stew, which they would finish the next day. Then she prepared to go to bed.

As she stood and watched Marion sleep, Emilia struggled to capture her thoughts. She imagined her emotions were racing as quickly through her as the fever was raging through Marion's weak body. Overcome by the fear of losing Marion that night, Emilia bent to sit down on the bed, then knelt beside it to bring her daughter to her Heavenly Father.

Emilia put her hands on her daughter's hot limbs, but she couldn't find the right words to convey the ache in her heart. She could, though, look up pleadingly into her Father's face. She was comforted that her Father God knew this was an hour of deepest need, even though she could not put words to it. He, out of the wealth of His love and not according to her capacity to ask, was willing to bless her.

Finally, some appropriate words formed and Emilia could pray aloud. 'All I can do is lift up Marion to You and ask that You make her well. I can't stop thinking how dreadful it would be if Marion died. You know that I gave up everything I valued most to marry Charlie. I gave up my inheritance, I'm no longer fully accepted in my own family and I've lost links with my people. You know it took me months to discover that I could keep going on in this life without dear Charlie by my side. Now it seems that I will be alone again. I can accept that You had to take Charlie away to make me see You, but what value is there in taking Marion away from me? I have already committed myself to You so I can't see how her death would change that.'

Her knees were getting sore, so she moved to her mattress on the floor and prayed again that God would heal Marion. After some time she raised her head and said to herself, 'Perhaps it's time I went to sleep. What is the time anyway?' She was saved from getting up to find her watch, because George's clock in the drawing room started to ring out the hour. Emilia counted eleven chimes.

'What date is it? Didn't Emily say this afternoon that we were now in March?' Emilia's thoughts turned to the day before. When she had paid the plumber, he had written '5 March' on the receipt. Suddenly Emilia cried out. Charlie had been taken from her at eleven o'clock exactly six years ago. Vivid memories of that horrid night returned.

Marion turned over in her sleep at the sound of her mother's voice. Emilia got off her mattress and sat down on Marion's bed to look on the familiar form of her sick child. Marion had been such a solace to her while she had struggled to live without Charlie. Was Marion to be taken from her too? This little life hung in the balance but Father God held the balance.

Emilia bowed her head but, as before, she was too stricken to pray until she felt Father God's peace fill her soul and her thoughts calmed down. Then she yielded her daughter up to God, believing that He knew best.

Emilia did not know what God would do, but His peace so filled her that she was able to sleep until she heard the birds greeting the morning sun.

Whenever Emilia looked back on that dreadful experience, that moment of absolute submission to the Divine Will, that was when she felt that God, in His grace, gave Marion's life back to her. Twenty years later, whenever Emilia had reason to remember His grace to them both, she would tell herself that Marion was still her joy and solace.

CHAPTER 51

Caulfield
March 1877

EMILIA RECOGNISED DR BERNARD'S KNOCK ON THE FRONT DOOR AND so opened it to greet the faithful doctor with a large grin on her face.

'You are smiling so Marion has made it through the night. Let me see her.' Emilia followed the doctor down the passage. He entered the bed room before Emilia did and gasped.

'How has that happened to you, Marion? You were so ill yesterday and yet you are clearly much better today. It is marvellous how God has answered our prayers for you. I and many other church folk went to the prayer meeting at Mr Macartney's house last night. No doubt your mother prayed for you too. Now, may I examine you to see what has happened?'

After his assessment, Dr Bernard suggested that Emilia give Marion whatever she wanted to eat today. She could play with her toys but still had to stay in her bed room and keep away from other children while she recovered

Soon after the doctor left, the mother sat on the bed and told her daughter how much she meant to her. Emilia emphasised that God's answer to her fervent prayers showed how much He loved them both. Her faith in, and love for, her Father God was strengthened after seeing His love and mercy in action for Marion. Many other experiences at this time in Emilia's life proved God's power and grace to her.

Because the parish of St Mary saw how God had answered their earnest prayers, they took a special interest in both Marion and her mother. Emilia often received home-grown flowers, vegetables and fruit from the parishioners and Marion was invited to play with the children of many church families. Mrs Porter made a special effort to invite Marion to play with her children because they were of similar ages.

Three weeks later, once Marion was restored to health, Emilia enrolled her in the school near the church. Emilia also reconfirmed the arrangements for her son to attend Wesley College and board with his Aunt Suzette's friend. Only then did Emilia begin her ministry to the Jewish community outside the house.

Within weeks, Emilia and Hussey were sure that, like St Paul, her mission was to the Gentiles.

CHAPTER 52

Melbourne
Early April 1877

EMILIA LOOKED OUT FROM THE CENTRE OF THE LUNCH ROOM UPON thirty or so women, some no more than girls, who had set down their seats to form a double half-circle about her. It was she who, with her first words, must break the expectant hush that had descended on them. It was too late now to protest unworthiness as the Jewish head of their department had introduced her, resumed her seat and smiled encouragingly.

There was nothing for it now but to take a deep breath and ignore the tremor in her voice. 'Mrs Weinbeck and ladies, I must thank you for this opportunity to address you all in your luncheon hour. I am pleased to see so many gathered to hear what God has to say to us; today we shall be looking at the subject of Worry. If you have come with Bibles, please turn with me to Philippians chapter four verse six.'

Half a dozen girls found their places, laid open their Bibles on their laps and looked up. Mrs Baeyertz was not tall. She had a slim build, a striking presence and a pleasant face with brown eyes, a firm chin and a distinctive nose. Her brown tresses were pinned in the manner of the day beneath a sober hat. Her attractive black dress had little ornamentation and her collar was buttoned up to her throat.

Her audience silently approved of Emilia's choice and cut of cloth. They all faced the conflicting challenges of fashion and careful stewardship of their wages so wore reliable garments of enduring style and long-wearing fabric, some made by tailors and some at home.

Mrs Baeyertz had a well-educated voice and manner, suggesting a wealthy family, yet here she was, away from the upper classes of Melbourne. What was her accent? From somewhere in England or Wales, or Europe perhaps?

Never before had Mrs Weinbeck arranged for a visitor to talk to the young women about something other than work. Furthermore, the men and women who instructed them about correct factory practices implied their authority had been earned from hard experience. In contrast, Mrs Baeyertz seemed rather young to be giving important advice. Yet she was highly recommended by Mr Macartney so the women made the most of this unusual occurrence.

'In nothing be anxious, but in everything by prayer and supplication let your requests be made known to God'.

Emilia raised her eyes from the Bible in her hand to look again at her audience. All, including Mrs Weinbeck, were experienced in the cutting, stitching, and finishing of women's undergarments. Emilia, who had never been able to pride herself on her needlework, had a respect for these women that would have surprised them, had they known.

Emilia began to refer to familiar passages from the Word of God: 'Casting all your care upon Him; for He careth for you' and 'Even the very hairs on your head are all numbered'. There came a steadying calm and all her nervousness fled.

'All this tells of One who loves us with an unchanging love, and we grieve Him when we give way to fret and worry, even though in our circumstances there may be apparent cause for anxiety. Worry must be confessed as sin, and we must seek deliverance from it as any other sin. There is only one way of deliverance and one Deliverer. The first step is to commit the whole trouble to the Lord. If there is sin in connection with it, true confession must be made. Put everything into His hands and ask Him to enable you to leave it there. Tell Him that you want to obey Him, but you can no more deliver yourself than you can create a world.

'Then, refuse absolutely to look at it. The Lord can put Himself between you and the trial, and make Himself so real to you that He will be as real as the trial, and He will comfort you, and rest you, until His own peace shall be in your heart and you will know by experience how true it is "As one whom his mother comforteth, so will I comfort you and you shall be comforted".

'Trust, with a persistent unwavering faith. Do not, I beg you, be discouraged if deliverance does not come instantly, but keep trusting. The devil will dispute every inch of the ground with you for we wrestle not against flesh and blood but against wicked spirits. Hold onto Christ. Victory is certain through Him!'

Emilia looked down at her watch and saw she had more time. As she told of an eagle learning to fly, and of Hagar and Ishmael, and of Elijah and the widow of Zarephath, the girls noticed that Emilia enunciated her words clearly and projected her voice effectively above the incessant noise of the factory. She spoke directly and avoided subtle arguments.

She then told of her own experience of discovering who Jesus was. When her whole face smiled with the memory, her audience saw that she was, indeed, a beautiful woman.

'O come to Christ anew this afternoon and surrender all; trust Jesus for everything, and He will give you blessed rest and freedom from worry. Because it is all in His hands; try it! I do not say sorrow and trouble will not come, but in the trial you will have Jesus to comfort and deliver you.

'The last passage we'll turn to is in Matthew chapter fourteen. Jesus has been feeding the multitude, and He constrained His disciples to get into a ship and go before Him unto the other side while He sent the multitudes away; but the ship was now in the midst of the sea, tossed with waves, for the wind was contrary. And in the fourth watch of the night Jesus went unto them, walking on the sea. Peter is, perhaps, standing in the stern of the boat straining his eyes through the darkness for the first glimpse of Jesus. Once before they had been in a storm, and Jesus had rebuked the wind and waves, and there was great calm; but now has He forgotten them? Does He not care? It's all dark, dark. Ah! It may sometimes be too dark to see Jesus, but it is never too dark for Him to see us.

'And now Peter sees the vision he has longed for, but is it Jesus or a spirit? He cries out for fear, but across the storm there comes the sweet voice known and loved, "Be of good cheer, it is I; be not afraid". That voice draws out his heart, and he cries, "Lord, if it be Thou, bid me to come unto Thee on the water", and back across the storm comes the word of power, "Come".

'What a moment in the life of Peter—to commit himself absolutely to a path of uncertainty. As long as he is in the boat, he can feel the planks beneath his feet; he can try and steer for himself. But, he will go and leap into the waves at the call of Jesus. Is it a risk? We read—"And when Peter came down out of the ship he walked on the water to go to Jesus"; he is committed absolutely to a walk by faith, and he does walk on the water. How dependent he is now upon the Lord, the power for that walk comes from Him, and from Him alone. As long as Peter looks to Christ he does walk, but when he looked at the circumstances he was afraid, and beginning to sink, he cried, "Lord, save me," and immediately Jesus stretched forth His hand and caught him, and showed him the secret of failure—"O thou of little faith, wherefore didst thou doubt?"

'To many of us there comes a time when Jesus calls us to such a walk, to go out into an unknown future and untried path, a path of uncertainties; this tests our surrender, can we venture? Oh, yes, let go of the old life, heedless of consequences, and trust that He who has called you to this life will maintain you in it, as long as you look to Him in an utter abandonment of helplessness. Don't wait until the chance of going to Him, or the water is over us for ever; a few years (less than that it may be for some of us) will see the last chance ever of following Him.

'Oh, for more devotedness, more abandonment, to let Him have all His own way with us, and so to be delivered from fret and worry. Yield your will day by day, and let the doubtful things go that would hinder your walk before God. Listen, Jesus speaks, "Lovest thou Me more than these?" Tenderly, He looks into your face for the answer, an answer to be given with our wills. Shall it be—"Lord, Thou knowest all things; Thou knowest that I love Thee."

'There is very little time left to us now, so in closing, I simply ask that each one of you ponders these things. Then, next time I come, I pray that there will be some who shall say to me that they have taken this vital step of casting all your cares upon the Lord Jesus.'

As the girls resumed their duties, Emilia was escorted to the baize door.

'How is it with you, Mrs Weinbeck? Are you saved?'

'Well,' she said, 'if you'd asked me before your meeting, I would have said "No". I did profess once but went back; now I have received Christ. He is my Saviour. He died for me!'

Later that very day, Mrs Weinbeck became quite ill and so was taken to the hospital by her staff. While waiting to be given a glass of water, Mrs Weinbeck fell back on her bed and left this life for one more glorious.

CHAPTER 53

Caulfield
Mid-April 1877

ON HER USUAL DAY OF THE WEEK FOR TEA AT THE VICARAGE, EMILIA was told that Hussey was visiting Mrs Weinbeck's mother as she was feeling poorly. Emily was hopeful that he would join them soon.

Emilia found that she was not the only guest. Mrs Macartney introduced a young Scottish woman, Mary Thomson, and then went on to explain. 'My husband is endeavouring to persuade Mary to take on the responsibility of opening a Chapter of the Young Women's Christian Association here in Melbourne.'

To Mary she said, 'He has no doubt mentioned Mrs Baeyertz to you. It is not long since she commenced meetings during the luncheon-hour for factory women in the district.'

Mary turned her head of elegantly braided hair towards Emilia. 'Yes indeed! I've heard of your work and am delighted to meet you at last, Mrs Baeyertz. If I am to take on the task of Secretary of the YWCA, I will stand in great need of help from ladies such as you.'

Emilia was not sure she had heard right. Her eyebrows lifting, she replied, 'Help from me? But I do not at all see how I could help you. I have no experience whatever in the work of such an organisation.'

Miss Thomson smiled charmingly and said quietly, 'Even though there is still more work to be done before the YWCA can be established here, I know of several young women who are ready to attend Bible Classes. They work in various factories in Melbourne and could attend a nearby class directly after they finish work. I am hoping that you would be willing to teach one such class on Wednesday evenings in the next few weeks. Mr Macartney has recommended you highly, and I would be so grateful if you would agree to be responsible for a group of girls, just a small group if that is what you would prefer.'

Before Emilia could give her answer, the tea tray was brought in and, for the next few minutes, everyone was busy with dispensing tea and passing plates. It was only when she could take her ease with a dainty cup of tea in one hand and a finely cut cucumber sandwich in the other, that Emilia was able to give thought to Mary's request.

The idea of taking a girls' Bible Class in town was not displeasing or unfamiliar to her. In fact she found the prospect rather stimulating but, of course, her daughter's needs would have to come first. If she became convinced that the whole enterprise was in the will of the Lord for her, she would willingly offer her assistance. Emilia was about to make this known to Mary when another interruption occurred, with the hurried entrance of Mr Macartney.

After seeking the indulgence of all present for his late arrival, Hussey accepted a cup of tea from his wife and gratefully sank into a comfortable chair before saying, 'I have just come from the bedside of someone known to you, Emilia. You will remember Mrs Weinbeck, I am sure?'

Emilia replaced her cup in its saucer. 'Yes, of course. She died soon after I'd spoken to her employees at the factory. It became apparent to me that my visit had been arranged by our Heavenly Father.'

'I hear that you also know Mrs Weinbeck's mother?'

'Yes, when I attended the funeral, her mother asked me to visit her home to explain what I had told her daughter when I visited the factory. We spent a most profitable afternoon together.'

'You may not know, Emilia, just how worthwhile your time in that home was. Her elderly mother was taken ill and has spent some days in hospital. When I visited her today I was determined to discover just where she stood in spiritual matters. The moment I began my enquiries, she said to me, "Oh, you do not need to fear for my eternal safety, vicar! Since I have had the Scriptures explained to me by Mrs Baeyertz, I have made my peace with my Redeemer, and I know that all is well with my soul."'

Emilia, delighted to hear this, asked, 'How was the lady when you left her today?'

The vicar replied, 'The doctor said her health was improving and he asked me to tell her friends and family that she would welcome visitors.'

Emilia said, 'I shall visit her myself.'

Emily added, 'No doubt she would appreciate a chat about the Bible and some prayer for her illness. How good God is!' she said softly. 'We must do all we can to make life as easy as possible for Mrs Weinbeck's poor mother.'

'It seems to me,' her husband remarked to no-one in particular, 'that the same good God has placed in our midst someone who is especially gifted in making His goodness known so that those who hear of it will not rest until they possess the Giver for themselves.'

CHAPTER 54

Tarryever, Victoria
April 1877

My dear Emilia,

Today I have the pleasant task of replying to your letter about Marion's dramatic recovery from scarlet fever. I was so pleased to read that God answered your prayers and those of the parishioners at St Mary's. I have still not met your darling daughter and long to see her now that I know I nearly missed the opportunity.

In return for your news, I have some of my own, which I do not doubt will at the very least raise a smile, if not an eyebrow. Yesterday, Saturday, was the long-awaited day of Tarryever's annual cricket match away to Dungower, our arch-rivals. Early that day, as soon as we were ready, Cousin Will drove Tommy and me to the Dungower cricket ground. Beside us was the largest hamper you are ever likely to see, filled with sandwiches, cold fowl, sliced tongue and other delectable picnic food. We were followed by the rest of our cricket team.

As the weather was fine and there were no delays, we arrived at Dungower in good time for the start of play. I went at once to renew acquaintances with the Dungower ladies, and was deep in conversation with them when I felt an impatient tug at my sleeve. It was Tommy, who was bursting to tell me something and hardly able to wait for me to offer my excuses before he dragged me away saying, 'Come and see who's here!'

When we reached a group of Dungower players, Tommy introduced one to me with 'Miss Wait, whom, of course, you know'. I looked up and saw—can you guess who, Emilia? Dressed in cricket creams was, shall I have to tell you?,

Dr Langmore from *Empire of Peace!* Can you credit it? I could scarcely believe my eyes, and for the space of several breaths could not find my voice to respond to his greeting. The match was about to start so we could not talk for long, and once the first ball was bowled it took all my concentration to keep the score, which was the task I had been given. Tommy was twelfth man so when he wasn't needed could station himself beside me to make up for my lapses with, 'Two more runs to them, byes though, don't add them to Jimmy's score!', and similar necessary promptings.

At some time in our innings, Dr Langmore took a spectacular catch, and I am afraid I did not altogether meet with Tommy's approval when I joined in the applause a little too heartily. Will upheld the family honour by making a respectable score, and the match proved to be a close one with suspense being sustained to the very last ball. We lost by two runs, which did little for poor Tommy's peace of mind!

Afterwards there was all the food to be eaten and Dr Langmore, who insists that I call him Martin as we did on the ship, took the opportunity to bring me up to date on the happenings that had led to his being so far west in the colony rather than on the high seas or in Melbourne. Here I must interrupt myself to tell you that he asked after you and George and seemed most interested in all I could tell him of you both.

Martin explained that he had come to Dungower as a favour to a medical friend, who had returned to England for family reasons. It was convenient for the two simply to exchange positions, and the friend sailed in his place as ship's doctor, while Martin took on his work at Dungower where he is the only doctor for many miles around. It seems likely that he will be here for a year, if not two.

He looks older than when you and I first met him, but I am sure I appear to be an older woman, as thirteen years have passed since we arrived at Sandridge. Otherwise, Martin is the man we met at sea. His grey-green eyes are the same, but there are grey hairs amongst the brown hair on his head and in his wheat-coloured beard. He has grown a little plumper, as most of us have. He remarked that he prefers the rural life to life on ship where he constantly watched his step.

Martin said that, in my next letter, I was to be sure to send his greetings to you and through you to George whenever you see him next. Do let me have news of your brother from time to time Emilia, as I should be delighted to hear what he is doing.

Fond remembrances from Will and Tommy. And from me, my very warmest love to you and Charles and Marion, and greetings to all your family.

Nancy

CHAPTER 55

Melbourne
Early May 1877

EMILIA CLOSED THE FRONT DOOR OF MRS PORTER'S HOUSE AND SMILED at having just seen Marion run upstairs to join Alice's children. Their mother had reassured her that she was happy to care for Marion while Emilia went to teach the Bible Class in the city. Alice had said, 'Indeed I don't have to do much to look after Marion because my children keep her fully occupied. I only see them if they've accidentally scratched themselves while playing or if it's meal time. You've got to walk some distance to catch the train, so go along now.'

While Emilia walked down the road to Elsternwick Station, she looked in her bag for the tenth time to confirm that she'd put her class notes into it. On seeing papers with her handwriting, Emilia felt assured and raised her head just in time to avoid walking into another pedestrian. She reminded herself that she'd already spoken to many young women in the factories and so Mary Thomson's group would be no different. In fact, it would be much easier to teach them because they were not meeting in a factory.

During the previous weeks, Mary had made a careful search for a suitable meeting place for Emilia's Bible Classes. She had found just the right room in a building near Collins Street. The room was available on Wednesday evenings and the landlord had assured Mary that the fire and lights would be lit in good time. In addition, there was room for growth with dozens of chairs and several tables.

The meeting room was one of the best she could find in other respects. Its proximity to the railway stations meant those young women who would take the train home would not have to walk far. In addition, Miss Thomson had searched for a building where the route between the front door and the meeting room did not take visitors through areas where other people worked. Mary had noticed that when girls gathered they created much noise; they conversed and whispered but also laughed and squealed.

Emilia found Mary standing inside the front door to assure her she'd found the correct building. In the meeting room, the two women arranged several chairs around a table and then discussed their plans for the Bible Class. Emilia asked Mary to introduce the young women to her and to open the meeting with prayer. She was also eager for Mary to participate in the Bible study as that would encourage the others to join in. After committing the evening to their Father God in prayer, Mary returned to the front door.

A few girls were slowly walking down the street while comparing building numbers with the details on her invitation. When they recognised her waving at them, they were elated at finding the right place. She had to calm them down before they reached the meeting room.

Emilia could see that Mary had received instruction on leading groups because she helped the six women feel at ease and supported the Bible teacher too. Emilia fell into her natural pattern of guiding her audience to see Bible truths for themselves. She also noticed that the conversation developed quickly when she didn't have to compete against machinery. When it was time to leave, the girls all happily said they would return the next week and one or two asked if they might bring a friend.

CHAPTER 56

Melbourne
Early July 1877

IT WAS JUST AS WELL THAT EMILIA WAS AHEAD OF TIME FOR HER BIBLE
Class that evening, for the room was already over-flowing. The question
uppermost in Emilia's mind was where they could possibly be accommo-
dated. Then Mary Thomson arrived, for the first time in weeks. She stood at
the front of the gathering, waved her arms and called out 'Quiet please!' It
took a little time before everyone stopped talking.

'Mrs Baeyertz, ladies, it is now most evident that you have outgrown your
present accommodation where, regrettably, there is no room for further
expansion. Fortunately, I am pleased to be able to tell you that from now on,
the Women's Bible Class will have use of the Assembly Hall on Wednesday
evenings. You'll remember that it is beside Scots' Church, near the inter-
section of Collins and Russell Streets. We must leave at once to walk there.
Should anyone not be familiar with our new location, may I suggest that you
follow those of us who are? Thank you.'

Emilia repeated, 'The Assembly Hall!' to herself. Surely she could not
address her audience in such a large hall? Her fear lasted only a moment
before the Word of God came to mind and strengthened her. She blessed
God for giving her an opportunity of telling out His glorious salvation to so
large a number of souls.

Dodging clusters of young women, Mary reached Emilia. Then arm in
arm, as they all walked up the hill, she assured Emilia that she would be
heard clearly in the Assembly Hall.

As the last women to arrive found a seat, Emilia looked out at her audience. She was confirmed in her opinion—the young women occupied but a
fraction of this cavernous hall that could seat 300. Their new quarters were
not at all what she would have wished.

As the numbers of women attending Emilia's Bible Classes increased, Mr
Macartney mentioned this remarkable woman to the Christian leaders he
met during his daily rounds. On returning to their homes, many of the men

asked their wives and daughters about Mrs Baeyertz. The women eagerly related stories they'd heard.

In July, John Singleton, a doctor and founder of many practical charities around Melbourne, invited Mrs Baeyertz to speak each week at the Mission Hall he had built on Little Bourke Street. Emilia enquired as to the audience he had in mind. Once he had assured her that the meetings were for women only, Emilia accepted his invitation.

CHAPTER 57

Melbourne
July 1877

ONE WEDNESDAY, EMILIA TRAVELLED INTO THE CITY EARLIER THAN usual. She had been invited to afternoon tea with her favourite brother at his place of work. Emilia walked out of Prince's Bridge Railway Station and then found her way through the throng and up the footpath on the eastern side of Swanston Street. At Collins Street, she turned left to walk, past the elm saplings, down to Elizabeth Street.

As she crossed on the wooden footbridge, Emilia held on to the handrail and watched where she stepped. She remembered having to do the very same thing when she had first arrived, thirteen years before.

One could be injured falling into William's Creek, which flowed down the centre of Elizabeth Street. Rain tended to wash the street surface into gullies and mingle with sewage that escaped roughly built cesspits. It puzzled Emilia that land and passage salesmen travelled around Great Britain boasting of Marvellous Melbourne, knowing full well that one of her principal streets was such a danger to her inhabitants. She mused that some of that tax raised from gold mining could have been used to improve the drainage of the street.

On the far bank, Emilia turned first right along the street then, at the corner of Little Collins Street West, she turned to her left into a street only half a chain wide. She smiled with pride when, outside number 15 on the north side, she found the sign she sought: ROSENTHAL, ARONSON & CO., JEWELLERS.

Once through the door of the solid three-storey building with under-stated façade, Emilia found herself in a carpeted show room. The outside sounds of the street and manufactory were muffled. Although the front windows admitted sunlight, her eyes still needed to adjust to the dimmer light inside.

A well-dressed gentleman walked towards her and asked, 'May I help you?'

'I am Mrs Baeyertz and I have an appointment with Mr George Aronson.'

'Ah yes, Mrs Baeyertz. I remember George saying you were coming this afternoon. Please wait here while I go to get him.'

Emilia could see several timber and glass display cabinets distributed around the room. Five comfortable chairs were positioned around a low table where customers could consider the merits of one piece of jewellery over another. A desk and chairs were positioned to one side of the room for the salesmen.

She stepped up to the closest cabinet and saw that brooches, chains, rings, earrings, lockets and studs had been arranged to present the best view. The sign said 'Jewellery from Germany'. In another cabinet, the sign stated 'Colonial Jewellery'.

When a familiar voice boomed out, 'My dear Emilia, how lovely to see you', she turned towards its source. Soon George was embracing her and exchanging kisses.

'Walter, we'll have afternoon tea in my office before I take Mrs Baeyertz to see the manufactory. Please ask Mrs Jones to bring us a tea tray.'

'I'll see to it, George.'

As they entered the office, Emilia exclaimed, 'Before I forget, the most recent letter I received from Nancy asked me to give you her greetings. She also passed on the greetings of her cousin Will and his son Tommy. They've celebrated Tommy's twenty-first birthday this year. I'm sure we'd both be quite surprised at how tall Tommy has grown since we saw him last.'

'I'm sure we'd all be astonished at how much older we've all grown in the last thirteen years.'

'Oh, and I must tell you that Dr Martin Langmore is also a resident of the Western District of Victoria now.'

'I'd wondered what had happened to him. I realised he was no longer a ship's doctor when I travelled on a ship of the line he worked for and they didn't have much news about him.'

'Nancy's letter said that Martin swapped positions with a doctor at Dungower who needed to return to England. Now let me look at this lavishly appointed office. I knew you were the Residential Partner now, but I didn't realise that you had the use of this magnificent room.'

'Don't let appearances fool you, my dear; this is not where the most important work is done. I've been blessed because I arrived back in Melbourne at a time when David and Saul wanted a third partner. David Rosenthal's business began to grow when he began to manufacture in 1871. Saul married David's sister and became his partner. They asked the architects Barnes and Reed to design a three-storey building behind this one where we can make our own jewellery. Four years later, David and his family have left for Europe by way of Ceylon, the origin of many of our gems, leaving Saul to manage the business.'

There was a knock on the door and when George had called 'Enter', a woman carrying a tea tray came in and placed it on the low table. 'Ah, Mrs Jones, thank you for bringing it so promptly. Let me introduce you to my sister, Mrs Emilia Baeyertz.'

They shook hands then Mrs Jones asked, 'Are you the lady my daughter Lizzie talks about? She goes to hear Mrs Baeyertz explain the Bible on Wednesday nights.'

'Yes, I am that lady. I am frustrated that I can't personally meet all the women who come to my Wednesday evening meetings for there are too many. Please ask Lizzie to introduce herself to me.'

'Lizzie will be that excited and jealous when I tell her. She speaks very highly of you, you know?' Mrs Jones bobbed in a brief curtsey and left the room.

'I'm still astonished that so many ladies of all ages come to my talks. I don't really know what makes my talks special. No, I didn't come here to talk about my work. I wanted to see my favourite brother again. Please tell me about Saul. The children met their Uncle Saul at their Aunt Eliza's house last year when we came to Melbourne to visit Wesley College. I was looking forward to getting to know him better and so were the children. Yet, before I could move from Geelong, Saul packed up his house to sail to London. I thought that there would be four Aronsons residing in Melbourne again. Now there are only three.'

George replied, 'Three is better than one, Emilia. Saul and his wife were living in St Kilda before they went to Europe in January. Saul and David consider it beneficial for Rosenthal, Aronson & Co. to have a branch in London. Saul can buy jewellery made in Holland, Belgium, Germany and England and send it to us. He can also sell our jewellery there.

'It is a curious thing but immigrants only want to buy fine imported jewellery, while people born here eagerly search for colonial jewellery and gold ornaments with a higher gold content. Increasing demand for colonial products prompted David and Saul to build the manufactory. Fortunately, many jewellers and metal workers have been migrating from Europe.

'Leaving me in charge of the business doesn't seem so foolhardy when you consider what we all learned by experience in Bangor. Furthermore, David and Saul have employed outstanding people who have skills in every aspect of the trade. I only see how many people are linked to our business at our company picnics. About 150 ladies and gentlemen came on the boat to our picnic at Mordialloc this year. Let me pour you a cup of tea. Please help yourself to the cakes.'

'I've been distracted, let me return to Saul. He's only been in London for a few months and has not yet completed all the tasks required to establish a business in that city. I expect Saul will return to live in Melbourne someday. But, I don't think you'll have to wait long before more of the Aronsons join us.'

'Which Aronsons are you talking about, George? Mama and Papa are getting older now. Lewis is running their business. Neither would I expect Julia or Emily to travel out.'

'You are right about our sisters, but Frederick, Charles and Nuriel were thinking about coming out to the colonies when I was last in Bangor.'

'I shall look forward to welcoming my brothers if they do come to Melbourne. Now months ago, I read a story in *The Argus* about you catching a thief and I have not seen you since. At the time I hoped the article would not discourage your customers.'

'Thanks for your concern. Fortunately the story only made customers feel they could trust us.'

'I'd like to hear the story from you.'

George leant back in his partner's chair and began. 'At the end of last year Otto Brinkmann, who manages the goldsmiths and the apprentices, noticed that gold pieces were missing from the zinc box where we keep the clean scrap. We set a trap.

'Otto marked two gold sovereign blanks in my sight with a chasing tool, put them in the box and then locked it into the drawer in his office. A fortnight later, the blanks turned up. Another jeweller nearby, Thomas Young, was alert for the blanks, so he paid with a cheque for £19/11/6 and then notified Police Detectives Hartley and Edleston.

'It turned out that one of our apprentices, John Coley, had sold a total of forty pieces worth £150 to Joseph Ralph Smith, a fence with a long record. The trial was in the middle of February. Smith went to gaol for seven years hard labour, but Coley only got two. John's a good lad, though a fool. If he'd confessed to me beforehand I could have saved him for the sake of his parents. He'll be out early with remission if he behaves himself. I trust he will have learnt his lesson and be an honest worker for the remainder of his life.'

'Well done for apprehending the thief, George!'

'It was a joint effort. Thomas, Otto and I had to appear as if we knew nothing yet we were fairly certain that we were working with a thief. It was harder for Otto because he works alongside the men every day.'

'We'd better not spend the whole afternoon talking. I'm looking forward to that tour of the manufactory.'

'Emilia, just before we go, I have some good news for you.'

'I wonder what that could be about?'

'I am too excited to play the guessing game. Do you remember the Solomon family whom we met when we were both much younger and living with Eliza and Abraham?'

'Solomon ... the name sounds familiar but as I've been meeting so many people this year I can't put faces to the name.'

'You'll remember when I tell you that they are a Jewish family that have been in Melbourne from the early years of settlement.'

'Yes, that's helpful. They hosted a dance in our first year here, didn't they?'

'You are right about the dance. Well, ever since I returned to Melbourne I have found the company of Miss Philippa Solomon to be most pleasing. I have spent time with her whenever I was invited to a ball or dinner or some such.'

'Oh, George!'

'Just wait a moment. I've met many lovely women during my travels here and at Home. I'm glad I waited until I returned though, because Philippa has matured into a special woman. I hope I've also matured. I wrote to her father for his permission to propose to her. Last week he approved. I agreed to his terms. Philippa said yes. We announced our engagement soon after that. Our wedding is planned for next year. Eliza and Abraham know but I asked them to keep it a secret from you. I wanted to tell you myself.'

Emilia jumped up and hugged George. 'Well done! Congratulations!

I pray God's blessings will go with you both now and every day in the future. Where's my handkerchief?' She pulled it out of her pocket and wiped the tears that slipped down her cheeks. 'Thank you so much for telling me yourself. I have missed you and Eliza more than I'd realised. It is so much nicer living in Melbourne where I can visit either of you occasionally.'

'I intend to introduce you to Philippa at a dinner hosted by Eliza.'

'That sounds a lovely idea.'

'Do you have time to look at our manufactory?'

'Yes, but do I look presentable? I've been crying, you know.'

'There is a mirror hidden in this cupboard for that very reason. We partners have to look our best.'

When they were standing outside the three-storey brick and stone building, George said, 'I warn you that there will be a lot of noise and heat. Some of the men may also use words that a lady shouldn't hear.'

'I appreciate your concern, George, but I've been in many factories since I started visiting women in their lunch breaks. I've heard, felt and seen a lot of things that I'd had no reason to know of before. I expect to encounter many more.'

'Because of the noise, I'll tell you now what we are going to see. There is a furnace on the ground floor, so we'll get very hot as soon as we walk in. On the first floor there is a stamping press where metal is stamped into a die. You'll also see the large press, the storage for the dies, the lathe and the vice bench.

'On the second floor, you'll see thirty-five workbenches where the goldsmiths create the jewels. You'll also see Mr Brinkmann sitting at his desk.'

While George led her through the building, Emilia marvelled that anything as delicate as the jewels she'd seen in the display cabinets had been produced in a place like this.

After Emilia had farewelled George, she stepped into a tea room to have another cup of tea and eat a freshly made sandwich. She had to prepare for her meeting at the Assembly Hall that evening.

CHAPTER 58

Caulfield
Late July 1877

My dear Nancy,

As you know, I always look forward to your letters for they are a pleasure to read, and until the one that came for me today, I would have said they were all of such a high standard that I could not choose any one above the others. But having read your latest one, I must admit that its content lifts it head and shoulders above the usual, and in spite of the fact that it has left me quite breathless, I cannot rest until I have written in reply.

First of all, please convey my very warmest congratulations to Dr Langmore! What amazing good fortune that he should have won for himself the prize of such a fiancée as Miss Nancy Wait. As for you, my dearest friend, I am so very happy for you, for I am persuaded that Martin, above all other men, comes closest to being worthy of you. I look forward to telling Eliza and Abraham of your engagement because they have often asked about you.

I quite agree that there is no good reason to delay the announcing of your engagement, as you have no-one but yourselves to consider. I would be grateful to learn the date you have in mind for your wedding, although I can't promise to attend.

As for myself, I cannot explain why it should be so, but I am receiving invitations to conduct women's meetings not only in the city and suburbs, but also out in the country! It seems I am being talked about. As you can see by the cutting from a Melbourne weekly paper I have enclosed, I am being written about as well!

I hope I am learning, Nancy, to first seek the will of the Lord regarding meetings, so that I might not accept any that do not accord with His will. For instance I cannot think it right to take meetings where I must speak to both men and women, since there are enough to keep me busy where only women and girls attend. The halls are full!

However, I have received so many invitations from church ministers who want me to speak to mixed audiences that I have decided to make it a matter of prayer. Please pray for me too that God will make His guidance clear to me.

Charles, Marion and I visited my parents-in-law in Brighton last weekend. Both Mr and Mrs Baeyertz were pleased to see us and were most impressed by the height of their grandson and his interesting conversation. He's been going to Wesley for nearly a year now and he's ten years old. Marion had her eighth birthday in March and she delights everyone who meets her. Whenever we visit their grandparents, Charles and Marion have most pleasing manners until they overcome their initial awkwardness. Then they become lively and I have to go out into the garden with them to prevent them causing mischief in the house. Their grandparents are no longer as sprightly as they were when we all lived in Colac.

Marion, Charles, and their mother send Nancy their fondest love, and if Eliza and Abraham had known of this letter, they too would have asked that their warmest regards be conveyed to you. Be assured of my loving prayers.

Ever your friend,

Emilia

CHAPTER 59

Caulfield

Spring 1877

WAS IT THE STORIES ABOUT MRS BAEYERTZ IN THE NEWSPAPERS? OR was it that many of the women gathered at the weekly meetings were surrendering their lives to the Lord? Whatever the causes, invitations to speak at churches arrived in ever increasing numbers and brought with them a question Emilia was finding difficult to answer.

Could it be pleasing to God that she, a woman, should address meetings at which men were present? At first Emilia had refused all such invitations, and this kept her from unwelcome controversy. She knew most people believed women should not teach men in public meetings. Though the ministers who invited her to speak to their congregations would support her, her reputation might be ruined for further ministry. More importantly, she did not want to bring shame to the name of Christ or go against God's desire.

On explaining these concerns to the clergymen who'd invited her, some of them pointed out that men far outnumbered women in this colony. Mrs Baeyertz could better influence people in Victoria for Christ if she welcomed men into her audiences.

During this time, Emilia found, to her horror, that she was experiencing a heaviness of spirit such as she had not known in her Christian life. Her soul seemed enclosed in a cloud of stifling darkness. The radiance that had shone forth from the day she had first trusted herself to the Lord had dimmed, shading the peace that had been His gift to her. In utter bewilderment, Emilia asked what this could mean. Had she stepped out of His will for her life? If so, could that be due to her refusal to conduct meetings made up of both men and women? In anguish of soul Emilia sought her Lord and, having poured out her doubts and questions before Him, waited for His answer.

Emilia also wrote a heart-felt letter to Bob, her trusted friend in Geelong. The distance of fifty miles between friends would not impede this important matter. In her letter to Bob, Emilia explained her confusion over the heaviness of spirit that persisted even though she felt her actions honoured her Saviour.

Some days later, after the housework was done, Emilia heard the postman on his afternoon rounds, stopping at most of the houses down the street. Into her letter-box, she heard him put something heavy. On lifting the lid, she saw a parcel bound with brown paper and string. It was from Bob. Emilia was expecting to receive a letter only, and not for some days. While wondering what could be more valuable than Bob's considered opinion, she picked up the parcel and hurried back into the house to find the scissors. Inside the wrapping she found the letter, clippings from English newspapers and a book called *Our Coffee-Room* by Miss Elizabeth R. Cotton.

Emilia set a tray with the makings of afternoon tea and retired to her favourite arm chair. While she turned the small book over in her hands, Emilia saw few signs of wear on the boards and pages. Bob's letter explained that an English Christian paper, to which he subscribed, had included exciting stories about a temperance coffee room. He had written to a friend in London asking for more and was sent a copy of Miss Cotton's book. Bob could see that her story would help Emilia and asked only that Emilia put the book to good use and return it when the time came.

The clippings revealed that Miss Cotton had been born in Tasmania in 1842. During her childhood in Madras, her father, Sir Arthur Cotton, had been a British irrigation engineer. He had built dams and canals on major rivers in southern India to avert famine for countless communities. When Sir Arthur retired, the Cotton family had settled in Dorking, a beautiful town in the English county of Surrey.

Emilia, wondering what guidance the book could offer, began to read from the Preface. Miss Cotton had taught the Bible to a small class of obedient little girls, while her heart was heavy with concern for the untaught boys. Many of the boys worked as couriers to support their families and Sunday was their only day off.

Sir Arthur helped pay the rent for a room in which a Scripture reader taught classes to the boys. However, they were unruly because they didn't understand his lessons. When the Scripture reader accepted a job in a distant town, Elizabeth could not find another suitable teacher. When she suggested to the villagers that she teach the wild boys herself, she was advised that 'such work is not for a young lady' and to 'let others who are more fitted undertake the task'.

Eventually Elizabeth, supported by her parents, volunteered to teach the Bible to a class of a dozen boys for just one week. Her style of instruction suited the boys so they begged Miss Cotton to teach them again the following week. They also told their friends, 'There's a young lady what cares for boys, and she is coming to teach us'. After several weeks, so many boys were attending the Sunday lessons that Sir Arthur rented a larger room. About this time Elizabeth added hymns and prayers to her simple Bible stories about Jesus.

On returning to their homes each week, the boys told their parents what Miss Cotton had said and soon the men and women were begging the Sunday school teacher to teach the lessons to them too. Aware, as she was, of the general belief that it was improper for women to teach men in meetings, Elizabeth tried to find other ways for the parents to get suitable instruction. These people said they went to church occasionally, but left the services as confused as they were at the beginning. The Bible teacher's cultivated sermons used unfamiliar words which spoke of things they did not understand. In contrast, their sons returned home from Elizabeth Cotton's Bible Classes with stories that touched their hearts.

Miss Cotton's voice leapt out of the pages. Emilia eagerly looked for the passages that explained how prayers were answered for a woman who had sought guidance on these matters before her.

Emilia learnt that God had answered Elizabeth, not by providing a man to teach, but by providing what she needed to establish a temperance coffee room in the village, including a suitable building, qualified managers and solutions to the many other problems that arose as the ministry developed.

More rooms were added as the needs of men and boys were different. In the boys' room, they read, played games, drank coffee and studied the Bible. In the main room, the men read, discussed, played board games, sang hymns, ate hot meals and drank hot and cold beverages but no alcohol. Other ministries developed such as a night school, a penny bank and a shoe club.

The main room was also where Miss Cotton held the Sunday meetings for men and women at the same hour as the evening services in the churches. She wanted to encourage non-church-goers to attend her meetings rather than have the seats filled by those who willingly went to a second church service on Sunday. She also wanted people to spend their spare hours on Sunday evenings in profitable activities instead of entertaining themselves drinking and gambling.

By the time Emilia was halfway through reading *Our Coffee-Room*, the Holy Spirit had clearly revealed to her soul the mind of God on this matter. Kneeling down Emilia gave up her reputation to His keeping, even if it meant being misunderstood by the entire world. Yes, she was prepared to go anywhere He might send her, speak to anyone He identified and be ready always for whatever work there would be for her to do.

Not long after she had made her decision, an invitation arrived from a Congregational minister asking Emilia to address his Sunday School and his workers, both men and women. Without hesitation Emilia went to her desk to write an acceptance letter, and an hour or so later was immersed in the preparation of her message for that occasion.

The day arrived and, while she was still far off, Emilia was amazed and horrified to see that a good crowd was gathering around the church. Once inside, she could see that in a very short time the building would be packed to the doors. On her way to the platform, she was astonished to meet no fewer than three ministers from nearby churches. Despite their best intentions, with their solemn faces, long black coats and huge white starched ties they loomed like sons of Anak in her path.

During the introductory notices, Emilia gazed out upon the sea of young and older faces before her. She judged that a third of these were men. She could feel her breath quicken, and her hands in their neat grey gloves clench and unclench. Yet when she heard her name and knew the time had come for her to step forward, she was conscious of a mantle of calm falling upon her. Everything but the opening remarks she had prepared faded from her mind.

Afterwards she could recall little of the afternoon's proceedings apart from the two side rooms filled with children and their parents, who sought to be shown from the Scriptures how they might find peace for their souls.

When Emilia saw how many people came forward to accept the offer of salvation, she was not proud. She remembered the prayer retreat in Geelong. There she'd asked her Father God for His holy power so she could speak for Him but He had not given it to her then. Instead, He had shown her the ugliness of sin. This had strengthened her resolve to explain to others why they needed to give up their old ways and turn to God.

Since that retreat, Emilia had learnt to rely on her Heavenly Father for every aspect of her ministry. Later, she saw that she had not been ready to receive His power when she'd first prayed for it. Now, by the grace of God, she was. God had spent the years preparing her for this new vocation. She was now being called 'Mrs Baeyertz, The Lady Evangelist'.

CHAPTER 60

Hobart Town, Tasmania
January 1878

TOWARDS THE END OF 1877, A LETTER ARRIVED FROM THE ASSOCIA-
tion of Christian Workers in Hobart Town inviting Emilia to provide Bible
Lessons for their summer children's programme. She was pleased to see that
the Independent and the United Methodist churches had joined the Association for this mission. Arrangements would be made for her to talk in several
large halls. Plates passed around at each meeting would collect donations
to defray costs and provide for Emilia, for the labourer was worthy of her
reward.

In previous weeks, Emilia had received another request to speak at
churches in Launceston. She could fulfil both invitations if she arrived in the
colony before Christmas and stayed into the early months of the following
year.

She wrote letters of acceptance and organised her household for the
months she would be away. Emilia would take both children with her. They
would sail to Hobart Town after school had finished for the year and before
Christmas Day. Emilia asked their teachers for lessons she could give her
children until she could find schools for them in Tasmania.

The family all looked forward to spending summer near beaches in the
cooler climate. Emilia planned to swim in the sea when she could.

On arrival, Emilia discovered that the Association had arranged for them
to stay with the family of Mr and Mrs Edwards who were delighted to share
their Christmas festivities.

During her stay, Emilia gradually saw that the Association was one of
God's instruments through which He blessed that community. Instead of
placing advertisements in *The Mercury*, volunteers visited every house with
a leaflet advertising the meetings in which Emilia was the guest speaker.
Meeting halls filled with eager audiences.

The Association advertised for volunteers willing to help at the evangelistic meetings and received many responses. Men and women swept floors,

moved chairs, ushered people to seats and provided cups of tea in smaller meetings. Singers, eager to become choristers, used the Association to locate rehearsals. People experienced in guiding enquirers in the faith were rostered so that Emilia was not alone in counselling new believers in the after-meetings.

Emilia's first opportunity to speak was on the afternoon of Sunday 30th December in the Schoolroom in Brisbane Street, attached to the Memorial Church, which belonged to the Independents. The hall was crowded with Sunday School children, teachers and friends.

Mrs Baeyertz introduced her eleven-year-old son and eight-year-old daughter. The audience listened with marked attention as their mother described the healing of Marion from scarlet fever. Emilia went on to speak about her husband, whose death had made her investigate the Holy Scriptures for herself. Her story prepared her listeners for her teaching that followed.

That afternoon, Emilia's sympathetic approach to the children won their allegiance. Her attitude implied they mattered to God and her beautiful manner held the children's attention while she explained spiritual truths in words the youngsters understood. She clearly approved of the idea, newly abroad in the community, that children weren't simply little adults whose short stature allowed them to climb around factory machines. Instead she spoke about things that concerned the youngsters. At the end of her talk, some forty children stayed behind to learn how to gain salvation in Christ Jesus.

The first public meeting for adults was held on New Year's Day, at 7.00 p. m. in the People's Hall in Bathurst Street. The great bulk of Hobart Town's population was out of town or engaged in amusements on this public holiday, so Emilia and the Association were surprised to find the hall completely full. Mrs Baeyertz spoke about the distinctive characteristics of the offerings of Cain and Abel. Numerous people stayed after the meeting to speak with her. Many of them saw that Jesus is the true and living way.

For much of the month, Emilia spoke on Tuesdays, Thursdays and Sundays at the People's Hall, the Memorial Church or the Ebenezer Chapel in Murray Street, a property of the United Methodists.

The Mission Committee met each Monday to discuss plans for that week. On 21st of January, once the Chairman had led them through the reports,

Emilia took the opportunity to explain that she was tired and needed a rest. She'd spoken at ten meetings so far and the calendar showed five more to be held that month.

She'd also spoken at the Congregational Chapel in New Town, a couple of miles to the north. She'd been invited to speak again at New Town and the good folk at O'Brien's Bridge, three miles further on, wanted her to speak at their Chapel too. Since it held two hundred people, she felt it would be irresponsible to refuse the invitation. She hoped to visit O'Brien's Bridge during February.

By the previous week, her feet had begun to hurt at the beginning of her teaching times, rather than by the end. She did not think she would be able to stand up through five more meetings.

She had found it easy to project her voice in a crowded hall because she'd learnt the skill in her childhood. However, she'd been speaking in large meetings every second or third day and to individuals and groups in the after-meetings. Her throat was sore after each public meeting and she feared she might lose her voice. Her fellow Committee members began to sympathise with her but Emilia would not be interrupted.

'Please let's gather facts rather than deal with one concern at a time. You see, this is the first time I've spoken so often and to such large crowds. Admittedly, I have to compete with machinery noise in factories, but they are usually short meetings. I volunteered to speak every second or third day here, but I have over-estimated my abilities. I've now learnt that this programme requires a great deal of stamina for my voice and feet.

'When I take my children for a walk to Battery Point or Sullivan's Cove, we only go a few steps before we are recognised and someone wants to ask me a question. I should delight in their interest in spiritual matters. Yet, I find myself feeling annoyed at the questioner. I expect I am just tired. The children are also disappointed that they can't share a walk with their mother alone. I try hard to reflect the loving patience of Father God. I welcome your suggestions.'

The Chairman began the response. 'We would never have guessed. You appear to be made of iron because you stand tall whenever you teach the Word of God and your voice carries smoothly throughout your teaching time. Some of us had been wondering how you were able to do these things, so we are comforted to know that you are just like us after all.'

'It is the Holy Spirit who keeps me going', Emilia replied. 'I rely on Him to give me the Father's message when I prepare and when I speak to the crowds. In the last few meetings I've been relying on the Holy Spirit to help me with the physical aspects too. That is why I've been able to keep standing and speaking His truth.'

One of the women on Committee said, 'Well, we can find you more comfortable shoes, and treatment for your feet, and a chair to speak from, for that matter.'

'I'd like to take you to my doctor for an examination of your vocal cords', said a well-to-do woman who had been concerned about Emilia's health for the past week. 'If he says we need to grant you rest, then the people of Hobart Town will have to accept the doctor's orders.'

Mr Brian Harris, a farmer sitting further around the table mentioned that four or five days a week he came into Town to deliver vegetables to the greengrocers.

'Mrs Baeyertz, I invite you and your children to come home with me for a few days. I 'spect you'd like the ride and your boy and girl would probably like the horses and my farm. Most of our animals are friendly to children and my girls would get some fun out of showing Charles and Marion around. Edna would be glad to provide meals and beds. She'd be even happier if you were interested in her garden. I'm mighty proud of that garden. Edna has put that much work into it, but not many people come to visit because we're not on a main road.' As he spoke, several other people commended Edna for her green thumb and the wide variety of plants she had established.

The Chairman offered, weather permitting, to take them up Mount Wellington to see the magnificent view of the town and the harbour.

The Secretary consulted his diary. 'There are six more meetings if we finish as planned on 3rd February. We will have to go ahead tomorrow because we don't have time to get the word out. However, it would be reasonable to cancel the meeting planned for this Thursday. We could ask Mrs Baeyertz which of the remaining three meetings she wants to lead and then finish on the 3rd.'

The gentleman who led the prayers at the meetings said, 'I've been praying for Mrs Baeyertz before each talk but my focus has been on her message. Now we will also pray for her physical needs. I won't tell the folk that she is feeling poorly, rather I'll remind them that standing still and speaking loudly for an hour is an effort.'

The Committee discussed further changes they could make. Those who'd offered to take Emilia to see specialists exchanged calling cards. The Chairman then closed in prayer, after a number of people had lifted Mrs Baeyertz to their loving God.

After thanking them sincerely for their concern, Emilia returned to her lodgings with a lighter heart. Mrs Edwards commented on the change she immediately recognised in her guest and enquired as to the source. Emilia told her about her sore feet and strained vocal cords. Mrs Edwards was aghast that her guest had felt constrained about admitting her problems. Mrs Baeyertz should have spoken up sooner because the hostess had a wealth of family remedies for these ailments. She did not think any less of the lady evangelist because she'd been privately wondering how anyone, even a worker for God, could speak to such crowds so frequently.

Towards the end of January, Emilia was overjoyed to hear that Mrs Sarah Perrin had arrived in Hobart Town.

Many residents of Tasmania had a deep sympathy for Mrs Perrin, because her husband, Mr Charles F. Perrin, had been working as an itinerant Bible teacher in northern Tasmania until he had died suddenly three years before. He'd only been 33 and had left Sarah with their children. Emilia could readily empathise with a woman whose husband had died unexpectedly of consumption and who was now a preacher with children.

When Emilia asked Mrs Edwards if she could invite Mrs Perrin for afternoon tea, the invitation was promptly issued.

On Sarah's arrival at the home of Mrs Edwards, Emilia greeted her like an old friend and introduced her to their hostess. Soon after, during tea and cake, Emilia showed Sarah a letter from the Association. It was an invitation to them both to speak in the same evangelistic meeting the following week. Their expenses would be covered.

Emilia looked at Sarah and said, 'I will always be happy to introduce people to Jesus. However, at this time I'm reluctant to speak for too long because I may lose my voice or become ill.'

Sarah replied, 'I know what it's like to have to project your voice into a crowded hall. However, I would be glad of the opportunity to inform people that my memoir of my husband will be published later this year. Whenever I am in this colony, people frequently tell me how his teaching changed their lives. Perhaps we could share the work? I preach to the converted and you address those yet to make a commitment.'

'That is an excellent idea', replied Mrs Baeyertz.

'In order to save your voice, Emilia, we'll ask the choir to present a special hymn and also lead us in a few more songs than they have done for your other meetings.'

Emilia happily agreed so they conveyed the plan to the Association.

Their meeting was held in the People's Hall. The choir was seated on the stage beside Emilia and Sarah and the audience filled every seat in the hall. Mrs Perrin received a hearty applause when she stepped up to the lectern. She announced her forthcoming memoir and spoke of the relationship between a Christian and Father God.

After the choir presented the special hymn, Mrs Baeyertz too received a warm welcome. Her appeal to the unconverted was interspersed with vivid anecdotes of how people had recognised they needed Jesus as their Saviour. The choir and congregation then sang several anthems with great enthusiasm. To conclude, Emilia invited those who wanted to know more to stay behind. About fifty people kept their seats while the ushers distributed leaflets to everyone else as they left the hall.

CHAPTER 61

Hobart Town
February to April 1878

THE FINAL MEETING OF THE SUMMER MISSION WAS ON THE EVENING of Sunday 3rd February as planned. The seats and standing places in the People's Hall were full, long before the start time. As Mrs Baeyertz addressed the crowd inside, a volunteer distributed 750 tracts with the story of her conversion to those turned away from the front door. He returned to the store room for another boxful to be prepared for the enquirers at the after-meeting.

Emilia felt an extra measure of the Lord's peace when she stood up to deliver her last message. In her preparations, she had examined the 'I will' sayings of Christ. She explained what she had learnt and concluded her talk with the 'I will of the sinner'. This was when a person realised the state of their spiritual life and decided, like the Prodigal Son, that 'I will arise and go.' At some point during her delivery, she sat down on a chair at the front of the stage. At the end of her talk, Emilia returned to a chair further back and the choir led the congregation in a final rousing hymn.

Before the final prayers were offered, the gentleman leading this evening's meeting explained to the audience that Mrs Baeyertz was in need of a good rest because she had toiled for a full month in the Lord's work.

He continued, 'Indeed the Holy Spirit has helped her with the message and with the ability to speak frequently in our large halls. The sacrifices she has made in her physical comfort show us the depth of her commitment to the spiritual well-being of our souls. Our spiritual lives will have far reaching consequences when compared with her sore feet. Nevertheless, you have seen how much Mrs Baeyertz has given to the people of Hobart Town. Pray then that God will restore Mrs Baeyertz to full health and keep her and her children safe on their travels around Tasmania.

'Before she leaves, Mrs Baeyertz has invited all those who have been converted during her mission to attend a gathering this Tuesday 5th. She would like to provide some ideas on how to grow in your faith in Jesus.

Ministers from the churches who have participated in this mission will also be in attendance to answer any questions and invite you to join their congregations.

'After a short rest, Mrs Baeyertz will visit some of the churches beyond Hobart Town. Next Sunday, Mrs Baeyertz will speak in Richmond. I expect she will be most interested to see the bridge that the convicts built in 1823. She has also been invited to return to New Town and O'Brien's Bridge to speak in their chapels. God willing, Mrs Baeyertz will also visit South Bruny Island, Port Esperance and New Norfolk, where she might speak in one of their large hop-picking fields.

'On behalf of the Association of Christian Workers, I wish to thank Mrs Baeyertz for all the work she has done for us during this summer mission. We have seen many remarkable ways in which God has used her to change the lives of the citizens of Hobart Town and, indeed, of much of southern Tasmania. Please accept this bouquet of flowers and a basket of products that have made this region famous.'

When the clapping subsided, he continued, 'Now I'll tell you about tonight's after-meeting and then we will pray for Mrs Baeyertz.'

Grasping the gifts, Emilia returned to her seat at the back of the stage, grateful that a competent man of God was going to conclude the meeting in such a way as to keep the audience thinking about their relationship with Jesus rather than wonder where she might go for her holiday. Her thoughts turned to Brian and Edna Harris who had invited her and the children to stay with their family. Since the Harris farm was not on a main road, she could look forward to receiving only a few visitors there.

As the last enquirer left the building, the volunteer with the tracts counted the remainder and so estimated that as many as three hundred people had been in the after-meeting. His fellow volunteers would later report that many others had opened their hearts to Jesus.

Charles and Marion adapted quickly to life on the Harris's farm. There were so many jobs to do. With the Harris children, they got up early in the morning to help collect chicken's eggs and milk the family cow and then go to school, knowing that there would be more tasks when they returned home each afternoon.

Edna had instructed Emilia that she was required to do neither house-work nor cooking. Neither was she to feel guilty for not helping with the household because Edna's sons and daughters shared the tasks. Emilia was encouraged to take naps, sit in the garden, read books and do her needlework.

After two weeks of rest, Emilia was able to travel to the nearby towns, as planned, and then return to Hobart Town for the Tuesday evening of 19th March. For the second time, she asked folk who had been converted to tell their stories of what God had done through the summer to draw them to Himself.

The parents of one family explained that they had brought one of their adult daughters to a meeting early in the month. She'd stayed for the after-meeting and was spoken to by a Christian sister who explained God's way of salvation. It pleased the Lord to open her eyes to the truth and the young woman accepted Jesus as her Saviour.

Those parents brought another daughter to the next meeting to listen to Mrs Baeyertz and she was converted. A third daughter was taken to a later meeting by her parents and she too claimed Jesus as her Saviour. The son was the only member of the family who was not yet a Christian. He went along to a meeting with his friends and listened carefully to the message. Later that night he gave his life to the Lord. The whole family was rejoicing in their new faith.

Other people explained that it was helpful to hear Mrs Baeyertz speak on a range of topics over the four weeks. Unbeknown to her, Mrs Baeyertz had dealt with their various objections to accepting Christ. A large number of men and women said they'd attended several meetings before they realised they had no more complaints about God's method of working in their lives.

Emilia realised that Father God often drew people to Himself through a series of encounters. A mission of several weeks was effective because people could attend numerous meetings and hear how the Good News addressed their different problems. On recognising the value of conducting a mission over many days, Emilia began to pray that He would show her how to remain healthy while doing such strenuous work.

Mrs Baeyertz and Mrs Perrin were not the only witnesses 'unto the utter-most part of the earth' that year. Mr Thomas Spurgeon, a son of Reverend Mr Charles Haddon Spurgeon of the Metropolitan Tabernacle in London, visited Tasmania in the early months. Another evangelist, 'Butcher' Varley of Lincolnshire, arrived in early autumn. Both men began their missions at the small town of Perth, south of Launceston, as guests of William and Mary Ann Gibson.

Mr Henry Varley had arrived in Tasmania with a fine reputation from his tour of Victoria. Emilia was as curious about his style of speaking as he was of her approach. The Association made arrangements for each to hear the other speak at public meetings and then invited them to meet for afternoon tea one day.

Over tea and cake, Mr Varley asked after her health and that of her children. They then compared experiences and found that they had spoken in the same churches and had common acquaintances. He assured Emilia that they were both preaching a similar message to that preached by the famous D. L. Moody in America and England.

'No doubt, Mr Varley, you will be pleased to hear that the Sankey and Moody hymn-book has been introduced to the churches here in Tasmania. Indeed, some of their hymns have been sung in my meetings.'

Henry replied, 'They will quickly become favourites. I have known Mr Moody for many years. Once, in Dublin, I happened to suggest to him that the world has yet to see what God will do with a man fully consecrated to Him. He has rather taken that to heart.'

On Friday 12th April, Emilia, Charles and Marion in turn hugged Mr and Mrs Harris, and their sons and daughters, and then turned to the Edwards family to embrace and thank them for their warm hospitality. The waiting train expelled some steam to hasten the farewells. After the family had climbed aboard and waved their final goodbyes, the train pulled out of the station on its journey to Launceston.

Earlier, at the farewell morning tea, Emilia had asked her friends in the Association to pray once again that, after a few talks in the north of the colony, she would get ample rest before sailing home to Melbourne in a week or so.

CHAPTER 62

Launceston, Tasmania
April 1878

SOME WEEKS LATER, HER FRIENDS IN HOBART TOWN WERE SURPRISED to read that Emilia had not yet left Tasmania. Her planned public meeting at the Launceston Public Gardens that Sunday afternoon had led to many more. That meeting had been advertised as chiefly for children and young people, but people of any age were welcome to attend. Some twelve hundred people of all ages squeezed into the spacious Pavilion. Those who could not find any room inside had remained outside rather than return home. A large offering was taken up.

The following day, *The Examiner* wrote of Mrs Baeyertz, 'She has a very pleasing appearance, and speaks in a sufficiently distinct tone of voice to be heard by a large assemblage'.

When they were at home in Melbourne the previous year, Marion had begun cutting out articles from *The Argus* and other papers about her mother's talks because it was special to find their name 'Baeyertz' in print. During the weeks in Hobart Town, Marion had cut out many articles about the summer mission from *The Mercury* and the Christian paper *Willing Work*. Once they learnt of Marion's hobby, her hosts in Launceston read their newspapers promptly to make them available for her.

On the morning of the following Wednesday, their hosts showed Marion a letter in *The Examiner*. She then showed it to her mother.

> 'Sir, —Have our ministers in town become superannuated that we actually need women from a distance to come and preach to us? ... I think Mrs Baeyertz and others of the same stamp should be "keepers at home", their proper sphere, and endeavour to train their children in the fear of God.' ...

Emilia looked up to see concerned faces watching her. She said, 'This is the very reason why I hesitated to accept invitations to speak to men and women in public meetings. It is also why I brought you children with me; I am acutely aware of my responsibility as your mother.'

Marion asked, 'Why should that man be upset at you speaking here? These other articles have mostly liked your message.'

Emilia stretched out her hand and pulled Marion to her side. 'Some people don't like ladies preaching. They say that a lady's job is to stay at home to look after her children and husband. I quite agree that a woman must care for her family but God wants me to tell men and women about Jesus too. I have to obey our Loving Father. I am quite tired and I could easily be upset by this letter. I won't take it to heart though. We saw the crowds of people who crammed into the Pavilion and into the Mechanics Institute to hear my messages. I also know God has blessed people because I obeyed Him.'

Their host said, 'I'm glad you have taken that approach. While it may be said that many of the people who went to the Pavilion were curious to see a woman preaching, you are not the first lady to visit us this year. You will know, I'm sure, Mrs Perrin was here.'

'Indeed, Sarah and I preached together in Hobart Town. So many people stayed for the after-meeting that we felt sure God had used their curiosity to let us show them how Jesus could meet their needs.'

That evening, Mrs Baeyertz spoke at the first of two meetings for women only, in Mr Price's Tamar Street Congregational Church. The seats filled quickly at the beginning and emptied slowly at the end. Some women got halfway to their homes before they returned to the after-meeting.

The Baeyertz family accepted an invitation, from Mr Henry Reed, Esq., and his wife Margaret, to spend a short time at their property before Emilia gave her last address in Launceston.

When their carriage arrived at Wesley Dale, forty miles to the west, Emilia was astonished to see Mr Reed come out of Mountain Villa to greet them. She had heard of his wealth and generous support of evangelists and new churches, but she had not expected that a man of such great stature would be so humble as to greet them before they had alighted from their carriage.

When the time came for the Baeyertz family to return to Launceston, all three were reluctant to leave the home in which they had experienced much affection. Henry and Margaret promised that Emilia and her children were welcome to visit whenever they were in northern Tasmania.

The Baeyertz family then went to Deloraine, thirty miles west of Launceston, where Emilia spoke at four meetings in the Town Hall.

At last, on Friday 3rd May, Henry Varley and Marion, Charles and Emilia Baeyertz boarded the *Mangana* at Launceston. From the deck they waved at their new friends gathered on the wharf. These folk had shown the depth of their gratitude for the work of the evangelists by coming to bid them farewell. As the ship left the wharf those assembled sang three of Ira Sankey's hymns.

The Reverend Dr Alexander Somerville and his son visited Tasmania that June. They discovered that their role was to follow on from Mrs Baeyertz and four other evangelists who had toured the island colony that year. They were not the pioneers that they had expected to be. Nevertheless, they had come all the way from Glasgow to the other side of the world, so they completed their mission in the colony.

CHAPTER 63

Melbourne
Winter and Spring 1878

EMILIA, CHARLES AND MARION RESUMED THEIR DAILY ROUTINES AT home. Charles and Marion each had plenty of stories to tell at their schools.

Now that she had time to consider her work in Hobart Town and Launceston, Emilia pondered what had been most successful so she could better prepare for future ministry. She decided that after-meetings would be an essential part of each public address. It was important to allow enquirers to speak to an experienced Christian who lived in the same community. She would also hold a special meeting for new converts only after her last public meeting.

She could develop a variety of talks that would suit each phase of a mission. By repeating her talks, the content would remain fixed in her memory. This would allow her to refine her delivery, extemporise and select illustrations to suit. For each new audience, she would learn of the local concerns by reading newspapers and consulting the committee before her presentations.

Her exhaustion during the month-long mission in Hobart Town taught her to pace herself. She would make the Saturdays days of rest. Emilia also decided to hold missions by the coast during the summer months, where the sea breezes would benefit everyone—and she could go for a swim most mornings.

Back in Melbourne, Emilia visited factory workers in their lunch hours. She also taught at women-only Bible Classes, on the first Wednesday evening of every month, in the Assembly Hall in Collins Street.

Both of those ministries were carried out during the working week, so Emilia found she was free to visit churches on the weekends. On a Sunday in August, she spoke at St Kilda Town Hall to both the unconverted and also the faithful. She presented a new talk about the seven cries of Jesus on the cross and gave a vivid portrayal of His crucifixion. Having shown what Christ suffered to redeem them, Emilia asked, 'What shall we do with this

Jesus called Christ?' She urged non-believers to make a decision now as none of them knew what would happen tomorrow. She also challenged believers to give up worldly ways that were stumbling blocks to others.

CHAPTER 64

Tasmania and Victoria
Summer to Winter 1879

THE FOLLOWING SUMMER, THE FAMILY RETURNED TO TASMANIA where Emilia spoke in the crowded halls of Hobart Town for a month. She used her new talk about the seven cries of Jesus in some of her meetings.

Her first talk in Launceston was held in the Mechanics Institute Hall on Regatta Day, Tuesday 25th February. This public holiday was popular among the people because it offered entertainment outdoors. The aquatic events on the Tamar River and the country fair beside it were ample diversions for town folk to spend the whole summer day by the water.

Some used the public holiday to attend to spiritual matters. At the Hall, Mrs Baeyertz spoke of her affection for the residents of Launceston. During the previous months she'd longed to return to Launceston to be with them. Her text for her teaching was the word 'Come' as it was used in God's invitation to believers in the Gospel of Luke. After she had spent two weeks teaching in various venues, her family returned to Melbourne.

That May, Emilia received an invitation from the Sandhurst United Prayer Meeting to be their guest speaker for a three-week mission during July. The letter explained that the mission was supported by several churches in the central Victorian town. Emilia accepted their invitation. She considered that Sandhurst was to be her first 'proper' mission. It would provide her with an opportunity to apply the lessons she'd learnt in Tasmania.

She entered into correspondence with the Secretary of the group and approved of their programme. She agreed to speak at three meetings a week: on Sunday afternoons and on Wednesday and Friday evenings.

In July, Emilia and Marion travelled by train to central Victoria. Emilia was encouraged by the enthusiasm she found in the Mission Committee of the Prayer Meeting. It was clear they had been praying earnestly for God's blessings and that they'd advertised the meetings within Sandhurst and in the hamlets of the surrounding country. They had reserved the Masonic Hall for all the meetings because it was reputed to seat 700 people.

A crowd of about 800, which included a section set aside for members of the Jewish community, filled the hall at the first meeting on the afternoon of Sunday 6th July. Similar crowds occupied the hall in subsequent meetings. The Committee was pleased to accept offers of other halls that could seat larger audiences.

Emilia also led a meeting for women only and a separate session for children in the Masonic Hall. She gave the youngsters three texts to remember based on the first three letters of the alphabet. The first bible passage was 'All we, like sheep, have gone astray', the second was 'Behold the Lamb of God' and the third was 'Come unto Me all ye that are weary and heavy laden'. A great many children stayed behind to attend the after-meeting and several professed to be saved.

At the meeting for women, towns-folk were astonished to see twelve hundred women and girls fill the Masonic Hall and the large number of late comers who were turned away. Never before had Sandhurst seen so many women gathered in the one place. Mrs Baeyertz addressed her audience about the word 'Come' in the Bible. She chose the passages 'Come into the ark', 'Come unto me and rest' and 'Let him that is athirst come'. She also gave thrilling anecdotes about how God had worked in women's lives. At the end of the meeting about one hundred women and girls stood up to show they were seeking the Lord.

The Friday evening meeting, on the 18th, was held in the Wesleyan Church in Forest Street which could seat 1,200 people. Half an hour before the meeting commenced, Emilia invited several Christian women to pray with her in the Vestry. God answered their prayers for a special blessing that night—so many men and women wished to have a personal conversation about their souls that they filled the vestry for the after-meeting.

The mission committee was grateful that Mrs Baeyertz was willing to accept invitations on some of the days she had set aside for rest. She agreed to speak at the Princess Theatre on the Sunday afternoon of 20th July. The 2,200 seats filled quickly and more people sat on steps and stood in vacant spaces, so eager were they to hear Mrs Baeyertz. Half an hour before the advertised commencement time the doors had to be locked.

On Thursday, Emilia preached the Gospel at the Presbyterian Church in Eaglehawk. The following night at the Masonic Hall, she gave her address about the seven cries of our Lord Jesus Christ on the cross.

Many people had travelled long distances to attend the Sunday afternoon meetings during the mission, but some were unable to get seats in the Hall. So that as many people as possible could attend at least one meeting, Emilia gave an extra talk on the final Sunday.

More than two hundred people professed to having received God's new life during the three weeks of mission. Members of the Mission Committee spoke with them. Those whose faith was considered authentic were given tickets, bearing their names, to attend the meeting for new believers. On arriving at the meeting, the following day, their tickets were given to ministers from the church that the converts had previously attended. In this way, the new Christians would receive spiritual food and encouragement to continue on in their faith and the churches happily supported the mission.

During the meeting for new believers, Emilia identified Bible passages that gave practical advice about living as Christians and drew their attention to a booklet about the power to overcome sin through Christ.

The Reverend Mr Gregson, a missionary recently returned from India, described many things that new believers there gave up when they became followers of Jesus. When compared to their sacrifices, the self-denial Christians had to practice in Sandhurst was a mere trifle.

Over subsequent months, Emilia developed a number of talks that she could present whether the missions were for one day, ten days, a fortnight or three weeks. After travelling by train to wherever she had been invited, she would make the most of the available days and then rest awhile between missions. Several times, when she was unwell or tired, local evangelists substituted for her.

Longer missions often featured lengthy lectures on Tuesday and Thursday evenings. The ticketed meeting for new believers became known as the 'testimony meeting', often on the Monday or Tuesday after the two final meetings on Sunday. Some meetings were for women and girls only. Evening talks addressed the complexity of the Christian life. Weekday afternoons were often devoted to Bible Readings, where Emilia would read and expound her chosen texts.

CHAPTER 65

Melbourne
Spring 1879

FOR THE LATTER HALF OF 1879, EMILIA INFORMED HER SUPPORTERS IN Melbourne that she would not travel for a while. Instead, she would hold her meetings for women weekly on Wednesday evenings, rather than monthly. The pastors and friends who had a high regard for Emilia's teaching skills hired the Assembly Hall for the meetings which would start at 7.00 p. m.

Soon, Emilia was regularly speaking to 150 women each week. At the start of October, the congregation was told that they may not be meeting at the Assembly Hall for much longer, because the rental rates had recently been increased. At the end of October, Mrs Baeyertz and the women arrived at the Assembly Hall to find it locked; they had expected to use the hall for one last time that evening. There had been a misunderstanding.

Fortunately a member of the crowd was able to direct the women to the building of the Young Men's Christian Association, to which she had a key. Mrs Baeyertz could present the talk she'd prepared about 'Christian Steadfastness'. At the end of the meeting the women were invited to return to the YMCA the following week, by which time new arrangements would have been made.

The supporters of Mrs Baeyertz considered her teaching ministry so valuable that they would not let it cease. A new home was found at the Protestant Hall in Stephen Street, at the eastern end of the city. People who wished to contribute money towards the rent of the hall were asked to take their donations to the nearby Tract Repository office at 113 Russell Street.

CHAPTER 66

Tasmania and Victoria
Summer 1879 to Winter 1880

ONCE AGAIN, EMILIA SPENT THE SUMMER IN TASMANIA, PREACHING IN the communities of Hobart Town and Sandy Bay. In March, Emilia was found in the north speaking in Deloraine and Longford.

After Emilia returned home to Caulfield, her sister visited to tell her that their father had written from England to ask for help now that their mother had recently passed way. Eliza and Abraham would be the ones to make the move Home.

A notice appeared in *Willing Work* informing readers that Mrs Baeyertz's Wednesday night meetings for women would recommence. The first meeting would start at 7.30 p. m. on 12th May at the Assembly Hall, in Collins Street. Christians who prayed for this mid-week ministry were invited to donate towards the rent of the Assembly Hall. Her work was not supported by any particular organisation, but funded only by her friends and the collection plates. Donations could again be left at the office of the Tract Repository.

In May, Emilia was delighted to receive a letter from her old friend Pastor Chris Bunning. He had baptised her by immersion at the old Aberdeen Street Baptist Church during her time in Geelong. Now he was inviting her to lead a two-week mission in their new building.

Mrs Baeyertz was warmly welcomed back. People from all social classes came to listen to her Gospel addresses. Many people told Pastor Bunning that they'd never heard the truth so plainly put before them. He wrote in *Willing Work* that, 'The most powerful impressions on the people have been made by simple statements of doctrinal truth enforced by scriptural illustration'. In the same article, Pastor Bunning also commended Emilia to all the churches in Victoria: 'We think that our sister belongs to and should receive encouragement and support from every denomination of Christians in Victoria. We believe that in a short time this will be the case, for we hear of many applications for her services which will be made.'

On the evening of Sunday 18th July, the throng in the new church building was so great that people were nearly crushed. Mrs Baeyertz completed her talk and then spoke to people as needed. She then walked two doors down to another waiting congregation at the old church and presented her talk again. Many stayed behind to be reassured.

While in the Corio Bay region, Emilia spoke to two meetings at Queenscliff before briefly resting by the sea.

In mid-August, she proceeded north to receive enthusiastic greetings from the people of Ballarat. Most of these meetings occurred in the Baptist Church which held between 900 and 1,000 people. The school room could only accommodate 250 to hear her Bible Readings. When the Sunday evening meeting was conducted at the Academy of Music, which seated 2,300, so great was the press of people in the street that the police had to close the road to traffic. At the end of the fortnight, Mr William Clark, pastor of the Baptist Church, was given the names of 140 people who professed to have been led to Jesus through the ministry of Mrs Baeyertz.

CHAPTER 67

Adelaide, South Australia
Spring 1880

PASTOR BUNNING REPRESENTED THE VICTORIAN BAPTIST UNION AT the South Australian Baptist Association Annual Meeting, held from 14th to 16th September. In his report, he spoke highly of Mrs Baeyertz. He listed many ministries she'd undertaken in the name of Jesus, both in Geelong and Melbourne. He also described the great blessings that had accompanied her recent mission in Geelong. Mr Bunning felt sure that Mrs Baeyertz would consent to visit Adelaide for a mission, if invited.

On the morning of Friday 17th, forty or fifty ladies and gentlemen of the Association travelled to Mount Lofty for a picnic at the generous invitation of Mr Fowler. There, the gentlemen held an open air conference on the topic of evangelisation and decided to invite Mrs Baeyertz to conduct a mission in Adelaide for as long as her strength would permit.

When she received the telegram, Emilia calculated that, by travelling on ships that regularly sailed between the colonies, she could conduct a three-week mission in Adelaide and still be home before Christmas.

When Emilia and Marion arrived in Adelaide in mid-November, they found the leaders of the Baptist Association to be pleasant and organised but lacking zeal. Emilia wondered why these folk were half-hearted because the meeting halls were crowded with people. She prayed and left the matter in her Father's hands while she persevered in preaching about Jesus the Christ.

Meetings for mixed audiences and for women only were held in the city at the Town Hall and at Flinders Street Baptist Church. The North Adelaide Baptist Church also hosted Mrs Baeyertz. Large congregations attended every meeting and some people stayed behind at the end of meetings in response to Emilia's challenges.

At one of the meetings for a mixed audience at the Adelaide Town Hall, so many people came to hear Mrs Baeyertz that a great crowd was still on the stairs when the meeting began. They could not hear the proceedings but remained in the foyers of the ground and first floors, hoping for an opportunity to experience her ministry. When the congregation vacated the large hall at the end of the meeting, the waiting crowd refilled the seats. There was no alternative; Emilia had to give her talk for a second time. She rejoiced that twice as many people entered the Kingdom of God that day than she'd hoped for.

As was now her usual practice, Mrs Baeyertz held a meeting for the converts on the last evening of her mission. About 120 people were admitted by ticket to the Lecture Hall of the Flinders Street Baptist Church. After tea, a meeting was held in the adjoining church where Mrs Baeyertz spoke and the converts were also invited to give a public testimony. Pastor Silas Mead and two local men welcomed the new believers and invited them to join their churches.

On the morning of Thursday 9th December, Emilia stood with her new friends from Adelaide on the wharf. The Secretary of the Mission Committee gave Emilia a letter and said, 'Please consider when you can return to us again'. Emilia passed the envelope to Marion and turned her attention to the ladies who wanted to thank her. One woman described to Mrs Baeyertz the great joy she had experienced during the mission and said she spoke for others too. Her friends smiled warmly and agreed.

Emilia and Marion waved farewell until they could no longer see their friends from the ship. They then searched for comfortable seats out of the wind and Marion opened the envelope and gave the letter to her mother.

Emilia unfolded it and read aloud to Marion.

> 'We cannot allow you to leave our shores today without
> giving expression to our sincere and grateful appreciation
> of your visit amongst us. On our part there have been grave
> shortcomings. We have had before today evangelists in our
> city, and we have not always been able to look on their work
> with full satisfaction. That was to your disadvantage on your
> arrival, and we did not enter with you on your work with that
> degree of expectant sanguine faith with which we ought to
> have co-operated with you.'

She silently read the remainder of the letter then gave a summary to Marion.

'The Mission Committee eagerly hopes that I will speak around Adelaide in addition to the country districts of South Australia. They promise to share the burdens of the mission with me. They want me to return as soon as the summer is over.

'I've committed myself to a two-week mission in Launceston at the start of February next year. I expect to spend the whole month in that region. I have some letters on my desk inviting me to visit towns in western Victoria. I've hesitated to reply because some are beyond the reach of the railway. We'll have to go there by ship.'

'Tarryever is in western Victoria, isn't it?' When Emilia nodded yes, Marion continued, 'Will we have the time to meet Nancy and Martin on a return trip to Adelaide? That would be exciting.'

Her mother replied, 'Actually, this is our best opportunity as Tarryever is quite close to Portland. Perhaps we could visit after I speak at the Port of Belfast? We'll look at the map and the calendar when we arrive home and enquire of our friends and family who have travelled that way.'

The sound of a loud wave smashing against the ship interrupted their conversation. Emilia tucked the letter into her purse and looked up to see Marion trying to stand. 'We should probably stay in our seats at the moment; it sounds like the sea is rougher than usual. Let's watch the waves from here.'

CHAPTER 68

Melbourne
January 1881

BEFORE DEPARTING FOR LAUNCESTON, EMILIA MADE MANY ENQUIRIES about moving a family to Adelaide. George explained how best to transport trunks between the colonies. Emilia then advised the Mission Committee in Adelaide that she accepted their invitation to return. Emilia also replied to the churches at Warrnambool, Belfast, Koroit and Stawell with a proposed itinerary. Next, she wrote to Nancy who promptly replied.

> My dear Emilia,
>
> Thank you for your recent letter which I read aloud to Martin, little realising the startling effect it would have upon the man. Would you believe that he actually jumped up from his chair? He cried out, 'If she's going to be at Belfast and Warrnambool, we must have her stop here to speak to the people of Tarryever and district!' He insisted that I write to you immediately to invite you to come here to take meetings, at the same time assuring you that a welcome of huge proportions awaits you. He is convinced that by the time you arrive we will have sent notices to villages near and far and a great crowd of people will come to hear the famous Mrs Baeyertz. We get the Melbourne papers here, even if they are several days late, and a number of people have commented on the stories about 'Mrs Baeyertz, the Lady Evangelist'.
>
> So my dear friend, as you see, I have done as I was told, and must add that Will and Tommy are already looking forward to your coming. As for the children attending my school—they have heard so much about you that I'm afraid they will be expecting someone larger than life. Please do not disappoint them! I hardly like to mention others such as

myself, whom you may not wish to disappoint, but there, now I have done it.

We eagerly wait to hear the most convenient time for you to come.

Very affectionately,

Nancy

CHAPTER 69

Melbourne
Early March 1881

EMILIA SAT DOWN AT HER DESK WITH THE MORNING'S MAIL. A FEW days earlier she had returned from Launceston. She now had to prepare for her long journey to the west.

As she considered the many things to do, Emilia caught a movement from the corner of her eye. She swung round in her chair and saw that it was Charles who had entered the room. She held out her hand to him, for she knew that he liked to seek her out when she was alone, and she wanted him to know that he was always welcome.

'Come, Charles', she said, pushing the envelopes from her. 'Bring a chair and sit here by me.' Emilia turned her back to her crowded desk; her correspondence would have to wait. 'I'm glad you've come here for I have wanted to speak with you about school. You celebrated your fourteenth birthday last December so you could go away to boarding school if that is what you would like. What do you think of that?'

Emilia thought she had caught a mulish expression, but could not be sure, for her son had his head down, studying his boots. 'What I would like most of all is to live with you, Mama.'

'Well, Charles, my first preference would be to have you and Marion with me. I've been making plans to return to "The City of Churches". That will keep me away from home for months, maybe longer. I wondered if we could work out something so we could be with each other during that time.'

Seeing that she now had his full attention, she went on. 'If you can attend a good boarding school in South Australia, we would be able to see one another from time to time whereas, if you waited for me in Melbourne ... ' Her shoulders rose and fell.

'I wrote to two boarding schools in Adelaide that were recommended while we were there; they have each replied with a prospectus. Mr Boehm's School is in Hahndorf, a Lutheran settlement in the hills nearby. He teaches in English to German immigrants. He has a fine reputation as a music teacher.

The other option is Prince Alfred College which is like Wesley College and close to the City of Adelaide. Do you like the idea of coming with me?'

His head was up now and there was a smile. 'Yes please, Mama. A boarding school near you would be better than a school here.'

Emilia pulled two envelopes from a pile of papers. Each displayed a school crest. 'Tell me what you think of these.'

'I plan to find a school for Marion too. She is quickly learning the skills of a young lady.'

As she smiled back at him, she was silently thanking her Lord for the gift of this precious son. When Charles left to tell his sister the news, she watched him until he was lost to her view then turned, with a small sigh, back to her letters.

CHAPTER 70

Tarryever
May 1881

THEY BEGAN THE DAY AT BELFAST AND TRAVELLED BY SEA TO PORT-land. Charles and Marion were excited because they were going to Tarryever. When they stepped onto the wharf, the children heard their mother gasp. She was staring at the young man who was walking towards them.

'Tommy Blackland, you are so tall! Why am I so surprised? Perhaps it's because the last time we saw one another, you were eight years old.'

The children were delighted with Tommy's entertaining stories and songs during the long wagon trip to Tarryever. There, Tommy introduced them to children of their own ages. Then he took Emilia and the children to the Langmores' home where Emilia hugged Nancy and Martin.

The women said they felt that the years had melted away and they had only just left Eliza's house in St Kilda. Charles and Marion were excited to meet Nancy—she wasn't just a make-believe story that their mother had kept up to amuse them. Nancy, in her turn, was just as pleased to meet these children of whom she'd heard so much. She made arrangements for Marion and Charles to attend some of the classes she would teach during the days to come.

After dinner, once Emilia had tucked Marion and Charles into bed, she drew her chair up to the bright fire that had been thoughtfully lit in their bedroom and allowed her thoughts to take her back over the long day. Then, before weariness overtook her, Emilia reached for her Bible and began her evening devotions.

Residents of Tarryever and district set aside their usual Sunday afternoon tasks to go to the meeting at which the lady evangelist would speak. It was not often that a famous stranger visited the region so they meant to make the most of the event. Quite a number of people arrived early so they could get a good seat.

From the vantage point of her chair on the podium, Emilia watched people enter by the door at the back of the community hall. They would each pause to accept a hymn-book, look for an empty seat, then walk there and sit down.

When the hands stood at ten to two on the clock face, three groups of men walked through the door. She recognised one group as the Blackland men. Will walked over to the back of the hall but was stopped from sitting down by Tommy. She saw him say something to his father and point to the front rows of seats. Will replied to Tommy and sat down at the back.

At five minutes to, Martin stood up from his seat, beside Nancy in the second row, walked up to the podium, climbed the stairs and stood beside their pastor who was visiting for the day. Their pianist, who had been playing tunes to familiar hymns, calculated how she could finish playing at exactly two o'clock.

Out of the corner of her eye, Emilia noticed that Will was following Tommy down to the front. They slipped into the second row and sat down beside Nancy. Emilia wondered why they'd moved, since Will had been reluctant to sit at the front. She would have to find a way to speak with him.

The pastor welcomed everyone who had come to the meeting then called on Dr Langmore to introduce Mrs Baeyertz. Martin told stories of first meeting her on *Empire of Peace*, how she had become an itinerant evangelist and how God had used her ministry to bless others. The pastor then invited everyone to stand for the first hymn.

Singing from memory, Emilia picked up her Bible and notes from the seat beside her. After she placed them on the lectern, she looked out at her audience. Most people were watching the newcomer with curiosity, but some seemed uncomfortable in her gaze. One of them was Will.

Forty minutes later, Emilia sat down in her chair. The pastor introduced the last hymn and explained that those who had questions were welcome to stay behind. Dr Langmore and other counsellors would stay at the front of the hall with Mrs Baeyertz and he would farewell all at the door.

Mrs Baeyertz returned to the lectern and gave an impassioned call to repentance. Her challenge caused some in the crowd to dab their eyes with pretty handkerchiefs, while others lifted their voices in praise for Jesus the Saviour.

The pastor proclaimed the meeting closed and recessed to the back door. Most people stayed in their seats to think, or to whisper to their companions. The pianist replayed the tune of the last hymn while Emilia walked down the stairs to join the counsellors.

Several people came forward and were intercepted before they could reach Emilia. She took advantage of the lull and leant across the first row of seats to ask Will if she could speak to him that night. Tommy, sitting by his father, asked if he could speak to her. They agreed to meet at the Langmore's home after dinner.

Emilia sat down at the dining table and placed her Bible beside her. Will and Tommy chose chairs opposite her. The happy voices of Marion and Charles talking with Mr and Mrs Langmore in the neighbouring room drifted into the tense atmosphere at the table.

'Thank you very much for agreeing to talk to me this evening, Will. I noticed that you seemed uncomfortable during the meeting this afternoon and I expect you are uneasy about being here too.'

'I'm here because Tommy asked me to come along. I don't believe in God or Jesus or in heaven or anything like that. Tommy will choose for himself what he believes, but can't expect me to follow.'

Tommy saw an opportunity. 'I went to Sunday school when I was a boy and now I go to church to hear Uncle Martin preach. You said some new things about following Jesus tonight.'

'Well, I'm happy to discuss them, but first I'd like to ask your father why he doesn't believe.'

'I'm angry at God because he could have kept my wife alive after she gave birth to Tommy. The doctor came to see Sally and the midwife kept her alive for two days. I prayed as hard as I could that God would make Sally better but she died in my arms. I didn't understand why God had let that happen after all I'd done to be a Christian. I'd obeyed the Ten Commandments and gone to church most Sundays. The Bible lies when it says that we can pray anything we want to and God will answer our prayers. After that, I couldn't see the point of reading the Bible and going to church.'

Emilia's heart was deeply touched by his despairing tone. She herself had spent days at her husband's grave asking God why the man she loved more than life itself was taken from her. 'You are clearly distressed and miss her deeply.'

'I'd hoped that by coming to Victoria, I'd stop thinking about Sally. We've been here for seventeen years now, but I still think about her most nights.'

'Oh Father. I didn't know you were still so sad about Mother', said Tommy. He reached across to touch his father's hand.

Emilia said, 'You can't ever stop thinking about the person you loved so much. The pain I had when Charlie died has become a dull ache, and there are still times when my memories of him are very clear.'

Will replied, 'When I see other women caring for their husbands and children, I remember the way Sally looked after me. She did a lot of things to prepare for our baby. She made clothes for you, Tommy, to wear when you'd just been born. She made other clothes for when you were older. Every time I dressed you I cried because I remembered how much Sally had wanted a child.' This time, Will reached across to touch Tommy's hand.

Emilia said, 'I don't understand why God allows such dreadful things to happen in our lives, Will. For reasons that are hidden from us, the Lord took Sally to be with Him. But He did not leave either of you on your own. Will, he gave you the gift of a son in Tommy, and to Tommy he gave a loving father. Will, I have seen evidence of how well you have cared for Tommy. He has grown into a kind and thoughtful young man.'

Will asked, 'Are you talking about that wagon ride home from Portland?'

'Yes. I've thought about our travel that day and I realise that Tommy deliberately found ways to distract Charles and Marion. He could guess that the trip would be too long for them if we had just sat and looked at the scenery.'

Tommy said, 'I have to go into Portland often. I need to keep myself interested to stay awake on such a long trip.'

'Well, you certainly succeeded yesterday. The children didn't have time to get bored. We've lived in a city for so long that the children were eager to learn anything you could tell them about the country. I was also amazed at your patience with them. Thank you so much for all you did to get us here safely and happily.'

Tommy smiled, 'I was pleased when Martin asked if I could meet you at the wharf yesterday, because Nancy had told us so much about you ever since we last saw you in Melbourne.'

'We can talk more tomorrow, Tommy. For now, let me talk to your father. God gave you to each other and more valuable gifts can scarcely be imagined. It is this same God who has given you and me, in fact the whole world, the gift of His Son. Father God knows what a precious possession a son can be. How much more is this true where His Son is concerned, His Son who can be our Redeemer from sin? I'm aware that the things I've said tonight may not change your thinking straight away, Will. You have held a grudge against God for so many years. That habit will be difficult to change. I'm going to pray that God will soften your heart and help you to see the things He has done for you because He loves you.

Before she prayed, Emilia said, 'Will, I'd like to have a longer talk about that passage in Matthew chapter 21 when Jesus says, "If you believe, you will receive whatever you ask for in prayer". If you are happy to do that, can you find the time in the next few days?'

Will said he would be pleased to and suggested that they all turn in for the night. Emilia agreed. 'We all need to think over these things. Let me hold your hands while I pray for you.'

The following day Emilia was glad to see Will and Tommy eagerly enter the hall for her second meeting. They quickly found seats up the front beside Nancy. Before the meeting began, Tommy leant forward and told Emilia that he and his father had talked long into the night about many hurts and joys. An even stronger bond was forged between them and now they wanted to hear what she had to say about Jesus.

Compared with those in Launceston, the audiences at Tarryever were small. Still, more people had come together in the hall than had for many years. Emilia reminded herself that it was not the size of the crowds that counted for eternity, but the genuineness of heart of those who committed themselves to the Lord. She was pleased that in the early meetings, most of those who were counselled showed evidence of a desire for an earnest relationship with the Lord.

At one of her later meetings, both Will and Tommy stayed behind for instruction. Emilia made sure she spoke with Will herself and rejoiced with him when he was drawn into a saving relationship with Jesus. Both father and son soon showed a splendid witness to the men among whom they worked and proved an encouragement to many.

Before Will set off with the Baeyertz family and the mailbag to Portland so both could catch the train to Ararat and Stawell, Emilia found time to write one last letter.

> My dear Eliza and Abraham,
>
> If you have written with news from Home, I haven't seen it yet. Your letters will have been forwarded to Adelaide. I will write to you from South Australia with my new address when I know it.
>
> How can I possibly describe to you the welcome that was waiting for us here at Tarryever? Suffice to say Charles, Marion and I were left in no doubt that our visit had been longed for over many months. The excitement, when we were driven up to the house at dusk, overflowed in abundance. The next day, the welcoming party included people of every age, some having come great distances, and a right royal time we had of it! Decorations were much in evidence, and so was food of every kind, though why such a fuss should have been made at all, I dared not ask.
>
> The children were as pleased to finally meet the fabled Nancy and Martin, as Nancy and Martin were to meet them.
>
> It was sheer delight to see dear Nancy again. It was a pleasure to see how well she and her cousin Will and his son Tommy have all adapted to the life that is available in the country. They have no regrets in making Tarryever their home and they are only sorry that more of their relatives have not had opportunities to migrate to Victoria.
>
> When we were all passengers on *Empire of Peace*, Tommy was a boy. He has matured into a capable young man and does his father proud.
>
> I had the pleasure once again of shaking the hand of Dr Martin Langmore. You'll remember I told you of Martin,

the doctor on our ship. He accepted a position as doctor in Dungower and that's when he renewed his friendship with Nancy. They were married the same year Marion and I moved to Caulfield.

It was Martin who was the moving force behind the meetings here. I have enjoyed speaking because they have been well organised and everyone is most interested.

Our time here is not all taken up with meetings. We are being driven about the countryside to view the many beauties of the place—lakes, mountains and river lands. It will not be easy for us to leave, but I promised to visit Stawell on our way to Adelaide.

The children asked me to send you their love. I add my love for you too.

Your affectionate sister,

Emilia

Emilia put her folded letter and a note from Nancy into an envelope addressed to Eliza in Edgbaston in England. As she was about to seal it, there came a knock on the door of her room. In response to her call of, 'Come!' the door opened to admit Nancy.

'Oh, I am glad it's you. I was about to go looking for you, as you have the mailbag.' Not until she had finished speaking did Emilia notice that her friend was not her usual smiling self. 'Sit down, Nancy. Is something the matter?'

Nancy sat as she was bid, her eyes downcast, and for a while she was silent. But then at last she said, 'I have to speak to you for if anyone can help me, you can'. Only then did she lift her eyes briefly to meet those of her friend, and it was plain to Emilia that she was deeply troubled.

'I will help you in any way I can. You know that, Nancy. Just tell me what I am to do.'

Once again Nancy's eyes evaded hers as she said in a low voice, 'It may be that not even you will be able to help me.'

Emilia spoke more sharply than she intended. 'How am I to know whether I can help you or not if you do not tell me your difficulty?'

Nancy raised her head at last and began hesitantly. 'Emilia, you know that I have attended every one of your meetings here. I have listened carefully to each word and I have been forced to the conclusion that I am not acceptable to God the Father!'

Emilia was stunned. 'Why not, Nancy?'

Emilia, waiting for her answer, saw Nancy dissolve into tears and, when she did speak, her words were interspersed with sobs. 'I have drifted far from the Lord. I don't read my Bible, haven't done for years, and I pray only when I particularly want something, which is not often. The Lord was once very real to me, Emilia, but not now. I seem to have lost my way! Help me! My father was a fine Christian gentleman and Martin is too. I want to be my father's daughter in the truest sense, worthy of him and of Martin too. I know I've not been that for a very long time.'

Emilia went to kneel by Nancy's side. 'But that can all be remedied, Nancy, if you are sincere in your desire to be restored to the Lord.'

'There is nothing I want more desperately, Emilia!'

Her friend reached for her Bible and, as she turned the pages, said, 'What I want to show you is here in 1 John, chapter one from verse seven: "If we walk in the light as he is in the light, we have fellowship one with another", meaning, of course, that we have fellowship with Him, "and the blood of Jesus Christ his Son cleanseth us from all sin. If we say that we have no sin, we deceive ourselves, and the truth is not in us. If we confess our sins, he is faithful and just to forgive us our sins, and to cleanse us from all unrighteousness." So there it is, Nancy. Nothing could be plainer, and you do not need to wait for me to tell you what you must do.'

Now when their eyes met, there was a dawning of hope in Nancy's eyes, and when she bowed her head this time, it was so that she might speak to her Lord in prayer. While Emilia listened, Nancy asked forgiveness for all the lukewarm years during which she had followed Him from afar. She thanked Him that He always heard and forgave truly penitent sinners such as her. She continued in prayer by asking that when Father God had cleansed her heart, as He had promised He would do, He would then come to reign as her sovereign Lord for as long as she might live. His word, which she knew she could trust, assured her that after this she could look ahead to an eternity in the very place which He was even then preparing for her in heaven. She also thanked Him for the many blessings He had given her as they were proof that He loved her like a Father.

PART SIX

A World to Win

1881 to 1889

CHAPTER 71

South Australia
Winter 1881 to 1883

THE BAEYERTZ FAMILY ARRIVED IN SOUTH AUSTRALIA IN JULY 1881. FOR the remainder of the year, Emilia held missions in churches in the Adelaide suburbs of Norwood, Parkside and Mitcham. She was also pleased to return to the Flinders Street Baptist Church in the city.

During this time, one Baptist minister commented to Emilia that far fewer men came to the meetings than women and children. Emilia said that was a common occurrence wherever she spoke. She added, 'Among the poorer classes, where both father and mother can't very well get away at the same time, one can come one night and one another.'

'Can't we do something,' the minister replied, 'to get the men to come? What do you say to one meeting for men only?'

'The very thing about which I have been seeking guidance: I'll do it.' Even though some people criticised the event, Emilia's first meeting for only men proved to be a great success.

Charles, at the age of fourteen, attended Mr Boehm's boarding school in Hahndorf for a short time. He then moved to Prince Alfred College, a Methodist boarding school. He found that its location in the City of Adelaide enabled him to see his mother often. The College permitted him to leave the campus to play the piano or organ in some of his mother's meetings. Twelve-year-old Marion travelled with her mother and attended a local school whenever they stayed in a town longer than a few days.

In January 1882, while reading the death notices on the front page of *The Sydney Morning Herald*, Emilia was surprised and upset to learn that her father had died at his home in England.

During that year, Emilia held missions in more suburbs and at Mt Barker in the Adelaide Hills. She also took Marion on northerly trips to towns in the Clare and Barossa Valleys. At Gawler, Emilia had to make it clear that, although she had been invited by the Baptists, she would include the Wesleyan, Primitive Methodist and Congregational churches.

On Yorke Peninsula, a hundred miles to the northwest of Adelaide, the evangelist spoke at Moonta and Moonta Mines. With some twelve thousand people, Moonta was then the second-largest town in South Australia, with more Cornish copper miners than had remained at home in Cornwall. Her next trip was to North Rhine, another copper mine, this time fifty miles northeast.

In the early months of 1883, Emilia and Marion returned to the Adelaide Hills. Emilia held a second mission at Mt Barker and went on to Nairne, Kanmantoo and Woodside. During April, they went back to the Clare Valley and based themselves in Burra. Emilia worked with the Methodists in their Kooringa Circuit and her three-week mission kept alight a revival fire that had been burning for sixteen months.

While she was there, Emilia received news that Charles had been diagnosed with typhoid fever. She and Marion returned to Adelaide to find that Charles had been banished from school. Their friend, Lady Mary Colton, had arranged for doctors and nurses to tend the sixteen-year-old youth in isolation, at a hotel in Norwood near her home.

During June and July, Emilia helped the medical staff to nurse and feed Charles. It seemed the disease would prove fatal, but she and Marion were not the only ones praying for him. All over the colony, people to whom Emilia had preached were praying for Charles and his mother. Finally, the Lord was pleased to restore Charles to full health.

In late August, Mrs Baeyertz recommenced her evangelistic work by speaking in Magill, near Adelaide. With her daughter, she then travelled 137 miles to the Mid-North region of the colony where Emilia held a mission in Terowie and then spoke in three other towns as she worked her way west to Port Pirie.

CHAPTER 72

Melbourne
March 1884

THEY RETURNED TO MELBOURNE IN THE NEXT YEAR TO DISCOVER AN enormous demand still for Emilia's ministry. Exhausted from her years in South Australia, Emilia undertook only one big ministry during the first half of the year: preaching in the large Theatre Royal on Bourke Street every Sunday night.

The Baeyertz family found a bright little house to rent at 9 Studley Park Road in Kew, near the road junction, railway station, post office and shops. They took great delight in making the house their home and rejoiced that they would no longer be moving from town to town every month. Marion would celebrate her fifteenth birthday so this was to be her last year of school.

'Mama, where have the Exhibition Buildings gone? Only the Hall and the annexes are still standing. We've visited many towns, but this Great Hall is still the biggest building I've ever seen.'

They had drawn level with the Hall while walking up Exhibition Street. Emilia slowed her walking pace so she could look more closely at the buildings then stopped at the best view to survey the Carlton Gardens around them.

Emilia replied, 'When it was built, this was the greatest building in all of the Australian colonies and the tallest in Melbourne. The pavilions that have disappeared were made of timber and corrugated iron. They were always going to be pulled down after the International Exhibition. Joseph Reed, the architect, also designed these gardens which were planted in their place.'

The Baeyertz family were ambling around the city on Emilia's birthday, Saturday 29th March, curious to survey the changes made while they were away. Emilia relished this pastime on her special day.

Marion said, 'The World's Fair seemed to fill all of these gardens when we came to see it. The buildings stretched from here up to Carlton Street.'

'I remember our visit to the Exhibition too!', said Charles. 'We didn't spend long enough there to see all eight of the courts from different countries. I was really looking forward to seeing everything.'

'My dear Charles, I knew you'd be disappointed even as we purchased our tickets. I was grateful for the donations I'd received from my missions, because we could afford to go for a few days. We were unable to return more often because we had so many other things to do then. I was preparing to go to Adelaide, by way of Tarryever. I didn't know how long we'd be in South Australia. Your aunts and uncles were a great help to me in making decisions. I hope that one day you'll be thankful we could go at all, rather than frustrated as you are now.'

Marion asked, 'How long was the Exhibition open for, Mama?'

'From the beginning of October to the end of March 1881, and then, because it was so popular, another month.'

Marion said, 'That makes it seven months all together. What will happen to those buildings that are still standing?'

Emilia replied, 'I imagine that such magnificent buildings will last for ages. They could be used for other important events such as, God willing, the Queen's Golden Jubilee in three years. If she lives to celebrate fifty years on the throne, she will be one of only three English monarchs to have reigned for half a century.'

Marion asked, 'Does that mean she's an old lady now?'

'No, she's not very old. She became queen when she was eighteen. That's not much older than Charles is now. Do you think he'd make a good king?'

This led to some jovial banter between the siblings until Charles began to tease and Emilia interrupted. 'No more, Charles. I know your years in boarding school have taught you how to answer back, but Marion is younger and there's no call for that.'

Marion asked, 'How old is the Queen now?'

'Let's work it out. She was born in 1819 and this is 1884, so that makes her about sixty-four. I am forty-two today, twenty-two years younger than Her Majesty. Let's see if there are other changes to buildings further on.' Charles and Marion each linked arms with their mother and fell into step with her.

Charles said, 'I must say, this city has grown busier since we were last here. I would never have guessed that so many new buildings would be under construction unless I'd seen it for myself. There seem to be more businesses opening and many more people about.'

Emilia replied, 'The Exhibition was such a success because it reminded everyone that Melbourne is one of the biggest cities in the world. Most people seem to be optimistic and excited about the way this city is expanding. Did you hear that my brothers are preparing to open two new jewellery shops?'

'I didn't know that!' said Marion. 'On which streets?'

'Oh, they won't be in Melbourne', replied Charles.

'Your Uncle Frederick is going to Sydney and Uncle Nuriel is going to Launceston. Oh dear, I forgot to call Nuriel by the name he uses now, Norman. He was only five years old when Uncle George and I boarded the ship to come to Melbourne. I'd expected to see him again back in Wales, but I met him here when we returned from Adelaide. It was astonishing to meet a man of twenty-five when my memory of him was as a little boy. It will take some practice to call him Norman.'

'You will only have to say that once a year if he does go to Launceston', said Charles.

'I hadn't thought of that. You know, I can't help thinking this has happened before—my brothers leave Melbourne just when I return to the city.'

'How many of your brothers and sisters have come out to Australia, Mama?'

'Well, there's Saul, George, Fred and Norman. And Charles, who is buried in the St Kilda Cemetery. And Eliza who has gone back. That makes six.'

Marion said, 'That means most of them are here now, with their families. If they'd remained in Wales, you wouldn't have seen them for many years, Mama.'

'Yes, I see your point, Marion. They've come to where I am; I haven't had to return Home. What a good thought that is. What sensible people my children have become. Well done, both of you.'

'Then there are Papa's mother and his sister and brother too.'

'You are right again, Marion. Grandmama is still living in Brighton and Aunt Suzette is nearby too. The last I heard from your Uncle John, he was in California.

'Now, Charles, a friend at church said there will be four concerts of sacred music on Good Friday. I'd like to go to one of them and that is only two weeks away. At the Theatre Royal last week, I saw a leaflet about their sacred concert with dramatic recitals and performances by renowned Melbourne singers. What have you heard about the others?'

'Mama, I've brought some flyers that I've been collecting for you. Here they are. The Bijou Theatre, in Bourke Street East, will present a similar concert of sacred music. The Melbourne Philharmonic is performing *The Redemption* at the Town Hall. That's an oratorio written by the French composer Charles Gounod and first performed in Birmingham just two years ago. He uses Bible stories about the creation and the death and resurrection of Jesus and the descent of the Holy Spirit on the Apostles.'

'That, I would like to hear—music to present the magnificent truths of Jesus. What else is there?'

'The Musical Union of Victoria is performing *The Martyr of Antioch* here at the Exhibition Building. It is a sacred musical drama about St Margaret set in the third century. Mr Arthur Sullivan wrote the music for the 1880 Leeds Music Festival. His friend W. S. Gilbert wrote the libretto. You may have heard of their recent musical theatre works *HMS Pinafore* and *Pirates of Penzance*.'

'I have. I wasn't aware that they wrote sacred music. That drama could be more enlightening.'

Charles said, 'It's remarkable that music arrives here so soon after it has been first performed in England. It shows that promoters believe Melbourne's population are familiar with the Arts.'

His mother said, 'I'm more interested in the fact that there are four recitals of sacred music planned for the same day. The promoters must believe that there are enough citizens to attend Easter concerts for them to be all worthwhile. Thank you for these leaflets Charles. I'll have to read them carefully before I decide which to attend. Would you like to come, Marion?'

'Oh, Mama, that would be wonderful. I haven't been to a concert for such a long time.'

Charles said, 'Of course, I want to come too.'

'Dear Charles, nothing would delight my heart more than having your company, and Marion's, at a concert of sacred music. Besides, I need your expertise to secure three good seats in the concert of our choice. After all, you've been to so many performances with your friends that you'll know the correct procedures and best seats.'

'The task will not present me with any problems, Mama. You will appreciate the music. The musicians who've travelled from Europe are the best in their profession. More importantly, they play pieces from the highly respected composers. I have not yet found a performance that could dissuade anyone in the audience from faith in Jesus. I admit that there are some concerts you would not enjoy, but those are not the ones I speak of now.'

'All things are lawful, not everything is expedient, Charles. You know my views on attending concerts for the mere entertainment. If the concerts do not educate or direct my thoughts towards the Lord then they would be an unwise use of my limited funds.'

'Yes, Mama, I've heard you say that many times. Surely God gave composers the skills to create music that directs a listener's thoughts to His greatness. Music without words based on the Bible can be used by God to bless the audience.'

'Charles, I spent many years going to concerts, both at Home and in this colony. They could be enjoyable and provide opportunities to meet other people my own age but rarely prompt me to consider my spiritual life.'

'Perhaps that was because you had settled your thoughts about your spiritual condition.'

'Now that I am aware of my true spiritual state, I've found many passages in the Epistles that warn believers to avoid all forms of worldliness that will distract them from the Lord. You've heard me tell many new believers to consider this verse "Wherefore come out from among them, and be ye separate, saith the Lord, and touch not the unclean thing; and I will receive you".'

'But, that doesn't mention music at all!'

'That's right, but it does forbid participation in every kind of ungodliness. Christians have always debated what the Apostle Paul meant by "the unclean thing". We know that the Torah explains what is unclean. Remember that we are the temple of the living God and God will dwell in us. Are we who have been born again to mix with the world and its amusements? No, we are to come out from among them, and to touch not the "unclean thing". I encourage new believers to avoid dancing, playing cards, the theatre and concerts.'

'But why do you call concert music "unclean"? Handel composed music for the Church. Think of J. S. Bach. All his music was written to the glory of God.'

'Yes, you are right, of course. Not all music is unclean. There is religious value in beautiful music. That's why I am delighted that concerts of sacred music are being performed in Melbourne. I will enjoy going to one.'

'Charles, I don't think you will get Mama to change her opinion about other music today,' said Marion.

'You're not much fun. I don't think God is that strict. And He has given me the talent for music', replied Charles.

'My dear ones, I have changed my mind about many matters. Still, I must practise what I preach. I'm aware that people all over the city recognise me and they will compare my actions with what I teach. I spend much time in prayer and thought so that my life and teaching are consistent. The great miracle of Christianity is its regenerating power today. It enables me, through the Holy Spirit, to live an upright, earnest, holy life.'

'Mama, I wasn't aware you have to be that careful about what you say and do', said Marion.

'Perhaps it is a good thing I told you both. Now you know why I am more reserved in public than I am at home. Charles, I can't stop you going to the concerts of your choice and even arranging your own.'

'Thank you, Mama. I'll try not to embarrass you.'

CHAPTER 73

Victoria

Winter 1884 to Summer 1885

ALTHOUGH CHARLES HAD LESS SYMPATHY FOR HIS MOTHER'S VOCA-
tion than his sister, he loved his mother dearly. He had returned to
Melbourne at the age of seventeen, having finished school, and was now
cultivating the life of a young man about town. An accomplished pianist, he
was choir master in church and sometimes the organist at St James' Cathe-
dral. He enjoyed the wide variety of local and visiting musical performers in
Marvellous Melbourne. Charles also joined a football team where he gave
good service to the forwards.

Emilia had noticed that her beloved son did most things slightly better
than his peers and enjoyed their accolades. However, he was inclined not to
pursue a ministry, trade, profession or indeed any vocation that provided
steady work or reliable income. Instead, Charles preferred to borrow to
invest in the rising property market, like hundreds of others in Melbourne.
His uncles had introduced him to prudent businessmen and bankers.

Emilia remained a member of the Church of England, yet would preach
in churches of many names. She, Charles and Marion most often attended
the nearby Kew Baptist Church which was led by Kerr Johnston. In addition to his congregational duties, Mr Johnston supported several evangelical
inter-denominational agencies and had established a mission to seamen
called Victorian Bethel Union.

Kerr and Eliza Johnston and Emilia Baeyertz recognised in one another a
common approach to their Christian faith—the service of God by both proc-
lamation and practical action in their community. The Johnstons welcomed
the Baeyertz family into their circle and so Marion and Charles became firm
friends with their children, especially twenty-six-year-old Isabella.

One of the Johnstons who had already left home was Sarah. She had
married Daniel Matthews and joined him, and his brother William, on a
station near Barmah on the Murray River. There they had established the

Maloga Mission School in 1874, around which a village had grown as a refuge for some Aboriginal people who had been separated from their land.

Emilia's estimation of Daniel rose when she learnt he was a Methodist who ran Maloga by a strict temperance policy. She volunteered to help if her travels took her that way.

In the second half of the year, Mrs Baeyertz began again to accept invitations to travel to missions.

One was from the Stawell Minister's Association, who asked her to return in July as there was more to be done in their town since her first mission three years earlier. This second mission would be unsectarian, members of the various churches would give aid wherever needed and the two weeks of meetings would be preceded by a week of united prayer. Emilia was delighted to accept. By the end of that mission, people of all ages stood at the testimony meeting to thank Mrs Baeyertz for her work among them. A Woman's Prayer Union and a Girl's Union were soon formed.

Emilia and Marion then returned to their home in Kew to prepare for a two-week mission at the West Melbourne Baptist Church during August.

In September, they travelled by train to Sandhurst for a twelve-day mission then, in October, onto Echuca.

Charles was already on the platform at Echuca to greet his mother and sister from the train and introduce to them a neatly-dressed man. Mr Daniel Matthews turned out to be an affable person who did not consider any task too difficult. After they had exchanged first names and handshakes, and comments about the railway, all four went to find the ladies' trunks. Charles loaded their baggage onto the buggy that Daniel had brought from Maloga and then they all climbed aboard.

Daniel directed the horses out into Annesley Street and they proceeded north. 'I've been asked to take you to the meeting with the Mission Committee, but I've got enough time to show you Echuca's wharf.'

As they rolled along the streets, the new-comers looked carefully at the buildings and people. Emilia exclaimed, 'Look at that street sign. It says "Annesley Street". I've been corresponding with the minister of the Wesleyan church on this street.'

'You are most observant, Emilia. We'll see the church on the left as we go. We won't stop now because the minister won't be there. He's off looking into matters about the mission.'

'I expect the kind gentleman has quite a bit to do because my first meeting is in three days. Besides, I'll probably spend quite a bit of time in that church.'

When they reached the wharf, Charles commented, 'There was more activity around the train station than there is down here.'

'Is your whole family observant? Charles, you've seen one of the big changes occurring here. The connection of the railway and the river made Echuca the largest inland port in Australia but now farmers and wood cutters have started to send their wool, grain and timber to Melbourne and the world by rail rather than by river. Naturally, the steamboat owners are wondering what will happen to their businesses. Perhaps we did the smart thing when my brother and I sold that store over there. We used to sell provisions for the paddle steamers. Did you hear that whistle? It's from a departing boat. Here's some shade for the horses to rest in while I briefly show you around.'

After the tour, as they returned to the buggy, Marion expressed her desire for a steamboat-ride. Emilia promised to ask her hosts to see what they could arrange.

Later, Daniel delivered Emilia, Marion and their luggage into the care of two more of their correspondents from the Organising Committee. These men, of the local Young Men's Christian Association, had wisely brought the Temperance Union, the Wesleyans and the Baptists into the mission. Before Emilia and the Committee began their discussions, Charles took his leave. He knew what missions involved and was keen to return with Daniel to Maloga where he had been staying.

From the first day of the Echuca Mission, people eagerly filled the churches and the Temperance Hall to hear Mrs Baeyertz speak. A report in *The Riverine Herald* declared that Mrs Baeyertz was a 'good evangelist' and a talented 'expository teacher of the great truths of the Scriptures'. Many people reported new faith and great blessing.

One evening during the third week, members of the Echuca Gospel Temperance Union were astonished to see some prominent inebriates enter the Blue Ribbon Mission at their Hall. Some ushers suggested to them that they had mistaken the gathering for a hotel. On the contrary, they said, they had come to hear the guest speaker. Mrs Baeyertz did not hesitate to speak plainly about the value of pledging a life-long commitment to give up the grog. To that end, they could sign a certificate on which they promised 'in the strength of God, Father, Son, and Holy Spirit, to abstain from all kinds of intoxicating liquor as a beverage, and to discourage as much as possible the drinking customs of society.' Some duly signed and had their pledges witnessed. Emilia and the Union rejoiced and prayed for them.

On their way home, some of the Temperance supporters met a sober man leaving a pub who told them that some of the pledgers had immediately gone there for a few ales. The publican had mounted their pledges on the wall. The missioners were indignant! The reporter from *The Herald* soon heard of the story, spoke to the participants, reported the facts and offered this opinion: 'Such conduct is certainly most reprehensible and discreditable.'

Some people who had flocked to the meetings of Mrs Baeyertz felt that the mission ended too early. Her winning manner had endeared her to them and she had raised a great interest in spiritual matters within the community. At the final meeting, on the evening of Thursday 23rd October, a member of the YMCA presented Mrs Baeyertz with a purse containing twenty-five sovereigns, the net of the collections taken up during the meetings, after all the expenses had been paid. The audiences had been informed that Mrs Baeyertz did not make any charge for her teaching and preaching, but depended on the Lord to provide for her needs.

The following day, Daniel Matthews returned to Echuca to collect the Baeyertz ladies and transport them on the twenty-mile trip to Maloga by carriage. They talked excitedly of crossing the border between the colonies of Victoria and New South Wales. Daniel spoke lovingly of the iron bridge because it had proven to be the safest way to cross the river since it was built.

The city-dwellers asked far more questions than Daniel could answer at once. He suggested that they wait until they were out of town.

On the north side of the river, in New South Wales, the road from the bridge directed all traffic into Moama. The businesses, vehicles and pedestrians showed that the township was an important centre for wheat farmers. Once the carriage had passed through, Daniel asked that the questions be repeated.

Some miles on, the horses turned right into Barmah Road and then, after a few more miles, into Gilmour Road and directly to Maloga Station Their trip was shorter than Emilia had anticipated, but perhaps that was due to the lively conversation and pretty road-side scenery. There was no need to enter Barmah this time; they would cross the river to visit that town later in the week.

Emilia was not surprised when she heard that Charles intended to spend three months with the indigenous tribes. The Yorta Yorta people appreciated this whitefella who would sit with them, beneath their favourite trees, learning their language and the stories they chose to tell him. His ability as a linguist was greater even than his grandmother's had been.

Emilia might have liked to remain in the district for as long as Charles, but she could only stay two weeks for she was committed to speak at the anniversary services of Brunswick Baptist Church on Sunday 16th November.

Emilia did not go to Tasmania for her summer holiday at the end of 1884. Instead, she accepted an invitation to speak in Mornington, on Port Phillip Bay. At her nine-day mission, which began on Sunday 25th January, 1885, crowds of eager people filled the hall to hear her teach. The Lord's people also received rich blessings through the consecration and holiness meetings in the afternoons. On the second Sunday night, the Mechanics' Institute was filled with people—on the platform, in the anteroom and outdoors.

Once this mission was over, Marion and Emilia could enjoy the beaches on the Mornington Peninsula before returning to Kew to settle into their routine for the coming year. Invitations to speak kept arriving from all over Victoria. Marion began to help her mother with the correspondence required for each visit.

At home, Emilia saw to the everyday needs of her family, housework and obligation. Outside the home, there were their friends, church, neighbourhood and city. Emilia helped care for the destitute, homeless and orphans through the Salvation Army, supported the YMCA, YWCA and Aborigines visiting from Maloga, wrote to the newspapers, provided hospitality, knocked on doors and prayed.

CHAPTER 74

Melbourne
Summer 1889

EMILIA'S SPIRIT QUIVERED WITH HOLY DESIRE TO ENCOUNTER THE
Living God. 'Lord, my Lord, how can I get nearer to Thee? How may I prove
my love to Thee?'

The Lord's reply was so distinct that Emilia felt she would see her Saviour
if she opened her eyes. 'Will you go to New Zealand and America for me?'

She frowned and wondered how to respond to Almighty God. If she'd
thought that His answer would be a commission to leave her precious family
and friends, she would never have asked. Now her excitement ebbed into
anxiety as her thoughts turned to what she had been avoiding.

For years now, she'd been receiving letters from Mary Thomson, who was
now Mrs Downie Stewart, inviting her to tour New Zealand starting with
the Dunedin YWCA. At first, Emilia had been attracted to the idea but, since
the birth of her grandson, she was unwilling to leave Melbourne. And then
there was the picture. One of her friends had brought back from America a
picture of women kneeling and praying in the snow. She desired the courage
of those temperance crusade women.

God's request returned to her thoughts and Emilia realised she had not
yet replied to her Heavenly Father. 'America, America, dear Lord, as well as
New Zealand! But I know of no-one in that far-away land.'

Emilia remembered afresh the character of the One to whom she spoke.
The lines of a consecration hymn came to mind so she replied with the
familiar words, 'I'll go, Lord; I'll go, Lord, I'll go where you want me to go'.
She was immediately filled with peace. She recognised that it was the peace
only God could give her.

She opened her eyes, silently got up off her knees, sat back on her seat and
looked about. She was surrounded by believers who were with God in prayer.
In the beginning of this special time she had felt the Spirit of God moving
mightily upon the silent, listening, waiting souls. Now she could hear some

people whispering, while others dabbed at their tears and some restrained their joy at the Spirit's touch.

Emilia smiled as she looked at the bent form of her friend on the platform. Although he was one of the leaders of this conference, Hussey too had knelt in prayer. She remembered some of the ministry she'd undertaken with him and Emily in Caulfield twelve years earlier.

As more people around her finished praying and returned to their seats, Emilia thought of her son Charles and his wife Isabella Johnston. They had wed over two years ago and were living nearby. In February, Emilia had joined the celebrations of the first birthday of Carl, their first child and her first grandchild. His full name was Charles Kerr Johnston Baeyertz.

Marion was now twenty years old, a stalwart support to her mother in maintaining the house and their correspondence, and a valued companion when Emilia's missions took them away. Whenever they returned home to Kew, they always looked fondly at their cottage, thankful they could call it 'home'.

As Emilia sat in the church, she wondered what to do with those invitations to Queensland and New South Wales. Did God want her to go north before she left for New Zealand?

'Thank you for unlocking the door for me Marion. I am ready for a cup of tea now. Please make us a pot while I put away my coat and hat. Travelling by train is so much quicker than the other option: taking the cable tram to the bridge and then the horse-drawn tram up the hill.'

When Marion brought the laden tray into the morning room she was full of questions. 'Who was at the conference? What happened there today? Did God speak to you during the prayer time?'

'Hussey led the prayer meeting today. It was a joy to share with others in the work.'

Marion said, 'I can usually find Mr or Mrs Macartney's name on the list of the organising committee for any new event. They are such dedicated workers for the Lord.'

'Yes, they have achieved much for the Kingdom, so faithful friends to evangelists here and there. Ever since our days at St Mary's, they have given us wise counsel.'

'Would you like me to refill your teacup, Mama?'

'Yes, please, and put a second biscuit on the saucer too. Thank you. Now Marion, several people sent their greetings to you. I wrote their names in my note book. Before I show you, I must tell you what God said today.'

'Mama, He spoke to you? How did you hear Him? Did He catch you up in rapture? Did He send a great wind?'

'Nothing like that, but I did feel as if Jesus was right beside me speaking in a quiet voice.'

'What did He say?'

'I fear you will not like my answer to that question. He asked me to do the most difficult thing I could ever conceive.'

'Oh, whatever could that be?'

'He asked me to go to New Zealand and America.'

'Oh, Mama, why did God ask you to do that?'

'You know that Mrs Stewart has been writing from New Zealand.'

'Yes, I gave up waiting for that trip years ago.'

'I haven't received clear guidance till now. I was busy enough here and I didn't want to uproot you. Then Charles and Bella married.'

'Why America? We don't know anyone there.'

'There is your Uncle John in Los Angeles. He manages a warehouse like his father did.'

'I meant, we don't know anyone there who would invite you to speak'

'True. Yet, if God wants me in America, He will find a way. See that picture on the wall that shows the crusade women in the snow?'

'I wonder what that would be like. We don't see that much snow here.'

'There must be grand stuff in women such as those. God bless the crusade women of America.'

'Haven't you left home often enough for Him? I thought three years in South Australia was too long. I was terribly lonely until I made new friends. You kept saying that God's love for me was more important than my feelings, but that always upset me. I doubted God really did care for me. I also doubted that He cared for you too. You worked so hard that you were frequently ill. When we returned to Melbourne we were all tired. You took many months to fully recover.'

'Well, Marion, I learnt from that experience and I've spoken at fewer missions in recent years.'

'Mama, since we've been here I've been much happier. I've made many friends at church and Bella's brothers and sisters are like my own family too. Since Charles married Bella, I've even had my own sister. We've become a normal family. It's been wonderful.'

'Whatever do you mean by a "normal family"?'

'As well as visiting my Johnston brothers- and sisters-in-law, we have stayed in the one house, hung our clothes in the same wardrobes and slept in the same beds. Charles is now living in his own home with Isabella, of course, but they are not far away.'

'I would agree with you, dear, that we've been much healthier since we've lived here. It's been a delightful period in our lives.'

'What did you reply to God in the prayer time? You didn't say you'd go, did you?'

'It is difficult to say "No" to God, you know. I preach about the way Jesus sacrificed everything He had to give us eternal life. It seems petty to tell God I don't want to leave home because my grandson is only one year old.'

'Mama, it's so unfair of God to ask you to leave while you are a new grandmother. Just the other day, Bella told us that she is having another baby at the end of the year.'

'Let me assure you, I don't want to go for that very reason. I expect I'll have to ask the Lord to give me the desire and courage to go to New Zealand and then America.'

'Well, I don't want to go with you! It's been difficult to go with you to missions around this colony but I've always known we were coming back. But America? We might never come back home. North America is so much bigger than South Australia.'

CHAPTER 75

Victoria and Queensland
Autumn to Spring 1889

THE INVITATION TO BRISBANE WAS SO EVIDENTLY OF THE LORD THAT Emilia dare not refuse it. Marion confirmed with her correspondents that Emilia would arrive by train in the last week of August.

Before then, Emilia had time for three missions in Victoria. In April, she and Marion went to Alexandra, in July to the South Preston Wesleyan Church and to the Eaglehawk Presbyterian Church in early August.

On Monday 15th April, the Reverend Mr T. B. Swift of the Presbyterian Church had welcomed Mrs Baeyertz and her daughter back to Alexandra. Mr Swift anticipated that her eight-day mission would be as successful as her first visit, the previous April, when 157 people had professed conversion. He had promoted this year's mission in his preaching circuit from Alexandra, to Yarck and Taggerty, but fewer people came than he had planned. Interest was high but the almost continuous rain that fell for the first three days had made travel unpleasant and, in some cases, dangerous. Despite the smaller congregation, seventy-three people had found a saving faith in Jesus by the end of the mission.

On their return to Kew after their sojourn in Eaglehawk, the time had come for Emilia to pack for her 2,000 mile return journey to Queensland. The warm humid weather would only require summer-weight clothing but she would be away for eleven weeks. She'd promised to speak in Sydney and Albury on the way home. Charles suggested she take the least luggage possible because she would have to change trains at least six times.

Although dining rooms in the railway termini served meals, neither dining cars nor beds were available on the trains. Emilia hoped there would be empty seats beside her so she could stretch out.

Marion only had to prepare enough food for one traveller, because she was unable to accompany her mother on this trip. Emilia had no qualms about leaving her daughter to manage domestic tasks alone, but she doubted her own ability to conduct missions without her daughter's support.

As she organised her papers, Emilia was disturbed by the thought of going anywhere alone. She had to frequently remind herself she'd given her whole life to the Lord Jesus and she was resolved never to turn back. Emilia wrote down her concerns in a note book so she could pray about them rather than worry. She knew the train trip would take some eighteen hours and that was just to Sydney, halfway to Brisbane. There would be ample time to discuss these matters with the Lord.

On the day of her departure, Marion, Charles and Bella and their son Carl accompanied Emilia to Spencer Street Railway Station. They assured her of their confidence in her ability to manage alone and saw her find the seat shown on her ticket.

After Emilia had stored away her bags and spoken cordially to fellow passengers, she settled down and opened her diary. She confessed silently to her Father God that she feared being lonely during the four train journeys to Brisbane. She prayed for people in neighbouring seats who were sympathetic to her work and agreeable companions.

Her next prayer request was for her recovery from public speaking each day. After presenting her message to a crowded hall and ministering to those who asked questions, Emilia usually returned to her room ready to collapse on her bed. Marion's presence and loving help had been a great comfort to her. How could she expect an acquaintance to give her such support? Emilia asked God to provide compassionate and supportive women throughout the missions.

When she came to pray about America, Emilia groaned quietly. Outside the window the countryside sped by. She recognised some regions from her earlier travels, but her thoughts were on the future. Was this trip a foretaste of the years to come? Marion had not changed her opinion and was determined to stay in Kew. Her mother did not doubt that God could change her daughter's mind, because He had altered her own. She had come to accept that it was time to take her ministry beyond these colonies. Nevertheless, she was still distressed at having to leave the Baeyertz and Aronson families, and her Christian friends. Travelling alone in America would be unpleasant and burdensome. She pleaded with God that, if He was to send her so far from home, He should be pleased to send her daughter too.

At Albury, half way to Sydney, Emilia gathered up her belongings and disembarked with everyone else. The railway gauge in Victoria was five feet three so passengers had to cross the platform to board another train on the New South Wales gauge of four feet eight and a half. The luggage was transported from van to van by the porters.

At Redfern, the terminus near Sydney, a porter helped her, and her luggage, find their correct places on the correct train for her next journey.

Later, fellow passengers looked out excitedly as they crossed a bridge that had opened only three months earlier. They assured Emilia that, before the opening of the Woy Woy Tunnel and Hawkesbury River Railway Bridge, train travellers had to endure a three-hour paddle steamer voyage from Hornsby to Gosford.

When, at 6.30 p. m., the train pulled into the platform on the east side of Wallangarra, the tired and hungry passengers were looking forward to their three-course dinner in the station dining room. While they lingered at their tables, the porters transferred all the mail, luggage and cargo. When the clock hands showed a quarter to eight, the Station Master asked the passengers to board the three-foot-six-gauge Mail Train to Brisbane from the west platform, on the Queensland side of the border.

Emilia, like her fellow passengers, experimented until she found a posture that might let her doze in her seat during the long hours ahead. Whenever she opened her eyes, she saw that other passengers had shifted positions in their seats and the night sky still blackened the scenery outside.

Half an hour before sunrise, Emilia was woken by the steward's call as he ambled along the passage. 'It's five o'clock. The train is on schedule to arrive at Roma Street at six. Please be ready to alight promptly.'

The pastel light of the sun's first rays illuminated the fields and the roads that ran parallel to the train line. Emilia gradually woke up and prayed that God would go before her into this new day. She wondered what He was going to do in this place.

Soon after, Emilia was greeted warmly by the Mission Committee on behalf of the Brisbane churches and taken to her accommodation. Her hosts were a retired clergy couple who were familiar with the itinerant life. She saw in them an answer to her prayers.

*

Emilia maintained her habit of reading the local newspapers. From them, she could learn about the city in which she was a guest and how her missions were promoted and reported. She found her talks advertised in the Classifieds of *The Brisbane Courier* and other papers a few days in advance of the meetings. Emilia also found her name in the Overland Passengers column of *The Queenslander*. The intended destinations of everyone travelling by train through Wallangarra were listed a few days after they had been there. She guessed that her name would reappear after her departure.

The evangelist conducted two missions in Brisbane that were each ten days long. The meetings of Emilia's first mission, which began on 31st August, were held in the Wesleyan Church in Princess Street, South Brisbane, and in the Baptist Church in Wharf Street. She also conducted a noon Bible Reading in the YMCA Hall every day.

The Mission Committee hired larger halls for her second mission. Emilia returned to the Wharf Street Baptist Church for some meetings, but others were held in the larger Courier Hall and the Brisbane Opera House.

The numbers of people who came to Emilia's missions followed the pattern she'd observed in the southern colonies. Her first talks were mostly attended by small groups from the churches who had invited her. Audiences grew larger at subsequent meetings as stories about her presentations spread amongst Brisbane's residents.

It was just as well that the final meeting, on Sunday 15th September, was held in the Opera House, because Courier Hall would not have been large enough to seat the throngs. Such a congregation had never before assembled in Queensland to hear an evangelist's address—every class of person in Queensland society was represented.

The Evangelistic Choir assembled on the stage and sang several 'Moody and Sankey' hymns. Mrs Baeyertz began by reading Isaiah chapter 6 and Revelation chapter 20 and then developed her talk about The Great White Throne. After urging the unconverted to accept Jesus as Saviour, she invited everyone with questions to stay behind to speak with an experienced Christian counsellor and accept a Bible with passages marked for their future guidance.

Emilia spoke warmly to those who had remained in the hall and made sure they received tickets to attend the meeting for converts the following

Tuesday. It would be held at the Opera House again, when Emilia would speak about The Lord's Second Coming.

In later years the strongest memory of her month in Brisbane was receiving a letter from Marion which startled Emilia considerably. She was certain it was written in Marion's hand, but there was one sentence that did not seem to reflect her daughter's opinion. It said, 'I do wish you would accept the invitation to New Zealand, and then go on through the States, home to England.' Emilia had to read it several times before she understood that God had answered her prayers.

Marion had realised they could go on to Britain from America's east coast. Emilia had not thought that far ahead but she could see the sense in returning to Wales. No doubt Marion would like to visit Bangor and the country her aunts and uncles fondly called 'Home'.

Her daughter's letter also said she'd written to Mr David Walker, the Secretary of the Sydney YMCA, to explain that she would meet her mother in that city and to ask for accommodation. Emilia would have to wait a few more weeks to learn what had altered Marion's mind because she had promised to hold a mission in Ipswich, twenty-five miles southwest of Brisbane.

Emilia discovered from her hosts that she was the third woman to visit the Town of Brisbane recently to talk about the Christian life. The first was Miss Lydia von Finkelstein whose task was to educate her audience about everyday life in the Holy Land now and at the time of Jesus. She displayed artefacts and costumes from the Levant, described the people's customs, gave dramatic portrayals of Bible stories and explained their meaning.

Another travelling speaker was Miss Jessie Ackermann of the Women's Christian Temperance Union, the WCTU, from the United States of America. In fact, she was still in Brisbane. This was Emilia's chance to hear and meet an American Temperance Crusade woman.

Miss Ackermann's temperance lecture, on Saturday 21st September in the Ipswich School of Arts, was poorly attended. People seemed to prefer to perambulate the streets on Saturday evenings. Despite the paucity of numbers, Mr A. H. Barlow, a Member of the Legislative Assembly and several members of the Ipswich WCTU were pleased to sit on the stage with their guest speaker.

Miss Ackermann explained that she had been sent by her American colleagues to promote their cause around the world. She revealed that when she had departed the shores of her native land, a few months earlier, she felt she was going amongst strangers. However, her opinion changed when she was warmly welcomed by people in New Zealand. She discovered that they spoke the same language and looked very much like the people she'd left at home.

Chuckling rippled through the audience.

Miss Ackermann said that since arriving in the Australian colonies, she had received the greatest hospitality everywhere and she felt now that she was one of them. On learning that there were many Temperance Unions in Queensland, she felt they were more than cousins: they were, in the great work they had at heart, brothers and sisters.

Her audience congratulated themselves at being found equal to the Americans who were so committed to temperance work and thus clapped loudly at the end of Miss Ackermann's speech.

While others were leaving the hall, Emilia was introduced to Miss Acker-mann. They agreed to have tea and scones together the following day.

Each woman approached the afternoon tea with many questions about the other's ministry. They had no trouble beginning a conversation and found they had many experiences in common. They asked for a second pot of tea and more scones.

Emilia and Jessie had each pulled a notebook and pencil out of her own bag to record names of suitable people and addresses of organisations that the other had recommended. They also found solutions together to some problems they'd encountered as guests in people's homes. The time passed quickly and soon they had to return to their hosts. Before they parted, Emilia and Jessie prayed for one another. They also thanked their Father God that He had made arrangements for them to be in the same towns in the same weeks.

Emilia found that her Ipswich Mission was unlike those held in Brisbane. The meeting halls were crowded from the very first day, on Monday 23rd September, and they remained full throughout the ten days. People in Ipswich had clearly heard from their Brisbane friends.

On Thursday 10th October, the train tooted its horn and began to pull away from Roma Street Railway Station. New Brisbane friends waved to Mrs Baeyertz from the platform and sang a favourite hymn from her meetings. Emilia returned their farewells and noticed the bitter-sweet feeling that rose in her chest. She was sad to leave the community of faithful believers but also relieved to be reducing the distance she was from home. Admittedly, she would not see Marion for a few more days yet, but she was on her way south.

CHAPTER 76

Sydney, New South Wales
October 1889

THE EVANGELIST WAS NOW LOOKING FORWARD TO A HOLIDAY. SHE had arranged her programme so she could spend two weeks in Sydney to recover from her hard work in Brisbane. Not knowing if God would allow her to come back, Emilia wanted to see the biggest city in the colony of New South Wales and to visit Christian leaders there.

On Friday 11th October, the train pulled into the terminus at Redfern Station. Emilia collected her bags and disembarked wearing the brooch she had described in her letter to Mr Walker, General Secretary of the Sydney Chapter of the Young Men's Christian Association.

She stood and examined all the men who walked by. After some time, a prosperous older gentleman with an assistant approached her. 'Are you Mrs Baeyertz?'

'Yes, I am. So you must be Mr Walker. I recognise you from this photograph in *The Illustrated Sydney News*. A friend sent me the February edition in anticipation.'

'What a pleasure it is to meet you, Mrs Baeyertz. Please call me David.'

'Please call me Emilia. Thank you for your invitation to speak at your YMCA. I've heard a great deal about Sydney. We will talk of those matters later, but I must go to the luggage hall to retrieve my trunk.'

'My thoughts exactly. Please put your hand into my arm as we walk. It will be much easier to keep together in this crowd if we are linked.'

'Thank you.' Emilia saw he was a tall man and his white sideburns gave him a distinguished appearance. The whiskers grew longer than his chin and blew aside in every breeze that passed through the station.

David Walker guided Emilia to the luggage hall where his assistant loaded her trunk and bags onto a trolley and transported them outside. The waggonette waiting for them had YOUNG MEN'S CHRISTIAN ASSOCIATION written on the sides. The young man neatly placed her baggage in the vehicle, assisted Mrs Baeyertz and Mr Walker into their seats and took his seat at the reins.

Before they set off, David Walker gave Emilia a telegram.

When she opened it, she read 'ARRIVE REDFERN 12 OCTOBER MARION BAEYERTZ'. Emilia looked up and asked, 'What time does the Melbourne train arrive tomorrow?'

'The same time as your train today. The lady with whom you are to stay has two beds in her guest room, so you need not be concerned about accommodation for your daughter.'

'Thank you, David. Your efficiency does you credit. I am looking forward to seeing Marion again. I have not seen her for nearly two months. '

'I would be delighted to meet your daughter too, I'm sure.'

While they drove through the streets of Sydney, Emilia told herself to think about Marion later and take notice of the buildings around her. After all, this was the capital city of the oldest colony in Australia.

After she had met her hostess and left her luggage in her bed room, Emilia was delighted to accept Mr Walker's invitation to show her around Sydney. They returned to the waggonette and set off for a tour.

During their trip, she noticed that the streets did not conform to a strict grid pattern. When she commented that Sydney was thus unlike the capital cities in the other colonies, David Walker reminded her that this was established as a penal settlement, not as a colony to be subdivided by free settlers.

Their driver took them east to a park where Emilia walked around the headland to gaze at the views of the harbour. As they sat on Mrs Macquarie's Chair, she agreed with David that Sydney had the most picturesque location of the cities she had visited in Australia.

The following day at the terminus, Mr Walker witnessed the joyous reunion. His assistant had collected and transported Marion's luggage to their hostess's home while Marion, Emilia and Mr Walker shared a delightful lunch. After the driver had a quick bite of his own, he returned with the waggonette to take the three to the imposing YMCA building at the corner of Pitt and Bathurst Streets.

Mr Walker showed them into his office. He said, 'It is delightful to see how happy you are together. The world would be a happier place if all mothers and daughters smiled so frequently.'

'Perhaps other mothers and daughters are not engaged in the vocation that God gave to us. Speaking at missions is tiring and I am uncomfortable at having to depend so much on acquaintances when I'm exhausted.'

Marion added, 'I missed being with Mama. I would have liked to visit Brisbane too as I hear it is much warmer than Melbourne.'

David replied, 'Sydney is usually warmer than Melbourne too, so I hope you enjoy our climate. Now Emilia, we need to discuss your plans. Then you will be free to see the sights.'

'We would be most interested to look around this building. The wide staircase to this first floor and the stained glass windows imply impressive rooms.'

'I would be delighted to give you a tour but let us first confirm your plans.'

He picked up a page of typewritten details. 'Let me see. In our last correspondence you confirmed that you would hold a meeting for men only. You also gave us the dates you would be here to allow us to pick one for our meeting.'

Emilia said, 'I gave as much information I could.'

'Thank you for your thoughtfulness. We usually hold evangelistic services on Sunday evenings, so we have allocated your meeting to 20th October. We'll have the meeting here because our lecture hall is the most commodious and best arranged in the colony. Advertisements have been placed in the newspapers and in Christian papers. We have also sent letters to other Christian organisations and many churches around Sydney. I expect announcements will be made in church services this Sunday.'

Mrs Baeyertz replied, 'That will give me eight days to prepare my talk. That's ample time. I've given the talk many times before, of course, but I like to become familiar with the city in which I am to speak so that my stories are relevant to my audience.'

'I am pleased our date meets with your approval. Now, I see you are holding a copy of your list of people you wish to meet.'

'Yes, David. Have you been able to communicate with them?'

'We have heard from most of them. My secretary can tell you more about the arrangements she's made. You can speak with her presently. Before you do, I've got a question for you.'

Mr Walker picked up different papers. 'I've been preparing my notes about your many achievements, Emilia, so I can introduce you correctly at our meeting. I was hoping that I could inform the men that you will return next year to conduct one of your longer missions here. When would you be able to come back?'

Emilia and Marion smiled at one another. David said, 'I see you know something I don't.'

'I've been wondering when I should tell you of the next ministry God has called me to. Now you've given me the opportunity.'

'I'd be very pleased to hear of your new venture.'

'God has asked me to go to New Zealand and then America!'

'In that case, I doubt you'll be returning to Sydney.'

'I would like to come back to Sydney but God has clearly asked me to go to New Zealand. That's why I've been fitting in as many missions as possible this year. I've even agreed to hold a ten-day mission in the Temperance Hall at Albury on my way home.'

'I'm not surprised to hear you'll be going to other countries. I remember reading that the evangelist John Wesley maintained that the world was his parish. It seems that in a short space of time you will be able to say much the same thing.'

'It is rather daunting to be compared to Mr Wesley. I've been following God's leading each step of the way and He has only told me about New Zealand and America thus far. When I left home to go to Brisbane, Marion had not agreed to come with me to New Zealand. Neither of us wants to leave home. My son and his wife have an eighteen-month-old son and are soon to have another baby.'

Marion spoke up, 'But God showed me how we could go on to England and Wales. Mama grew up in Wales and I would love to see her childhood home, her school, her father's shop and where she went to her débutante ball.'

'It is an all-encompassing venture and I confess to a little fearfulness in regard to it. God has answered my prayers about Marion coming with me, but we know of no one in America who could give me permission to preach in a church. Will you keep us in your prayers for the whole of that time?'

'I shall do that, Mrs Baeyertz—if you will let me know in good time when and where you expect to take meetings, so that our prayers can help prepare the ground in advance.'

'We will be delighted to send you letters knowing that prayer will follow.'

'Now let's start our tour. I'll show you the hall in which you will be speaking. The hall and enquiry room are on this floor. We can also look in at my secretary's office so you know where to find her later.'

The women saw that the early history of the YMCA in Sydney had guided the design of the building. The Association's work had begun in a suite of small rooms in the neighbourhood. When they had the opportunity to provide for their own needs, they constructed this multi-storey building. An auditorium had the latest equipment. The first floor also contained a reading room for periodicals and a parlour with a well-stocked library. Classrooms, two dining rooms and a private conversation room were on the second floor. A gymnasium, with the latest exercising equipment, occupied the top floor so that the apparatus could be suspended from roof joists.

Emilia was astonished at the size of the rooms and the amount of equipment in storage until David explained that, since the building had opened, the Association had gained more than 1300 members. He assured her that the rooms were in use every day and night of the week by young women as well as young men. She had no doubt that the YMCA would succeed in its goal of increasing the physical, intellectual and spiritual wealth of young men in the colony.

On Sunday 20th October, the lecture hall was crowded with men who came from all over Sydney to hear the converted Jewess deliver her address on The Unpardonable Sin. The audience listened intently to Emilia's anecdotes about God's dealing with individuals at many of her public meetings. A large number of men remained at the end to obtain clearer explanations of their personal experiences. On the following day, *The Sydney Morning Herald* published a brief report.

CHAPTER 77

Kew, Victoria
November 1889

WHEN THEY RETURNED TO KEW FOR THE LAST TIME, EMILIA AND Marion contemplated the blessings provided by their cherished home with fresh pangs. Their dwelling had always looked bright, peaceful and home-like, even more so after long journeys. Now it took on an extra glow when they realised they had completed the last of their missions in Victoria.

The ladies visited the Macartney home for afternoon tea to discuss their new venture. Emilia explained that she would have access to pulpits in New Zealand through Mrs Downie Stewart, but she did not know how she would get the opportunity to preach in the United States of America. She knew no one with the authority to invite her to speak in public.

After his friends had returned home, Hussey sought the suggestions of fellow church leaders about a practical way they could help. If only she could preach one sermon in any of their churches, he felt sure the Americans would recognise her as one of God's evangelists and invite her to conduct a mission. After some thought and prayer, he and his colleagues decided to invite minis-ters Emilia had worked with to sign a joint recommendation for Emilia to carry on her travels.

Before she announced her new plans in public, Emilia wanted to speak of them to her family in private. Even though they may not have fully supported her activities throughout the years, they had not prevented her public speaking. Mary Anne had become a Christian through her daughter-in-law's ministry, and accepted that God had a great work for Emilia to undertake. Even so, she was tearful at the news that Emilia and Marion were to leave. She looked to her daughter Suzette and her grand-children for comfort.

The Baeyertz ladies called on George and his new wife, Charlotte. Weeping and long embraces followed Emilia's revelations. They also wrote to Eliza so the rest of her family would know they were coming.

Of their closest friends, the Johnstons gave the greatest support. They recognised the necessity of obeying the Lord but they also understood

Emilia's struggles. They would have been distraught if they also had to depart from Charles, Bella, Carl and the new baby.

Soon Mrs Baeyertz could announce, in one of her public meetings, that God had called her to go to New Zealand and America and that she and Marion would leave Melbourne on New Year's Eve. The news in Christian papers and the secular press was discussed around dinner tables, after church services and during prayer meetings. As the date drew nearer, her friends arranged a thanksgiving and farewell meeting at the Baptist Church in Collins Street.

No one was in any doubt that Mrs Baeyertz was an obedient servant of the Lord. She spoke about her departure with assurance, frequently mentioning God's new commission as a matter of fact and refusing to change her plans despite the urging of kind friends. However, when she walked through the front door of her home, Emilia privately doubted that she would be able to leave Melbourne. Marion would greet her warmly and promise to bring tea and cake as soon as she could make up a pot.

One memorable day, Emilia entered her little study—scene of so many wrestles with the Lord. His present call was her biggest challenge since Colac. Now, every time she thought of leaving Melbourne, Emilia trembled inwardly.

Her usual practice of praying while kneeling by her chair seemed inadequate. This time, she lay face down on the carpet and asked God for the strength to obey Him. Her thoughts turned to tears as she sobbed.

'I cannot go Lord; I cannot leave Charles and Bella and Carl behind. I don't know when I will see them again. I don't want to leave my friends who have helped me with Thy work either. I'm also worried about Charlie's mother. She's been a widow for ten years.'

The Holy Spirit reminded her of God's provision for Mary Ann in recent years. He would continue to care for her family. Emilia's simple task was to obey the Lord. Then she prayed, 'Yes, Lord! Thou art with me! Thou wilt be with me all the way and I'll go, Lord, where you want me to go!'

Emilia heard a shuffle at the door. Marion pushed it open with her elbow. 'Here's your tea and cake, Mama.' She entered her mother's study to put the tray on the occasional table. 'Oh, I'm sorry. I didn't know you were praying.'

'It's quite all right, dear. A cup of tea will do me good.' Emilia got up on her hands and knees and then used her chair to help her stand up.

Marion sat down and arranged the cups on the tray. 'Mama, I thought you didn't need to plead with God after I agreed to come. You told me in Sydney that God had shown you that new audiences needed to hear your story.' She poured milk, filled the cups with hot tea and put a teaspoon of sugar in each.

Emilia sat down in a comfortable chair and picked up a teacup. 'Visiting Bella and little Carl today made me shrink back from obeying God. Bella said everything is going well with the baby due next month. God willing, we'll see the baby before we leave.'

'We could look after Carl while Bella gets help with the birth', offered Marion.

'What a good idea! I'll talk to Bella. Their lease in Burke Road will finish at the end of this year. They are moving into this house for the cheaper rent now the property market is so uncertain. It's still near Bella's family and church. We can leave Charles to decide about furniture and the rest.'

Marion replied, 'Well, that's an answer to my prayers.'

'I see it as further proof that God is arranging matters.'

Her daughter replied, 'Now I'll have to ask for His guidance on the things I should take with me. We don't know how long we will be travelling.'

'I have the same problem, my dear.'

CHAPTER 78

Melbourne
December 1889

ON 14th DECEMBER, CHARLES BROUGHT CARL TO HIS GRANDMOTHER'S home while the mid-wife was with Bella. The active twenty-two-month-old toddler kept Marion and Emilia occupied until his bedtime. They prayed for Bella, Charles, the midwife and the baby then turned in. When they took Carl home the next day, they found a healthy baby girl in the arms of Bella. Maida, the newest member of the family, was welcomed joyfully.

On the evening of Tuesday 17th, the Baeyertz ladies went to a show at the Athenæum Theatre in Collins Street that had been recommended when Emilia was in Brisbane. Miss Lydia von Finkelstein did not disappoint. This was her big farewell to Australian shores. Emilia noticed that the American visitor was an experienced performer. Her descriptions of the people who presently lived in the Bible lands engaged her audience. Emilia could also compare Lydia's explanations of the culture and traditions of the people in the Old and New Testaments with the insights she'd gained from her own people.

Two nights later, Emilia and Marion returned to Collins Street to enter the Baptist Church, which was two doors up from the Athenæum. This gathering was also a farewell event for an inspiring woman who gave meaning to Bible stories, but Emilia's intent was to transform people's lives more directly through the Word.

The Baeyertz ladies had arrived well before the starting time, knowing that Emilia's meetings often attracted more people than could fit into the building. Marion chose a seat beside Charles, Bella and the Johnston family; Emilia was invited to sit on the stage. As she climbed the steps she recognised clergy and laity, both men and women, from several denominations. She was delighted that the meeting was open to all who wished to attend.

Emilia looked out at those sitting patiently in the hall. She recognised many people who had accepted Christ as their Saviour during one of her missions. Matthew Burnett, the Yorkshire Evangelist, was there taking notes.

His presence reminded Emilia that God had many servants in the colonies; she would not be leaving a void.

Dr Campbell, a prominent Presbyterian minister, occupied the chair and so was the first to speak. He said he did not usually approve of women being public speakers, but he recognised that Mrs Baeyertz had been commissioned by God to address both men and women. He certainly had no authority to hinder Mrs Baeyertz in her valuable ministry, particularly when she had led hundreds of people to the Lord Jesus and given glory to God. He then invited the evangelist to make some remarks.

Grasping her notes, Emilia stood up and went to the lectern. She could not speak until the audience ceased their generous applause. She thanked Dr Campbell for his kind words and then described the events that led her to conclude God wanted her to leave the colony to teach in New Zealand and America.

Ever since a dear sister in the Lord had returned from a visit to America with that picture of temperance women and urged Emilia to preach there, the evangelist had considered going. However, she was keenly aware of her responsibilities to her children and felt constrained from asking them to leave Melbourne so soon after they'd returned from South Australia. Besides, she'd received enough invitations to keep her busy preaching around the colony for the last five years.

Earlier in the year, God had clearly asked her to go to New Zealand and America and now was the moment to go. Her daughter's willingness to travel with her was confirmation. Emilia said nothing of her struggles to leave her grandchildren.

Emilia asked for prayer for her new ventures. She was acutely aware that it was only the prayers of the saints that made every service in the Lord's name bear fruit. Emilia promised to pray for the Christians in the colony of Victoria and looked forward to hearing how God had used them to bless every town and city.

She did not hesitate to teach from that pulpit about how to live as a Christian. She urged her audience to cultivate love and kindness for others, even in the seemingly trivial rounds of daily life. God would accomplish His own work in people's hearts when they were shown His love.

As an example, she shared from a letter she'd received from Mrs Henry Reed of Launceston, that very day. Margaret Reed had written a few thoughtful words which had lightened the recipient's heart and been a sweet song to her ever since she'd read them. She and Marion had been invited to visit Mrs Reed in Tasmania that January. Margaret had been her firm friend since Mr Reed had invited the Baeyertz family to stay with them at Wesley Dale in early 1878.

After some farewell remarks, Emilia sat down to a great applause.

Miss Sarah Booth, Honorary Secretary of the YWCA, was invited to the lectern. She reminded the audience that Mrs Baeyertz had worked amongst the women of Melbourne before their YWCA Chapter began. She explained that those engaged in Christian work know that grace is required to persevere for fourteen years. It was only through the Lord's help that Mrs Baeyertz had been so able. This was the highest tribute that could be paid to her work.

Mr Dimant, of Beath, Schiess and Co., a garment factory in Little Flinders Street, made suitable remarks when he presented Mrs Baeyertz with a purse of sovereigns from her friends. Another gentleman in the audience gave five pounds to Mrs Baeyertz as a thank offering for the blessings he'd received through her work.

Emilia's ability to work with many denominations was illustrated by the ministers from the Baptist, Wesleyan, Methodist and Presbyterian churches who gave short talks. Mr Swift, the Presbyterian minister at Alexandra, had travelled over 100 miles to attend this meeting. He reported that 230 people had converted during the two missions Mrs Baeyertz had held in his town.

Christopher Bunning, now a pastor at West Melbourne, stepped to the pulpit to speak. Emilia smiled at the memories. At Aberdeen Street in Geelong, Pastor Bunning had been one of those who nurtured her early faith, taught her biblical theology, encouraged her church and visiting ministries, supported her when she preached, and recommended her to the South Australians. Indeed, he spoke on behalf of the Baptist churches of South Australia to commend the work of Mrs Baeyertz in that colony.

The chairman concluded the meeting with the benediction. After Emilia left the stage, she was surrounded by people who wanted to speak to her. Most lined up to shake her hand, explain how her teaching had touched them and promise they'd pray for her. She was overwhelmed by their kindness and encouraged by their willingness to pray for Marion and herself.

*

Family celebrations in Melbourne were particularly meaningful that year; for some it was to be the last time they would see Emilia and Marion in this world. As usual, Emilia and Marion accepted the invitation to join Kerr, Eliza, Charles, Bella, Carl and Maida Johnston for their Christmas meal. They also shared a farewell meal with their Aronson family.

After Christmas, Emilia and Marion were visited by a small group of their most faithful men and women supporters. Before they prayed, John MacNeil presented the circular letter that Hussey Macartney had organised for Mrs Baeyertz. It was signed by fifteen leading ministers who affectionately commended her as 'an evangelist of exceptional power ... to the Churches of Christ, wherever in the providence of God she may be led.'

Emilia was surprised. 'My dear friends, I knew nothing of this but I see that you have responded to God's promptings. I could not understand how I could speak in America when I know no one to introduce me there. It has been my fervent prayer for many weeks that God would provide a means through which I would be recognised as His servant by Christians in America. Now I see that He has answered my prayer through your generous gift. I can show these qualifications to my brothers and sisters wherever I go.'

Tears streamed down Emilia's cheeks while she hugged and prayed for her only son in her cabin. She had been dreading this moment for months. Tomorrow she and Marion would steam away on SS *Pateena*. The time had come to leave Charles and his family behind and to pray for them, trusting in the Lord. That was the best farewell present she could offer.

Epilogue
1890 to 1926

Tasmania,
January 1890

THEY HAD GIVEN UP MANY PRECIOUS THINGS TO OBEY GOD'S CALLING, but not yet their summer holiday in Tasmania. SS *Pateena* arrived in Launceston on New Year's Day. Emilia, with Marion, spent much of January visiting the men and women who had supported her missions, perhaps for the last time.

The Baeyertz ladies were delighted to stay with Mrs Reed. Her magnificent home, Mount Pleasant, was said by some to be the finest house in northern Tasmania. Emilia particularly enjoyed this period of ease because she expected to be engaged in tiring missions in the months to come.

Emilia's last address in Australia was delivered on the evening of Monday 3rd February, at the Sailors' Home in Hobart. The Committee provided tea for their guests, the crew of the survey vessel HMS *Rambler* and other members of the seafaring class. She gave her address about Lazarus and the rich man, to which her audience listened with great interest.

New Zealand,
Autumn to Spring 1890

ON TUESDAY 11th FEBRUARY, EMILIA AND MARION DESCENDED A GANG plank to meet Mr and Mrs Downie Stewart on the wharf of Port Chalmers on the South Island of New Zealand. After a warm reunion with Mary, they all travelled by train to the Stewart family home in Dunedin, where the Baeyertz women would stay for several weeks.

Emilia's first mission there was under the auspices of the Young Women's Christian Association in Dunedin, the first Chapter in the colony. Good reports about her meetings at the YWCA Hall, Trinity Wesleyan Church and Garrison Hall appeared in the newspapers.

Mary Stewart sought invitations for Mrs Baeyertz from churches throughout the country. She sent letters, with printed copies of Emilia's circular letter, to various denominations. Offers arrived from churches on both major islands, so Mary made arrangements for Mrs Baeyertz to work her way north, starting with missions from March to June in Oamaru, Christchurch, Ashburton and Nelson.

In many ways, New Zealand was like the Australia she had left. The economic depression was just as bad. Workers had lost jobs and some would go out on strike. Yet, many families found the same hope in Emilia's words. She introduced the methods and messages she had used in Australia and received similar responses in New Zealand. Numerous people remained after meetings to seek guidance in the enquiry rooms. As a result, many men, women and children joyfully acknowledged Jesus as their Lord and Saviour. The organising committees took up offerings to cover the expenses and often gave a donation to Mrs Baeyertz.

During her afternoon meetings, hundreds heard Emilia use the Bible Readings to explore how a believer should live. Articles in local newspapers explained that, unlike earlier evangelists, Mrs Baeyertz ministered to the Christian as well as to the unsaved. The papers' summaries of her talks encouraged more citizens to attend. A lengthy interview of Mrs Baeyertz by a reporter appeared in *The Nelson Evening Mail* of Tuesday 24th June.

In July, Emilia and Marion crossed Cook Strait to the North Island to find high expectations in Wellington. Mrs Baeyertz spoke to large audiences in the Opera House, the Central Hall and the Salvation Army Barracks until her mission finished in mid-August. From late August to the end of September, Emilia spoke at meetings for the YMCA further north, in Wanganui and in Auckland.

In Auckland, her afternoon bible readings now attracted over a thousand listeners. Her evening lectures were even more popular, so much so that newspapers published summaries the following morning and warned parents to leave children at home for the sake of safety. One of those publishers, Henry Brett, printed a booklet with three of her lectures and the story of her conversion.

A new theme in Emilia's talks was the return of the twelve tribes to the Promised Land. After one of those talks, the Rabbi of Auckland made a point of thanking her.

At the conclusion of that Auckland mission for the YMCA, Mrs Parkinson provided a bountiful tea for eight clergy and 300 converts. The committee presented Emilia with a morocco leather case, beautifully tooled in gold, with the words of an address thanking her sunk into the boards, surmounted by sea views and an emblazoned border. Mrs Baeyertz cordially acknowledged that the gift would be useful in America to satisfy people that she was not an imposter (laughter). Mrs Baeyertz gave a brief practical address that was followed by brief testimonies from 170 converts and a word or two from seven dignitaries.

In New Zealand, Marion began to manage all of her mother's correspondence. Mr Walker had sent her the address of Mr McCoy, General Secretary of the San Francisco Chapter of the YMCA. Marion passed on that address to John MacNeil in Melbourne who then placed a note in *The Southern Cross* 'for those who wished to send a line of cheer in that strange land'. She also replied to Mr Walker that they would travel on the mail steamer SS *Zealander* to San Francisco.

On Monday 6th October 1890, the Baeyertz ladies were farewelled by hundreds of people on Wellington wharf. As the steamship left, the crowd sang, 'God be with you till we meet again'. As she listened and watched the crowd waving, Emilia's heart leaped upward in grateful love for the expressed affection of all. She said to herself, 'Goodbye dear Australia! When, oh, when shall I see you again?'

North America,
Fall 1890 to Spring 1892

SS *ZEALANDER* DOCKED AT SAN FRANCISCO ON MONDAY 27th OCTOBER. At their hotel, Emilia prayed, 'Lord, what wilt Thou have me now to do?' Mr Walker's note came to mind so she asked Marion to find it. When they had the address of Mr McCoy, Emilia dictated a letter for Marion to send to him.

Mr McCoy promptly visited the Baeyertz ladies. As they shared a pot of tea and some cake supplied by their hotel, he was shown the circular letter from Melbourne and the morocco case from Auckland. He very kindly thanked the women and then candidly explained that he represented the Young *Men's* Christian Association. There was no opening for a lady.

After he had departed, Emilia asked Marion, 'What does this mean? Have I mistaken God's leading?'

While Marion pondered, her mother supplied the answer. 'No! God would not let me so persistently mistake Him as to bring me here and leave me with every door closed against me.' Yet, there was no light, no opening. However, there was the word of her God to her soul amid her difficulty— '*Stand still* and know that I am God!'

After two days, Mr McCoy returned to their hotel. 'I have heard from Sydney, Mrs Baeyertz. Mr Walker writes that your services are much blessed to young men. Now, next week is our week of prayer for them. Will you consent to hold meetings every night for men only?'

Emilia promptly accepted. Now it was Mr McCoy's turn to wait and see the result of plans which God had begun several years earlier. By the end of the week, fifty men had claimed Jesus as their Saviour. God had opened doors to Emilia; Emilia had opened doors to God.

Her second invitation in San Francisco was from the minister of the First Baptist Church. A marvellous time followed as the congregation experienced God's ministry through the previously unknown evangelist.

The ladies were to spend twenty months in North America. On leaving San Francisco in 1890, they spent November and December travelling through California, visiting Sacramento, Monterey, Pacific Grove and Los Angeles.

Their stay in Los Angeles during 1891 took on extra significance as they were able to meet a relative they had not seen for many years: John Baeyertz, Emilia's brother-in-law and Marion's uncle. He was now Chief Clerk at the Santa Fe Railroad Freight Depot and soon to marry a lady named Olivia Phelps.

Mrs Baeyertz received a request to speak at the Los Angeles YMCA. She was not widely known, so her first audience was merely a few score. Within two weeks, an excited crowd of 4,000 flocked to hear her Easter address at the Simpson Tabernacle, the largest church in the city.

The news was not all good, however. Marion fell ill from malaria. Emilia stopped teaching to tend to her. While the days stretched into weeks, they received papers and letters that brought more bad news. The era of Marvellous Melbourne was over; land prices had crashed. Charles, who had borrowed heavily, lost heavily and had to try his luck as a travelling tea salesman until his mother's good reports of New Zealand led him to leave for Dunedin on 24th February 1891. Two days later, his grandmother, Mary Anne Baeyertz, died at her home in Black Street, Brighton. That May, Bella and their children joined Charles in Dunedin where the economy was no better but he did find some work as a musician.

By midsummer 1891, Marion had recovered well enough to travel, by stages, with her mother through Chicago to Hamilton, Ontario. After Mrs Baeyertz spoke there they went on to the YMCA at Toronto.

They then turned to the eastern United States. Emilia had been invited to speak at the well-known church of the Reverend Dr J. A. Gordon, in Boston, Massachusetts, where her mission was warmly received.

Boston also interested Emilia as a tourist for, in the suburb of Cambridge, they could visit Craigie House, which had been the residence of one of her favourite poets. Henry Wadsworth Longfellow had died nine years earlier. The house was then occupied by his oldest surviving daughter, Mary Alice Longfellow.

Boston is well-suited to tourists for another reason—it is by the sea. Emilia chose a resort where she and Marion could swim, walk barefoot through the waves and enjoy the cooling sea breezes. Their coastal activities eased away the exhaustion of public speaking. This season of rest was a great physical blessing.

While in Boston, Emilia received a letter from the Toronto YMCA requesting that she return for another mission. She replied that she would, if they opened the whole of Canada to her. They agreed. Emilia and Marion arrived in the Fall of 1891 to remain in Ontario and Quebec until the Spring. Emilia never forgot the Canadian style of generous hospitality they experienced, nor her deliciously novel and exhilarating sleigh ride in London. This had been the first time she'd been on snow since her childhood in Wales.

Britain,
Spring 1892 to 1904

ON 13ᵗʰ APRIL 1892, EMILIA AND MARION BOARDED WHITE STAR LINER *Teutonic*, in New York, bound for Ireland. Their ship arrived in Queenstown in early May. On the first Sunday after her arrival, Emilia gave her first Gospel address in Ireland in the Parochial School House.

Emilia's first standard mission in the British Isles was held in Cork. In the crowd was a lad of fifteen, named Tommy. At the suggestion that those who had received a blessing from the Lord should write their names in the Minute Book of the YMCA, Thomas Chatterton Hammond did so. Soon he was known as 'The Boy Preacher' and became an enthusiastic evangelist and author in the Church of Ireland. Decades later, in Sydney, New South Wales, the Reverend Dr T. C. Hammond would reinvigorate Moore Theological College as Principal.

After the Cork mission, Emilia rested by the sea at Glengarrif, visited the tourist town of Killarney then continued to other missions in Ireland.

Emilia was fifty years old and her daughter was twenty-three when they arrived in England in July 1892. They established a base in London which they found to be good for meeting old friends. Henry Varley, whom they had first met in Tasmania fourteen years before, introduced church ministers to Mrs Baeyertz. For the next twelve years, Emilia travelled around England, Scotland and Wales to conduct missions in hamlets, towns and cities.

In New Zealand, Charles Nalder Baeyertz found enough interest in theatre and music to establish a successful journal. In April 1893, he published his first edition of *The Triad, a Monthly Magazine of Music, Science and Art*.

In Edinburgh, Marion married James Kirkland, a doctor from New Zealand, on 29th October 1895. They lived in England and had three children. Emilia was able to participate in the lives of some of her grandchildren at last.

Australia,

1904 to 1906

IN 1904, DR KIRKLAND MOVED HIS FAMILY, WITH EMILIA, TO PERTH IN the new state of Western Australia, for 'reasons of health'. Soon Emilia was conducting missions in the towns that she could reach by rail.

Emilia received a request to return to Melbourne. After a sea voyage, she arrived on 30th March 1905. Great joy was shared amongst beloved relatives and the co-workers with whom she'd toiled in the previous century. Emilia also praised God when told that many hundreds of the people she had led to Christ were still faithful disciples making significant contributions to their communities. Indeed, a number of them had become ministers of God's grace at home and abroad. Emilia accepted invitations to hold missions in five churches in Melbourne's suburbs and two churches in Ballarat.

In November 1905, Emilia sailed to Tasmania for one last summer. In Launceston she held a mission in the Henry Reed Memorial Church and another in the Hobart Baptist Tabernacle.

In February 1906, Charles sailed from New Zealand to Hobart to see his mother for the last time. On greeting her son, Emilia found a confident thirty-nine-year-old man who was a musician, a performer and an arts critic with influence in New Zealand and Australian society. He would continue to publish *The Triad* until June 1924.

Emilia returned firstly to Melbourne, then to Perth, after an eleven-month absence, and then back to Britain.

Britain,
Summer 1906 to Spring 1926

EMILIA STILL HAD THE ENERGY TO RESUME THE ITINERANT LIFE. SHE spent a further twelve years travelling to communities around the British Isles to teach believers and non-believers what God required of them and why they should acknowledge Jesus as their Christ, Saviour, Redeemer and Lord.

In 1918, at the age of 76, Emilia ceased public speaking to stay home in her terrace house on Streatham Hill, south of London. Now, instead of travelling with a trunk all the time, she could enjoy the company of the Kirkland family who lived nearby. After eight years of retirement, on Monday 26th April 1926, Mrs Emilia Louise Baeyertz died in the care of her daughter, Marion.

Amanda's tribute to Mrs Emilia Louise Baeyertz

MRS EMILIA BAEYERTZ BELIEVED GOD HAD GIVEN HER THE GIFT OF evangelism and that He frequently gave her instructions on how and where to use it. Her life was shaped by this belief and her commitment to obeying the Sovereign God of the Universe.

Emilia constantly studied the Bible for herself and gained new insights into many passages, even the ones on which her talks were based. She looked to Father God for more discoveries and developed new talks to share her recent findings. She had a vibrant relationship with God because she depended on Him in every aspect of her life.

The longer she was a Christian, the more Emilia submitted her will to Father God. She often asked God to make things happen in a certain way. Eventually she would give up her expectations and accept that God would do things His way. This is what she meant by giving up her will. After accepting God's will, she often received a sweet consciousness of His presence. Emilia believed it was only through complete submission to Him that she would gain His approval and assistance in every venture He set before her. Emilia also believed she only received God's power because she recognised her true status before Him. That was why she was not arrogant or boastful. The idea of complete submission to God's will is not fashionable in some parts of the Christian Church today.

Despite her desire to obey God, Emilia often struggled to do as He asked, because His requirement either cut across her personal values or her society's values. When God instructed her to speak to men and women in public, she had to disobey a fundamental value in Victorian society. To keep the status of an acceptable woman, Emilia should have remained the mistress of her home circle and confined her opinions to her family. By entering into the public sphere, she challenged her society's standard that only men had the right to teach both men and women in public.

After hearing Mrs Baeyertz speak in a new town, locals often debated the correctness of her behaviour. They could see that her ministry was blessed by a power over which they had no control and they interpreted her success as evidence that the Sovereign God enabled her. The grumblers often concluded they had no right to prevent Emilia from speaking in public. If hundreds of people had not responded favourably to her, she may not have been allowed or encouraged to conduct missions.

At the same time, the suffragette and temperance movements challenging the status quo in the British Isles, Australasia and North America benefited Emilia's ministry by helping to bring acceptance of women undertaking significant roles outside their homes.

Why was Emilia's ministry so successful? In the first instance, Emilia gave Christians new access into a Jewish world view. She explained Old Testament and New Testament ideas through the glasses of her Jewish heritage.

Audience members with a Protestant interpretation of Jesus' teaching received a clear Jewish Christian perspective of what He had said.

Her public talks were also captivating because of her vivid illustrations, some of which came directly from her own experiences. Emilia suggested that ordinary people could encounter the Holy Spirit. She explained how to gain a deeper relationship with God and benefit from His power. Her life and ministry showed it was possible to live a more satisfying life as a Christian. Emilia offered hope that there was more to human existence than the usual round of daily life.

Was her close relationship with God an adequate compensation for the things Emilia had to give up? Despite His presence in her life, Mrs Baeyertz still experienced loneliness while she was away from home. She did not like having to depend on strangers for support when public speaking exhausted her. Although she always had a home of her own, she spent long periods of time living in other people's homes and in hotels. Emilia may not have been able to develop close relationships with key people, or to have the comfort of belonging to one church and one community. She also missed participating in the lives of her son's children. We would now consider most of the things she did not have as desirable, perhaps essential, to a well-balanced life.

Emilia had to find other ways to maintain her sense of self, develop supportive friendships, find ways to adapt, depend on God to provide her security and recognise that God had His own ways to meet her needs.

During her lifetime, from 1842 to 1926, extraordinary changes occurred in most fields of human endeavour. The structure of societies throughout the world altered and the way people lived and thought also changed. Through it all, Emilia told the old, old story without sensationalism and insisted that it was still relevant.

Emilia Louise Baeyertz lived a remarkable life. Her ability to obey Father God meant she touched the lives of thousands of people for the better in the English-speaking world. Until recently, the Christian community in Australia had forgotten about this remarkable woman. Thanks to many people who have contributed to this book, many more can now celebrate Emilia's achievements.

We can also look for the ways God has used, and continues to use, His faithful disciples in every age to intervene in human history and reveal the Kingdom of God here on earth.

The Immediate Family of Emilia Baeyertz

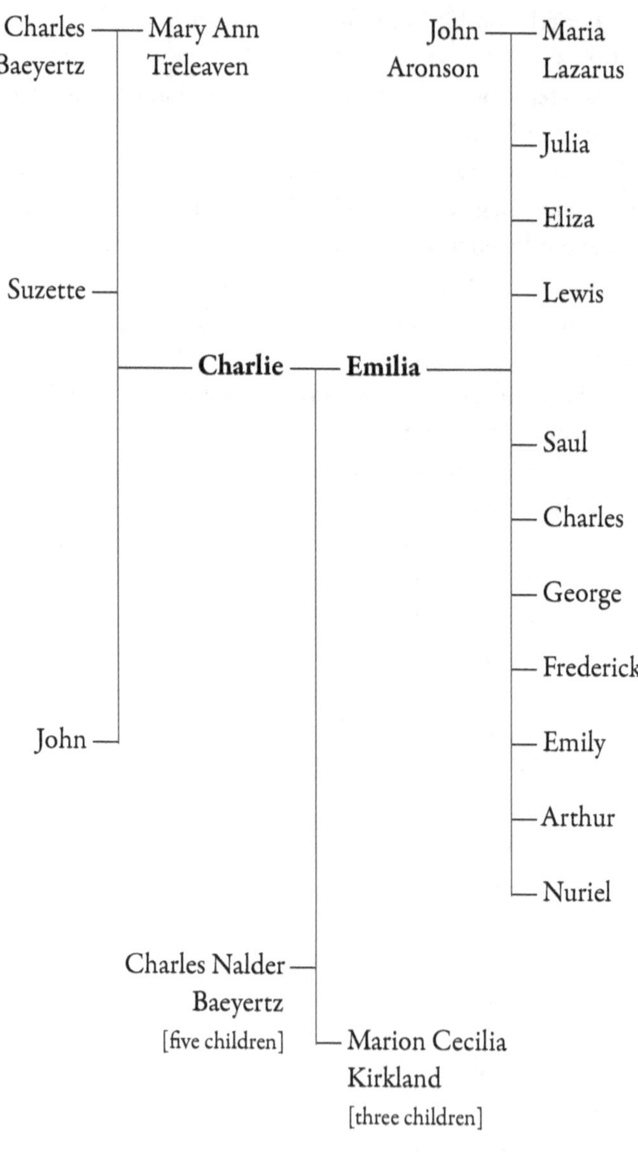

Glossary

Afikoman. The 'dessert' is the middle broken, larger, piece of Matzo of three Matzot at the Seder table. It is eaten at the end of the Passover meal as the unleavened bread was eaten with the sacrificial lamb before the Temple was destroyed. It is 'hidden' by the head of the house at the beginning of Seder. The youngest member in the house is rewarded for the finding of the Afikoman. From Greek.

Bar mitzvah. At the age of thirteen years a Jewish boy becomes an adult. He then observes the commandments of Judaism by taking responsibility to perform all the duties. From Hebrew meaning 'Son of the commandment'.

Charoseth. Apples, nuts, wine and spices pounded together to represent the clay used by the Israelites to make bricks for Pharaoh's builders. From Hebrew *Haroset*.

Chuppa. The canopy supported by four poles, fixed or held by relatives, under which the groom and his bride stand to be married. A symbol of the new home to be built for their personal lives. From Hebrew *Huppah*.

Goel. An office held by a near relative to accept the duty of continuing the preservation of the family such as line, property or good name. From Hebrew Gaal meaning 'To redeem'.

Haggadah. The text for Seder from Talmudic literature formulated after the destruction of the Temple. From Hebrew meaning 'Narration'.

Ma'ariv prayer. The evening service which is to be recited every day of one's life. From Hebrew.

Matzo. A thin, perforated square cake of unleavened bread made of flour and water and quickly baked to stop fermentation. It is called the 'bread of affliction' and is eaten at the Passover meal as a symbol of the affliction of Israel's slavery in Egypt. From Hebrew. See Exodus 13:6.

Meshumadim. Jewish people who, of their own free will, forsake Judaism and embrace another faith. From Hebrew.

Pidyon haBen. A first-born son, unless a Levite, is redeemed at the cost of five shekels to a Kohen (a priest) thirty days after the birth. From Hebrew.

Seder. The ceremony held in Jewish homes on the night of Passover as a reminder of the Passover meal and the offering of the Paschal lamb which is celebrated in March or April on 15 Nisan of the Jewish calendar. From Hebrew meaning 'Order'.

Second Seder. A second ceremony held on 16 Nisan in many Jewish homes outside Israel.

Sit shiva. A period of grief for the death of a close relative. Family members neither wash nor shave, nor wear cosmetics or new clothes. No work is performed and family members sit on the floor or low stools. A child who marries outside the Jewish faith is accounted as dead. From Hebrew.

Yarmulke. A skull cap worn as a head covering by male orthodox Jews in recognition that life is always lived in the presence of God. From Yiddish. The Hebrew word is *Kippah*.

Merle Roseman

Authors' Notes

Without the information contained in the book entitled *From Darkness to Light—The Life and Work of Mrs Baeyertz*, by Sydney Watson, we today would know almost nothing of Emilia's childhood in Wales and early life in Australia. She gave Mr Watson what was suitable to promote her message and to give people at her meetings some understanding of Emilia's background and experience.

It was not until she began her public ministry that interviewers asked personal questions of her and reports were published giving her testimony. I have photocopies of eighteen of her messages which were taken down by Hansard reporters as she gave them at her meetings.

It has been my privilege to meet a member of the Baeyertz family, Dr John Baeyertz, a great-grandson of Emilia and Charles living in New Zealand. He put me in touch with a member of the family by marriage in New South Wales, Mrs Lois Baeyertz, who graciously allowed me the use of a Baeyertz family scrapbook containing newspaper clippings from New Zealand, Canada, the United States of America, and United Kingdom, as well as the Australian colonies.

This has allowed me to give brief excerpts from the newspaper cuttings of her day in the historical novel. Unfortunately, the name of the newspaper from which a paragraph came has not always been attached, nor has the date (in some cases not even the year) been available. But these two sources, Sydney Watson's book and the family scrapbook, have been almost my only means of building up the true story of this most remarkable and godly woman and I freely acknowledge my indebtedness in this regard.

I have had a most comprehensive view of Emilia's worldwide ministry and the response it provoked in each place.

Throughout her public ministry, Emilia found that the spelling of her name Emilia caused some difficulty to journalists and others. So much so, that when she was in Cork, she was happy to be known as Emily Baeyertz.

But her marriage certificate, of which I have a copy, clearly gives her name as Emilia Louise, as does the family tree, which was kindly sent from New Zealand. The spelling difficulty continues however, for her will gives her name as Emelia Louisa, and it would be well for us to let the matter rest there.

Where fact is interlaced with fiction, it is not an easy matter for the reader to assess how much of this story is true, so it must be said at the outset that this book is solidly based on fact.

Wherever I have known characters' correct names, I have used them in the narrative.

Betty Baruch

Betty wrote those words for her Author's Note in 1998. Since then, some pertinent events have required changes to her book. I, Amanda, have many questions for Betty (and Emilia and Charlie) which won't be answered till we meet in heaven. Now I have access to a few of Betty's notes and letters, but not her library nor her research. I have Betty's manuscript, her summary of Emilia's life and her copies of her selected scraps from the Baeyertz family scrapbook, but not the scrapbook itself. I have gleaned much from historical material from Internet sources like Trove at the National Library of Australia. Later editions of *From Darkness to Light* and much more have been collected, collated and analysed by Rev. Robert Evans.

This Is My Beloved is based on historical people. Consider their names. Novelists sensibly avoid using the same name for two different people except for effect. In Emilia's world of the nineteenth century, we meet real people with common names such as Charles (eight), Maria/Mary (six), John (five), Thomas (five), Emily/Emilia (three), Sarah (three) and variations on Elizabeth (six). What editor would allow that in a work of fiction? Just how many Marys are there in the Gospels anyway?

Nevertheless, *This Is My Beloved* is a novel. Betty and I have each imagined how events might have been. Betty took liberties with history to add colour, drama and romance. I have largely kept Betty's descriptions of Jewish life and relevant historical detail while pruning and grafting the rest. My husband, Garth, has helped me find fascinating historical documents. Where accounts clash, I have adopted a likely resolution. Often I have had to rely on a single source.

No doubt, by the time you read this, someone will have digitized another newspaper into Trove that proves me wrong in some respect. I trust that all such discoveries are to the glory of God.

To the Aronson, Baeyertz, Baruch and Berens families, I apologise for any offence. None is intended. The keepers of your family histories know much that I will never know.

Emilia deserves a properly researched biography which covers her whole life and ministry. I have written, not a biography but a novel with a Companion. If you were to build on these works and those of Sydney Watson, Robert Evans and others in the bibliography, you would find enough for another book or two, and maybe a PhD or movie, of your own.

I haven't gone far into analysing Emilia's theology, spirituality or sermons. These topics have been nicely covered by Robert Evans.

Mines into which I have not delved include Royal Navy, Welsh Newspapers Online, *Jewish Chronicle*, Jewish Museum of Australia, records of Geelong churches, *The Missionary at Home and Abroad*, Public Records Office of Victoria, Tasmanian Archives and Heritage Office, *New Zealand Graphic*, Library of Congress, British Library, Bodleian Library and *The Triad*. Does anyone have a copy of Emilia's paper *My Authority as a Woman for Preaching the Gospel*?

We trust that you have been built up by reading Emilia's story. If you want more, I suggest that you start by reading *This Is My Beloved Companion*. There you can find notes for each chapter, more selected historical accounts and talks, lists of places, people and times, and a bibliography from which you can select your next text to read.

Amanda Coverdale

The Story Behind the Story

In 1986, *The Jews in Victoria 1835–1985* by Hilary L. Rubinstein was published. In it she briefly mentions Emilia Baeyertz, an evangelist to the Christians, amongst the *meshumadim* in Victoria. David Perry soon brought this observation to the attention of Betty Baruch, his friend in Melbourne, who then set out to discover what she could of Emilia.

Betty wrote to John Baeyertz, whom she found in a New Zealand phone book. She found a copy of Emilia's authorized biography *From Darkness to Light* in a Special Collection of the Baillieu Library at Melbourne University. Out of her research came a manuscript for *This Is My Beloved*. Betty had written fiction before and, as historical details were scarce, a novel based on history became her way to tell Emilia's story. In her draft Acknowledgments, Betty wrote:

> The author wishes to express her great indebtedness to David Perry who rediscovered Emilia and gave invaluable help with research for the book, and the Baeyertz family, in particular Dr John Baeyertz of New Zealand and Mrs Lois Baeyertz of Sydney. They were both willing to loan the author a family scrapbook listing Emilia's meetings throughout the English-speaking world and containing interviews in many places she visited.
>
> The author must also acknowledge her heartfelt thanks to Lance and Sandra Hodgson for all the work they have put into preparing the manuscript, Valerie Hipe for typing and retyping, and others who helped get the typing onto computer.
>
> **Betty Baruch, 1998**

Many others helped Betty with her book project. Merle Roseman wrote a useful Glossary and tried to find a publisher. Amy Chalmers typed some more.

Shortly before Betty's death in 2000, she entrusted her manuscript to her friends at the West Clayton Cell Group of the Clayton Church of Christ Fellowship in Victoria, Australia, who agreed to get it published, somehow. Between them they had great skills and experience with many things, but not with publishing books.

Trudy Snyers, Betty's trusty friend, 'kept alive' Betty's desire to see Emilia's story widely known. Many read and commented on the text, including Mark Warren and Joy Hunting of David House Fellowship and Win Morgan. Lawrence Hirsch wrote a gracious Foreword. Generous donors created a small fund. Legal advice was commissioned. Prayers were offered. Encouragement was given. Quotes for layout, cover design and printing were obtained. 'All' they needed was a publisher!

One international organisation was keen for hundreds of copies, so offered to publish the book. After a year of consideration, that organisation declined. They weren't publishers after all. One publisher declined because the book was 'derivative'. Another didn't 'do fiction'. Betty's sister decided not to publish.

The Cell Group was stuck till one of their members, Gwen McKelvie, received the Christmas 2006 newsletter from me, Amanda Coverdale. Gwen and I had been missionaries together in Papua New Guinea some years before, and now I was going freelance as an editor. *This is My Beloved* became my first book editing project.

The Baeyertz scrapbooks had long since been returned to the family without having been photocopied. The author was not available for consultation. The biography commissioned by the subject has been out of print for a century. Most writings on and by the subject were ephemeral.

I polished *This is My Beloved* for publication, while changing and charging as little as possible, and then moved onto other books for other authors.

We kept looking for a publisher. We are grateful for those who gave the work due consideration. For a book that was neither fully fiction nor fully fact, no publisher appeared to have a suitable genre let alone an imprint.

The time drew near for the cell group to disperse. So Betty's friends decided to publish the book themselves. They incorporated the Emilia

Baeyertz Society (EBSI) to which they could collectively assign the copyright and through which they could arrange for publication.

Friends who volunteered to help included Val Hipe, Lance Hodgson, Sandra Hodgson, Gwen McKelvie, David Soffe, Dorothy Soffe, Kwee Sin Phua and Carolyn Yong. Betty, Gwen, David and Dorothy had been students together at Melbourne Bible Institute. Those serving on the Management Committee of the Society have included Lance, Sandra, Gwen, David, Dorothy, Kwee Sin, Ron Emilsen, Miranda Starkey, my husband, Garth, and me.

Garth mentioned to a graphic designer friend that we were having trouble finding the designer who had quoted on the job years before. Our friend then offered his graphic design services. This was a blessing. He showed the edited manuscript to his employers and they offered to publish the book. We were away! After a long negotiation, we had a contract.

Only then did they pass the manuscript to their assessor. The book didn't suit their style after all. It was neither history nor biography. Characters and events in the book clashed with known history. We knew all that. Betty said so in the back of the book. That hadn't bothered Betty in the slightest. Betty had woven weft of history and gospel through warp of romance and crime. Yet, many readers who like blends of history and story demand that verisimilitude not be lost by jarring encounters with what they know cannot be true.

For the third time, the project had been on hold for a year while waiting for someone to decide not to publish.

The EBSI Committee sent me back to the editing screen to rework the book, trim fat and falsehood, add what relevant history could readily be discovered and revise the endpapers. Incrementally, I made the transition from editor to co-author and Secretary and Garth became editor and President. We were excited when we found vivid history in our research and also disappointed when that meant we had to cut or adapt Betty's stories.

Garth became integral to this project. Without his assistance, editing, research, leadership and constant encouragement, this novel may never have been published.

Now, as we worked on the manuscript, we could refer to the biography of Emilia's son, Charles Nalder Baeyertz, which Joanna Woods had published in 2008. More useful still was the help from and extensive research by the Reverend Robert Evans OAM. For an analysis of Emilia's theology and impact, and for a collection of contemporary sources for her life, we recommend that you read his book *Emilia Baeyertz—Evangelist, Her career in Great Britain and Australia*. You can buy a paper book, hand-crafted by the author, or download a PDF, through revivals.arkangles.com. Robert also lent us his collection of sources which includes the latest edition of Sydney Watson's *From Darkness to Light* and some of Betty's letters.

We expanded the 'List of Missions' created by Robert Evans into a detailed Chronology of Emilia's life as we collated Evans' collection, Watson's vagueness, Betty's imagination and Trove's immenseness. We replaced half the book, added a map and family tree, dropped the Foreword and added Notes and Appendices which we later moved to *This is My Beloved Companion*.

The committee met, often in Room 4 at Clayton Church of Christ, to keep the project moving. More people commented on more drafts—thanks especially to Carlyn Mathews, Patsy Coverdale, Kwee Sin Phua, Diana Summers, Carolyn Yong, Miranda Starkey and Jackie Brady. A field trip to Colac was especially productive due to help offered by the Colac and District Family History Group, the Colac and District Historical Society and Anthony Bright of Rod Bright and Associates. A later trip to Echuca proved useful too.

Now that the Internet is ubiquitous, the challenge is not so much where to find information, but when to stop looking. Yet this is not a new challenge; 'there is no new thing under the sun'. In the words of The Preacher, 'of making many books there is no end: and much study is a weariness of the flesh. Let us hear the conclusion of the whole matter: Fear God, and keep his commandments: for this is the whole duty of man. For God shall bring every work into judgement, with every secret thing, whether it be good, or whether it be evil'.

This Is My Beloved has been written and published, as Betty Baruch stated on the title page of her manuscript, 'With help from Above'.

Amanda Coverdale

About the Authors

Betty Baruch was born into the Jewish faith in 1927. She migrated, with her family, from Poland to Australia when she was five years old.

After school in Horsham and Melbourne, she began studying pharmacy but transferred to primary school teaching. During her first teaching assignment in Gippsland, she recognised Jesus was the Messiah and committed her life to Him.

On completing her teaching assignment, Betty set out for India, expecting God would show her where to serve. Eventually, Betty was led to Dr Graham's Homes in Kalimpong, West Bengal, where she taught Anglo-Indian children for two years. She returned to Australia to study at the Melbourne Bible Institute (now Melbourne School of Theology) during 1959–1960. Subsequently, Betty served in Dr Graham's Homes at Kalimpong for a further four years. In 1965, she returned to Melbourne after her father died, and she remained in Australia to care for her mother.

Under her pennames, Tova David and Jennifer David, Betty wrote four short evangelistic fiction books set in places she had lived.

God opened doors to Betty in a variety of ministries other than formal teaching in schools. Wherever she lived in Melbourne and Brisbane, Betty found ways of caring for her neighbours, encouraging Christians and working with Jewish people.

Each week for fifteen years, Betty and a team of helpers handed out literature to pedestrians on Acland Street, St Kilda. Another of her ministries was with the Baptist New Settlers Association. In 1992, Betty attended the Lausanne Congress on World Evangelization and became the representative for Jewish outreach in the South Pacific.

While Betty lived in a unit at Trinity Close, Oakleigh, from 1993 to 1998, she wrote her fifth book *This Is My Beloved* and received great support for this project. Following a stroke in September 1998, she became a resident of Oakmoor and later Darvell Lodge. Betty went to be with her Lord Jesus the Messiah on 19th June 2000.

May her soul be bound up in the bundle of life with God.

Like Emilia, Betty was of the tribe of Levi, migrated to Melbourne by sea, yielded herself to the Lord Jesus at about the age of twenty-seven and proclaimed Jesus to the end of her long life.

Amanda Coverdale was born in Wapena-manda in the Territory of Papua and New Guinea and moved to Australia at the age of fifteen in advance of her family.

She has served in administration, writing, editing and research roles for archi-tects, doctors, libraries, schools, churches, publishers, missions and authors including the Evangelical Church of Papua New Guinea, Asia Pacific Christian Mission, *Alive Magazine* and Mission Avia-tion Fellowship.

Amanda has an Advanced Certificate in Professional Writing and Editing from CAE, a BA in Art History from La Trobe University, both in Melbourne, and an MA in Cross-Cultural Studies from Fuller Theological Seminary in Pasadena, California.

For the Curious Reader

For the curious reader who wants to research Mrs Baeyertz, or simply know more about her, the Emilia Baeyertz Society has also published a companion book. Some of the documents we found while researching her life are too valuable to ignore and some are enjoyable to read in their own right.

This Is My Beloved Companion includes our selection of historical extracts, reports, letters, interviews, pictures and talks.

Our complete list of characters in the novel reveals which are historical and which are fictional.

If you look through our list of places where Emilia preached, you may be surprised to see your town. Then, in our extensive chronology of her life and times, you may see your church or hall. You will also better understand the events in *This Is My Beloved* and get some idea of what we had to leave out of the novel.

Notes for each chapter give more detail of the background, incidents, characters, sources and references. A bibliography will help you find our sources and works that we would have liked to find. We included several of Emilia's talks so that she can speak to you and challenge you today!

In the next few pages, we present a sample of historical documents from *This Is My Beloved Companion*.

MELANCHOLY ACCIDENT

A MELANCHOLY ACCIDENT OCCURRED ON SATURDAY afternoon by which Mr. C. Baeyertz manager of the National Bank narrowly escaped a fearful death.

He left the town about 4 o'clock and proceeded to the racecourse paddock to shoot quail. While in the paddock Mr. Woodward of the Stoneyrises passed up the road and observing Mr. Baeyertz called to him and he came to the fence dividing the paddock from the road; he placed the stock of his gun on the ground and reached over to shake hands with Mr. Woodward when suddenly the gun went off, the charge entering between the left shoulder and breast and passing out at the top of the shoulder. He made some exclamation and then fell to the ground.

Information was immediately brought to town and so as soon as possible he was conveyed to his residence at the bank, and Dr. Rae being in attendance shortly afterwards, he prescribed for the unfortunate gentleman in the circumstances of the case admitted. A telegram was despatched to Geelong for Dr. Reid who arrived in Colac at 3 o'clock next morning having changed horses on the way. After an examination was made it was thought amputation would be unnecessary, but when daylight came, and the extent of the injuries could be better arrived at, the doctors, after consultation, decided that amputation was compulsory in order that life might be saved; this was performed on Sunday morning close up the joint of the shoulder, and the patient bore the operation with great fortitude.

On Sunday he was well as might be expected, but at night violent vomiting took place which had a very weakening effect. Yesterday he was very low. It appears that the charge when it entered the shoulder struck the bone and glanced off in almost opposite directions thus rendering the wound of a more jagged nature. This is the second accident the unfortunate gentleman has met with while shooting having on a previous occasion shot two of his toes off.

All those who are acquainted with Mr. Baeyertz will read the above particulars with profound regret, as he was a gentleman esteemed by all; as a business man he was strict to the letter, and as a townsman has given many instances of his enterprise. We sincerely trust he will soon be restored to health and strength and occupy his former position among us.

Since the above was in type the unfortunate gentleman has gone to his long home having expired at 11.00 p. m. last night. From an early hour this morning a gloom was cast over the town, and when it became fully known that death had ended his sufferings, one by one the inhabitants drew down their blinds or put out their shutters and it needed not a very perceptive eye to observe some melancholy event had occurred, one which was felt by every resident of Colac. Sales were postponed and for a time all business appeared to be suspended; and a feeling possessed many as if they had lost a dear friend.

Many an expression of heartfelt sorrow was given for the deceased gentleman, who young in years and strong in body and mind, was so suddenly called from amongst us, without we may say, a moment's warning; cut off in the soundest of health and in a career of usefulness. Truly 'in the midst of life we are in death.'* As a townsman none other was higher esteemed; of a happy disposition he was a good husband and a kind parent, and those who were dearest to him will lose a warm protector. Much sympathy is expressed for the young widow, and two children, and we believe we but re-echo the sentiments of Colac, when we say that his melancholy death will be deeply regretted by everyone who knew him.

We transcribed this account from microfilm of the *Colac Herald* generously made available by the Colac and District Historical Society. *Colac Herald* is still Colac's weekly newspaper.

*In The Order for the Burial of the Dead, the priest by the graveside would say, 'In the midst of life we are in death: of whom may we seek for succour, but of thee, O Lord, who for our sins art justly displeased?' (*Book of Common Prayer*, 1662/2015).

QUAIL JOTTINGS

IT HAS NOT BEEN, I SHOULD SAY *IS* NOT, A VERY BAD season for quail this time, after all. Notwithstanding the almost utterly empty bags with which most sportsmen that I have any acquaintance with returned to their homes on the opening and following days, better things have come to us with the advancing year. Breeding has become much prolonged. Not only has the handsome little painted quail raised, as usual with us, several successive broods (these lay generally four eggs only), but several other species, notably our very best substitute for the home partridge, and which commonly rears a brood of over a dozen, have kept on, where undisturbed, pairing and diligently repeating their kind.

Even now, beginning of March, hundreds of small fledglings are to be found, more especially in quiet, well-grassed districts; and a Colac correspondent tells me that quite recently (middle of February) he found, to use his own words 'numbers of cheepers, unable to fly'. So who shall presume, after all, to fix dates for the close season for quail which shall be applicable to all years?

…

The pleasantest afternoon must have an ending, and the darkness came down upon us when, of course, the birds were well on the feed and readier found …

But had we not enough … and had the powder not for once as a rule proved straight, and the dogs worked well, and, in short, what on earth was there lacking to our happiness?

Cantering home afterwards, in the cool of the evening, upon the old stock-horse, I found myself arriving at two sage conclusions. One was … the Game Act* has not by any means proved a failure … Further, I proposed, seconded, and carried a private resolution, that little beggars as they might be, there certainly were worse ways of passing a nice cool afternoon in the month of February, than in shooting quail.

N.B.—Little thought I, when penning yesterday the 'quail jottings' above, that an old friend and comrade, than whom no sportsman ever knew a truer, and to whom I made allusion as my 'Colac Correspondent', was lying on a bed of agony, stricken down by an accidental discharge of his gun while pursuing his favourite pastime. Should it not teach the lesson to us, one and all, that however old and experienced we may be in the use of firearms, we cannot exercise too much care with them?

Cartridge

[Shortly after the above article was in type we learned with extreme sorrow that Mr. Charles Baeyertz, the Manager of the National Bank at Colac, a keen sportsman, and an occasional valued contributor to our columns, has died from the effects of the sad accident above mentioned. SP ED]

This is the top and tail of a long article in *The Australasian* describing a day's shooting by Cartridge and friends that we found in Trove, the digital repository of the National Library of Australia.

*The *Protection of Game Act 1867* regulated the hunting season.

I HAVE A DREAD OF WHAT IS BEFORE ME

I HAVE A DREAD OF WHAT IS BEFORE ME. IT IS HARD TO leave all that is dear and go amongst strangers, appearing cheerful and happy when your heart is breaking!

Ah, I hope you will make a better thing of your life than I have done. I am a desolate, lonely woman, feeling that my life has been a grand failure, although I must always have the comfort of feeling some good has come out of it in the knowledge of Jesus Christ. I would not change to be the happiest wife in Christendom without Him.

Mrs. E. L. Baeyertz

This is an extract from a letter collected by H. C. N. and published on page 151 of 'A Supplementary Chapter' to the 1910 edition of *From Darkness to Light—The Life and Work of Mrs Baeyertz*, by Sydney Watson, published in London by Mrs Baeyertz.

MELBOURNE, VICTORIA, 1877

LOCAL CHURCH NEWS

MRS BAEYERTZ, A YOUNG JEWISH WIDOW WHO WAS brought to the faith some years ago, is a flame of fire. She visits the factories, and has now over four hundred young women in her Bible Class at the Assembly Hall each Wednesday evening. With but few exceptions these have all received God's gift of eternal life.

For some months she has addressed crowded congregations at the newly erected Mission Hall where over a hundred have found the Lord under her ministry within a very short time, whilst regular Church attenders have been revived under her clear, earnest holding forth of the light of Bible Truth.

In the next few weeks, Mrs Baeyertz has been invited to speak to women and girls at the Gospel Hall Blanche Street, St Kilda, followed by similar meetings at the Presbyterian Church Clarendon Street, Emerald Hill.

Dr John Singleton

This undated and unattributed article from 'a weekly paper' was selected, and possibly edited, by Betty Baruch from Emilia's scrapbook. Sydney Watson (*From Darkness to Light*, 1894/1895, pp. 63–64) quotes from a similar article by Dr Singleton, published by *The Christian* in London, England, on 31st January 1878.

THE LADY PREACHER

A LARGE CROWD OF SUNDAY SCHOOL CHILDREN ASSEMbled in the pavilion, Public Gardens, yesterday afternoon, the announcement that Mrs. Baeyertz, of Melbourne, would deliver an address being sufficient attraction to fill the room to overflowing. This lady has been holding a series of evangelistic services in Hobart Town, and has drawn large numbers of people together, those attending in the first instance merely out of curiosity to 'hear a woman preach' being impelled to frequently repeat their visits by her simple yet earnest and forcible language. She has a very pleasing appearance, and speaks in a sufficiently distinct tone of voice to be heard by a large assemblage.

The service yesterday began by singing one of Moody and Sankey's hymns, the harmony being led by Miss Price, who presided at the cabinet organ. A very earnest prayer was then offered up by Mrs. Baeyertz, after which another hymn was sung. The preacher then read portions of the tenth chapter of St. Mark's gospel, the account of the rich young man who desired to inherit eternal life, but who when required to give up all his possessions and follow Christ went away grieved, forming the basis of her address. She pointed out in clear language that it is not by rigid observance of the commandments that we can obtain salvation, but by becoming new creatures. Her subject was well handled, and was illustrated by many anecdotes, which were pointedly put.

Upon commencing to read the scriptures, she reproached very severely some whom she observed laughing, and reminded them of the solemnity of the occasion. Her discourse was mainly devoted to laying before her hearers the terms upon which salvation can alone be obtained, showing how condemnation rests upon all, and she concluded by saying that she washed her hands of the blood of her hearers if

they failed to seek that salvation. She could but show the way;
she could not do more.

Altogether the service was a most profitable one. The lady
invited any who felt seriously impressed to remain for further
instruction, and a number of her hearers accepted this invitation. Several other announcements were made, but being
uttered during the bustle caused by a large audience rising
from the seats, they were not heard by the great majority of
the congregation. Mrs. Baeyertz will deliver another address
this evening in the Mechanics' Hall, to which all are invited.

From *The Examiner*, still Launceston's daily newspaper.

VISITING PREACHERS

17th April

To the Editor of *The Examiner*,

Sir,

Have our ministers in town become superannuated that we actually need women from a distance to come and preach to us? Our place got the name of being dead or somewhat like it, and it appears to be true.

I think Mrs. Baeyertz and others of the same stamp should be 'keepers at home,' their proper sphere, and endeavour to train their *children* in the fear of God. If she and others have time to spare let them visit our lanes and alleys, where their services (if they are Christians) might do great good.

D.

[There is work enough for all.—Ed.]

18th April

To the Editor of *The Examiner*,

Sir,

It is quite true that 'there is work enough for all'; still it seems to me unseemly that women should be public preachers of the Gospel, and if I understand the New Testament aright St. Paul thinks so too.

D.

19th April

To the Editor of *The Examiner*,

Sir,

Are you not sad at the wrongs of 'D.'? Poor fellow! It is really too bad that one strolling preacher after another should intrude here, and wind up with a *woman!* What makes the matter worse is, that members of poor 'D's' church and congregation should patronise these objectionable people.

Suppose our ministers (some of whom would be much better 'superannuated') were to go and hear for themselves, and learn the secret by which these women draw such crowds of attentive hearers, many of whom will *stand* for two hours at a time fascinated by the beauty of these Gospel addresses. Let 'D.' only hear Mrs. Baeyertz once, and, if he is not too conceited to learn from a woman, his future sermons may be the better for it.

E.

LETTER TO MRS BAEYERTZ

Dear Mrs. Baeyertz,

We cannot allow you to leave our shores today without giving expression to our sincere and grateful appreciation of your visit among us. As the Committee who have acted with you in the services you have held in this city we are sure that we speak, not only for ourselves but also for each worker who has taken part in the meetings, in saying that we are devoutly grateful to God for directing your steps into our midst.
We are equally confident that we are only expressing the thoughts and feelings of a very large number of Christians in Adelaide and suburbs in testifying not only to our esteem for you as a sister in Christ Jesus, but to our conviction that God has eminently endowed you with gifts for the setting forth of His precious truth both to Christians and non-Christians.

We are aware that you feel specially called to minister the Gospel of Salvation to the unconverted, and we rejoice to know that during these recent meetings it has proved to be the power of God unto salvation to many unsaved ones. We trust that you will still make the salvation of sinners through faith in Christ the distinguishing aim of your labours, and we pray and will pray that our gracious Lord and God may give you wisdom and power to win for His glory many thousands of souls from the thraldom of sin and Satan.
At the same time, we know both from experience and from the earnest and unanimous testimony of large numbers of Christians that your very clear unfolding of the foundation truths of the Gospel have been most helpful, stimulating, and edifying to the great bulk of believers. May you still be greatly honoured by God in ministering to the saints, though this be not your first aim. We rejoice to believe that your steadfast

adherence to and love of God's Word has made the Bible a more precious volume to many of us.

On our part there have been grave shortcomings. We have had before today evangelists in our city, and we have not always been able to look on their work with full satisfaction. That was to your disadvantage on your arrival, and we did not enter with you on your work with that degree of expectant sanguine faith with which we ought to have co-operated with you. Your own faith has rebuked our lack of faith. We want to confess this before God as well as to you. Had we been more believing, doubtless the results would have been larger. Nevertheless, we are intensely grateful that so large a number of souls have been saved, and that so much real spiritual good has been accomplished.

You know—at least we hope you in part understand—how ardently we entertain the hope of your returning to labour afresh in and around Adelaide as well as in the country districts. Rest assured, we and others will earnestly strive to promote in every possible way the true and highest success of your second visit. Will you permit us to urge it on you that with the existing feeling and expectation it would be best if you could return to us as soon as the summer is over, say in May next? We will ask the Lord to send you back to us soon. Meanwhile our prayer is that He will more abundantly and graciously bless you than we have language to express.

Yours in the faith of the Lord Jesus,

The Committee

This letter from the South Australian Baptist Association was published in the January 1881 edition of *Truth and Progress*, the South Australian Baptist monthly, with this introduction: 'The subjoined letter was handed to Mrs. Baeyertz on the morning of her departure from Adelaide by the Committee which assisted in the direction of the services. Several of the members of this Committee waited on Mrs. Baeyertz and personally expressed the great joy which they in common with others had experienced in connection with her visit.'

LETTER TO THE EDITOR

Sir,

To do aggressive work and build up the various Churches, we need an Evangelist, and one that has proved his call to be one by the fruits following his teaching. If such a man can be found we should engage him for the Association work, but if we cannot find a MAN we can find the WOMAN who has proved her call to the work of an evangelist. And I would respectfully request that, with all the evidences before us of the fitness of Mrs. Baeyertz to do this work, an effort be made to engage her services for the Association, if it be possible to do so.

The testimony given from all the Churches where she has laboured is so conclusive as to the great good done that we should at once try and secure her before her plans are matured for leaving the Colony, as I believe she is contemplating doing after this year.

Hoping this will set the Churches a-thinking and acting,

I remain, yours truly,

A. O. Chambers

From *Truth and Progress*.

'LET HIM THAT HEARETH SAY, COME'

Dear Sister,

During the ensuing month (July) we intend, as an 'association,' to hold a fortnight's special mission services. These services will be conducted by Mrs. Baeyertz, the converted Jewess and lady evangelist, whom we all know and love. As we were praying last month for a special outpouring of the Holy Spirit, we hope during these mission services to see the result in a great ingathering of souls. And now, dear sister, what is your part in the great work of winning other lives to Jesus? You have heard for yourself the Master's loving invitation, 'Come unto Me.' Gladly your heart responded with the cry, 'Lord Jesus, Thou hast bid me come take me just as I am, and save me now.' Then, in that glad hour, you knew for the first time what it was to 'come' to Jesus.

'Let him that heareth say, Come.' Will you not obey the loving command, and carry the message to some other weary soul? Look around you in your own home circle. Is there not someone close at hand waiting for you to bid them 'come?' Ask Jesus Himself to direct you, and you will not long be left in doubt. Have you ever tasted the joy of carrying the message to some weary, waiting soul—to one who has been longing for it as the parched traveller in the desert longs for a draught of cool water? Then we are sure it will thenceforth be your highest ambition to be constantly employed in carrying the Master's invitation. Will you try this month, dear sister, to make a special effort to win one soul for Jesus? Also, we would ask you to help us by your prayers (and in any other way open to you) to make our first Young Women's Christian Association mission a great success.

Mrs. Baeyertz will commence the mission services on Sunday night, 12th July, in the upper hall of the Young Men's Christian

Association building, Russell-street (as we cannot have the Assembly Hall on account its being otherwise engaged), and will hold meetings on Tuesday, Wednesday, and Thursday nights of each week, also on Monday and Friday afternoons at half-past three. Hoping to see all our members, if possible, at these meetings.

We remain, your loving sisters in the Lord,

S. C. and E. W. Booth*

P. S. Replies gladly received.

Robert Evans (2007, p. 180) found this Monthly Letter of the Young Women's Christian Association in *The Spectator and Methodist Chronicle*, 17 July, 1885, p. 349.

'Let Him That Heareth Say, Come.' Revelation 22:17.

*Sarah and Lila Booth were sisters who together ran the YWCA in Melbourne.

CIRCULAR LETTER

Brethren,

Mrs. Baeyertz, the bearer of this letter, has long been known to us as a devoted and gifted servant of our Lord Jesus Christ.

She has faithfully served the Churches of Victoria and of the other Australian Colonies during the past thirteen years as an evangelist of exceptional power.

Her meetings have invariably been crowded, and the spiritual results of an abiding character. There is not a city, and scarcely a town or hamlet, in Victoria, where men and women won to Christ through her instrumentality are not to be found.

In addition, it gives us pleasure to say that our sister has, since her conversion from Judaism to Jesus, maintained a high level of Christian consistency, and of whole-souled consecration.

We affectionately commend her to the Churches of Christ, wherever in the providence of God she may be led, as a sister worthy in every way of their confidence and esteem, and as one eminently qualified by the great Head of the Church to be their helper in the work of the Lord.

John G. Paton, Missionary, New Hebrides

H. B. Macartney, jun., St. Mary's Vicarage, Caulfield

Henry A. Langley, Minister, Church of England, St. Matthew's Prahran, Archdeacon of Gippsland

A. J. Campbell, D. D., Presbyterian Church of Victoria

Samuel Chapman, Collins Street Baptist Church, Melbourne

John Watsford, Wesleyan Minister, Richmond, Victoria

Samuel Knight, Brunswick Street Wesleyan Church (late of South Australia, to which this letter is equally appropriate)

Allan Webb, Albert Street Baptist Church, Melbourne

Alfred Bird, Baptist Minister, Hawthorn, Melbourne

Wm. Christopher Bunning, Baptist Minister,
West Melbourne

D. O'Donnell, Congregational Church, Malvern

W. Lockhart Morton, jun., Presbyterian Church, Malvern

John MacNeil, Evangelist of the Presbyterian Church
of Victoria

Silas Mead, LL. B., M. A., Flinders Street Baptist Church,
Adelaide (in whose church she held services continuously for
over two months with great success, accompanied with many
signs of God's blessing).

This circular letter (Paton, et al.) was presented to Emilia at her private
farewell from Melbourne. The text is from a footnote by Sydney Watson
(1910, pp. 83–84).

LOCAL AND GENERAL

A SOCIAL GATHERING OF THE MEMBERS AND FRIENDS OF the Young Women's Christian Association was held in the Garrison Hall on Friday night in honour of Mrs Baeyertz, who has been conducting an evangelistic mission in Dunedin for the past few weeks. Tea was provided in the hall by ladies of the association at about half-past 6 o'clock, nearly 350 persons partaking of the repast. After the material wants of all had been satisfied Mr Brunton's choir rendered a number of sacred selections in their usual tasteful manner.

Mrs Baeyertz subsequently addressed the meeting on Christian work, pointing out that all might and ought do some work for Christ. She indicated that people might work for Him by visiting the sick at the hospital, by making up bouquets of flowers and taking them to that institution, by teaching at the Sunday Schools, by 'winning souls to Christ', and by holding intercourse with men and women, and in other ways.

She also said that if God called women to preach, let her go, but take care that no women went out on her own account. When she did that God's name was dishonoured; but wherever a woman was really called by God to preach she was never in a hurry to obey the call.

We found this snippet from *Otago Witness* (p. 32) in PapersPast, the digital newspaper archive of the National Library of New Zealand.

PACKED TO THE DOORS

A MONTH AGO IT WOULD HARDLY HAVE SEEMED POSSIBLE for a lone woman, a converted Jewess, to have come into this city, unknown and almost unheralded, and begin a series of Bible readings and doctrinal sermons to a few score people in the unfinished Y. M. C. A. Hall, and in two weeks' time pack to the doors the largest church in the town with over four thousand people. Yet such is the case, and Mrs. Baeyertz is the woman. Nor was it newspaper notoriety. Almost nothing appeared in the papers; the growth came from the interest excited by the merits of the woman herself. Her profound knowledge of Scripture; her spiritual perception of its truths; her soundness in the faith of Christ; her aptness, grasp, pathos, boldness, hard common sense, freedom from cant, made one feel that they were listening to a Jewish prophetess. The Scriptures are a new book to many through her teachings, and the unity of the Old and New Testament in testifying to the Lord Jesus as the Messiah who is to restore all things is fully established in their minds.

... Mrs. Baeyertz's closing meeting at the Simpson Tabernacle, where she addressed over 4,000 people on the Easter subject of Dead unto Sin and Alive unto God (Romans vi).

... her phenomenal success here, or on the marvellous escape from a panic in the crowded assembly by the repeated cry of 'fire!'

... created a deeper and more lasting impression than any evangelist or lecturer over here, not excepting Moody ...

We obtained these extracts from *Los Angeles Churchman* from three sources: Sydney Watson (1894/1895, pp. 97–98) in England, who quotes from a clipping in Emilia's scrapbook, Betty Baruch (1998, p. 11) in Victoria, who quotes from a clipping in the Baeyertz family scrapbook, and Robert Evans (2007, p. 239) in NSW who quotes from a copy of a clipping in the C. N.

Baeyertz Collection in New Zealand. They may all be quoting overlapping parts of exactly the same clipping in one well-travelled scrapbook!

A HEBREW PROPHETESS

WE COUNT IT AMONG THE MOST SIGNIFICANT SIGNS
of the times that so many women are moved by the spirit
of God to tell out the story of redemption, and to lend
their help in the work of the gathering of the harvest of
souls.

At home and abroad as missionaries and evangelists, as Bible readers and tract distributors, the number
of Christian women who are doing the Lord's work is
constantly increasing. The psalmist's prediction seems to
be literally fulfilled before our eyes—'The Lord giveth the
word: The women that publish the tidings are a great host'.

...

*We believe, in spite of the seeming prohibition of Paul,
that the Spirit of God calls and commissions women to be
evangelists, and to tell out the story of the cross.* What else
can be the meaning of the words of Joel, reiterated by
Peter on the day of Pentecost, 'And it shall come to pass in
the last days, saith God, I will pour out of My Spirit upon
all flesh: and your sons and your daughters shall prophesy,
[and your young men shall see visions, and your old men
shall dream dreams:] And on My servants and on My
handmaidens I will pour out in those days of My Spirit;
and they shall prophesy'. 'Prophesy' means not to foretell
necessarily, but to *forthtell*, to witness for Christ unto the
people.

...

We rejoice that in these days of lax theology and feeble
preaching of the doctrines of grace, such a witness has
been raised up; so sound, so clear, so fearless in her setting
forth of the utter ruin of human nature, and salvation
alone through the vicarious death of Jesus Christ, 'who
is over all, God blessed for evermore'. We wish her great

success and in her future missions, and pray that God will greatly use her, as in the past, to strengthen Christians, and to win the unsaved.

Rev. Dr. J. A. Gordon

These excerpts from *The Watchword* were reproduced by Sydney Watson (1894/1895, pp. 105–106). Dr Gordon quotes from Psalm 68:11 (Revised Version), Acts 2:17–18 and Romans 9:5.

WOMEN EVANGELISTS

THE PROPRIETY OF EMPLOYING WOMEN EVANGELISTS, which has lately been discussed a good deal in Christian circles in the United States and Canada, seems to have been pretty effectually settled in the affirmative in Montreal, by the recent visits in close succession of three or four very eminent women speakers. There was, first, Mrs. Booth Clibborn, of the Salvation Army, a woman who inherits the singular powers of her remarkable parents, who had also the privilege of calling out Lady Henry Somerset, otherwise silent in Montreal. Then there was Miss Blanche Cox, another of the Salvation Army heroines, whose thrilling tales of devotion were calculated to renew the lives of many. And lastly, with the same message of complete personal consecration, came Mrs. Baeyertz, the converted Jewess.

Facts are often more convincing than argument, and few who heard any of these holy women could doubt that God had given to them, as well as to consecrated men, the evangelistic power of drawing and deeply infecting large audiences with their own spirit of Christian consecration.

The Protestant community of Montreal is known to be very conservative in religious matters; and nearly all of the many evangelists who have laboured here unite in the statement that Montreal Christians are about the least impressionable people to be found on the continent. Even Mr. Moody had to acknowledge that a comparative defeat attended his labours in Montreal, and he has since shown considerable reluctance in renewing them. It was scarcely to be expected that an almost unknown evangelist, and a woman at that, would in one short week turn the tide of Christian sentiment here from a cold indifference, if not aversion, to an overflowing enthusiasm, such as has rarely occurred in this city …

Whence, then, is the power which drew the thousands towards St. James's Methodist Church, which was taken for the occasion, being the largest church in Montreal, last Sunday evening, and which on Monday evening filled that large church with two thousand five hundred Christians, admitted by ticket? Where is the sober believer in the New Testament who will venture to ascribe this attracting power to other causes than that which drew the crowds to hear the Apostles on the day of Pentecost?

Watson (1894/1895, pp. 129–131) describes his source as 'a press leader entitled "Women Evangelists" which appeared in the Montreal papers'.

MRS BAEYERTZ AT ABERGAVENNY

VERY GRACIOUS HAVE BEEN THE MISSIONS HELD IN THE past in this town, but none has excited such interest or awakened such concern as the mission just held by this Jewish lady. The interest has increased day by day, and the buildings have been taxed to the utmost, very many at times being unable to gain admission.

The Sunday services were held in the Town Hall, the meetings during the week being held in the various chapels, kindly placed at the disposal of the Y. M. C. A. for the purposes of the mission. The men's services were greatly appreciated, and attracted large numbers, particularly on Sundays, and resulted in several men confessing Christ.

The first week-night service was held in the Wesleyan Chapel, which was crowded out, and as the interest deepened the attendance increased so much as to necessitate an earlier migration to Frogmore-street Chapel (the largest chapel in the town) than was originally intended. The first night, when Mrs. Baeyertz gave her address on the Passover, this was over-crowded. The afternoon bible readings have been a rich treat. They were well attended by the ministers and Christians of the town, and were much appreciated for their invigorating, strengthening, and helpful spiritual influences.

The last Sunday's services will be long remembered, both for the numbers who crowded the Town Hall, and by the exceedingly powerful and solemn address on 'The Master is come and calleth for thee.' Many were convicted. The following meeting being the last, such great numbers attended that Frogmore-street Chapel was too small, and an overflow meeting was held at the Presbyterian Church. Many were moved to tears in the after-meeting, and during her address on Romans vi. The Christians felt it was a time to reckon themselves 'dead indeed unto sin, but alive unto God,

through Jesus Christ our Lord.' The holiness meeting afterwards was a rich experience to all present.

The Y. M. C. A. has had the privilege of sending to the
various ministers the names of over 200 individuals who
passed through the inquiry room, and also the names of about
seventy children, who desired to follow Jesus, to the Sunday-
school superintendents.

Thos. Tom King, President,
Winfred Rose, Vice-President,
Abergavenny Y. M. C. A.

This is from *The Christian*, a journal published in England.

THE OUTCOME OF A LITTLE INCIDENT

A VERY INTERESTING INCIDENT HAPPENED AT MRS BAEY-ertz's mission in Edinburgh a short time ago, showing how God works through 'little things' to bring about His own ends.

A man was left by his master in charge of the house while the family were away and, feeling very dull and lonely one afternoon, he began to look about for something to pass the time away.

Pulling open one of the drawers in a kitchen table, he saw a dilapidated copy of a book, which turned out to be *From Darkness to Light—The Life and Work of Mrs Baeyertz*. He began to read it, and soon got so deeply interested that he could not put it down until he finished it.

Soon after, one of his mates came to see him, and he gave him the book, telling him how deeply it had influenced him.

'Why!', said his friend, 'I believe that is the very lady who is preaching up at Chalmers' Territorial Church every day, just now', and, rummaging in his pocket, he produced a handbill of the meetings. Comparing this with the book, they both decided to go and hear her that very night, and the result was that both were savingly converted. But it did not stop there, for they brought their wives, and they too were converted to God.

Sydney Watson

Sydney Watson first tells this story in his 1904 edition of *From Darkness to Light*. What the man found in the drawer was an earlier edition of the same book.

CLIFTON HILL

THE LAST MISSION HELD BY MRS. BAEYERTZ IN
Melbourne was at Clifton Hill, one of the northern suburbs.

Much prayer was offered in all the churches and in many
homes that the spirit of indifference, which has always been
very evident in previous missions held, would be removed.
The Hill is acknowledged to be one of the hardest places
in and around Melbourne to move, but the blessing that
attended Mrs. Baeyertz's labours in other places was manifested here.

The oldest workers say they have never seen the place so
moved. Night after night there were such crowds that the
largest building procurable was not capacious enough, and
although the stewards filled every available space—the pulpit
steps on both sides being packed—scores of disappointed
people were turned away. And what shall we say of the
after-meetings—such deep conviction of sin, such definite
reception of Christ! It has been soul-inspiring. Among the
numbers who turned to God were men and women who up
to this had no thought about their souls, and who for years
had never entered a church. Many times we had to adjourn to
the church, as the inquiry-room was too small for the number
of seekers.

A most encouraging feature of the meetings was the
number of young men who came out for Christ. At one
meeting alone there were thirty and we were stopped again
and again in the streets by those who had found the Saviour,
and who told us they were trying to get their friends and
companions to come to the mission.

About twenty-five years ago Mrs. Baeyertz was mightily
used of God in a district not very far from here, and it was
most delightful to see those who were converted then seeing
their children, and in some instances their grandchildren,

brought to Christ through the same honoured instrument. One minister was heard to say, as an envelope with fifty names was handed to him: 'Ah! These cards mean something, as we ministers know what is lasting. We are always coming across those who were converted through Mrs. Baeyertz in the old days and these will be the same, we are sure.'

Over 300 persons were dealt with and professed to trust the Saviour, and ministers and workers are organizing meetings to help these babes in Christ. We are devoutly thankful to the Lord for sending Mrs. Baeyertz to us, and unceasing prayer will go up for her life to be spared for many years to witness for her Master.

John Carson,
Minister, Baptist Church, Clifton Hill, Melbourne.

From *The Christian*.

MRS BAEYERTZ AT NEWBURY

AT THE INVITATION OF THE Y. W. C. A., MRS. BAEYERTZ recently conducted a mission at Newbury, where the power of God has been manifested in a wonderful way. From the first day the Bible-readings were well attended, and many testify to the fact that through the unfolding of God's Word and its searching application by the Holy Spirit, their lives had been lifted to a higher level. One said: 'My Bible has become a new book to me.'

People came from miles around. One woman, whose father had been to one of Mrs. Baeyertz's missions nineteen years ago, walked four miles with a friend. Both were converted and went home rejoicing.

From *The Christian*.

CATTAC PRESS
cattac.com.au